Praise For A Girl Like That

"We take our wine and wander out onto the front porch and watch the last of the sunset. Birds flutter toward dark trees, settling in to roost for the night as cicadas and crickets begin their evening serenade. My mountains are beginning to take their deep exhale."

— **Elle McLarin in...** *A Girl Like That*

"Author Mary Flinn, also exhaled deeply, and the resulting breath became the novel, *A Girl Like That*, which takes her craft to the next level. Like a well-savored summer vacation, the reader follows Elle on a journey from the mountains of Valle Crucis to the sea at Wrightsville Beach and Wilmington, North Carolina. The reader will fall in love with the free-spirited Elle and root for her as she navigates her life-changing journey to find change, forgiveness, acceptance...and love."

— **Tim Swink, award-winning author of** *Curing Time*

"Gritty, gut-wrenchin₁  , the bad girl, is back, and she's on a m   t. Moving from the small-town moun   ever let her live down a near-tragic ch₁   ₁ay be relatively easy for her, but keeping her past from ruining the good start she's made in Wilmington may be next to impossible when temptations are everywhere to let bad choices rule her life again. Mary Flinn's *A Girl Like That* ties up all of Elle's loose ends in a neat and satisfying package worthy of a celebratory piece of cake."

— **Laura S. Wharton, award-winning author of**
The Pirate's Bastard, Leaving Lukens,* and *Deceived.

"Mary Flinn's new novel *A Girl Like That* is the kind of story that leaves you wishing it will never end. I was totally caught up in former bad girl Elle's efforts to reinvent herself as she opened a bakery and took a chance on love again. It's been a long time since I laughed so hard or felt so deeply when reading a novel. Like the wedding cakes Elle decorates, this book is layered with feeling, mixed with a variety of fascinating episodes, and frosted with love by its author."

— **Tyler Tichelaar, Ph.D., and award-winning author of**
Arthur's Legacy* and *The Best Place

"*A Girl Like That* is the story of the girl we love to hate—Elle is the bad girl hell-bent on making trouble. As Flinn's characters so often do, though, Elle surprises us with a complexity and humanness that make her sympathetic and even likable. She is good and bad, hard and soft, sweet and saucy—and we recognize Elle's battle very clearly because we all know girls like that, or truer still, because in some way, we are all girls like that."

— **Sabrina Sells Stephens, author of**
Banker's Trust* and *Canned Good

A Girl Like

THAT

A Novel

Mary Flinn

Mary Flinn

A Girl Like That
Copyright ©2015 by Mary Flinn

Address all inquiries to:
Mary Flinn
mflinn@triad.rr.com
www.TheOneNovel.com

ISBN: 9780990719779

Editor & Proofreader: Tyler R. Tichelaar, Ph.D.
Cover & Interior Layout: Fusion Creative Works, www.fusioncw.com
Cover Photo: Mary Flinn
Cover Photo Model: Jessica Flinn
Author Photo: Jessica Flinn

Printed in the United States of America

First Printing 2015

For additional copies, visit: www.TheOneNovel.com

"I am the true vine, my Father is the gardener. He cuts off every branch in me that bears no fruit, while every branch that does bear fruit he prunes so that it will be even more fruitful."

John 15:2

For Jessica and Shelby.
You are my prize and joy.

Acknowledgments

Many heads went together to put the notorious Elle McLarin's character in a believable place. Thanks to my editor, Tyler Tichelaar, for planting the seed in my head a few years ago about writing Elle's story in the first person. I was hesitant in the beginning, but I believe this is the best writing I have done, so as usual, you were right. I needed help from a criminal attorney so Peter Romary, Partner and General Counsel/Managing Partner with QVerity Legal, and co-author of the newly released *Get the Truth*, stepped up to the plate. Thank you, Peter, for sharing your knowledge and wit throughout the process of uncovering Elle's legal issues. Fellow author and banker, Sabrina Sells Stephens, answered my banking questions and general inquiries about life in Wilmington, NC. Thanks, Sabrina, for being a kindred spirit and sharing your knowledge with me, especially telling me about the L-Shaped Lot. Thanks to Lauren Rayle, of Let Lauren, who told me all about the daily life of a baker and the baking business in general. Call her if you need something sweet and delicious or a meal to go after a busy day! Kathy Williford, retired guidance counselor from Davidson County Schools, was gracious enough to answer my questions about Elle's probable high school experiences in relation to her crime. Nate Metcalf of Mojo Outdoors shared so many of his experiences as a field producer with the hunting shows I've seen on the Sportsman

Channel that I had to name my male protagonist after him. Thanks, Nate. You are Great. And finally, thanks to Vickie Plott and Jonathan Danner, PV2 of the Army National Guard for answering my questions relating to emergency leave, uniform, and general experiences with basic training; your information was invaluable in developing Joey's character.

None of my books would be what they are without a stellar editor and an extraordinary graphic designer, so my heartfelt thanks goes out to Tyler R. Tichelaar, Ph.D., editor, author, and owner of Superior Book Productions, and to Shiloh Schroeder of Fusion Creative Works for making *A Girl Like That* the best it can be. I am so fortunate to be able to work with you both.

Thanks to my fellow authors and manuscript readers, Laura S. Wharton, Sabrina Sells Stephens, and Tim Swink for their support, testaments on my behalf, and for taking the time to read this book. Your efforts are always valued and appreciated, as well as your friendship.

And thank you, thank you to my family and my readers for hanging in there with me. This one may be the one you've been waiting for.

Chapter 1

I Need a Hero

My past can be a deal breaker in a relationship. In fact, it usually writes the end of my happily-ever-after all by itself. I've watched it happen time after time. It's as if I fall into a sinkhole on a regular basis, like in that movie, *Groundhog Day,* when Bill Murray wakes up every day and the same stuff keeps happening to him, over and over again. When I finally allow myself to get close to a person, eventually I have to tell my side of the story, even though I never want to tell it. Sometimes it's just best never to get that close. But if I do, it's better that the person hears it from me than from some other source so at least he get the facts straight. In my experience, people love to dish the dirt about a person, embellishing the tale as they see fit, especially when they think they know all the details. People are quick to judge you when they think they know all about you. Growing up like I did, people knew way too much about me for my own good, so I didn't stand much of a chance of keeping my business to myself. Part of it was my fault. Part of it wasn't. This is my side of the story.

Not many people in my life have had my back. The ones who did are rapidly disappearing one by one, the way a favorite song eventually goes off the radio, making me want to keep singing it for the feel-good effect.

So after my grandparents passed away and my son decided to join the Army, I needed a hero. Sometimes a girl just needs somebody to pick her up off the ground. Marcus Gilmer is my hero. He's rare—one of those men who is always trying to help a girl like me, down on her luck with something compelling and mysterious about her to prompt his good deeds. And I didn't even sleep with him.

I *did* sleep with his son Michael, a while ago before he got run out of town by his baby mama who showed up with a seven-year-old daughter he didn't even know he'd made. *Small world*, as everybody loves to say. Anyway, I met Marcus at Michael's apartment one day. Before I'd discovered that Michael had left town, I'd stopped by to see him and found his wrought-up father cleaning out Michael's shit so the property management company could rent out the place. I became so captivated by Marcus's rants about Michael that I ended up hanging around and helping him clean. We bonded that day—over scrubbing toilets and taking turns trashing his son—along with a bottle of Jim Beam we'd come across, and we've been friends since then. I never heard another word from Michael after he split Boone. Michael's far from a hero. I'd call him a douche bag actually. Even Marcus agrees with me on that one. But then, I'm a douche bag, too, if I'm running around with guys like Michael. I suppose I can't help myself.

Now, two years later, as I'm walking into the coffee shop on this Sunday afternoon, I spot Marcus reading the local newspaper at a table by the window. He's already bought my coffee so I join him wordlessly, dropping my purse strap over the chair back and seating myself across from him. For the North Carolina mountains, it's sweltering, unusual for May, too hot for coffee, but he was nice enough to meet me when I'd called to say goodbye. His brassy head emerges from the paper as he folds it and tosses it aside. Large, patrician features make his face memorable under that mass of wavy hair; there is no gray in it, although he is old enough to be my father. Because he's big and loud and commanding, he captures the attention of everyone wherever he goes, just like a politician, but he's not one, really. He just happens to own most of the prime real estate in Boone and the surrounding areas, including his most recent acquisition, my grandmother's mountain house. I cross my legs and look dully at him. He chuckles.

"So, Elle…how was the send-off?"

I shrug, rolling my eyes, giving my buttery blond hair an effective toss over my shoulders. He loves it when I do that. He loves me. I can tell by the way he's eyeing my good figure, always weighing the possibilities. "Well…Aiden and I took Joey to lunch at Panera; he sulked the whole time, and then he shook hands with his daddy, tossed his duffle bag in the van with the rest of those boys, and they drove off for Fort Hood, Texas. Didn't even give me a kiss goodbye. And you could hardly call it a hug…. He and Aiden are still pissed at me for selling the house." Or something. Joey has been hollering at me since he emerged from my womb eighteen years ago.

Marcus takes a sip of his coffee. Mine is scalding; I can feel it through the cardboard sleeve. I'll have to cool off, emotionally and physically, before I can drink it.

"Basic training. I remember it well. Maybe he's just scared shitless like I was. Don't worry. He'll figure it out."

"Figure what out? That deep down inside he really loves me? Or that he will never forgive me for selling Granny's house and leaving the mountains for something better?" *Sell this house. Take the money and run,* Granny told me fervently the day before she died about a year ago. *Start over with a clean slate somewhere nice.* "Hmph. Joey couldn't leave fast enough. It's not like he wants her house or anything to do with this town. And he can stay at Aiden's when he gets leave and wants to come home. Aiden's never going anywhere."

Aiden works for his daddy's grading company and will be content to spend the rest of his life driving a dump truck while living down the dirt road from his mama and daddy, his aunts and uncles, and about fourteen million cousins, but I can't wait to get away from all of that inbreeding. I've read books. I know better. I've seen enough movies to know there's more to life than this little town, its clannish inhabitants, and all the Florida snowbirds—the retirees who have discovered our mountains halfway back to their native northern states, and have chosen to stay and eat up our land. I want out. So does Joey. I don't blame him.

Aiden Caffey is Joey's father, though he never married me. He knew better; I knew better too. He didn't love me, and I sure as hell didn't love him. We knew we didn't want each other after our couple of rolls in the hay back in high school, but for some reason, Aiden wanted Joey when he found out I was pregnant. Aiden is a lot of things I don't like, but he is a good man, and he is a good father. Given my circumstances at the time, there wasn't much I could do about being pregnant so Aiden and I have always had an agreement that he would be a part of Joey's life. It was never written down on paper, but it was an agreement we made, like a pact sealed in blood, and it's worked out well for all of us, in spite of his mother and her opinions about me. (She hates my guts and usually refers to me as *trailer trash*. God! What a bitch.)

I'd never have thought Aiden would have stuck with Joey and me like he did. But despite his mother and everybody else, he did, and now we've all paid our dues. All three of us are free. Incarceration for all of us is over. And for me, that's a really big deal. Joey couldn't wait to jump in that van and leave the mountains and be rid of me. Fine. It goes both ways. He wasn't the easiest kid to raise up. I suppose Joey thought that eventually Aiden and I would get married, ending his suffering with all the crap he took from the other kids about me, but that was never to be. Even Aiden has suffered in his own way, being single and not having the girl he really wanted—Kendra. She was a bitch anyway. More on her later.

Marcus studies me while I ruminate like he's expecting me to cry, but good luck with that.

"Honey, one day Joey'll come around. The Army's good for that. The Army teaches a man respect and responsibility."

"Phfft!" I snort, rolling my eyes again, and trying a sip of my hot coffee. If Joey didn't learn respect and responsibility from Granny and Pa—not to mention Aiden and me, then he sure won't learn it in the Army. Maybe he's mad because we were never the kind of family he wanted. None of us got what we really wanted. Life is like that sometimes, but you suck it up and move on. Still, Joey had it rough; we both did, losing Pa and then Granny.

"So you ready to head out for good?"

"Yep. My car's packed tighter'n a tick. Your friend, *Ah*-yunne Borden Mont*gom*ery," I say, drawing out each syllable in her name and then some, the way she does, "is expecting me to roll into Wilmington about eight tonight, so I'll be leaving in a few minutes." Who talks like that? I think, blowing on my coffee, knowing I'm about to drive eastward across the entire state of North Carolina. It will take me near six hours, the way I figure it. When I look at Marcus, suddenly that familiar flood of self-doubt rolls sickeningly through my belly again. I've never lived on my own, truly, without Granny and Aiden for support, and I'm about to take on an uncharacteristically honorable challenge.

"So you think I can really pull this off?"

"What? Run a bakery, or be a good girl?" Marcus scoffs. *A good girl.* He knows me better than most, and better than I'd like him to. But it's a comfort that he knows me and still likes me. Most folks don't when they get to know the real me.

I screw my face up at him in mock irritation, making him chuckle at me. Still, he needs thanking for all he's done.

"Both," I finally shrug, giving in. "And I want you to know I'm really beholden to you for helping me get set up in the bakery down there and all." Marcus lived in Wilmington before he married his second wife (who kicked him out of the Hamptons—I guess being a bad boy runs in the family) and he knows people. Marcus knows *a lot* of people. "I just hope I can do the right things when I need to and not self-destruct as usual when people piss me off."

"Oh, you'll be fine," he reassures me. "You've kept your nose clean as long as I've known you, Elle. You really don't give yourself enough credit." He props his pointy chin on his hand, rubs it a bit, and looks at me again with unusually serious eyes. "I wouldn't have offered to help you if I didn't think you could pull it off. Plus, you remind me of myself. I wish I'd had somebody to lend me a hand back in the day. I sure made my share of mistakes."

"You never got caught for anything you ever did, did you?"

"A time or two I did," he grins, a sly glint in his eye, and he snickers through his nose. I wonder what happened with his ex-wives. We don't talk about it.

Marcus and I are akin in what we want and how we go about getting it. We both have that primal need for power; it's almost sexual. Knowing you can manipulate a person is a powerful thing, a thing I learned early on. I was hopelessly corrupt in school. It was so easy then, and there was such a captive audience. I could act my way into whatever I wanted, actually believing I was the person I played. That particular talent served me well on the high school stage. It also gave me something to do.

I knew back then that the things I was doing were wrong, but I couldn't seem to stop myself. Being bad gave me such a rush! Like blowing spit wads at the clock in our geometry classroom. There was a sound they would make if you hit the dome cover just right—*PONG!* It still sends me into fits of giggles when I think about it. I was better at it than Rocky Santoro. We'd have contests to see which one of us could piss the teacher off more without getting caught. The poor man almost had a stroke one day. We were just awful.

I was wild and out of control, except for when I was at home with Granny and Pa. They'd not allow me to try any of that shit with them. For years, I've tried to squash my inner self, that mean girl I was in high school; the boys liked to call me Badass Barbie. But the internal dialogue between Good Elle and Bad Elle just won't go away! One day, I'm afraid I might just explode with all the pressure of trying to keep the bad girl down and be good. I get so fucking tired of having to bite my tongue when it would feel so good just to lash out at people, throwing flames out of my mouth like some bizarre circus performer. No wonder Joey is such a mess. *The apple doesn't fall far from the tree*, as Granny used to say. That's a telling statement about my mother, then me, and ultimately Joey, but what does it say about Granny? She didn't deserve any of us. Lord, the three of us must have worn her to a frazzle. Poor Granny tried her best to raise me up right. What do you expect, though, when my good-for-nothing teenaged mother named me after a fashion magazine and left one day to go shopping with some motorcycle hoodlum, never to return again? I don't like to talk about that either.

Obviously, I didn't have the best of starts in life, but people say that's no excuse for any of the things I've done. Regardless of whether I believe that or not, I've never been able to make it right in this town; everybody knows me, what I came from, and what I did, and none of them would ever let me forget my past transgressions, especially my relatives—with the exception of Granny, Pa, and my cousin Judy. But now that my son is out of my hair, and Pa and poor Granny (God rest her sweet soul) are gone, I have nothing to lose and only myself to live for. I have a chance to start all over with a clean slate for the first time in almost nineteen years. I'm a damn good-looking, hard-working, thirty-seven-year-old felon with a burning desire to reinvent myself. So I'm pulling up my bootstraps—and my roots—and moving on.

Today.

Chapter 2

....

THE TRIP

....

Two hours later, I'm cruising down Interstate 40 near Greensboro, realizing I will have a lot of time to myself from here on out, something I'll have to get accustomed to. There are many advantages to all this alone time: I have a business plan to go over in my mind for when I arrive and start in to work on my new bakery, not to mention my new digs. I have Marcus and Judy to thank for all of it. On the other hand, the quiet is a bit unsettling. Too much thinking can be dangerous, especially at night when I'm trying to go to sleep and the demons come back to haunt me, keeping me up when I should be getting my beauty sleep. But I have sleeping pills. I'm not stupid. Drugs were invented for a reason, and I use them when I need to. But all this quiet new self-reflection might turn on me. I hope I like myself enough to make my new life work.

Joey…what are you thinking? I sigh, pushing thoughts of my son away. I've lost him and that's that. What did I expect? I couldn't make myself into the person I wanted to be, so how did I expect my son would turn out any different? It's that apple thing again. Screw it. Screw them all.

Anyway, I love the beach. I've been three times in my life, and I love that feeling of riding fast over a bridge with the wind whipping through my hair, listening to the *ka-thunk, ka-thunk, ka-thunk,* as I roll over the seamed pavement, breathing in the salt air and leaving my bad self be-hind, becoming a different person on the other side, someone no one knows. The last time I went to Wilmington, I was with Marcus, flying down the highway in his fancy something-or-another sports car, as if there were not a state trooper working anywhere in North Carolina. And when a cop did come into view, it was as if Marcus had sniffed him out ahead of time, slowing to an acceptable speed. He is such a master at avoiding disaster! At the reminder, I check my speedometer, hoping for similar luck.

For Marcus, living in the fashionable, coastal town of Wilmington and having a wild social streak with the ladies afforded him several ties he has put to my advantage, like the woman who owned the bakery I've just bought. She was a friend of a friend he'd met at a party, who'd come down with a strange illness—Lyme disease or something—which debilitated her to the point where she couldn't work. The young lady had no family or friends to take over the bakery for her, so she had to sell it. Networker that he is, Marcus heard about it and thought of me. Her misfortune was serendipitous for me; I've been working fulltime in my cousin Judy's bak-ery for years, catering all kinds of special occasions, including multitudes of events at Marcus's businesses, especially the Snow Drop Inn, his quaint little bed and breakfast in the chic tourist mountain town of Blowing Rock. (More on that later too. *Ugh!*)

Granny had just passed, and Marcus knew I was considering selling her house, a picturesque little cabin with a willow-twig front porch that Pa had built for them back in the 1950s on four acres of family land in the heart of Valle Crucis—prime real estate. It is just the kind of place people will kill for now—that quaint but rustic second residence they'd buy for a vacation home to escape the rat race of whatever city they need-ed to flee for a weekend respite, making them think they're roughing it with all the comforts of home. I've heard the snowbirds talk. (It's amazing what information you can pick up, putting plates of food in front of rich people, pouring their wine, and refreshing their martinis.) It is the kind of property that would have gotten snapped up in twenty-four hours in the normal market.

In our mountains, it's an act of treason to sell family land, but I did it anyway. My aunts and uncles were furious with me for selling it to Marcus, the "outsider," but what else was new? They disowned me once and for all after the sale of the cabin. I didn't give a shit about any of them because they never lifted a finger to help me when I needed help. That was always the way it was, like I was an outsider myself, even with my own family—except for Judy. Still, I have to admit I was sad to leave the cabin. It was my home for more years than it wasn't, and I will always love my mountains. The house needed some repairs and general fixing up after Pa passed on, but still Marcus gave me almost half a million dollars for it, and most of the furniture. I kept some of the special pieces in storage before I left. He's planning on renting it out, and although I'll never be able to buy it back from him, he's offered to let me stay there for free whenever it's not rented out. Marcus is generous that way—more generous than I deserve. It's what you call a win-win. At least I'm out of there and starting over. And I have money in my pockets—more money than I could possibly know what to do with. I feel compelled to bury it all in Mason jars in the backyard, but I don't have a backyard.

Anyway, as Marcus says, *location, location, location.* I'm beginning to understand what he means, as my eyes fall on the less than spectacular landscape of what's called the piedmont; nary a hill nor a holler in sight, and too many ugly buildings and busy roads everywhere for my liking. I can scarcely concentrate on my driving for all the cars zooming in and out around me. This new flat land is straight and boring. I will miss my lovely, peaceful valley. But I can't think about that now, so I will focus on my bakery.

I learned the baking trade in prison. There, I said it. *Prison.* I lived in the North Carolina Correctional Institution in Raleigh for twelve months back when I was eighteen. I don't like to talk about it, but at least I did learn a trade. Granny told Vada, my caseworker, that I liked to bake, and I'd worked at Judy's bakery in high school, so Vada sent me to the kitchen where I learned more culinary skills. After Joey was born (during my incarceration), Granny took him home with her. Since I'd quickly learned to behave myself and look like a good reform candidate, I was allowed to go out into the community under the supervision of my caseworker, to attend classes at a community college, where I got started on my baking and pastry arts degree. It took me a year and a half to finish it up after I came back home to Pa and Granny's. I had Joey to take care of while I waitressed a few nights a week to pay my tuition at our local community college.

Aiden helped out with the babysitting so I could finish school, but it was hard. Joey was a colicky baby and didn't sleep much, so neither did we. It all seems like a blur. None of us laughed much in those days. I guess Aiden figured the more he could do to get me working steady, the less he would have to do in the long run; plus, he seemed really focused on Joey, and he had much more patience with him than I did. He loved him the way I didn't. I loved Joey, don't get me wrong, but it was different with Aiden; he felt a reverence for our son; I guess it was because he helped make him. To Aiden, Joey was a blessing. I wanted to feel that way, but I didn't; still, I made the best of my situation that I could.

At the time, it seemed like we were always tired, but I never complained; I knew better, with all the help I was getting. Granny and Pa helped me out with Joey at night when they came home from work. Granny worked her own job at the post office all day, and Pa was a linesman for the local power company until he retired when Joey was twelve. Then Pa died—fell slap over of a heart attack in his vegetable garden, right in the middle of the tomatoes, that big, strong bear of a man with hands the size of shoeboxes, I used to think. And then Granny and I were on our own, raising up Joey with Aiden's help.

So here I am, riding down the road, waiting for my bridge, the salt air, and that deep, cleansing breath of relief that I'm counting on to transform me into someone else entirely. I turn up the radio, tuned to the local country station at the moment, and sing as loud as I can so I won't think. The songs are all the same—about horny boys sitting on their truck tailgates at night, drinking moonshine, and lusting after pretty girls in sundresses; girls like me who knowingly tease them to the brink of pain, eventually taking them on rewarding, moonlit skinny-dips in the river on hot summer nights. I was that girl in high school, so I can sing these songs with the feeling only a certain level of knowledge can impart. But who am I now? Skip the blur of the last eighteen years and I still don't know. I'm just me, wanting more.

Acting in plays, watching movies, and reading books and fashion magazines were the ways I escaped into the life I wanted. Like every woman, I suppose I have always wanted the same things, to be successful and happy, to have a man love me, be kind to me, appreciate me for more than my looks and my body, to run his fingers through my hair and touch my face with tenderness. But I have never had any of that. I'll bet even married people don't have that after the honeymoon. You can just tell.

The list begins again in my head, and I find myself falling silent as the song on the radio goes on—that invasive list in my mind that climbs like poison ivy up a tree, denoting all the things I haven't done for one reason or another, ticking off my regrets like the holes in a belt: I've never been to summer camp, never flown on an airplane or ridden on a bus. Apart from a handful of towns in Tennessee, and Myrtle Beach, I've never been much outside the state of North Carolina; I've never even paid my own rent; I've never heard the words, *I love you,* from anyone other than Granny…. *Oh, stop it, bitch!* The bad girl is back, squashing all that nonsense inside my head like a square slap in the face. If I'm going anywhere in this life, I will need a thick skin to wrap around me.

Soon, I've passed Raleigh (where my knuckles went white while I gripped the steering wheel in all that traffic!) and a sign alerting me to the Neuse River watershed. Like the Blue Ridge escarpment that I drove down a few hours ago, I remember that second transitional landmark from social studies classes in school; the falls at the Neuse River comprise the separation point between the piedmont and the coastal plain, like the escarpment separates the mountains from the piedmont. I feel as if I'm really getting somewhere now. Noticeably flatter, the transformed road takes me into rural North Carolina, past farms and fields, newly planted with tobacco, soybeans, and corn. Small sandy roadside stands are set up with painted wooden signs, advertising strawberries and boiled peanuts for sale. I resist the urge to stop, wanting only to reach my destination and find that liberating bridge.

Driving becomes a frenzied occupation, and I stop at a gas station only to pay my coffee toll at last, and fill the tank of my old Honda CRV. In Boone, most of those cars are littered across the back with bumper stickers, proclaiming all kinds of liberal nonsense. Mine's not. I can't vote, so I don't bother with politics anyway, but I also have a thing about not letting anybody else know what I think. It's none of their damn business, and probably best that they don't know! So I have no bumper stickers anywhere on my car, and it looks pretty good that way. Who wants to see all that crap?

Finally, I hit the city limits of Wilmington, the idyllic southern port city, in which I'm hoping to nail down my future happiness. I come to an intersection that requires me to stop at a light so I put down my window and breathe deeply. There is no salt air just yet, only gas fumes and humidity, even for the late hour. It's seven o'clock and I have an hour before Anne Borden Montgomery is expecting me. It occurs to me that I'm hungry, so I pull into a Taco Bell, park, and go into the air-conditioned fast food restaurant for a taco and a large cup of ice water. I wolf it down as fast as I can, and I'm in the car again.

Looking over the directions I've scribbled on a torn out sheet of note-book paper, I realize that I'm going to have to pass my new home to get a whiff of the ocean, so I steer my car onto Eastwood and put down my window for the ride. Tall bushes I can't identify, filled with crimson or white blossoms, line the median and add to the novel feel of this place—my new home! I feel a little shiver of excitement, knowing I'm almost there. After cruising through a few more green lights, I pass my street, Waters Edge, and glide toward the bridge that carries me over the Intracoastal Waterway to Wrightsville Beach. My deep breath rewards me with everything I've craved—the thick pungent scent of warm mud, marsh grass, and spawning fish, awakening that visceral, stirring feeling inside of me that tells me I made the right move; finally, confirmation that I'm doing the right thing on my own terms and in my own time, of my own accord—well, with a little, no, a *lot* of help from Marcus. The thought of him draws a smile across my face. Whatever his part, though, from now on, my future is up to me.

I drive on past Redix, a beachwear store that I note for future explo-rations. I'd forgotten there was a park here, just before the ocean will appear. There are so many people out, walking their dogs, jogging, and others out after a day's work, visiting and laughing with friends on the sidewalk that circles the park. I have to pay close attention not to run over the bicyclists who are also out in strong numbers, riding the loop as well. Which ones live here, and which ones are on vacation? I guess that will be a common question I will ask myself, much like I did in my mountain community, which was a haven for visitors from all parts, particularly Floridians during the summer months, as well as the local residents.

My heart skips a beat as I think of home, but then I come to the stop-light at the intersection that will require me to turn one way or another, and I glimpse and smell the Atlantic Ocean all at once. I breathe in and sigh dramatically, feeling my face light up as a grin I cannot contain takes over my face and I run all ten of my fingers through my hair. Two bare-chested college-aged boys in the car beside me leer ridiculously at me, as

I catch their eyes for an instant, and then the light turns green. I shift my gaze back to the road and turn left. They switch lanes to follow me, cutting off the driver behind me, causing him to honk his horn loudly. I chuckle to myself and shake my head. Oh my! Horny boys are everywhere!

Turning my head quickly and repeatedly to the right, while I navigate the out-to-dinner traffic, I can catch quick, thrilling glimpses of the ocean between the beach houses. The evening light is still bright enough to sparkle on aquamarine waves, and I'm glad I have chosen to take a peek at the beach before making my appearance at the house. Hopefully, I will be able to move in before it is too dark, but I don't have much to haul in, and I can certainly manage it all by myself. Anne Borden Montgomery doesn't look like the type of woman to offer her help anyway; she is all business and there doesn't seem to be a warm, fuzzy bone in *her* body, which is fine with me. I surely don't need a babysitter, and I picked her because she's the type who will leave me alone so I can get on with my life. Well, okay, if I'm being honest, I didn't *pick* her. She was the *only* person I knew who'd rent to me, courtesy of Marcus again. It's not easy getting an apartment when you have to answer that felony question. Thanks to her association with Marcus, I also have a place to live.

I've circled back around to the park, recognizing a few of the brightly-clad joggers who have looped it with me. Redix appears again, and compelled as I am, I pull into the parking lot in search of a retail fix. It's only seven-thirty, so Anne Borden is not expecting me for a few more minutes. Wandering into the store, I follow the female vibe to the right, finding myself in preppie clothes heaven. I make my way to the back of the store, to where the swimsuits line the wall. Checking a price tag or two, I let them drop from my hand like hot potatoes. This is a pricey little shop, but I remind myself that now I can actually afford these offerings—and more. In the past, I used to browse my stacks of fashion magazines for the latest trends, and then drive thirty minutes over to the Target store in Mountain City, Tennessee to search out the cheaper models.

My eye settles on a lobster-red bikini, and I find it in two sizes, along with a black, cotton cover up that could pass as a dress for running into a grocery store on the way back from the beach. In ten minutes, I am in and out of the fitting room, where I've newly discovered two things—one, that the expensive things always look the best and are worth their price in the long run; and two, I've dropped a size! I lost fifteen more pounds when Granny got sick. On the way to the checkout counter, I snag a pair of gold flip-flops in my size, pay for the lot, and click my tongue in satisfaction with my finds.

Back in my car, I return across the bridge and nose slowly down Waters Edge, heart pounding with joy, marveling again at the charming little street with the exceptionally lovely homes and their private docks across the street where "Private Property" signs discourage nosy tourists from making themselves at home to admire the views. It is even better than I remember from my last visit with Marcus. I can't believe I'll be living on this street!

It is almost eight o'clock, but I treat myself to a little tour of my own down the entire street, turning around in the cul de sac. Most of the homes are stately and lovely, seemingly designed to perfectly complement their settings, rich with local flora. One or two sad little houses stick out like sore thumbs, looking as if they were thrown in on bare, unadorned lots, as though an afterthought, by someone who wasn't as well endowed as the other owners along the street. (Listen to me, being all judgmental about it!) A small, brown rabbit darts around a corner of a garden, where I am finally to pull into the driveway of the most dramatic and eclectic house on the street. As my tires crunch softly over the sand that dusts the stone driveway, I admire the gardens in front of the large, whimsical home. The rich, green, front lawn is flanked tastefully by palmetto trees and gardenias. A rose garden is placed front and center. More of those unidentified flowered shrubs are planted here and there, with an unusual collection of perennials trimming the base of the shrubbery. Happily, I can hardly take it all in, here with the sun setting over the rooftop, tingeing the sky above the treetops with honeyed rose. Someone has indulged a funky fantasy over the years by adding a separate wing, linked by an upstairs walkway to the south of the main house, with matching white tongue-and-groove siding, all topped neatly with a cedar shake roof. In the back, viewed attractively through a vine-covered entranceway over the drive, is a matching guesthouse, resembling a doll's house that will be my new home, indefinitely.

Taking a nervous deep breath, I wonder how I rated this decadent place, however temporary it may be, silently thanking Marcus again; he was a friend of Anne Borden's husband, but apparently knew her well enough to prevail upon her on my behalf. All I need is to disappear inside the little sanctuary and I will be home at last. I stop my car next to the main house's front walkway, checking my phone to see whether I have received a message from my son, but there is none. When he arrives at the base, there will be no more phone messages, or communications other than letters. My heart does another flip-flop at the thought. Unbeknownst to Joey, I'm sure, I will worry about his safety until the day he is discharged from the Army. Glancing in the rearview mirror, I rearrange my hair and add a fresh coat of strawberry gloss to my lips. I look tired, but my appearance will have to do. Pinching color into my cheeks, and placing a shaky hand on the door handle, I will myself to muster some self-confidence and open the door.

Between the guesthouse and Anne Borden's three-car garage is another shady garden with a gurgling fountain, pouring into a pond under a canopy of mimosa trees. I glimpse the variety of flowers and the impeccable green grass as I step lightly along the stone walkway and up the stairs to the front porch where ceiling fans twirl coolly for no one. Anne Borden's color scheme is classic and charming—Delft blue and white, with a mingling of white wicker furniture and ferns on iron stands, arranged in a calming way, which is helpful, since my heart is thumping out of my chest! Large, red geraniums greet me in pots at either side of the front door as I contemplate whether to ring the bell or lift the brass pineapple doorknocker, which will signal my arrival. I choose the doorbell, wondering whether Anne Borden is hard of hearing; she is, after all, in her seventies if I've guessed right.

Taking another deep breath, I hear the click-clack of rich lady footsteps, and then the door flings wide open, revealing a woman about my height with clear, peaches-and-cream skin devoid of wrinkles, which makes me want to smack her, and blueberry eyes that look directly at me. Her hair is short and blondish, fluffed stylishly around her face in that no-nonsense way successful women her age like to wear theirs. One side of her mouth rises in a sort of forced smile, and she straightens her shoulders, gesturing me inside.

"Hello, Elle. It's nice to see you again." Her voice is relaxed and unemotional. This is business. She extends her hand and I take it. It is cool and plump, covered with the same creamy skin as her face, but I have noticed a few livery spots on the back of it. A large diamond ring glitters impressively on her other hand, catching my eye in its opulence.

"Hi, Anne…" I don't remember how Marcus had addressed her from our previous trip, and I am inwardly kicking myself for being unprepared. She smiles, maybe at my hesitation or at the sound of my twangy mountain accent; two words and I'm a laughingstock. Crap! My face reddens, but I pretend it hasn't. I take in her stylish clothes as well—a crisp white linen shirt with navy and white patterned crop pants. Her two-toned, Italian leather shoes look expensive. I've seen them in *Vogue.*

"Call me AB—everybody else does," she says in that deep, slow Southern drawl that is so different from mine. "Please, come on in. Are you hungry? I've just finished eating, but I've put together a plate for you to take with you, just in case." The house smells divine, a sweet pork and rosemary aroma wafting my way. Ah! She is pleasant and polite, but she has no intentions of having a chummy little dinner with me. I am her tenant. I did not expect to be her friend, just as I never expect to be friends with other women, regardless of their age. I am too competitive for my own good. Recognizing the familiar assessing looks we are sharing, I have just deduced that she is the same way. She wants to be done with me as soon as possible.

"Oh, thank you, but I've grabbed a bite to eat along the way already," I reply casually, letting her off the hook, memories of my pathetic taco being no competition for what is promised by these smells. Besides, I don't want to be beholden to her for anything else, other than the gracious lodging she's providing me out of allegiance to her friend Marcus.

Unaffected by my refusal of her food offering, she guides me through the living room, which is decorated in oriental elegance, in warm hues of spicy red, pale gold, and mossy green. Costumes from the seventeenth century are draped carefully over her fine furnishings, with one or two being worn by mannequins in her living room, making me realize I have interrupted her work. Anne Borden is a costume designer and works with the film industry in Wilmington. Marcus told me that her husband managed one of the local film studios here before he died. It was her husband Monty's wish to have someone living on the premises after he died so she wouldn't be lonely. I can hardly imagine that she would want my company though. She must be loaded, so why in the world does she still work? I don't get rich people.

AB waves a hand at the costumes on her way to the kitchen. "Please disregard the clutter. I'm working on a TV show and I often bring my work home. I tend to think better here, and after about eight or nine hours at the studio, I need a change of scenery!"

"Oh, that must be fascinating," I mutter behind her, looking around at all the outlandish artwork tucked here and there and on the walls, and the variety of crystal chandeliers and other ornamentation in the rooms we pass through. The place is like a museum! Even a glimpse into her decorous powder room makes me gawp like the hillbilly I must seem to her. I correct my posture and close my mouth before she catches me. She hands me a foil-covered Chinet plate and plucks a key off a hook by her kitchen door. Maybe I'll eat this later, whatever it is. It smells fabulous! There is more Delft blue and white here in her massive collection of china and crystal displayed on the backlit shelves, encased with glass doors to show it all off.

"Let's go out to the guesthouse and get you settled in! How was your drive?"

"Not bad," I say nonchalantly, as if I do this kind of traveling every day.

"Did you have a nice Mother's Day?" she asks, clearly making conversation about the day she thinks I had. She must remember I have a son.

"Oh, yes, it was great." The lie floats effortlessly off my tongue. (My high school acting talent is still finely tuned. A career on the stage was my plan until I became incarcerated.) "How was yours?" I beam when she turns to look at me.

"Oh, it was all right. I got a call from my daughter in Oregon and my son called me from New Jersey. It's nice to hear from them even though we can't be together."

"Mmm. I'm sure that's hard."

What would that even be like, having your children call to say they missed you?

AB has opened the back door, and out we go into the muggy twilight, where the small cottage across her courtyard has taken on a fairy-like appearance. Cicadas have started up a peaceful chorus that rises and falls from different areas of the neighborhood as we walk past more of her flowerbeds and her three-car garage. A little swell moves through my chest as I begin to pretend that this is my place already. Having seen all this before, the images are even sharper now that I'm really here. There's a little iron bistro table and chairs beside the cottage on the stone terrace. I notice my new address: 312-B is on the door in brass symbols beneath a dragonfly doorknocker. A window box is bright with pink and lavender petunias spilling over the sides, mixed with lime green potato vine. A metal watering can sits beside the doormat to remind me to water them. A memory of Granny tending her flowers hits me hard, bringing a sting to the backs of my eyelids, as I squeeze my eyes shut for just a moment behind my hostess, who is unlocking the door.

"There's a deadbolt on both of the doors, and I've installed a security system out here, too," she explains, as a scent of lavender, mixed with a little mustiness, greets my nose. It's not too unpleasant, and AB doesn't seem to notice, or care, perhaps. Sniffing, I think I'll open the windows to air it out after she leaves, even though I can hear the hum of the air conditioner, a swamp box unit, wedged in the window. "Here's the code," she says, handing me the key and a card with a four-digit code on it that I will commit to memory. The small house is much like I remember, simple and clean with creamy plastered walls and a remodeled kitchen, with new stainless steel appliances and muted aqua cabinets with marble countertops. She takes me on a tour of the bedroom, where the bed is stripped, but the red chalk-painted furniture is inviting and quaint. The style is shabby-chic. AB gestures to the bathroom, where I peek in to see the shower curtain draped inside the claw-footed bathtub that is equipped with a showerhead. There is a toilet, and a sink, embedded in a gold-painted antique sideboard, making me wonder when the house was originally built.

"It's small, but hopefully you will have everything you'll need," she says, eyes darting around to assess me some more. It will take some time for her to trust me, no matter what Marcus told her, especially if he's mentioned my jail history. Either way, I can tell she knows my kind.

"It's perfect. I absolutely love it," I say convincingly, hoping to impart my gratefulness.

"No wild parties or too many strange men in and out," she warns me, and then laughs. My own laugh blurts out in response. Her candor surprises me. At least I know where I stand.

"You don't have to worry about that. I came here to work so that's all I'll be doing," I say to reassure her. And sadly, it's probably true. Oh well.

"Okay. Do you need any help unloading your things?" she asks, but I know she's ready to get rid of me. Surprising me with her lack of curiosity about my work, she has asked nothing about my upcoming endeavor. We told her about the bakery before, so she must be bored already with such a mundane occupation. Still, it would be nice to get her business and sell her some cakes. I'm sure she throws some banging parties in that massive house of hers.

"No, thanks. I really don't have much. It's nothing I can't manage on my own. Thank you for the dinner."

"You're welcome." She indicates a note attached to the refrigerator with a starfish magnet. "Here's the phone number to the house, and my cell number in case of emergency. Mr. May is my gardener. You'll see him in the morning, and he can help you too if you need anything. He's here three mornings a week."

I nod and she looks like she is itching to go. "Thank you so much, AB. Oh, and here is your check for the first month's rent," I say, pulling an envelope from my purse. This exchange of money is all that will ever transpire between the two of us. Monty would probably have been so disappointed at our lack of camaraderie. She takes the envelope, poised to peel out of the door ASAP.

"Thank you. Well, have a good night. Hope you settle in well."

"Thank you, AB. Have a good night," I reply, as if she is a customer whose check I've just dropped off on the table.

I watch until she has gone back inside her kitchen. I hear the click of her deadbolt, and in a moment, the porch light goes on and the kitchen light goes off, so I exhale and begin unloading my suitcases, boxes of toiletries, and kitchen supplies from the back of my car. My knives are superior to the ones she's supplied so I switch them out, along with a few other pots, pans, and accouterments, packing her stuff in my boxes, and depositing them in the storage closet, along with a shoebox filled with memories, and Granny's vintage tablecloths. There is no table to speak of, so I'll have no use for them—yet. Deciding to save my welcome food for tomorrow, I tuck my dinner into the refrigerator where AB has graciously left milk, butter, and eggs for me, as well as a sleeve of English muffins and a package of bacon. There is a bag of French roast coffee beside the coffeepot. Disposable sea salt and black pepper grinders sit at the ready beside the electric range.

Then I unpack my linens, placing towels and toiletries in the bathroom, and making my bed with my own sheets. I top it off with a white cotton comforter, with flax-colored butterfly pillows. I turn off all the lights, except for my bedroom lamp, set my own deadbolt, and prepare to wash my face and go to bed when my cell phone rings. Maybe it's Joey finally. A glance at the caller ID shows me it's Aiden.

"Hey," I say into the phone, surprised and glad he's called. A memory of his lips set in an awfully straight line while Joey boarded his van morphs into my current vision of him. I imagine him talking to me, probably holding his phone with a hand jammed down in his pocket, the way he usually stands.

"Hey. You made it okay?" His voice is flat—the usual monotone.

"Yeah. Thanks. Have you heard anything from Joey?"

"Yeah, he called from Alabama just a little while ago. Still on the bus."

"Yeah, I guess he is." There's a brief aching silence, like Aiden wants to tell me something but he doesn't. *Hell of a Mother's Day, wasn't it?*

"You okay?" he asks. Like Joey, there's rarely much emotion in his voice or his conversation and tonight is no different. But still, I can feel there is something more in the pause. I know he cares about me. He doesn't love me, but he cares. After all, I'm Joey's mama. And he is losing

MARY FLINN

part of his family. Losing Joey to the Army is hard on him. We can at least share that.

"Yeah. How about you? How's your toothache?" I'm not his wife, but somebody has to remind him to take care of himself.

"Still hurts. I'm going to see the dentist tomorrow."

"Wow. That's a first."

"Gotta do it."

"Tell them to go easy on you. It's your first time and all…."

He snorts. Aiden's lack of oral hygiene was one thing that always got to me, if not for the disgusting nature of it, for the general lack of courage it represented for him not to face his fear of dentistry.

"Well. Tell Joey…I said take care."

"I will."

"Thanks for calling."

"Sure. Call me if you need anything…."

"Okay. Will you just…um, text me when he tells you he made it?"

"Yeah."

"Okay. Goodnight."

"'Night, Elle."

There is a pause and then a sound to indicate he's disconnected. We are disconnected. Listening to the silence, I can feel the freedom he's just been granted, making me envision his stoic face and the relief that's probably flooding over it, now that I'm gone. I know he's going over to Kendra's or maybe he's already there. He's probably out in the parking lot of her apartment building, smoking a cigarette and talking to me so she won't know about either of his bad habits. After her recent divorce, they've spent a lot of time together. I knew as soon as I left town, he would probably invite her to live with him in his little house down the

35

road from his family, and probably ask her to marry him. It's what they've both wanted for the past nineteen years, but she was mad at him for making me pregnant, and then sticking by me and helping me raise Joey. So for revenge, she got married and taught kindergarten over in Blowing Rock, until she was done using her husband. But now, she can have Aiden all to herself. Her husband is out of the way and Joey and I are gone. They can finally be together. Even from here, I can feel him grinding out the cigarette butt on the pavement with his shoe and going in to (hopefully) brush his teeth and have sex with her—the long awaited, forbidden love kind of sex. He's been waiting over nineteen years. It makes my insides ache.

I sink down on my bed in the lamplight of my bedroom, laying my phone on the bedside table. My eyes move about the room, taking in the small but pleasant surroundings, reminding me how glad I should be that I am here in this cute little place all by myself with nobody else in my business. And tomorrow, I'll buy my own bakery. Suddenly, I feel dead tired, but I know I won't sleep a wink tonight.

Damn.

Chapter 3

THE MAN I DIDN'T MARRY

Birds wake up at dawn. I can hear them now. I have closed my eyes during the night, but you can't call that sleep. Glancing at the clock tells me that dawn is cracking at 5:37 a.m. Today is such an important day that I didn't risk taking a sleeping pill and sleeping through my alarm; that would be no way to start my new life. I get up, slip into my comfy blue bathrobe, and stand. It takes a minute to stretch and get my bearings, and then I walk into my new kitchen to start a pot of coffee. AB likes the good stuff, I think, breathing in the smell of the French roast. We always bought the grocery store brand in the big cans that were useful in Pa and Granny's garden, or for holding Joey's markers and colored pencils when he was little. He was always good at drawing.

I plug in my TV and connect the cable. It takes some doing; I'm not particularly good at anything involving electronics, but being on my own and taking care of Granny forced me to learn a few things. I could always count on Aiden to help me if I really couldn't figure something out.

The morning news show is on, so I take my cup of black coffee to the couch, where I plunk down and prop my feet up on the coffee table. Two women are cooking something for a graduation picnic. One of the women is the cook, and she's placing a Boston butt in a Crock-Pot with a jar of those little pepper rings, and pouring apple cider over it all. Looks good. I should be writing this down. The other woman, the short perky brunette that's all dressed up, is the news reporter, throwing in her annoying comments for clarification every two seconds, like we're all a bunch of morons who can't figure out what the cook is doing just by watching her.

Perky Girl—Amy-something-or-other—keeps talking and interrupting the cook. I'd have slapped her by now. God! What a damn know-it-all! I hate a know-it-all. And she has those beady brown eyes and that grin pasted on her face that she's had since her high school cheerleading days. I know her type. I was a cheerleader. Still, I can't stand her voice so I turn down the TV and just watch. I got this. Slaw, pineapple rolls, baked beans…is this really newsworthy?

I get up to go to the bathroom, thinking I'll fix an English muffin. Back on the couch a few minutes later, I watch the six o'clock news while I eat my muffin, spread with the peanut butter I brought. Another woman and a man are sharing the anchor desk so I turn up the TV, hoping to catch the weather, which is looking promising from the clear sky that's starting to show itself outside my window. The news guy is talking about a police officer who's been shot and is now in critical condition at the local hospital. Then there was a drug bust last night, involving local smugglers who were caught bringing heroin into the city in a boat. Crime fascinates me—and what people will think they can get away with, and how stupid they are. Like the girls I was in prison with—convicted of food stamp fraud and other stupid stuff—who knew it was against the law to share those with your sister? Next, there's a boy's face with big sad brown eyes on the screen. He's smiling in the picture, but to me, he doesn't look happy. He's been missing four months, last seen at a big discount store parking lot with his mom; just seven years old. The anchorwoman takes over, discussing the primary election highlights, but I automatically tune it out, the way I usually do when it comes to politics. It's a good thing I can't vote; I always see things from both sides, so I would miss the election anyway, just trying to decide.

Then after some other depressing stories, the weather comes on. I rinse my breakfast plate, refill my coffee cup, and listen from the kitchen. No rain is in the forecast for several days and the high will be in the mid-eighties, a perfect beach day. They have to say that to cheer everybody up, after all that bad news! Perky Girl is back on with another report about something else—this time it's about what kids are wearing to prom this spring. Short dresses are in! Jeez, she's thrilled! Like *she's* going. She's at least my age, and she's already gushed about how her kids would love that barbeque, so give us a break! I take a look at the dresses on the girls they've obviously picked from the local high school to model the clothes. If I were a teenager, I wouldn't be caught dead in any of those horrible dresses. The colors are all wrong, and they should have fixed the girls' hair. Next, the guys come out in their tuxes. One of them looks like Aiden. Big as a tree with wavy brown hair and that same shy, self-conscious smile. And Joey. Two peas in a pod.

Aiden took me to my prom. Well, more like smuggled me in. I wasn't supposed to go, but he got me in so I could apologize for something I'd done. He was brave. Nobody else would have done that for me. I don't know why he was nice to me after what I did, but it was like he thought I deserved a second chance—that and the fact that we were having sex by then. I wasn't allowed to be at extracurricular, school-related events, after I'd gotten caught for slipping a roofie in Kyle Davis's drink one night at a party at my boyfriend's house. It was Kendra who turned me in, too. She was supposed to be my friend. All I wanted was to loosen Kyle up for a little fun sex in my boyfriend's mother's bedroom. Kendra was along for the ride, and was going to take a picture of us. The idiot filmed it, as in video-recorded it—me, sitting on top of Kyle, in Rocky Santoro's mother's polka dot bra and nothing else. I was drunk, and complaining about how I gave Kyle more than I should have, because nothing was happening. He was passed out cold, lying on the bed with his pants down and me sitting on top of him. We were lucky we didn't get arrested that night. Rocky's party got busted, but Kendra and I hid behind a large potted plant in his basement when one of the cops came in. Finding no one down there, he went upstairs and found Rocky and his friends trying to clean up, so it was then that we made our escape! Knowing we'd gotten away with it, we'd laughed our asses off, driving around the switchbacks up the mountain, where we picked up Aiden and Anthony English, another football player at the party; they'd both been hiding out in the woods to escape capture. Kyle was still passed out cold on the bed with his pants down in a sea of Mrs. Santoro's underwear, so the cops called an ambulance and had him hauled off to the hospital. *He could have died.*

Yep, I was awful and wild back then. I was also one of those dumb people who got arrested for doing a stupid date rape crime. Boys never get caught doing shit like that, but leave it to me to get tarred and feathered for it. They call it Murphy's Law. I should have known better. And I should have known that Kendra would turn on me. She was supposed to be my best friend. She left school one day with Kyle and his girlfriend and went to the police station with the evidence on her little digital camera to turn me in. I got charged with felony assault with a deadly substance, and that was how I landed in the slammer for a year. At least I didn't get charged with sexual assault. No one could really prove that Kyle didn't pull his own pants down. That was my story anyway. I said he passed out after consenting to have sex with me. Kendra was too drunk to remember—but not too drunk to video the whole thing.

Anyway, that day Aiden saw Kendra leaving school to go to the police station with Kyle and that bitch, Chelsea, to turn me in, so he found me at my locker with his hands stuffed down inside his jeans pockets.

"What?" I'd asked, seeing his apprehensive face. He didn't usually hang around me without Kendra.

He'd studied me for a minute, looked around, and said, "You're probably going to get arrested in the next half an hour. Wanna get out of here?"

My mouth fell open and I just stared at him. *Why was he helping me?*

"Kendra went off to the police station with Chelsea and Kyle to turn you in. I heard them talking."

I couldn't get arrested at school. Anywhere but there. I was the shit. I ran the place. "Shit. I don't have a car," I'd told him.

"I know. But I do. I can take you off for a couple of hours…." He shrugged. "If you want." He drove me up to a little place he knew about, up on a ridge, where we hiked and sat up on a flat rock, looking out over the mountains. It was freezing cold that day, but beautiful and peaceful up there, and I let him kiss me. He built a little fire and we stayed up there for hours, wrapped up in his blanket trying to stay warm. It wasn't until that evening when I got home that Pa called the cops, and they came back for me, handcuffed me, and took me away. Pa bailed me out, but he and Granny were really sore at me for what I'd done, so they kept me under house arrest until my court hearing. After school was out for the summer, there wasn't much they could do to keep a watch over me since they both worked, and they didn't trust me to stay home by myself, so that was the summer I started working in Judy's bakery. Who knew that would begin my new career?

So back to the prom—Granny made me promise to talk to Kyle and apologize to him for what I'd done. I *was* sorry, but not the way I should have been at the time. I didn't have a clue about true compassion and real remorse. She said she'd take me to do it, but I couldn't stand the thought of going to his house. His mother would have killed me, even with Granny there! I wasn't allowed to have contact with Kyle at school after my court hearing, so I didn't know how to get ahold of him in private. He sure wasn't going to meet me since I wasn't supposed to be anywhere near him. Granny said to call him up on the telephone, and I thought that would be the easy way out, except he'd probably just hang up on me.

Then prom rolled around and Aiden invited me to go out with him for a special dinner, all dressed up like we were going to the dance. Kendra was pissed off at him for taking me up on the mountain, so he didn't bother asking her. (He even told her we'd made out, which was the truth, but he should have kept that to himself. I guess he was proud of it.) So after dinner and a couple of slugs of his apple pie moonshine, we decided it would be a real gas to show up at prom and let everybody see us together. He said I looked real good, and I think he wanted to rub it in to Kendra that he was with me and to show me off to the rest of his boys. It was a reckless thing to do, a Bonnie and Clyde kind of move—showing up there like that. I wasn't supposed to go to extracurricular activities, so I could have gotten turned in to my parole officer. We knew we'd only have a few minutes to get in and get out, but whatever—we'd go out with a bang! Aiden was barely able to graduate, and I wasn't sure I was going to graduate at all, so what did either of us have to lose? We weren't like the rest of those stuck up kids who had everything going for them, like scholarships and cars, and the like.

So we went to prom, later in the night, sneaking in the back way, through the open terrace doors when the chaperones were standing around the punchbowl and dancing—what a sight *that* was! I got a glimpse of Kyle and thought, *Well, why not just go and apologize now?* I could make Granny happy, and I did kind of want to talk to him one more time. I knew I wasn't his favorite person, but I'd always been obsessed with him, so I took a chance and up I went for the big apology. Who knew? Maybe it would change the way he'd feel about me. Maybe he would forgive me.

I found him with Chelsea over on the side of the ballroom, away from everyone else, having a serious talk, so I went right up to him, interrupted whatever was going on, and started to apologize. It kind of hit me then, the way I saw them looking at each other, that he really loved her. Someone like me would never really have a shot at a guy like him. He saw something in Chelsea that I didn't see, but the way he was looking at her made me realize they would always be together. Maybe it was the way

Chelsea was looking at him, but it hit me then, too, that what I'd done really could have killed him, and that shook me up.

I guess the moonshine made me kind of sentimental and brave at that moment, so I told him I knew what I'd done to him was wrong, and that I was really sorry. I was. *Who would want to kill someone that hot?* Then I told Chelsea I was sorry for treating her the way I did. (I'd flirted with Kyle all year in spite of her. And I told her at a party once that she was flat-chested—well, not in so many words. But she was.) They didn't say a word, just looked at me like I had two heads. Anyway, I turned around and walked off; Aiden and I left, and I guess I thought I felt better. Granny was happy, so that was all that really mattered. And I can say that I went to my senior prom.

My coffee cup is empty again and I sigh, feeling that familiar flush of guilty heat from remembering my sins, and turn my attention back to the TV. Perky Girl is grinning again, standing with her arms looped with the high school models. Give me a break! She gets paid for this?

Switching off the TV, I turn on the water and navigate the claw-footed bathtub shower, holding on to the towel bar so I don't fall on my butt. I'd hate to start out my first day here with a broken leg! An hour later and I'm dressed, hair pulled into a neat ponytail. I don't have much in the way of business attire, so I'm wearing the sleeveless A-line dress from the suit I wore to Granny's funeral. Without the jacket, and with my coral beaded necklace that sets off the black dress in a dressy-casual way, the look is appropriate for a business meeting. I slip my feet into my favorite peep-toe heels and I'm suddenly professional. My plan for the morning is to stop at the bank and pick up the certified check I need for my bakery closing at ten o'clock. I glance at my nails, giving them a quick file with an emery board. People always look at your hands when you're signing papers. I didn't get to that manicure I wanted, but at least my nails are neat and clean. I fasten a fake gold bracelet around my wrist to complete the package. Ever since I left prison, I have always dressed up and worn makeup like I did before I went in. It's a sign that I'm out…and me again. Not that girl.

My cell phone rings before I can leave the house. *Joey?* It's Aiden again.

"Hey."

"Hey…. I wanted to let you know that Joey made it. He just called and said they were rolling into the base."

"Oh. Good. Well. I'm glad you called. You could've just texted me."

"I know. Well, look; have a good day, okay?"

"Yeah. I will. I'm about to buy a bakery!" I say with a little tingle inside that makes me giggle and smile.

"Yeah, you are," he says, and I know he's smiling, too.

"Oh, and good luck at the dentist."

"Thanks. I'll need it. Bye now."

"Bye…." I put the phone back in my purse, wondering why he'd called. He didn't sound like himself. Maybe Kendra heard him talking to me last night and kicked him out. Who knows with her? She'll always be jealous of me, even though I know there will never be a reason for it. Still, I can torment her from afar, it seems! I smirk. *Stop it!* Good Elle chastises me from somewhere inside.

Taking a deep breath, I grab my purse and keys and pull open my door, catching myself from almost tripping over a man on my welcome mat.

"Oh, good God!" I shout, clutching my chest at the shock of seeing him bending over with my watering can in his hand. "You scared me to death!"

A similar look of startled embarrassment catches him, too. He must be *eighty! Holy cow!* I could have given the poor man a heart attack! I try to recover so I don't send him into further apoplexy!

"I'm so sorry! I think I've scared you more than you've scared me!" I exclaim, hoping he can recover and not keel over right in front of me. What a way that would be to start my new life!

His mouth is shaped in a small O of surprise, but then the sides spread and lift until his face is transformed into a bright smile, and he laughs soundlessly, as if he cannot contain his mirth. His canvas porkpie hat, long-sleeved shirt, and long pants identify him immediately as Anne Borden Montgomery's gardener, and I find myself laughing with him. *What was his name?*

He chuckles, trying to compose himself, and then extends his hand, the one without the watering can.

"Hello! I'm Bernard May," he says in a very polished voice. "I'm Mrs. Montgomery's gardener. And you are...?" he asks.

I shake his hand graciously. "Oh, hi! I'm Elle—Elle McLarin. I'm sorry. I guess you weren't expecting me. I got in last night."

"Well...I should have known that. I see your car now. I beg your pardon; I was just getting ready to give your petunias a little drink of water. I tend to notice the flowers and plants, while ignoring the more important things around me," he says merrily, giving me another one of his smiles. "I sometimes can't see the forest for the trees!" I laugh along with him. I think Mr. May must have been quite handsome in his day, so I smile back at him. I often wonder what old people were like when they were young and robust.

"I thought that watering the petunias would be my job," I reply, wondering whether we are flirting.

He straightens, as best he can, and pushes up his darkened glasses. Granny had that kind—the ones with the lenses that darken in the sunlight. Clearing his throat and apparently thinking about his next line, he continues, "You may certainly water your own flowers if you wish, but I would be happy to save you the trouble."

"Oh, I'd actually love to tend these flowers. It'll remind me of my grandmother. She had flower gardens all over the place at our house."

"Well, then, I'll leave the can here for you; although you look as if you might be in somewhat of a hurry. Maybe you should allow me to do the honors today, and you can start tomorrow morning." His expectant smile expands further, brightening his face even more, making me grin. "Where are you off to so early?"

I giggle, forgetting to be wary of strangers. This sweet little man couldn't possibly hurt anyone.

"I'm going to buy a bakery!" I don't have to worry about what he thinks of me. He doesn't know me, and he doesn't know what I did. I am a new person. It feels like such a relief. Who in this town is going to ask me, "*What kind of crazy shit did you do back in high school?*" At least, not today. I smile back at Mr. May.

"Well, congratulations! Then I won't hold you up any longer. I hope we'll talk again soon. I'd like to hear about your grandmother's flowers. Have a wonderful day!"

"You too!" I say, walking across the drive to my car, still feeling his contagious smile on my face. I wonder whether AB has left for work. There is no movement from her house that I can see, and her garages are all closed. Mr. May tips his hat to me as I drive by. I am grinning from ear to ear. He's such a nice man. I don't know many truly nice men, but I believe he is one.

In twenty minutes, I am standing in the long teller line at the bank, waiting to deposit a sizable amount of money in my personal account, and to get a cashier's check for the balance on my bakery from my business account. The people in front of me wait patiently, filling the time by sipping store-bought coffee from paper cups, or checking their phones for messages, or reading the news. Glancing idly up at the counter, I notice a pair of sad brown eyes on a poster propped up between the tellers. It is the missing boy from the news this morning. Shivering, I look away.

I may not have been mother of the year, but at least I was able to hang on to my own boy until he decided to leave home of his own accord. *Barely*.

My mind drifts to Joey. I remember the way he used to wander off in a store and I'd run around, panic-stricken, looking for him. I'd tell him that was a good way to get snatched up by a mean person, but he'd just shrug, and say in that irritating way of his, "I knew you'd find me." He drove me so crazy. I wish our relationship had been more satisfying for both of us.

Why did a girl like me have to have an introvert for a son? What was I supposed to do with someone like that? Joey was like a visitor in my house after he turned seven, and I missed the loving little boy I'd had, who'd curl up in my lap, letting me read to him, or run my fingers through his hair. I suppose most mothers want the same unconditional love back from their children that they feel for them. As he got older, Joey became more and more detached or preoccupied, and he never gave back what I tried to give him.

Joey was quietly ashamed of me. His school counselor told me that the other kids taunted him about me, calling me a "jailbird," and how he was a bastard because Aiden and I had never married. It didn't help that I dated lots of men Joey didn't like. I know he'd heard the story of how my mother left me, and I think he always assumed I'd do the same to him. He craved being outdoors with Pa and Aiden, fishing and hunting, and camping in the mountains near our house. By the time Joey was in high school, he'd take to disappearing in the hills for a day or two at a time. Aiden would go looking for him in the places he and Pa used to take him. Once, they'd returned together, Joey carrying Pa's bow and a small, dead doe slung across his shoulders.

Joey liked to be off on his own, which I could understand, given the circumstances, but he took his detachment to a new and dangerous level after Pa died, leaving for longer periods of time, doing God knows what. Pa had been the only one who could reach Joey at times. If unprovoked,

Joey usually stayed out of trouble at school, but it seemed that the place he didn't want to be was home with me. With his frequent forays into the woods and his lack of interest in anything academic, his grades were never what they should have been, given how smart he was, and he expressed no desire to work with Aiden in his family's business, so we weren't surprised when he decided to join the Army. Only travel and adventures will ease his restless nature for now, it seems, but I wonder how he will take to being bossed around in the Army. If he didn't listen to Aiden and Granny and me, I can't imagine how he'll take to following orders. As Marcus said, the Army will surely make or break him. Still, he could have been that little boy on the poster.

I check my phone to see whether he has left me a message or sent an email; there are no missed calls, no messages, no emails in my inbox. I wonder when and if he will acknowledge the birthday present I managed to slip into his bag before he left. It was a week late, but I've been busy, and he did choose to spend his last few days with his father, not me. I guess it's natural that they should have had their last manly bonding together, since going off to the Army is nothing I want to understand. There will be no emails or messages now, only letters in the mail, but I can't see him wasting the time to write to me.

An hour and a half later, I shake hands with my realtor and the lawyer at the office where I've just purchased my bakery. They assure me that the power and water are on, and they wish me well, as I collect my portfolio of paperwork and head to my car, keys to the shop in hand. I try not to speed as I drive the eleven miles to the strip mall that will be my home for the next...well, maybe the rest of my life, if my business is as successful as Judy's. The back of my car is filled with boxes of baking supplies, towels and aprons, and a recipe notebook with all of our recipes for cakes, frostings, ganaches, petit fours, and whatever else I can sell to the public here on the coast. How different can it be?

Finally, I arrive at my destination. The storefront looks sad without a name above it; however, I am fortunate to be sandwiched between a specialty food and gift shop on one side, and a winery on the other. The Sandy Britches Winery takes up the space on the corner, where the owners have apparently added a new patio with tables, and a large burgundy awning, edged with white lights since my last trip. It's a strip mall, so it can't look that good, but they are trying, I'll give them that. Standing at my front door, I peer inside at the dim décor, which consists only of a few wooden tables and chairs, and display cases that separate the customer café area from the kitchen. My hands tremble with excitement, making it difficult to unlock the door. I walk inside and look around. *This is mine!*

Fumbling for a light switch, I try to remember where it was the last time I was here. My nose turns up at the Tuscan color scheme—persimmon and gold textured paint on the walls. I will have to change the paint job first thing. This is not a cheesecake factory, but a wedding cake bakery. I will prepare the finest cakes and cupcakes in town for anyone's special day. A pale lemon meringue color on my walls will be cheerful and appetizing, just girly enough without being the predictable pink. I may be Badass Barbie, but I don't do puke pink. I imagine a couple of subtle lime green and mango accents here and there to complement my logo—a simple, tiered cake with large, stylized black letters underneath. It's all here in my portfolio and on my laptop. I set everything down on the counter and run my hand along the display cases, which need cleaning. The lights are on, but I can't hear the hum from the refrigerator and freezer in the back. Their doors gape open in their state of inactivity. Satisfied after inspecting them for cleanliness, I plug them and close the doors, hearing them buzz to life. A double row of tables and stainless steel sinks are in place, with shelves above them for storage. There is plenty of table space for bakers to work simultaneously with decorators. A large walk-in pantry with a lock is in the back, beside a built-in desk with a bookshelf along the wall beside the fridge. Opening the pantry, I see the vault inside, along with plenty of storage for office supplies. Turning around to the front, I notice the counter where the customer command center will be. It's backwards from Judy's place but slightly larger and definitely more modern. I know exactly how to get started here. I'll place a consultation counter down the side wall, where customers will be able to sit and view my notebook with all the offerings that will be available, from birthdays to graduations, to weddings, and all the other kinds of celebrations in between.

The place needs a deep cleaning, a paint job, a telephone, and signage put in place before it will be ready for business. I need to order my food supplies: fondant, flour, sugar, butter, milk, eggs, flavorings, and lots and lots of chocolate! I'll have to contact a sign person and find a handyman who can paint better than I can. I could do it myself, but I want it to look professional. Besides, the faster it gets done, the sooner I start bringing in my cash flow. I wander back to the sink to turn on taps and check the water pressure and drains. Good, there are no leaks and the sink holds water. I check the bathrooms next. There is a toilet for the public, and a toilet in the back for employees. Both toilets flush, and the sinks work well. I'm lucky to have stumbled onto a new place like this.

Out the back door, there is a short walk to the dumpster in the parking lot for the merchants' cars. Surveillance cameras are positioned at each end of the building. I check the deadbolts to make sure I'll be safe inside. There needs to be a peephole, too, so I sit down at the desk with my notepad to add that to my list of things for my handyman to do. I need to look into getting a cash register system and a printer for my business laptop. There is a cable hook-up as well, so I make a note to call the cable company. This afternoon, I'll buy a frame to display my business license when it arrives, and I'll figure out a date for the grand opening. That will be a day to celebrate. I'll prepare for a grand opening celebration with press releases and ad campaigns I'll start as soon as I have a date. When I get things going, I'll have to hire a couple of employees. I'll need several, once we're really rolling. And then the sky is the limit! Maybe I can invite Perky Amy from the morning news show to come in and sample my cupcakes, and advertise my grand opening…. Surely, she can be useful.

As I sit, holding the pen to my lip, I hear the door open, and a chime alerts me that I have a customer. I jump slightly while I get to my feet and round the corner, not expecting company. An extremely tall, dark, and handsome man in his mid-forties in jeans and an Oxford shirt with rolled up sleeves is standing in the middle of the shop, looking my way. He grins the biggest, whitest smile I have ever seen. He runs a hand over his clean-shaven chin.

"Well, hi! I thought I heard somebody knocking around over here! Are you the new tenant?"

"Yes. I just bought the business about an hour ago. My name is Elle McLarin," I say, going to meet him with an outstretched hand. This day is getting more and more interesting!

He's still grinning at me, and his friendly blue-green eyes are twinkling along with those amazing teeth. His hair is dark and bushy with threads of gray at the temples, a nice complement to his tan. Everybody I've met here has a tan. Am I the only one not on vacation? He grasps my hand in a firm shake.

"Congratulations! I'm Brandon Dean. I own the winery next door. You should come over and have a glass—on the house to celebrate! Welcome to the neighborhood."

I will just do that! "Thank you, Brandon. It's so nice to meet you! How long have you been in business here?"

"We've been open about two years. People know we're here. We've had some great advertising. We're adding some music events on Fridays and Saturdays out on the new patio. That helps. What kind of business is yours?"

I gesture around with my hands. "It's still a bakery—cupcakes, wedding cakes mostly, and birthday cakes, whatever you want."

"Great! We get lots of folks in who are planning weddings and having lots of celebrations. We should work together—tag team it."

"Absolutely!" I give him my sweetest smile and make my own eyes twinkle as best I can. "When I get my business cards made, I'll bring some over. Be sure to give me some of yours."

"I will!" he grins again, reaching into his pocket for one. *Whew!* I'm getting hot just looking at this guy. I try subtly to check his left hand for a wedding ring and see nothing, not even a tan line. *Wow!* "So what's the name of your bakery?"

"Bake My Day," I say, watching for his reaction. The name kind of suits my personality. Judy didn't like it, but most men do. Brandon is no exception. He considers it for a moment, then throws back his head, and laughs out loud.

"That is priceless! I love it!" His hands are on his hips now, and we are both glancing out the plate-glass windows as people walk by on the way to his store.

"Ah, look! Business!" I grin back at him, showing him I'm pleased for him. "Do people usually come to drink wine this early in the day?"

"Oh, you'd be surprised. Lots of times they're just stopping in to price things, or pick up a few bottles for parties, but yeah, some of the tourists will stop in to have a tasting or sit out at the tables and have a glass before lunch."

"Serious wine drinkers, then."

"Oh, yes. Well, I'll leave you to your preparations. Let me know if I can give you a hand with anything."

He doesn't look in a particular hurry so I try to think of a way to extend our conversation. This is going to be so much fun!

"Brandon, who do you use for your business supplies, you know, like soap and paper towels and toilet paper?"

"Oh, I get all that at a wholesaler in town. I'll write it down for you," he says, taking a pen out of his pocket.

"Oh, let me get you something to write on," I offer, slipping quickly around the counter to get my notepad. He hands me a business card, pointing out a number.

"Here's our number too, by the way, in case you need us. Really, stop by later on if you can," he says, writing the wholesaler's name quite illegibly on my pad. I hope I can read it. I lean in to check and feel our shoulders touch for an instant. "Jewel will love to meet you! She'll be glad to have your company. There aren't any other young ladies in the mall."

"Oh? Jewel?"

"Yeah, she's my partner…and fiancée."

Great. *A man I can't have.* I don't mess with married men, after I found out about a little thing called *alienation of affection.* It's big in North Carolina. Well, when I find out they are married, I ditch them immediately—funny how that goes; they never think to mention it. I've extricated myself from a few engaged men as well, for obvious enough reasons, especially engaged men who work next door with their fiancées. I may walk on the wild side, but I'm not stupid. I have learned a thing or two in my time of penance.

"Great!" I say without missing a beat. "I look forward to meeting her. I'll be sure to stop by. Probably not today, but I will come by soon. Thanks for coming in!" I'll be giving old Jewel a *wide* berth.

"Yes, ma'am!" Brandon says and shakes my hand again. "You take care now," he says, and I could swear he gives me a little wink. Well, maybe he's the stupid one!

This could be trouble.

Chapter 4

RANDY

After calling to set up a phone line in the bakery, contacting Brandon's wholesaler, and setting up an account, I have gone by the paint store to pick up lemon meringue color samples and check paint prices. I stopped by the power company and switched the account over to my business. Then, feeling famished, I drove back to my part of town and turned down Airlie Road by the waterfront to find a place for lunch. No more tacos for me!

At the Dockside Waterfront Restaurant, a T-shirt clad hostess seats me on the deck at a table under a large blue umbrella and hands me a menu. I order an iced tea and peruse the lunch specials. Glancing around at the other customers from the safety of my sunglasses, I feel conspicuously pale and slightly overdressed for this casual, kicked-back kind of place, where people are obviously here for fun. I spot one or two folks who look like they might be having a business lunch among the vacationers, but then, business here seems to be more casually conducted than I would have thought. Maybe I will fit in, after all.

I've never seen so many different kinds of boats slipped in at the docks in front of me. The array of silvery masts mixed with white fiberglass and warm teak, sails draped in bright blue canvas wrapping, is both soothing and exhilarating. *What would it be like to sail off in one of those crafts with some seaworthy wonder of a captain?* I ponder, as I watch a sport fishing boat gliding quietly over the no-wake zone, a girl in a bikini basking in the sun on the bow while two bare-chested men steer from a center console and talk. Papery gulls circle and swoop, calling to each other above the boats. The smell of fish is heavy in the pregnant warm sea air, making me wish for a reciprocating, salty kind of man.

Reflexively, I reach in my purse for my tablet, so I can occupy myself while I eat my lunch alone. I make a note to find an accountant. A good lawyer would be helpful, too; maybe I'll contact the attorney from the closing to see whether he can recommend someone. Giggling erupts from the table behind me, where I glance around to see three sunburned college girls, sipping water and gassing about the party they were at last night. A stocky man in a long-sleeved white dress shirt and a tie approaches them, bringing each of them a job application. He's the manager, judging from the shirt and his lack of suntan. The owner is probably sitting in the shade at the bar, in a Hawaiian print shirt, and tapping away on a computer. Ah, I see him now! Damn, I've played this scene so many times, I know exactly how it goes. I could waltz in here and snap up a bartending job so fast it would make your head spin, making five times what these girls are going to make, hustling tables in the hot sun.

From their conversation, I can tell that the girls are too hung-over to fill out their applications. They are groaning at the questions and dragging out their wallets to write down their driver's license numbers. The manager passes me once, taking a look at my legs; then he buses a table, and he is back again to check on the girls. He knows their scene too, and I hear him sigh as he passes me again. More kids to babysit, he's probably thinking. He's at least my age and too hot in that shirt. He catches my eye this time.

"Has anyone taken your order yet?" he asks pleasantly, reminding me of a bear. He's big, with a soft belly that suggests he doesn't have time to work out and probably drinks and eats whatever the hell he wants. He has friendly brown eyes.

I remove my sunglasses to talk to him. "Not yet, but I think I see my server coming with my tea."

"Oh, okay. Let me know if you need anything...."

A thought occurs to me and my eyes take on a new gleam. "Actually, I think I'll have a Mimosa. I need to celebrate."

"Yeah, sure! What are you celebrating?"

"I just bought a bakery!" I say, giving him my cutest grin. I can see him checking out the dimple in my left cheek.

"Congratulations!" he says, grinning back at me, and he's not bad looking. His light brown hair is short and bristly, a good choice since he's going bald on the crown of his head, and he has a well-groomed short beard that makes him look distinguished. He needs to; he's the boss. He's definitely got the people skills. "One Mimosa coming right up!"

I watch his large butt walk away from me as my waitress arrives with my iced tea. I order a cup of the blue crab and corn chowder, and a side salad with vinaigrette dressing. A fly explores my glass so I shoo him away, going back to my tablet, where I'm investigating signage businesses. The girls behind me are guffawing over their vague memories of somebody puking up her PJ at last night's party. They're having the time of their lives, coming to the beach to work and play the summer away. Good for them. I never had the time of my life. Maybe it's now. I know as hard as I'm going to have to work, that this won't be the time of my life, but it's a whole lot better than what I had yesterday, so I'm as glad as they are to be here, no matter what's to come. Besides, I've passed the age when I could have gotten away with anything frivolous. Those girls suck.

Apparently finished with their applications, they are waiting for the manager to come back and talk to them, so they can start working here or move on to the next stop in their quest for employment. The manager arrives with my drink and I thank him graciously. He watches me take the first sip, and he looks like he's going to approach the waiting threesome behind me, but I think I'll distract him. Just long enough to piss them off. Besides, I need information, and since he's in the same industry....

"Do you have a minute?" I begin, taking off my sunglasses again and giving him a promising smile. The girls can wait.

"Sure," he says, pulling out a chair and joining me. I can hear the girls mutter their protests. The heat isn't helping their hangovers, but they're too stupid to roll out the umbrella at their table.

"I wondered if you'd mind sharing some of your resources. You're the owner, right?"

Seemingly flattered, he runs a hand across his beard. "No, but I'm the manager. What can I help you with?"

"Well, I'm new to Wilmington, so I was wondering if you know of a good sign company. I have something in mind—my own logo, but I want to get my signage up as soon as possible."

He nods. "Sure. Of course. I can get you a name, if you can wait a minute. What's the name of your place?"

"Bake My Day," I throw out confidently, aware that the girls are now trying to eavesdrop on our conversation. The manager looks unfazed, as if he's forgotten all about them.

"Wow! Very Clint Eastwood. I like it."

"Me too. I'm also looking for a handyman. I need somebody who can paint and do the heavy lifting, you know, general stuff."

Bear studies me for a minute. He looks out, over the water. "Yeah, I know a guy." He chuckles. His hands are clasped, and I watch his thumbs lift up and down. I raise my eyebrows. He meets my gaze dead-on. "You need Jimmy Burns."

Apparently Jimmy Burns is a somewhat controversial character, but then, so am I. I'm up for meeting him. "Can you give me his number?"

"Yep," he says, taking his phone from his pocket and scrolling through his contacts. I take mine out as well and he asks for my number so he can send me the contact. *Isn't he the slick one?*

"Great. Thanks so much."

"You're welcome," he says, standing, as my food arrives. "I'll get you that signage company's name and number as well." He's still holding his phone and I know he needs my name to add to his contact screen.

"Thanks. My name's Elle, by the way. Elle McLarin."

"Hi, Elle. I'm Randy."

Randy.

I freeze for a moment and then I force myself to move on. Randy and I shake hands, another business deal sealed. He puts his phone back in his pocket and I send him away with another *I'll-be-back* smile as I take a sip of my Mimosa. The girls are really pissed off now. They protest that he's walking away again, while here they sit in the hot sun. One of the girls is making ugly comments about me behind my back, telling her friends I should apply for a job at Hooters. They think he was interviewing me for a job? That's rich. Hooters, my ass! And I sure as hell don't wear orange anymore. I smirk and blow on my chowder under the shade of my umbrella, watching more boats slide by on the water. It's so lovely here.

Randy.

Randy's waiting while my mama rummages through the kitchen cabinet for a bag of potato chips. They always eat stuff after they've smoked their homemade cigarettes outside on the double wide's porch, the cigarettes that have that sweet musky smell that aren't like Pa's. Mama goes into the bathroom where we can both hear her peeing. Our trailer is so small you can hear through the walls. You can even hear inside the other trailers next door with

the windows open in the summertime, like they are now. I always hear Mrs. MacLeod hollering at her boys, twelve-year-old twins, Bryan and Eddie. They're always in some kind of trouble. Randy sidles up closer to me on the couch to see what I'm drawing, making me get stiff. I'm a good drawer and he watches me a lot. I've changed the dress in the magazine to have ruffles, and I've colored it lavender instead of pink. Purple is my favorite color. Then he notices my naked Barbie dolls on the couch beside me. Trying to dress them makes my fingers tired, so sometimes they have to go without their clothes. On TV, the fairy godmother from Cinderella *sings, "Bippety Bobbity Boo" as she's turning a pumpkin into Cinderella's coach, so I focus on* Walt Disney *instead of Randy. I can tell he's got his mouth on Barbie's bosom, sucking on it, the way I eat ice cream cones, but I can't stand to look at him doing that. Next, he takes both Barbies, pushes their legs apart, and presses their bottoms together, breathing hard and laughing quietly, so mama won't hear him. "Why don't your Barbies have nipples? Your mama has nipples. Girls are supposed to have nipples. Someday, little bit, you're gonna look just like one of these Barbie dolls," he says, like he can't wait. His breath smells like medicine when he talks so close to my face.*

I'm only five, so I don't think I'm supposed to be discussing this stuff with Randy. I back away, my eyes glued to the TV. He shouldn't talk about nipples. The fairy godmother wouldn't, and I don't think that nice Cinderella in the movie would like hearing him talk like that either. I sure don't. It makes me swallow a bad taste, and I wish he'd go away. My stomach is starting to feel funny again, the way it does when Randy comes over. It's dark outside, and I know he and mama are going to go back in her bedroom to play their games, the gross one where they laugh and make a lot of noise. It sounds like he hurts her, but she doesn't seem to mind going in there with him. I don't like it, but if I stay here and be real quiet, Randy won't get mad. He's little for a man, not much bigger than Mama, but he's got a big temper. Maybe it's because of all the black he wears. His dirty blond hair is pulled back in a ponytail, and his mustache looks like the handlebars on his motorcycle that's parked outside. Mama calls it Harley Davidson, like it's some really important per-

son I should know, but I don't like it either. It's loud and scary, and I wish he would get on it and ride off yonder to wherever it is he lives. I don't know why she likes it, or him, but at least they're back from their "errand" and I'm not by myself anymore. Mrs. MacLeod doesn't like him either. She scowls at him and Mama every time she sees us. She's always watching us over here. I wish Mama'd come out of the bathroom so he'd put my dolls down.

The bathroom door flings open and she's here. "Gross, Randy. Quit it!" she yells at him, and then she laughs. He returns the dolls to the couch and gives me a warning look. Wiping her wet hands on her cut-off jeans, Mama brings the bag of potato chips over and shakes some in a napkin for me on the coffee table where I'm trying to draw. "Be a good girl," she says, leaning over and giving my head a stroke, pushing my hair back over my ear. Randy looks down her shirt before she takes him by the hand and they go back to her bedroom where I hear the door shut and the lock click. As if I would ever go in there now! I blow out the candle on the table and lock the front door. Then I turn off the lamp and pull Mrs. MacLeod's afghan over me, just about the time that Cinderella makes her entrance to the ball. This is the best part....

I should probably keep on working if I want to open this bakery any time soon, but after my Mimosa at the Dockside, and the unpleasant memories I've chosen to cast aside, I feel the need to abandon business and reward myself with a celebration. After all, I am at the beach with a brand new bikini and no tan yet, so I decide quickly to return to my place, change clothes, and spend the afternoon on the beach. I used to get as brown as a hen's egg when I'd spend the summers swimming in the river, sunning myself on the rocks, and tending Pa's vegetables with him, but today, I am embarrassingly pasty. First, good sense makes me stop at the grocery store to stock up on fruits and vegetables and a few other items I'll need. As I pull into my spot under the crape myrtle, I notice something on my doorstep. Mr. May appears to be gone for the day, but someone has left me a Mason jar filled with lovely, unusual pink peonies. I've never seen this variety. Granny would have swooned and exclaimed over them, an image that makes me smile. I'm sure Anne Borden Montgomery did not leave these for me. Mr. May has welcomed me to my new home! I feel surprised and thankful to be in his thoughts in such a way. There is a dark, wet spot underneath my window box. True to his word, he took care of my petunias as well. He is indeed a thoughtful man.

A warm feeling spreads through me as I carry my little treasure inside, setting it on the kitchen counter that also serves as my dining table. Someone cares about me. Mr. May is too old to have anything kinky in mind, so I relish his innocent act of kindness even more. "*Having flowers shows you care*," Granny used to say. And giving them means someone has a good heart. To me, flowers are hope. I need hope. How could Mr. May have known that I prefer peonies over roses? A girl like me never gets roses anyway, and there are certainly enough roses on this property to have filled a mere mason jar without AB's notice—if that were the issue. So there is definitely something special about Mr. May. You can just tell. When I get my kitchen set up at the bakery, I will bake Mr. May a cake. He is a cake-worthy person in my opinion!

I glance at my phone again for messages. There is one from the signage company. A representative will meet me tomorrow at my shop to go over some options. Great. I plan on getting there early to start cleaning. Jimmy Burns is coming at nine o'clock, so I expect to have a full day. Staring at the phone, I wonder whether I'll sleep tonight. Pushing old thoughts out of my head, I reach for the plastic bag that holds my new swimsuit and begin to change clothes. It takes some rooting around in my bathroom cabinet to find my sunscreen, and I slather it on liberally, knowing that if I don't, there will be hell to pay in the form of an uncomfortable, and unattractive, sunburn. Smirking to myself, I wonder if those girls from the restaurant got jobs there. I will definitely return. Maybe they will wait on me so I can torture them further. *Quit it!* says Good Elle, and I just laugh at her.

After putting on my black cover up dress, and sticking a beach towel and a magazine in my tote bag, I slip my feet into my new gold flip-flops and head out the door to my car. It's another beautiful day here, just like the weather person promised this morning. I glance around at the flowers surrounding 312-B: lovely little clumps of coral bells and snow-on-the-mountain border the edge. I gasp with delight, seeing my favorite flower settled in their midst: the enchanting bleeding heart, with its slender arches of pink heart-shaped petals, lined up in delicate rows, each dripping pearl-like drops. It's a special sight to behold. Granny showed me a couple of her old love letters that she and Pa wrote to each other. She'd pressed bleeding heart blossoms into the folded pages of the ones she wrote to him. I can't imagine having a man who'd appreciate something like that. I can't even remember the last time anyone wrote me a letter. Who writes love letters anymore anyway? I've tried to imagine Pa as a young man, reading Granny's letters. I've seen pictures of her in her youth; she was a beauty. Their pictures and their letters are in the shoebox in my closet. I couldn't bear to part with them. Granny and Pa were lucky to find each other. Those were the days, I guess.

But then, here I am in this new place and no one knows me. I have all kinds of new possibilities. Someone has already given me flowers! And first impression flowers at that! There could be lots more fish in the sea than I'd previously thought, and I *am* going to the beach…so who knows? I start my car and head over the bridge, putting down my window and breathing in the salt air. This is it—my new start! Driving several blocks down Lumina Avenue, I snag an open parking place. Realizing that all the spaces are metered, I dig through my wallet, collecting enough quarters to spend an hour and a half soaking up the sun, and boy-watching. Excitement flows through me, as if I were twenty-one again, like those girls at the Dockside. *This is ridiculous!*

Hot, dry sand squeaks under my feet, and I walk quickly to the flatter, wetter part of the beach that's cooler to the touch. Spreading my towel on the sand, I make a mental note to buy a beach chair at the drugstore. No one is around to spread sunscreen on my back, so I will have to lie face-up. I glance around to check out the possibility of a lifeguard or any other male who could help, but I see no prospects over the age of fifteen. I'm no pedophile, so I give up and wander toward the ocean to check the water temperature. Tides splash and fizz, spreading over the sand like champagne. The remaining fan of bubbles leaves the impression of a wedding veil, and then it is gone, as tens of tiny fiddler crabs scurry into their holes, as the wet sand closes over their heads. The sandpipers come next, like a corps of miniature ballerinas lined up *en pointe* with their skinny little legs miraculously supporting their bodies.

The image reminds me of Chelsea Davis, Kyle's wife now, who is actually a ballet dancer, making me frown. The image of her lithe body wrapped in his competent arms suddenly makes me feel fat, so I suck in my stomach and give my head a shake, purging the thoughts of them, and move on to viewing the aquamarine water in front of me. The mid-afternoon sunshine throws sparkles on the water like thousands of diamonds. More wedding images and happily-ever-after thoughts are coming to mind, and I find it only mildly annoying today. Could they be a foreshadowing of what is to happen to me? *No way*, says Bad Elle, but I push her away and walk into the tide that laps at my feet. The water is startlingly cold, making my toes curl into the sand in response. There will be no swimming for me today, especially since I am by myself and there is no lifeguard here. Swimming alone in the ocean is not a good idea, although there are plenty of other people on the beach, sitting in groups together, or flinging Frisbees back and forth along the wet sand. *Would any of them rescue me if I were to drown?*

My sleepless night is catching up with me, fatigue driving me back to my towel, where I sit and eventually stretch out, closing my eyes, and letting the sun bathe me in its warmth. The warm, soothing breeze wafts over my face and my body. Why am I so conflicted about the possibility of happiness? Everything is here; I'm ready, but what is dragging me down? I have a strange dark sense of foreboding that pushes on a door inside my mind, and I push back.

The sound of the waves swelling, cresting and crashing, and then fizzing into the shore lulls me into semi-wakefulness. My thoughts are a jumble, making me realize I'm pleasantly drifting off. And then there is Vada's face peering into mine, her unexpected green eyes searching me.

"Elle, just let it go…."

Chapter 5

DARK VADA

Vada's office looks like crap. But it's the Taj Mahal compared to my cell. The musty old carpet, dented file cabinet, dirty windows, and piecemeal furnishings are apparently all you get when you're a caseworker for the state, but Vada doesn't seem to care. She sits at her desk, her impressive black hair neatly cornrowed into ropes that hang down her back. Watching her go through my file, I observe that her mocha skin is clear and without makeup, but I can see that she's licked off what remains of her lipstick. Suddenly, her eyes look up at me. They're green, startlingly green for a black person, and that catches me off-guard, so I immediately look away. I will not let my guard down in this place for one second, especially not with her.

"So what's your story, Elle?"

I try to look bored. After a minute of giving her my "you-dumbass" stare, I say, "You should know. You just read my file."

She doesn't react. "How'd you get the name, 'Elle'?"

Easy answer, and one I don't have to think about. "My mama named me after the magazine."

"I've read that one. Not bad. Your mama left you when you were five?"

"That's what it says...."

"And you've lived with your grandparents ever since?"

"Yup."

"And you never knew your father?"

Hmmm. *Did you miss the part where he got blown up in the meth lab before I was born? Yup, my mama could really choose 'em. Surely, Granny has filled her in on all the details of my past. Vada looks at me, trying to read my face, but I don't respond.*

"Where'd you get the roofie?"

Whoa. *Quick topic change. I'd never divulge Richard Spencer's name, if that's what she's after.* "A friend in college. He was gonna use it on me," I say, *giving her my most devilish smile.*

"No way! How'd you get hold of it?"

I remember homecoming weekend, when he'd returned from college to be my escort on the court. I wasn't the queen, but I had the best dress and the hottest date.

"I had my hands down his pockets tryin' to get me some of him, and I found it. Then he realized he didn't need to give it to me, and I asked him if I could have it, so...there you go."

"Aha," she says. "Did you think giving a guy a roofie would really get you what you wanted?"

Her question stings. The cops asked me the same thing. She's trying to make me look stupid, and I don't like it, so that's the last she's getting out of me. I wasn't going to give him all of it. I tried to break the pill in half and drop it in his drink to loosen him up, but the whole thing fell in. Nobody knows that. Things could have turned out so differently for me....

"Pretty, smart girl like you—why didn't you just jam your hands down Kyle Davis's pockets and work your magic on him?" she asks sharply.

My face flames red. She's trying to bait me so I look away, trying to look bored again.

"'Cause he wouldn't go for a girl like you, right? You're smart and pretty so you didn't understand why you couldn't get him to like you. He's too good for you so you had to go to extreme measures to get what you wanted. You always get what you want, don't cha? Elle. You do realize that you could have killed that boy?"

The cops told me that too; so did the prosecutor and the judge...and Pa. I'm sick of hearing it. She must have read my apology letter to the victim from the court file, not that he was even there to hear it that day, just his mother. Vada is not going to get one over on me. I can turn this around on her. "Why do they call you Dark Vada?" I blurt, but she does not react. Her nickname is ridiculous. It must have something to do with Star Wars, but hell if I know. "The other girls call you that. Doesn't it piss you off? Is it a Star Wars thing or just a racial slur?"

She probes me with her eyes, which remind me of the sliced green olives on top of Granny's potato salad. Then she starts a slow smile.

"It's because, baby, I'm gonna take you to the deepest, darkest places inside of you that you don't wanna go, but you will. Before you leave here, you will go there. You just have to learn how to let it go so you can get on with your life." Then she stands, so I guess our meeting is over. She hands me a book. "Read this so you can have dessert."

I haven't had dessert here. I don't know what she's talking about. I do know that she read in my file that I like to read. And I love a good chocolate cake. I'll bet Granny told her all that.

I look at the worn and dog-eared paperback she's laid on the desk and pick it up. It's the book we were reading in my English class at school. I missed the *exam when I left school that day with Aiden and had to take an incomplete. You can run, but you can't hide.*

The Awakening *by Kate Chopin.*

A ball hits the sand near my head, awakening me with a start. I wipe drool from the side of my mouth and right myself to a sitting position, in time to see one of the fifteen-year-olds careening toward me to scoop it up, and then he cuts sideways before he takes me out completely. *Holy crap!* I'm awake now.

I check my phone. I've been asleep for forty minutes or so. I blink and cross my feet in front of myself, as if I'm preparing for a yoga class, resting my palms on my knees. The phone in my hand is registering another message so I enter my code to read it.

"Made it to base. Thanks for the camera and the card." Joey.

My own tide is swelling and crashing inside, relief flooding through me. Until now, I didn't realize I'd been holding my breath for two days—two exhausting days. But no reciprocated words from my son—the two words I have rarely heard from him, the two words I wrote on his card under "Happy Birthday." *Love you.*

Still, I'm sure the camera was a shock. And it was a nice camera. We'd never been able to give expensive presents until after I sold Granny's house. I wanted Joey to have something nice, something lasting, that would show him how much I love him. We have always had our obstacles, but I have always loved him, and going into the Army just a few days after his eighteenth birthday is a big deal. He loves to capture pictures through drawing, the way I did as a child, but with all the traveling he'll be doing in the Army, a camera is something he'll enjoy using. Granny and Pa would have wanted him to have it too, and Aiden thought it was a great idea.

Tears from somewhere have made their way down my face and I remove my sunglasses to wipe them away. Getting Joey's message is a welcome distraction from the dream I was having. It's best not to sleep sometimes. Letting the relief register, I sit with my arms wrapped around my knees, watching the football being tossed on the beach.

Aiden played football in high school. So did all the other boys I knew. I was a cheerleader. I try to imagine Joey tossing around a football with his new Army buddies on the base. Maybe they'll play soccer. He grew up playing soccer. He needed the exercise the way the rest of us need air to breathe. He hated being indoors, something Pa had sensed about him early on, so he did his best to keep Joey occupied with all the things they did on the weekends and in the summer.

"What do you and Joey talk about when you're fishing?" I'd asked my grandfather, hoping to glean some insight into my son.

He'd thought a moment and said, "You know how it is. We don't say a whole lot. Don't want to scare the fish away. Besides, once you start tellin' a story, that's when you're likely to hook one. Then you'd miss it."

I wish Pa had taken me fishing more. Maybe he knew I didn't have the patience for it. As I grew older, I got into girly things like clothes and dancing and boys, none of which Pa wanted to think about. He didn't like it when I started wearing makeup and spending time with boys, my budding sexuality scaring the hell out of him. Granny thought if she prettied me up and had me singing and dancing in plays, people would like me better, I guess. It would have served me better if she'd made me concentrate on school; I was certainly smart enough to do something with my life, starting with a college education, but Granny and Pa didn't have that kind of exposure so they didn't know how to guide me onto that course. Plus, they had their hands full with me and my hormones.

The boys caught on quickly to what I was all about. I grew up too fast, which made Pa uncomfortable. We didn't talk about anything I liked. I felt like I had lost my grandfather forever back then, but he came around when I needed him. I suppose sometimes words are irrelevant, but there is a difference between being comfortable and quiet, and so conflicted that there is nothing to say.

I didn't have many of those special quiet times with Joey, except maybe when we were riding in the car, and there was just that peacefulness between us, but it never seemed to last. I'd ask about school and his test grades, and then freak out when he'd tell me how badly he'd scored, or he'd forget to turn in assignments he'd done, and his grades would suffer because of his lack of initiative. Then the silence between us would be edged with disdain and irritation. All Joey cared about was being outdoors. I thought he would eventually grow out of it, but there seemed to be more to it than just that. The school counselor tried to help me figure it out, but nothing showed up in their testing. She said he was smart but an underachiever and maybe a little hyperactive. I wasn't about to give him drugs; he was only a child. He didn't care about his grades, so I was at a loss for ways to help him, and Aiden couldn't do much better. At least Joey was happier with him; Aiden didn't stay on his case about school the way I did. I guess I failed him. I failed at being a mother. And now he's gone and I may never see him again. Maybe without me, he can finally be happy.

My celebration is over, I think, standing and shaking out my beach towel. Sighing, I fold it up and shove it back in the tote bag, along with the magazine I didn't get around to reading, since I fell asleep and dreamed about Vada. I haven't thought about Vada in weeks, but she's a part of me that I just can't shake. After our initial interview, I actually grew to like her. She was right; there was that invasive element to our talks, in which she did try to explore the inner workings of my consciousness, and after a while, I kind of got into it, like addiction in a way. There was nothing else to do in prison except listen to the other women tell me their troubles. And I told them mine after a while. We were a sorry little club, the kind of club you don't ever want to join. There are some sad, irresponsible, reckless, addicted, sociopathic, and just plain fucked up people in the state's prison system, and I realized real quick that I wasn't, or shouldn't have been, one of them. I guess most of us felt that way. I was really no different.

When I went to prison to serve my time, Granny and Pa were so disappointed in me; scared for me, but most of all so disappointed in me. Vada helped me rehabilitate myself after dragging me through hell and back, but it was worth the trip to have her feel good about me. Who knew I was a pleaser? Still, when I got out, I never called Vada. What would have been the point? She did her job and I did mine.

I remember the day in her office, a month after she'd given me the book, when I'd reread it and wondered about dessert.

"Well, what did you think of The Awakening*?" she'd asked, whisking around her desk and sitting down. She always smelled of sandalwood or one of those earthy, exotic fragrances.*

"Beats reading about black oppression," I said, giving a disrespectful shrug and getting no reaction from her.

"Why do you suppose you have to read that kind of literature in school?"

"So we won't forget about slavery."

"Right answer. And so we learn to treat each other with respect, as fellow human beings, regardless of our diversity."

"That's why we have to read about the Holocaust. I don't know any Jewish people, but I think I treat everybody the same way."

"Unless you have a mean girl agenda."

I shrug again. "Unless somebody has it coming to 'em. That Edna woman in The Awakening *took the lame way out of her problems. I don't understand how people can commit suicide. She had no balls whatsoever."*

"No? Did she really have a choice? She couldn't live with herself the way she was after her sexuality was awakened in her. Think of the way the moral code was back in her day. Sexuality, particularly extramarital sexuality, was more than frowned upon. Scandal had a much deeper meaning then than it does now. Plus, she was in love and she couldn't imagine her life without Robert."

I wanted to laugh, but I didn't. Why would someone like her give a rat's ass about that repressed, selfish little white woman who'd had an affair, and a repressed affair at that?

"Edna Pontellier was a wimp. She had a choice. You always have a choice. You always have to face the music."

"Another good answer. Facing the music is the honorable and courageous choice. But Edna did make a choice, although it wasn't the one you would have made. It's the choices we make that determine our character. It's not how we fall, but how we rise."

Like I don't already know this! "I wouldn't have done what she did. I'd have moved somewhere else and started over. I know—she left her children by walking into the ocean. She could have at least enjoyed herself, if she was going to leave them."

"You would have left your children? Isn't that what your mama did to you? And your daddy, in his own way? They did whatever they pleased, and you weren't even an afterthought."

She's trying to get to me through my parents' evildoings. I pretend not to notice. Would I do that? Would I leave a child? No. Granny and Pa didn't abandon me. They might not have wanted me, but they took me anyway. I would never abandon a child the way my mother did me. Still…. "Death wasn't her only option. It's a stupid book."

"So you would have done exactly what your mama did? She left you with your grandparents and rode off into the wild blue yonder with some moron on a Harley?"

"No! I would never leave a kid." She was really pissing me off then. I was starting to feel sick at my stomach, but at the time, I thought it was from what we were talking about. When confronted, it's always been my tactic to change the subject. And I sure didn't feel like throwing up.

"You told me I could have dessert when I read this book."

"Yes, I did. You get to make your own. We're going to the kitchen to see how good of a baker you are. Maybe you can put those skills to good use."

It's late afternoon by the time I've arrived at my driveway. AB's car is in the garage and the door is up. She drives a sleek little Mercedes—silver like lots of the Floridians we used to get up in the mountains over the summers, looking to escape the heat. I still wonder why she works. I wonder how old she is too, and why Mr. May is her gardener. They're so old that I hope they both don't keel over and make me call 911. It wasn't my intention to come down here and worry about people and take care of them, like I'm working at some old folks home! I sigh, thinking about Granny and how sick she was for so many months. The weeks and months went by like a blur. I can't do that again, take care of somebody like that again, at least not for a while. And I don't even know these people.

Not feeling like having a confrontation with Anne Borden Montgomery at the moment, I decide to take a little walk down my street. Noticing the "No trespassing" sign across from her driveway, I wonder whether she'd care if I sat out on her private dock. I do live here. It looks so peaceful out there. A large, dark bird glides in a circle over the water, fishing—an osprey, maybe? I need to look it up, and those flowers I can't identify. The tide is noticeably lower than it was earlier, and I can see people in the mud across the street near a dock, laughing and talking as they walk around in it with rakes and large white buckets. What in the world are they doing? The woman bends over and picks up something— a clam maybe—and drops it in her bucket. The man does the same and tries to toss his in, but he misses, which makes her laugh. "*Awww!*" She's nice about it and he laughs, too. *Married people.*

I walk farther down the street under the canopy of trees. The house beside ours is plain and sad-looking, with painted windows on the second floor. Why not curtains? Maybe some kid liked to paint; there are flowers and rainbows on the panes, and it definitely looks like a kid did it. There doesn't seem to be anyone home, although an old, tan Buick sits in the back of the driveway. The next house is nicer; it has the same white tongue-and-groove siding we have with a nice porch along most of the front, with gingerbread features nestled in its corners, and old rocking chairs. Although the yard is well-manicured, there are not many flowers, as if the owners don't have time, but they have the same colorful bushes that ring the yard and lots of trees.

A man stands with a woman in the driveway next to a car. I can't tell much about her, the way he's shielding her with his arm, but he's dressed in shorts and a T-shirt, with sun-streaked, light brown hair, and of course, a great tan. They're nuzzling each other and talking softly. She seems to want to get in the car, but she keeps going back for more nuzzling. I would too; this guy is *hot! An affair!* I'd know this kind of behavior anywhere. I've done it myself.

Her little slate blue Mini Cooper is a contrast to his weathered white pickup truck parked farther up in the driveway. I slow my pace, as if I'm too hot to walk any faster so I can observe them. He holds the car door so she can get in, and I can't help but notice the large angle of his shoulders, the cleft in his back, and his well-muscled legs, as he helps her in. He seems familiar. Then he leans over and props his arm on the top of the car so he can talk to her some more. They speak quietly to each other as I pass, but I can't make out what they're saying. *Why aren't they working?* Then again, I'm not working either, just out on the last leg of my little celebration before the onslaught begins tomorrow morning.

As I pass the house and move on to the next one, I hear her car start up and back out over the gravel driveway. Reaching the gray house at the end of the street, I notice there's a trail that takes off into the woods, but I circle around casually, naturally, as if I'm ready to head back down the street, listening to her shift the gears and then seeing her car point down the street. He's lingering, watching her, giving her that special smile that's meant just for her, and she waves before she drives away. Interestingly, there's one of those decals on the back window of her Mini—white stick figures of a dad, a mom, two kids, and a dog—the happy little obligatory family for a girl like her, but Mama's been screwing her brains out with my hot neighbor! Maybe she's another unfulfilled Edna Pontellier, leaving her children for the afternoon, looking for her own sensual awakening with my neighbor. This guy could definitely wake me up! Hmm…no sign of any toys in the yard; they don't live there together, and it's definitely an affair! At least I will have some youthful entertainment while I am here.

He's so oddly familiar. It's the shape of his head, the pleasing roundness of his face, even the ease and economy of his movements. He turns my way and gives me a short, acknowledging glance and then turns away to walk back into his house. And then it registers. The piercing blue eyes and gentle slope of his nose, the fullness of his lips and *damn!* He reminds me of Kyle Davis! Am I imagining this? After all, I've spent most of my time on the beach thinking about Kyle. Actually, there aren't many days that go by that I don't think about him.

Do you realize you could have killed that boy?

How is this fucking fair? I have moved six hours away from the only home I have ever known and the precious few people in the world who actually love me—along with a lot more who don't, all for the sole purpose of getting away from Kyle Davis and starting over, and here *he* is. Will I never be able to break free of Kyle, to get him out of my mind, and all he represents in my life? Why do I have to have this particular man here on my block, fascinating me by his all too familiar good looks and having a torrid affair with a married woman right under my nose? I try not to look at him again, or to call attention to myself as I pass his house and he walks back up onto his front porch, preoccupied with his cell phone. I resolve at this very moment that he and I will never meet.

Once years ago, when I was moonlighting at a rustic upscale restaurant in the mountains, Kyle came in with some other people on a business dinner. I was so caught off-guard and flummoxed upon seeing him that I acted like my pissy old self. I tried to be nice, but my defensiveness automatically brought out the bad girl in me. He'd just gotten married, and I weighed about two tons and my hair was awful—grown out at the roots. I couldn't have looked worse. How could I ever have a normal conversation with him after what happened? All I could do was turn on my Badass Barbie self and give him a hard time when we literally ran into each other coming out of the restroom. But what I really wanted was his forgiveness. I wanted to show him I *was* remorseful. In the back of my mind, I'd played out hundreds of scenes where I'd run into him, we'd talk, and everything would be okay. But that night, I ruined it. It wasn't okay then, and it never will be—at least, not on this planet.

Rattled and perspiring, I return to 312, fanning my face in frustration. I decide to check the mailbox. Maybe there will be a letter from Joey. Inside the box for 312-B, I find an envelope addressed to me. It's my business license. It won't be long for the junk mail to begin arriving, now that the mailman knows I'm here. As I wander back down the driveway toward my guest cottage, I see no sign of AB, and her garage door is closed. Mission accomplished, I think to myself with a sigh. Who will be my friends here? *No one, if you keep yourself closed off this way,* Good Elle says to me. *Shut up. I'm too tired to deal with you right now,* I retort silently.

I should call Judy to update her on my progress. I need to hear some kind words from a friend, and Judy is the one. Once inside my cool abode, I sniff for mustiness that is no longer there, only the scent of lavender from a dish of AB's potpourri. Glancing with pleasure at my jar of peonies on the counter, I deposit my beach bag at the door and pull out my phone, scrolling over my few favorite contacts for Judy's number. After several rings, I decide to end the call, but she answers, her husky friendly voice slightly breathless from hurrying to the phone.

"Hello!" she almost shouts.

"Hey, Judy! How are you?"

"Runnin' around like a chicken with my head cut off! How about you? I wanna hear all about it! How's your place?"

"Which one?" I laugh, releasing my hair from its confinement and fluffing it to dry from the heat and humidity.

"Uh, the bakery, *duh*!" she laughs back at me. I miss Judy. She shoots straight from the hip and has always been supportive of me, one of the few friends I have, whom I have chosen to leave.

"It's awesome! I have people coming over tomorrow to help me with the sign and the painting. I'll be giving it a deep cleaning all day."

"Well, what did you do today?" she asks, surprised that I haven't sanitized the place already and opened for business.

"Well, shit! I had to go out and celebrate since I just bought the place, and I had to check out the beach. I'm the only person in town without a tan."

"I know you. You were out boy-watching, weren't you?"

"Maybe. I think I've found the forbidden fruit right down the street." Thinking about my neighbor sends a little ripple through me. I can't even think about it.

"Look out, Wilmington! Elle's landed! Oh, lordy me! So are you still calling it 'Bake My Day'?"

"Yes, I am, and so far everyone loves it. You'll have to come and see it."

"I can try, but you know, wedding season is upon us, and I won't be coming up for air until Christmas, the way it is up here."

"I do know that," I respond. Mountain wedding season is long and fruitful, given our lovely, mild summers and spectacular autumns. "Maybe you could slip out for a day or two to come to my grand opening?" I throw out, hopefully.

"Not a chance, sister. My best manager ever just bailed on me, so I'm sunk until I can find a suitable replacement," she says, humor lacing her acidic comment, making me feel bad. Sort of.

"Hate it for ya. I hope I can get in on some of these summer beach weddings. Maybe the brides that are sliding in at the last minute will come to me since everybody else will be booked."

"There you go! Take out a Facebook ad. That's where you're gonna find 'em."

"Yeah, I thought about that." We've been over and over my business plan. Judy's been more than generous with her time and support. "Hey, I want you to know how grateful I am for all your help. And I'm sorry I bailed on you."

"I know you are, Honey Bun." I smile. She always called me that. Her daughter was Sugar and I was Honey Bun. "And you know I think it's okay. I hope you have loads of success. How's the traffic where you are?"

"It seems good from what I can tell so far. There's a winery next door, and on the other side there is a specialty food and gift shop. Then down the sidewalk, there's a sandwich shop, and a small art gallery on the other end. It all goes together really well, but it's a relatively plain-looking strip mall so it's not very charming. People are trying, though."

"Well, that's good. You'll need to go out and shop your competition."

"Yeah. I think I'll do that tomorrow after I get my cleaning done and get the painter going."

"Get some sleep while you can. It's going to be a long ride, Honey Bun."

"I know. Thanks, Judy. Sleep is overrated."

"That's what they tell me. Have you heard anything from our boy?" she asks apprehensively. She knows more than enough about my intrepid son.

"Yeah. He sent me a text saying he'd made it and he liked the camera."

"Unh. Nice of him. Well, just remember, as hard as you think you're working, he's gonna be working even harder."

"I know. I just worry about him, you know?"

"I know. It's not a good time to be serving our country, that's for sure. And you never stop worrying about your loved ones, especially the ones that are in harm's way. Write to him. He needs to know you love him."

"I will. Thanks, Judy. You're the best."

"I know it. Take care, sweetie."

"I will. You too. Bye now."

"Bye, girl. Be good."

The call is over, and I'm enjoying the sound of Judy's voice playing over in my head. Judy—plain and honest as the day is long. She remembers every customer by face and name that walks through her doors. All of them are so flattered, they keep coming back. She remembers numbers and prices and anything that needs remembering, except the bad stuff I did. And if she remembers, she doesn't continue to beat me up for it. She always made a place for me when my other relatives scorned me. The woman has a heart of gold, and she's taught me everything I know about being kind to people.

After all my years waiting tables, I never had the experience I had in Judy's bakery. Waiting on people in a restaurant can be rewarding if you play it right, but even so, some of them are indifferent. It always amazed me that people wouldn't stop talking when I'd arrive at a table to take their order, whatever the topic was; like how someone was cremated right after they'd seen him laid out in a casket the night before—ugh! *Like I'm not even standing there!* I'm a person, too, and I don't need to hear shit like that. People can be so rude and crass. Customers were strangers to me at first, so it was hard for me to let my guard down and be genuinely nice to them. But creating people's cakes is different. It's the same as growing flowers. It shows you care. It makes you feel good when people love what you bake for them. Judy's customers are customers for life. Mine will be, too. *Bake My Day.*

Maybe I'm not as conflicted as I think about my possible success in business, so I get up off the couch and retrieve AB's leftovers from the fridge and transfer them onto a proper plate. After popping the plate into the microwave and setting the timer, I set a place at my bar and pour myself a glass of wine. Sleep may be overrated, but I intend to follow Judy's advice and give it a try tonight. A warm shower, a good book, and a nice soft pillow are calling my name. I will have to find the public library soon.

I glance down at my phone and think of Judy again. Judy is always right. Picking it up, I check Joey's message again, thinking about the letter I'll write. Have I wasted eighteen years with my son? Going to my bedroom and opening a drawer in the bedside table, I take out my notecards and begin a letter. I'm bad at this too. It takes me forever to get the words out.

Dear Joey,

I'm glad you liked the camera. I hope you'll settle in and get used to the Army. I hope it's all you want it to be. I know our life wasn't what you wanted, but your daddy and I tried to make it the best we knew how.

I bought the bakery and I'm going to open in a couple of weeks when I get everything ready. I'd love it if you could visit when you get out on leave. You would like the beach. Please write to me and let me know how you're doing.

Love,

Mom

Chapter 6

JIMMY

I slept. I know this because I awoke in the same position in which I fell asleep. When my alarm sounded at six o'clock, I discovered that the book I was reading had fallen aside and the lamp was still on. For an instant, I had no idea where I was, and then it dawned on me that I was living my new life, and I had work to do. Rising to a sitting position and stretching, I'm pleased to realize also that I did not dream. How often does either of those things happen? And both the sleeping and non-dreaming were achieved without a sleeping pill! Life could be good.

I make my way to the bathroom, feeling stiff and groggy. My face, chest, and shoulders in the mirror are slightly pink, and my skin feels warm to the touch. Small, white impressions on my cheeks are left when I press my fingertips into them. An alien I am no more!

Putting my hair up, I give my face a light wash and brush my teeth. Since I'll be spending most of the day cleaning the bakery, I decide to wear a striped tank top and jean shorts with sneakers. A little makeup wouldn't be a bad idea either, I think, knowing I'll be meeting with the sign company's rep this morning. Jimmy Burns will be arriving at nine o'clock to talk to me about the painting and other things I need done.

I'm curious to see what he's like, remembering Randy's hesitation, but then his resolve to refer Jimmy to me.

After a cup of coffee and a quick breakfast of scrambled eggs and toast with some blackberry jam that Granny and I put up two summers ago, I make a list of cleaning supplies I'll need to purchase and keep at the bakery. I'll stop by the store on the way over to buy a bucket, a mop, and a squeegee for the floor. There won't be time for a real lunch, so I get out peanut butter and bread, make myself a sandwich, and toss it into my purse. It already feels as if I'm running behind schedule, so I grab my keys, a bottle of water, and head out the door, taking a look around for Mr. May so I don't knock him down again, when I realize he's not working today. Instead, I see AB walking to her car, a red leather tote bag slung over her shoulder, and a travel coffee cup in her other hand.

"Good morning, Elle," she calls out to me as I'm locking my deadbolt.

"Hi, AB. How are you?"

"Fine, thanks. How's it going?" She seems friendly, but there's no smile in her eyes. It's okay. I'm not expecting it.

"Great."

"Have a good one!" she says, waving, and beeping the unlock button on her car's remote. Before I can open my own car door, she's zipped out of the garage, closed the door, and nosed down her driveway.

"Have a good one," I mutter back.

In under an hour, I have plugged in my refrigerator and freezer again, and I am up to my elbows in latex gloves, scrubbing away at the inside of the display case, wishing I had music. What kind of music am I going to play here? I need to come up with a sound system. I'll go crazy without music. A song from *Frozen*, my favorite new musical, starts up in my head, and I start to sing the lyrics from "Let it Go." The sound echoes nicely in the open space, reverberating off of its tile and metal, so I let it rip as if I am on the stage. This could be my theme song!

"That sounds really good," says a male voice. Mortified, I extract myself from the case, pushing escaped hair out of my eyes as I look at the man who's talking to me. Fifty-something, with frizzy, blondish hair and a soft potbelly, Jimmy Burns is as nondescript as anyone I've ever seen. I couldn't pick him out of a line-up if I had to. I'm guessing he wore those jeans in high school, and maybe the T-shirt too, which seems to bear the colors of every wall he's ever painted. Under all the paint spatter, there appears to be some kind of advertisement about a rock festival from several decades ago. His arms are crossed and he stands, thoughtfully looking around my place, regarding me quietly. He's early. He shrugs. "I used to play in a rock band so I should know."

"Oh. Hey. Thanks. I didn't hear you come in. You must be Jimmy Burns," I say, peeling off a glove and going to shake hands with him.

"Right," he says in a twangy voice I recognize instantly as mountain. "You're Elle?"

"Yes. Elle McLarin. Welcome to Bake My Day."

He looks around some more, as if taking in the feng shui of my place. He nods, rubbing his hand along the opposite elbow that rests on his belly.

"This is a nice place," he says, allowing me a look at his coffee-stained teeth. "So you're wantin' it painted?"

"Yeah. I mean, this paint is relatively new, but it just doesn't suit me."

"What color are you thinkin' about?"

"I brought some samples from the paint store. I would have gotten the paint myself, but I wanted your opinion on the kind, and the color, how much to buy, and that kind of thing," I say, going to get my samples. "I wasn't expecting you until later."

"Oh, well, I was up, so I thought I'd stop on by."

"Here," I say, showing him a couple of the paint samples. "I like lemon meringue pie, and I think these colors remind me of that. I want something cheerful and warm and appetizing."

"Oh, I love lemon meringue. My mother used to make wonderful pies and lemon meringue was one of my favorites. I used to like to watch her whip the egg whites to make those little peaks. She was a real artist when it come to baking. And I loved to smell of it when it was baking in the oven."

His accent and his way with words make me feel at home.

"Where are you from, Jimmy?"

"I'm from western North Carolina."

"So am I. Valle Crucis. Do you know it?"

"I've heard of it. Never been there. I'm from Waynesville. Lived down here for twenty-five years, though. I like this color. You want to do the whole place this color?"

"Yes."

He looks around in the back, then returns to the front of the store, where the two-toned walls are, running his hand over the texture of the persimmon wall. Finally, he makes his pronouncement.

"I think five gallons ought to cover it. The same hue is going on top of this gold. That'll be easy to cover. The good new paint has a primer in it, so it covers really well. I think you can get away with five gallons."

"Oh. Good. When can you start?"

"I can go and get the paint right now."

"Will I be in your way, cleaning?"

"No. I can work around you."

"All right. How much will you charge for all this?"

He looks around again. "Two hundred sound fair?"

"You've got a deal." Randy deserves a big hug for this! And Jimmy Burns couldn't hurt a flea, so what was that all about? Maybe it was my imagination.

Jimmy looks around again and then rubs his arm. "All right then. I'll buy the paint and add that to the cost."

"Okay. Randy said you might be available to do some odd jobs for me from time to time—handyman kind of stuff."

"Yeah, I can do that if I'm free. I do carpentry and I'm a licensed electrician. I like to stay busy, so if there's something I can work in, I'd be glad to help you out."

What a nice guy. I checked too, to see whether he was bonded and insured and he was. It wouldn't do to have reprobates afoot! Jimmy leaves and I am alone again, contemplating how much it would cost to upgrade the light fixtures and maybe paint the furniture. I could paint it with black chalk paint and sand the edges to distress the tables and chairs, making them look vintage, which might give the place a bit more interest. I'm cleaning the plate-glass windows when the sign guy arrives. It takes a half hour to show him what I want on the storefront and on my glass door, and he takes it all down. My idea is simple and modern with lots of visual impact that will say it all—words and a cake. That's all I need.

I've cleaned the sinks, countertops, and both bathrooms by the time Jimmy returns, so I seat myself at my desk, poring over the offerings for all sizes of cake boxes, boards, cupcake liners, and logo stickers, letting him do his thing. Dreading the inevitable rock 'n' roll music he'll be blaring while he works, I soon notice that he's as unobtrusive as possible. He goes about his business with hardly a sound, arranging his drop cloths, positioning his ladder, and starting to cut his paintbrush into the top of my walls with hardly more than a slow *swish-swish* if I listen closely. As he comes around the corner where I can observe him, it is evident he is an artist, methodically but gracefully applying my delicious lemon meringue to each surface with the sanctity it deserves. He is going to make sure I love it here. I already do.

I watch for a while, and feeling a sense of calm fold over me, I finish placing my order. It is easy to work in this atmosphere of positive purposefulness. After having taken an inventory of the equipment that the previous owner has left, I move on to ordering baking supplies, tools, and ingredients to get me started. I can add more as my business develops. Next, I make a phone call to the department of agriculture to schedule the required inspection.

Munching on my peanut butter sandwich, I spend at least an hour evaluating the different cash register systems, and when I finally look up, I realize that Jimmy has outlined the entire inside of my shop in the yummy shade of yellow that looks even better than I'd hoped. Needing a break, I stand and stretch my legs, wondering about how to proceed through the murky waters of sales transactions. Brandon Dean may be just the man to assist me in this dilemma, so I decide to go next door for a consultation—and another look at Brandon. Jimmy seems only mildly aware that I have moved, and I am amazed that hours have gone by and he has not spoken a word.

"Jimmy, I'm going next door to Sandy Britches for a little second to see what kind of cash registers they use." He nods as he runs his paintbrush down the side of the doorway. Then it occurs to me that I should do something nice. A good girl would. "Do you need anything? I can stop over at the gift shop and get you something to drink."

"Oh, thanks, but I'm okay. I brought my water. It's almost lunchtime and I brought my lunch—out in the truck, so you go on ahead."

"Okay. I'll see you in a bit then," I say, remembering to order a neon "open" sign for the door as I push it open.

The polished décor of the winery next door reminds me of how much work I have to do to be ready to open, so I gasp apprehensively as I push open the door and step inside the charming ambience. There is an older couple perusing a section of red wines, set on top of a barrel. A woman at the wine bar is setting wine glasses in their places as I catch a glimpse of Brandon at the desk near the door, talking on the phone. He sees me come in and instantly breaks into that gorgeous smile. And there's that almost wink he does. I pause for a moment, waiting for him to finish his call, and gaze at the woman behind the bar. This must be Jewel. She's attractive, petite, and curvy, with that 1950s hourglass shape that's accentuated by the form-fitting lilac-colored top she's wearing with a coordinating set of matching glass beaded earrings and necklace. That matching jewelry is a sure sign of a control freak! Poor Brandon. Is he really the kind of guy who's going to let a little gal like that run his show? He looks too old to play that part. But you never know. I glance at him, but he's engrossed in his phone call, so I look back at her. Brandon's pretty young thing, hah! It's hard to tell how old Jewel is—older than I am maybe, though I always assume a woman is older than she looks, especially the way she makes herself up. Her hair is curly and sculpted perfectly in place, and I'll bet it looks that good every day. Her facial features are doll-like, as if they have been painted on in absolute symmetry. Even her dimples are symmetrical, I notice, as she greets the couple with genuine cheeriness as if they are old friends. Sickening.

Brandon is finished with his call. "Hey, there! I was hoping you'd stop in to see us! It's Elle, right?"

"Yeah. Hi, Brandon," I respond, trying to flash my own singular dimple, remembering to push out my impressive chest. In this tank top, I've got the goods on Jewel even though she is polished and poised. She continues to talk to the older folks, as if I'm not even here.

"So did you come over to join us for a celebratory tasting?"

"As tempting as that sounds, I actually wanted your advice on something. I'm looking for a cash register system, and with all the choices out there, I'm feeling a bit overwhelmed. I thought you could show me what you're using."

"Absolutely! Come here," he says, motioning me around the desk, and his voice sounds so casual and familiar that I find myself blushing. I walk around the desk where I can stand beside him so he can show me his machine. He wears that fruity, musky cologne I can't stand, so I'm reevaluating my opinion of him while I'm listening to Jewel cajoling the couple, finding out where they're from, and of course, it's her hometown, too! *Small world,* they're exclaiming. *OMG!* Brandon's showing me the features of this system, and he pulls out a little mobile card swipe device that works with it. "This'd be great for you, especially when you go out to make deliveries. You can accept payments on the spot—anywhere you are. How many stations will you need in your store?" His earnest blue-green eyes are so appealing, but it's his smile that's doing a number on my bad girl side. His towering height is also alluring, I think, since I have to look up at him. I like a man who reels me in but makes me work for it, too. *Girl—you do not need this,* I tell myself.

"Oh, I think just one. My place is small. When I worked in my cousin Judy's bakery, we got by with one. I like that card swipe thing, though. I think you're right; that would be really handy. I saw this system on the website. It seems reasonably priced—for what it is, you know?"

"Oh, definitely! It's easy to learn too—piece of cake! We love using it. We have two—one for the desk and one for the wine bar. See, it even has a way for your employees to clock in, and you can keep up with all of your transactions, inventory, which customers are buying what, and your employees' hours, all with the same program." He shows me how to access the screen and enter a sale. Then he deletes it. It looks so easy. "When you get yours, I'll teach you how to use it."

"That would be fabulous! And I need to know if you have an accountant you can recommend, too."

"Yeah, I do. Wait—I've got her name right here..." he says, scrolling through his phone contacts and writing down a name and number. "Tell her I sent you. Look; come on over and meet Jewel."

I follow Brandon reluctantly over to the wine bar, where Jewel is pouring a small amount of white wine into the couple's glasses.

"Hey, folks, how are we doing over here?"

"Great!" says the man, setting a shopping bag on the bar.

"Here; let me show you the hook for your packages under the bar," Brandon says, helping the man stow his bag.

"Well, isn't that clever!" says his wife. Brandon grins at her, too, and I watch her melt at the sight of those teeth. Maybe he has given her the almost-wink as well.

"Jewel, this is Elle, the young lady I was telling you about who's moved into the bakery next door."

"Oh! Yes! I'm so glad to meet you, Elle!" Jewel shoves her pretty, manicured hand across the bar at me, and I realize she has the matching bracelet as well. Super control freak. And—she's tan, big shock.

"Hey, Jewel!" I say, equally as enthusiastic, shaking her hand, which feels like one of those church ladies' handshakes: nothing to it, just a little squeeze of the fingertips to be polite, but her face is all into it.

"I'm so glad there's another woman on the block," she says, and I get the feeling she wants to say *and one my age*, but she doesn't, in deference to the sixty-something lady at the bar. I can foresee a post-wine tasting afternoon nap for these two customers.

I'm usually the prettiest girl in the room, but today, my disheveled appearance after all my cleaning has left me feeling inferior, so I want to bolt out of here as fast as I can. Now that I've checked out Jewel, I can see that she and Brandon are tighter than two ticks on a mule's tail, so I'll be leaving them to their own devices, but he sure is nice to look at. I'll definitely make this my go-to place for wine so I can enjoy Brandon's smile when I need some cheering up. They'll refer their customers to me, and maybe they'll buy their cakes from me as well.

"Well, it was nice meeting you, Jewel. And Brandon, thanks for showing me your system. Seeing you made me remember to go and order my business cards."

"So when are you planning to open?" Brandon asks as Jewel listens with interest.

"I'm planning on a few weeks from now if I can get everything done."

Brandon whistles. "Wow! That's soon. Let us know if we can help in any way."

"I sure will. Would you mind putting out my grand opening flyers?"

"Not at all," says Jewel. "We'd be glad to!" She gives me the double-dimple grin.

"Okay! Thanks so much! I'll see you both later on, okay?"

"Great!" says Brandon.

"Come back when you can sip and chat, okay? I'd like to get to know you better," Jewel says, and it sounds like she really means it. Maybe I should try to make friends. I'll need somebody to come to my rescue if I get robbed or mugged or something.

"Let me know if I can help!" Brandon says, and he walks me out, giving me another wink. Does she not *see* that?

Jimmy is wiping his brush and wrapping it in a plastic bag when I return. He has trimmed out the entire café area with the yellow paint, and I can see his roller and pan set up on the floor.

"Aren't you going to stop for lunch?" I ask.

"Yeah. I'll sit out in the truck and eat. I need to make a few phone calls."

"Oh, okay, but it's getting hot. You can eat in here if you want."

"Okay. Do you mind if I use your bathroom?"

"Oh, heck no! I cleaned it before you got here, so you can help yourself. I have a cash register to order so I won't bother you."

He nods and disappears into the bathroom while I sit down to my laptop and start to order the system online. A few minutes later, I realize he has gone out to his truck and come back in already with his own sandwich. I join him at the table where he's sitting.

The look Randy gave me is still gnawing at me, making me curious about Jimmy Burns. "What other kinds of work do you do, Jimmy?"

"Subcontractor work. I work regularly for Randy. I've been with him for about six years now."

"You work with Randy?"

"Yes," he says, sipping his water and wiping his mouth with a paper napkin from home. "Randy flips houses on the side, so I've been doing a lot of the reno work for him."

"Really?" I can't imagine how Randy could possibly find the time, but I guess he has nothing else to do.

"Yep. He buys foreclosures and short sales and does a little renovation and resells them."

"So you do the carpentry, painting, electrical work?"

"Exactly. I did my own house after I'd saved enough to buy my own foreclosure. It's small, but it's all I need."

"Hunh. That's an idea. I'd never thought of that."

"Do you own a home?"

"No. I'm just renting a place right now, since I just moved here and don't know the area, but it just seems like throwing money away." That's what Pa always said about renting.

"Yeah, it is…but sometimes you don't have a choice."

"That's right." I nod. I could buy a small place and pay in cash. There's no way I could get a mortgage from a bank with my record. Then, I could sell it and move to a bigger place if I wanted to. I could even have a kitchen table for Granny's vintage tablecloths, and grow my own peonies.

"Randy does right well with his business. I don't think he'll have to work at the restaurant much longer if he keeps doing as well as he is. But that Randy likes to work. He's a good man."

"I thought so, too. Hey, what do you think about painting these chairs? I was thinking about chalk-painting them black, and distressing them, and then staining the tabletops sort of a deep honey color...."

Jimmy looks around, imagining it. "Yeah, that would work. Want me to do it?"

"Do you have the time?"

"I can work it in. When are you planning on opening?"

"Maybe three weeks from now. I need to get in on the wedding season as soon as possible."

"I see. It's doable. Your place seems to be in real good shape. You seem to be a hard worker."

"I have nothing to do except work."

"No family?"

"Nope. I gave all that up in Valle Crucis, and came here to open this bakery."

Jimmy looks at me thoughtfully and nods. "I know where you're coming from."

You couldn't possibly. "No family for you either?"

"No," he says ruefully. "Not here. My family is all back up in the hills, and I get up there when I can, but there's nobody here."

"What brought you here?"

He shrugs. "A girl." He gives me a sad look and I know better than to pry. She probably dumped him and he feels stupid. I've heard that story a thousand times.

"Do you still play music?"

"Only when I go back home. I should though.... How about you? Where'd you learn to sing like that?" His eyes are sparkling, which I choose to take as a compliment.

"I sang and danced in plays when I was in high school, but I haven't done anything since then."

"Well…maybe you should get back into it. Get into a church choir or something."

It's a good thing I'm not eating. I would have choked for sure. I haven't been to church since I was five and punched Betsy Odell in the nose for saying that her mama said my mama was a druggie and a ho. I didn't know what a druggie was, or a ho for that matter, but the way she said it made me want to smack her down. Granny said if that's what Sunday school was going to be like, then I sure as hell didn't need to go, so she kept me at home after that. (Except for she took me to Christmas and Easter services, but only in church, never again to Sunday school, where she couldn't keep an eye on me.) That experience made me realize I had power.

I try to keep a straight face and twist my hair from the tip of my pony-tail between my fingers. "I'm not into church. Never was really."

"Oh. Well, you sing like an angel."

That would be the only resemblance. Still, Jimmy makes me smile.

"Thank you."

He wads his trash between his hands and stuffs it back into the paper sack he brought in.

"I reckon I'll get on back to work. Now that I'm rolling, I'll be finished today. Unless you want your trim painted?"

"I don't think it needs it, do you?"

"Nah, it's in really good shape. You got a nice place to start with. I've seen much worse. Do you want me to come tomorrow and paint the chairs?"

"Sure. You can help me. I'll get what I need when I go out again." Feeling as though I can trust Jimmy, I make a decision.

"I'm going to get out of your way and do a little comp shopping."

He looks confused.

"I'm going to check out some other bakeries in the area to see what I'm up against, so I can determine my battle strategy," I explain, letting my hair down and combing it out with my fingers. Then I rake it back up and put it back in the ponytail. Looking in the plate-glass window, I can tell that it's neater. I still look like Barbie. All I need is a bit of lipstick and I'll be marginally presentable. Still, I don't want to look like a slob, even though nobody knows me here. You never know whom you might meet. "Will you be okay here while I'm gone?"

"I should be fine. I ain't goin' nowhere."

"Okay, then. I'll be back in a couple of hours."

It takes less than ten minutes to drive back to my place, where I park and change into a sundress and sandals, perfect for my afternoon errands. A shower would be nice, but I can't afford the time if I'm going to be back to lock up after Jimmy. I'm in my car again, pausing at the end of the driveway while a car glides slowly past in front of me. It's the slate blue Mini Cooper. At the speed it's going, I can clearly see the driver. She fingers her short dark hair back in place and wipes a finger under her eye, while glancing at herself in her rearview mirror—my hot neighbor's mistress—and my mouth falls open in perfectly scandalized delight.

Why, it's Perky Amy Stainback from Channel 3 News!

Chapter 7

HOT NEIGHBOR

Was she crying? It is all I can do to close my mouth and force myself to turn right and not left, to continue on my business errands and do what I know I should do. *Hold on! Just take a wee little second and ride down there and have just a little peek!* Bad Elle is at it again, trying to sink me, yet I am so tempted to go with her just one more time! Just to get a glimpse of that delectable young fellow to see for sure if he really does resemble the bane of my existence. My insides are doing skin-the-cats right now just thinking about him, the way they always did in high school when I used to look at Kyle Davis. He had that irritating show of self-control that used to drive me so crazy, when all I wanted from him was just one little lascivious grin. Well, really, that wasn't *all* I wanted from him; I just needed *something* at least to work with, but it has taken me nineteen years to realize I was never going to get it, whatever it was about him that had me transfixed all that time. I cannot go down the other end of this street—*ever*—if I want to preserve my sanity.

Focus! I tell myself, coming to the stoplight and reaching for my list of area bakeries I will visit before I stop at the local big box store to purchase the supplies I'll need for tomorrow's painting project with Jimmy. Jimmy is solid. Jimmy will help me channel my energy where it needs to be. There will be no sexual distraction from Jimmy Burns, only a sacred kind of dedication to the work that I'm counting on to make me whole again. *Was I ever whole?*

Granny and Pa made me feel whole, and Judy did too, when I worked in her bakery. There is nothing like pouring your heart and soul into some bride's wedding cake and having her weep with gratitude upon witnessing your creation to make you feel whole. Quite possibly, baking cakes is what I was called to do, as vapid as it sounds. My calling was certainly not motherhood, nor apparently daughterhood either, nor anything else noble or remotely spiritual, but the simple act of presenting a cake to someone gives joy not only to the recipient, but to the creator as well. I was always so happy to have baked someone's day.

Still, I won't forget the day I was sitting at Granny and Pa's house, waiting for my mother to get back from her shopping trip, paging through the stack of fashion magazines Granny always kept beside the couch, looking for pretty dresses to draw. I could hear Granny and Pa whispering in the kitchen where Granny was stirring the stew. *I don't think she's coming back. What do we do? You should call the police.* I remember that we ate supper in an odd kind of silence, and then Granny let me put on my special pajamas she kept there for me, and I snuggled up beside her and her familiar red sweater on the couch and watched *The Sound of Music* until I fell asleep. I never left. I was glad to be there all the time. Once, I asked if my mother was coming back, and Granny said, "No baby, she's not." I said, "Oh," and that was that. I was happy.

As set in their ways as they were, Granny and Pa sucked it up and treated me like I was their little girl. Pa went to our trailer and got my clothes and toys. I didn't want my Barbie dolls anymore, so Granny let me put them in the trashcan. Pa gave me little horses he'd carved from wood, and he built me a small barn to keep them in. I drew lots of girls in pretty dresses. Granny and I didn't talk a lot, but we watched every musical ever made on the television, when Pa wasn't watching Clint Eastwood movies. I learned all the songs and performed for Granny and Pa in front of the fireplace with my wire whisk microphone. Granny signed me up for dance lessons and gymnastics classes. They came to all my plays. I had the lead almost every time. And then Kyle came to our high school at the beginning of senior year and derailed me completely.

I've pulled into a parking place at one of the bakeries, so I shake my head and reach for my notebook. I'll order a decaf coffee and a pastry, and sit inside and take notes. The place is old and comfy with upholstered chairs and lots of pretty lighting and yummy smells. A large blackboard suspended from the ceiling lists the menu items, including the cake of the day, the cupcake of the day, and the cookie of the day. I linger at the counters with the other customers, making mental notes about the flavors and the decorating, so when I have gotten my treats, I sit at one of the bistro tables and write down my impressions. There is a large decanter of cucumber water, and plastic cups on a counter where the wedding cake book is located. Several employees work behind the counter, and I can hear the bakers banging around in the kitchen. The phone rings and a girl takes an order. The busy atmosphere of this place makes me break out in a nervous sweat. I have a lot to do before opening day.

The next two places offer different ideas but are less impressive. One place is almost dead. It's pink; that's got to be why. Feeling as if I have enough information, I head to the big-box store for a diversion. I can make this happen if I do my own thing, and take it one step at a time. I find two telephones and a large blackboard to place in my shopping cart. Browsing through the chalk paint color selections, I exhale purposefully, making myself relax. I need to place an ad for some employees. As soon as my food stuffs arrive, we can begin baking and freezing some things to get started. I can do a cupcake campaign and go around to all the upscale places where my target audience shops and deliver cupcakes to the owners, along with my grand opening flyers. I need to order business cards, I remind myself. And I need an opening date, I think, adding paintbrushes to my cart, and looking at stain colors.

Back at my place, Jimmy Burns is rolling the café walls. The overall impression of my lemon meringue is delicious!

"Oh, wow! Jimmy! I love it! You've done a great job!"

Making my way around the corner, he looks over at me. There is not a speck of yellow paint on him anywhere. How can he be so neat?

"You like it? I do too! It looks really inviting and cheerful."

"I think so, too. Even on rainy days, it will look warm and cheerful."

"I'm almost done. Do you need anything else done today?"

"I don't think so. I bought phones. All I need to do is plug them in. I'll write down the number for you when I get it set up with the phone company. You have my cell number, right?"

"Yes 'um. What time do you want me here in the morning?"

"How about eight?"

"Sure. That'll be fine," he says in his calm, kind voice.

"Thank you for all your hard work."

"Glad to do it," he says, going back to his wall.

"Can I just pay you tomorrow, after the chairs are done?"

"Sure."

I set my bags down on the counter and go to work on installing my phones. Then, I group the chairs together and the tables in another area. Placing the large blackboard I've bought next to the counter, I set out the painting supplies for the morning and go over my list. In the time it takes Jimmy to clean up, I've ordered the business cards on my laptop, and started looking over my calendar to choose a date for the grand opening. June first. Eighteen days away. I feel a wave of nausea. We can do it. I'll have my permit from the city by then. Resting my chin in my hand, I glance around at the tables and chairs. I want little glass vases on each table with an orange flower in each one. I'll have flowers every day. Maybe Mr. May can help me, and if it's okay with AB, I can plant a little cutting garden of my own with zinnias and cosmos, and chrysanthemums for the fall.

AB is looking through her mail, ripping junk mail in pieces, and tossing it all in her garbage can at the foot of her kitchen stairs when I pull under the crape myrtle. She looks surprised to see me. Her red leather tote bag is parked on her shoulder.

"Hi, Elle!"

"Hi, AB! How was your day?"

"Oh, pretty good. You've certainly been working hard," she says, peering at me over her red polka dot readers.

"Well, I really want to get the place open soon. I don't want to miss the wedding season altogether."

"Time is money."

"Yes, it is." I remember what I wanted to ask her, but then she beats me to the next topic.

"Elle, I wanted to ask you about something. Do you have a minute?"

"Sure." She doesn't make a move to invite me in, so it must be a quickie.

"Mr. May's birthday is coming up and I wanted to give him a little party. He'll be eighty next week. Would you bake a cake for him?"

"Oh, absolutely! I'd love to. What did you have in mind?"

"Something with lots of flowers on it. Really colorful with kind of a *Midsummer Night's Dream* sort of theme. I'm hoping to have about twenty-five people, and we'll celebrate out here in the garden. It'll be fun. And I hope you'll join us. He thinks you're swell."

Swell? Me? Mr. May is so cool. I can't help but smile.

"Sure. I will be glad to take care of it. What's the date?"

"The twentieth. Will you be here?"

"Of course. I'll have it for you that morning. And—there's no charge. I think he's swell, too."

"Wonderful! We'll plan on partying about seven."

"Thank you for including me."

"Absolutely, dear."

"Is it a surprise?"

"Oh, no! I don't think Mr. May would come unless he knew people were waiting for him."

That makes me smile. Mr. May isn't the kind of person to let anyone down—a man of commitment.

"Oh, and thank you," she says with a wave, turning toward her back steps and disappearing into her house.

Wow! AB must think a lot of Mr. May to be hosting his birthday party. Maybe he doesn't have a wife. Who knows? I look down the driveway at all the flowers and new foliage that's emerging, promising future surprises for me as spring unfolds. The beauty of AB's garden is breathtaking, calling me to participate. The peonies and floribunda roses in varying shades of pinks, yellows, and reds beckon me to visit, like showgirls in a chorus line. I wander down the drive, looking at each one of them as they display their fluffy heads to the evening sun. Thinking to check my mailbox for a letter from my son, I continue down the lovely drive, belting out the title song from *Cabaret*. I glance over the unidentified hedge at the odd painted windows as my voice picks up the crescendo at the end of the song.

There is nothing in my mailbox, but as I am turning around, a large black dog appears, one pointed ear up, and one ear down. He must be a rescue pooch from the pound, but he looks friendly as he trots up to me, tongue lolling. Letting him sniff my hand, I talk to him as if he is another neighbor. "Hey, buddy. What's up?" His red collar is a good sign; he belongs to someone, but whom? He shouldn't be off the leash in this neighborhood, and he seems quite content to hang out here with me for the time being. He lets me pat his head. "So where do you live, huh?" I'm thinking about turning around to go back to my house, so I look around, trying to locate his owner. Maybe whoever it is could be across the street on one of the private docks. No one is over there. Maybe he's been down the street on the nature trail. I glance down the street, but I see no one. I hear an engine start, and I think maybe it's his owner coming to get him. The dog makes no move to leave, and as I turn and head down my driveway, he begins to follow me.

"Really? Where do you live, buddy? You need to go home," I say to him, leaning over to check his tag for an address or a phone number. At that moment, I hear a car coming up the street. Maybe this person knows the dog. I walk out into the street and the dog follows me. The car is coming toward me, but then I realize it's a truck—a tired-looking white pickup—and inside it is my hot neighbor. *Crap!* This is not supposed to happen.

If we have to talk, at least he might know to whom this dog belongs. *Oh, hell yeah!* says Bad Elle, while I roll my eyes inwardly at her. The truck pulls up in front of me without my having to ask, and the passenger window goes down. The driver is indeed my hot neighbor, fresh and clean-smelling from a shower, damp hair neatly combed, dressed in a button-up shirt and khaki shorts, a pair of expensive sunglasses dangling from a cord around his neck, and a black camera bag on the seat beside him. He has to lay his head back on the headrest and turn to look at me, and instantly, my feminine organs are turning inside out. In his overly suntanned face, those deep-set blue eyes are like two steaming hot tubs, calling my name. I can imagine slipping a foot in each one and sliding all the way in until that magic promise of him meets me in the middle and—oh, my God! My toes are curling just thinking about it!

"Hi. I see you've found Harley," he says, grinning, and oh, my God, I can't even breathe. He has that crisp intelligent-sounding voice that doesn't dawdle—the kind I love. "Or—Harley's found you."

"Harley." I raise my eyebrows at him—an old habit. Really, I am so stupid right now I can hardly talk. I'm trying to pass my expression off as aloofness. Kyle Davis had nothing on this guy!

"I know, it's not very original," he says and gives me another grin with a hint of naughtiness in it, or am I imagining that, too?

"Is he yours?"

"*She's* not. She belongs to Patsy down the street. I'd help you out, but I'm on my way to the airport—running pretty freaking late, actually..." he says, looking around, tapping his thumb on the steering wheel. "Oh, no worries, here she comes now."

I look down the street to see a tall and lumpy older woman with short, disheveled blond hair lumbering toward us in ancient white Reeboks, leash in hand.

"Oh. Okay. Well, thanks."

"All right. See you," he says, flashing those hot blue eyes and giving me that adorable bad-boy grin again, before driving off.

See you. Darn it. I didn't get his name and he didn't ask for mine. *It's for the best, Honey Bun*, Good Elle reminds me as I swallow my disappointment. He did say he was in a hurry, late for the airport. Where was he going? Patsy makes it up to my mailbox and greets me with the heaviest eastern North Carolina accent I have ever heard. "Heeyyy! Is Harley bothering youuu? I'm sooo sorry. We have one of those invisible fences, but she just busts right through it like it's not even there, and then of course, she duddn't wanna come back, so here I go every time and have to drag her back on hooome!"

"Oh, it's no problem! She's real friendly."

"Yes, she is that! I'm Patsy."

"Hey, I'm Elle."

"I live down in the gray house at the end of the street if you ever need to drag her back down there. I hope she won't be a problem. She just likes to go visitin'."

"Okay. I'll bring her home if she gets out again."

"Thank you. It was nice meeting you. Have a good evenin'."

"You too. Bye now."

"Bye-bye! Say bye, Harleeey!"

Harley gives me one last, long look and lolls her tongue again, as Patsy snaps the leash onto her collar and they are off toward the other end of the street.

My goodness! I realize I am almost shaking from my encounter with Hot Neighbor. I have to think about how long it's been since I have been with a man, and I realize it's been several months, after Granny died, but still, several months. A man like *that*, however, is a different story altogether. I have never been with a man like that. But I know he is bad news, and I can't let myself even entertain the thoughts of getting all worked up over someone who looks like that. *And someone who is in the throes of an affair should be strictly off limits!* Good Elle is shrieking in my ear. *But it was worth it just to have a little peek, wasn't it?* asks Bad Elle, and I have to agree with her.

It definitely was.

Chapter 8

JEWEL

Jimmy and I are getting a lot done. The sign man is putting a frosted style logo on my front window, but my big storefront sign won't be ready for another week. Jimmy has sanded and stained all four tabletops while I have chalk-painted the sixteen chairs black. Now he is painting the table legs while I sand the edges of the chairs, giving them a distressed, vintage look before we apply the wax. It excites me to see the progress we are making, and knowing that everything we do gets me closer to opening day only energizes me further. I am even forgetting to eat, so it's a good thing I have brought over peanut butter and a loaf of bread to keep here. Jimmy brought strawberries from a local farmer he knows.

I watch the skillful way Jimmy strokes on the paint. He definitely has a knack for what he does, making quick work out of the painting, and his concentration seems like prayer, so I try my best not to disturb him, even though I have so many questions—about his life, Randy, and the houses they renovate. This total absorption in what I'm doing is soothing for me too, making me forget about all my past transgressions, and reminding me that I am rehabilitated and decent, worthy enough to have this place and to make a go of it here, on my own.

I think about Joey and what he must be doing—lots of calisthenics and marching in the rain, or doing millions of push-ups while some task-master sergeant screams at him mercilessly. I wonder whether he thinks of me. Surely I was easier on him than what he's bound to be enduring now.

Jimmy doesn't ask me what I'm thinking about, so I am comfortable in my thoughts, not worrying about keeping up my guard. I think of Judy, and how her bakery must be hopping about now, with all the weddings in full swing in the mountains. I loved the baking, the decorating, the packaging, and even making the deliveries. The deliveries and the unveilings were my favorite part of what we did. That look of surprise, awe, and appreciation on our customers' faces made all the effort worthwhile. We always smelled of sugar and vanilla, or almond, or lemon, whatever ingredient we were using during the day. The smell got transferred into our hair and our clothes from the steam released by the cake, and even after washing, a baker always has that sweet aroma about her.

There is a serenity, I realize, in the ritual of everyday tasks, especially when they are done well and with love or whatever passion is put in. Washing dishes, stirring batter, counting change, it's all the same; the work of a life is made up of all these simple actions, even the contented, weary sigh at the end of a day. It is all good. It is all worth it. It is me.

I see Jewel before the door chimes to signal her arrival. As she moves past my windows, I can see her, wearing a red sleeveless dress and carrying a bag. She walks through my door, giving us that double-dimple smile and her friendlier than normal greeting.

"Heeyyy! Boy, you guys are busy! This place looks great!" she says in her squeaky, cheerful voice, looking around and taking in our work.

"We're getting there. How are you, Jewel?"

"I'm great!"

"Jewel, this is Jimmy Burns. He's the one who's done all this beautiful painting in here. Jewel and her fiancé, Brandon, own Sandy Britches next door."

"Hey," they greet each other but there are no handshakes.

Jewel presents me with the bag she's brought. "This is for you, Elle, from Brandon and me. We didn't know whether you liked white or red, so I brought both!"

"Oh! Thank you so much!" I don't usually like local wine, so this gift is doomed to sit around my kitchen for a while. Still, it's a nice gesture.

"We figured you've been so busy getting ready that you aren't going to have time to come over and have a tasting."

"Well, you're right about that. I've been trying to get things going. My kitchen is mostly set up. I'm waiting on the food stuffs to arrive so I can start baking. I've set a date for the opening, so now I just need to get my staff on board and do some campaigning."

"We'll be glad to help you. And you should call the TV stations to get them to come out and do a morning spot before you open. We had Amy Stainback from the morning news on Channel 3 come out and interview us before we opened and it was very effective."

"Oh, yes, I've seen her on the show," I say innocently, *and in my neighbor's driveway and in his arms!*

"She's great! I have her contact information if you want it."

"I'd love it." This will be fun!

"What are you doing for dinner tonight?"

"Well, nothing special." I'll be eating chicken piccata—again. Cooking for one can be boring if you make anything other than a salad.

"Come out with us, then! Brandon and I are going to the Dockside! Have you been there yet?"

"Yes, I have. That's where I found out about Jimmy, actually."

"Oh!" I wonder whether Jewel will think to include Jimmy, since he's probably *the help* in her book. She surprises me by coming back quickly with her invitation. "Can you come too, Jimmy? We're going over after we close at six. We'd love to have you join us."

"I actually have another job I'm going to later, but I appreciate the invitation," Jimmy says, extricating himself easily enough. Jewel seems genuinely disappointed.

"Well, if you can get away, you know where we'll be."

"Thanks," he says shyly. Who could turn down Jewel and her dimples?

I'll have to go home to shower and change, of course. I'm wearing shorts and a T-shirt with no makeup and a ponytail, my everyday outfit for this stage of the game.

"Can I meet you there? I live close by and I'll have to go home and clean up first."

"Sure! We'll get there about seven, so will that give you enough time?"

"I think so." I have total control over my schedule, so I know I can get there on time, but it's nice to make it sound as though I have to think about it.

"Okay, great! We'll see you then! It was nice meeting you, Jimmy!"

"Yeah, you, too, Jewel."

"Bye!" we all say to each other as Jewel heads out my door and down the sidewalk. People are going up and down, I notice, as a few of them stop to peek in my windows, now that the sign is up and there is activity afoot. The attractive tables and chairs will make it look like something is happening here. I wave at a young couple who are gazing in at us.

"You might have customers already," Jimmy comments, as he's closing up the black paint can, reaching for a rag and the finishing wax.

"Yeah, wouldn't that be nice?" I go to the door and open it so I can greet the onlookers.

"Are you open for business?" asks the girl. She appears to be in her mid-twenties, like her male companion.

"Not quite yet, but we're getting close. Are you looking for something special?" I ask.

"We're, uh…looking to order a wedding cake."

"Oh, I can help you with that!" I can certainly take an order. "When is the wedding?" I ask, holding the door open for them. I suddenly realize I have no order forms printed out and my wedding cake book is packed up in a box in the back of the kitchen.

"It's June 29th. I know that's soon, and all the other places are already booked up. We haven't been the best at planning, but we've had a death in our family and that's messed things up. I mean, you know, we were trying to put the more important things first, so the wedding kinda got put on the back burner…." The poor girl is going on and on, but I know how these things go.

"Oh, I'm so sorry!" I don't want to sound over the top like Jewel, but maybe that's how I should act. Nah. "Listen, I know how life gets in the way sometimes. My grandmother passed away not long ago, and I totally understand how overwhelming it can be."

"Oh, I'm sorry."

"What kind of cake were you thinking about?"

"Three-tiered, for about a hundred and fifty people."

"Okay. Where's the wedding?"

"At the Airlie Gardens. The cake just totally slipped our minds."

How do you forget the cake? I don't let her see my face as I'm rolling my eyes and walking back into the kitchen to dig out my wedding cake book from one of the boxes. I can't believe I'm about to take my first order! I don't even have order forms yet and people are beating down the door! I return with the book and my notebook. They are a cute couple—too young to be getting married in my opinion, but cute. They share the same brown hair and a variety of tattoos. You will never see an ink mark on *my* body! Tattoos and bumper stickers are not for me.

"I'll have to tell you, I've only been in the building for two and a half days, so I don't even have my business cards printed yet, but here's the phone number. I'm Elle, by the way."

I stick out my hand and the girl reaches for it first.

"Hey, I'm Lexi and this is Jacob," she says and they both smile as we shake hands and murmur our belated how-do-you-dos. Jimmy goes about his business, smearing wax on the chairs I've sanded and wiping it off with firm, clean strokes with the rag.

Lexi and Jacob and I go through the notebook on the checkout counter since I have yet to install the counter and barstools I want for the consultation area. She oohs and aahs over several of my best designs. I get an idea of their price range and what flavors they like. Lexi tells me her color palette and design preferences so I have something to work with. After a few minutes of conversation between the two of them, Lexi gets to pick. Jacob is complacent and doesn't have much of an opinion one way or another. He will make a great husband. We settle on the flavor, style, and colors, and the price seems to be surprisingly high, but they both suck it up and settle on their choice. I write it all down, and the date the cake is promised. They wait while I plug in my printer and print out a contract for them to sign. Jacob writes me a check for the deposit, which amazes me, since I didn't think anybody their age even owned a checkbook, but since I have no cash register or card swipe system in place, I am grateful that they are prepared. We shake hands and they leave. I've written my first contract! I have to calm myself down in order to get their names on my calendar, and I jot it down in my notebook. I will hang a white board in the kitchen with cakes and due dates so I can keep up with it all. The worst mistake I could make in this business is to overlook someone's wedding cake!

After they have left, I turn to Jimmy.

"That was awesome! Are you going to be free over the next few days?"

"I can give you some time. What's next?"

"I need you to build me a cabinet with a countertop over here so I can display my cake notebooks. I'll also need you to hang my blackboard and that whiteboard in the kitchen for my orders."

"Sure. I'll measure for it today before I leave."

"Okay. I think I want it painted black with a quartz countertop." The thought of having money to spend on whatever I want gives my insides a little rush. I've never had this experience and it feels good. "I'll go this afternoon and get a sample or two to look at. I'll need barstools and some paint to spruce up that blackboard frame. I might as well take my sleeping bag over to the Home Depot."

Jimmy smiles at me. "You might want to get some flowerpots and a bench for outside your front door."

"Oh, my gosh! You're absolutely right! That would look so awesome! I can put all that together while you're building the cabinet. And I need a decanter for the cucumber water…."

Jimmy laughs. "You don't have to do it all this week, do you?"

"No, I know, but it would be great if I could! You never know what else is going to come up, so I need to roll with it while I'm thinking about it. And I need to set up the office forms so I can take more orders. When can you have the cabinet and counter done?"

"I can have the cabinet built by Friday, but depending on how soon you can get your countertop, it could be a while."

"Hunh…. Well, can you build it with a wooden top to match the tables? It would be cheaper and faster, that is, if you've got the time. I'll do the painting and the staining."

"Sure. If you want to finish the chairs, I'll go ahead and design your counter. Where do you want it to sit?"

We go to the wall and I show him what I'm thinking. He goes to his truck to get his tape measure and a notebook and draws it out while I'm applying wax to the remaining chairs. By lunchtime, we've finished the tables and chairs and gotten the counter designed. Another trip to the big-box store is productive. I leave Jimmy in the lumber department while I go in search of four barstools I can paint and stain to match my furniture, a black metal bench, and two large planters that will work for my sidewalk appeal. I add two large bags of potting soil and choose several pots of flowers—petunias, coleus, and creeping Jenny. I find the white board, markers, and some colored duct tape that will look good for the black menu board frame. Jimmy and I load it all into the back of his truck and we deliver it to the bakery, where it all goes in the back door until tomorrow. Then, Jimmy and I high-five each other and call it a day.

Back at home, I turn on some music and take two pain relievers before getting into a warm shower, washing my hair, and shaving my legs. I put on the same chevron print sundress I wore yesterday, apply my makeup, and dry my hair, leaving it loose around my shoulders for the evening. With the right earrings, bracelet, and heeled sandals, I feel more dressed up than I was yesterday. I'll be competing with Jewel tonight in her red dress and matching jewelry ensemble, but I look pretty good—younger, too. I'm assuming Jewel and Brandon are somewhere in their forties, and I definitely look younger than they do. Maybe I will catch someone's eye tonight. *Wouldn't it be something to find someone?* I can hardly allow myself to think it. I'm sure I've been a disappointment many times around. Most of the men I've known have been equally disappointing to say the least, and the good ones aren't even ones I'd consider—I mean there's Jimmy and Mr. May, who are the salt of the earth, but I wouldn't *date* them! They are both way too old and not even my type. Still, it would be the icing on the cake to find somebody I could be with.

As if on cue, my phone rings. It's Marcus!

"I was just getting ready to think about you," I say, grinning.

"Hunh! Then I guess I should be flattered! How's it going?"

"Great! I'm coming along at warp speed and I just took my first wedding cake order today."

"That's fantastic! How's AB treating you?"

"Fine. We're not chums by any stretch, but she did ask me to bake a birthday cake for her gardener and she invited me to his party too."

"Well, then, life is good."

"Life is good. How are the mountains?" I ask, and I feel a surprising pang at the thought of home.

"Everything is going well. I've hired a contractor to go in and remodel your grandmother's kitchen, and we'll be replacing some of the facial boards on the outside. I'll bet you I'll have renters in there by the first of July!"

"You're amazing! Send me pictures, okay?"

"Will do. Have you heard from your boy?"

"Yeah, once. He sent a text message when he got to base. I guess that will be the last one I'll get from him. He'd found the camera I'd packed in his duffel bag for his birthday present."

"Well. Good. Have you been to the beach?"

"Yep. I got a bit of sun, so I don't feel too much like an alien. What else is new?"

"Oh...not much. I ran into your ex with a new girl the other day."

"Aiden? Oh, that girl's not new. He's had a thing for Kendra since high school. But she's newly divorced and he's free, so...whatever."

"Yeah, well, maybe when I get some time I'll come down and visit you."

"Please do! You'll have to check out my place when I have the grand opening."

"I'll do it! Let me know when."

"June first."

"Great! I'll put it on my calendar. You take care now!"

"Okay. You too. Thanks for calling. And thanks for everything."

"You're very welcome. Play nice, now."

"I will."

"Bye, girl."

"Bye, Marcus."

I stare out my window for a moment, watching the breeze stirring the crape myrtle branches, wondering about Joey and thinking I'll dash off another quick note to him tonight to let him know how things are coming along.

Randy is at the host stand when I arrive at the Dockside. It is hot and humid despite the dinner hour, so I feel sorry for him in his long-sleeved shirt. Why do they make him wear that? I'd buck the owner and go for the T-shirt like the rest of the staff is allowed to wear, which reminds me, I need to think about a uniform eventually for my own staff.

"Hey! You're back!" he says, grinning at me, a little rivulet of sweat running down each sideburn, kin to the beads of moisture on his upper lip that are dampening his mustache.

"Yeah, I had to come and say thank you! Thanks for sending me Jimmy Burns. He's amazing!"

"Yes, he is. I'm glad he could help. He's my right-hand man," he says, picking up a menu. "Are you dining alone or meeting someone?"

"I'm looking for my friends," I reply, glancing past him at the deck, which is filling up quickly with the dinner crowd. *Friends*. I have friends. This place must stay packed.

"Oh! Sure, Brandon and Jewel. They said they were expecting a pretty blonde lady. Now it makes sense. They're right over here," he says, putting down the menu and motioning for me to follow him. It's a small town, I remind myself, knowing that small business owners stick together like flies on honey. It is reassuring to know that all these people seem like good folks from what I can tell, and the fact that they are friends is a good sign. I need to be in with good people.

Brandon stands and holds out my chair when he sees me coming. We all greet each other and Jewel even gives me a smooch on my cheek. Good lord! She begins talking immediately.

"I can't believe you already know Randy, and what a small world it is that he and Jimmy work together flipping houses! Can you believe that? I've always wanted to flip houses. I love watching those shows on HGTV; don't you?"

"I…" I begin and shrug since I've never watched any of those shows.

"*The Property Brothers* is my favorite! I just think that Jonathan is the cutest thing! And I just love that girl, Nicole, on *Rehab Addict*. I love the way she whacks away, demolishing those walls with her maul! She's such a little powerhouse!"

"Can I get you something to drink?" asks a sunburned waiter in a faded blue T-shirt.

Thank God for the break! Is she ever going to shut up? Brandon watches as I glance over the beverage list looking for a craft beer. He reaches over and points at the bottom of my menu.

"They carry our wines; did you see that?"

"Oh. What do you recommend?"

"This one if you like white," he says, pointing out one, and feeling like they might be picking up my tab, I nod to the waiter. In this heat, the chilled white wine makes more sense, even though wine isn't calling my name at the moment, and I doubt I'll be spending much time in their winery. I know a lot about wine, but right now, I'd die for a good, cold Mexican beer with a lime, straight from the bottle.

"How's it going at the bakery?" Brandon asks, while Jewel sips her wine. I can already tell he has to time his remarks for when she takes a breath so he can get a word in, like trying to get your footing in the ocean between waves. Somehow, it doesn't bother him. I'd tell her to shut the hell up.

"Oh, it's great! Jimmy has painted the whole place and we redid the furniture—and I took a wedding cake order! I don't even have my order forms printed out yet, but I guess I'm off and running!" I wonder if they've planned their own cake yet.

"That's excellent!"

"Oh, you should see it! They've done a great job!" Jewel gushes. "I can't wait to see your cake designs."

"Of course! Come over and I'll show you. Have you planned your own cake yet?" I ask hopefully. Her heart-shaped face is perfectly proportioned with the tiniest, most delicate little features. I try to imagine Brandon on top of her when they have sex, and wonder how it is that he doesn't crush her. It must take incredible restraint!

"No, we haven't. We've just set the date—for October, and I've just nailed down the venue. My mother and my daughter and I are going wedding dress shopping next week, now that Megan is out of school—she goes to Carolina—and we're going to Mama's in Charlotte to go shopping. I just can't believe all there is to do!"

"Do you have more than one child?" I ask, aware that Brandon is checking his phone messages while we talk girl stuff.

"I have a son in high school. Brandon has a son in college, so we're almost a blended family. Megan will be helping us in the winery this summer so you will have to come and meet her too. I can't get Gray—my son—to come near the place. He's always off with his friends. He loves to fish and go to the beach. I guess that's just a boy."

Our waiter returns with my wine and asks whether we are ready to order. I have not even looked at the menu.

"We need a couple of minutes," Brandon tells him and he nods, turning to another table. After taking a sip of wine, which is not surprisingly disappointing, I decide I really wish I'd ordered that beer. I try not to make a face. Never go for the white blends.

Jewel starts in on telling me about Megan and college and what in the world she's gonna do when Gray leaves in the fall for Carolina too, and they're both so smart that they both got into Carolina, and you know how hard that is, and then she takes a breath. I can hardly concentrate on the menu with all that talking, and I wonder how I'll get a word in, or whether I'll have to. That might serve me well.

I quickly tune out her dorm vs. apartment dilemma and try to divert my attention to the menu so I will be ready when the waiter comes back. I glance at Brandon, who is looking once more at the menu before he lays it down on the corner of the table. Jewel is shifting the topic to me.

"So, tell us about your family, Elle." She props her pretty elbows on the table and clasps her fingers daintily under her chin.

"I have a son, too—Joey. He's eighteen and has just joined the Army."

"Nuh-*uh!* No way! I thought you were about *thirty!* How can you possibly be old enough to have a son that age?" Jewel is flabbergasted, and even Brandon looks surprised.

"Really! You don't look old enough to be the mother of a soldier."

A soldier. My son is a soldier. I feel a little catch in my throat. It wouldn't hurt for them to see a little tear in the corner of my eye at the mention of his name, but I'm too tired to fool with it now.

"Joey was born when I was young, right out of high school, actually." Right out of *prison*, actually, but they'll never hear that from me.

"Oh…" she says, her voice fading, as if she is unprepared to ask much more. I have thrown her off her script. She struggles for her next comment. "You must be so proud of him, going in the Army."

"Yes. We are. His dad lives in Boone, where I'm from—sort of, but yeah, we're both very proud of him." Leave it at that. I've said just enough.

Jewel is decidedly silent in perfect time for the waiter to come back and take our order. She starts us off by choosing the seafood lasagna, so I order it too, not having the benefit of thoroughly studying the menu.

"Make it three, sir," says Brandon, handing over our menus.

Jewel begins the story of how she and Brandon met. She was on vacation with her mother in Napa Valley while Brandon was there, studying winemaking. The wine train had taken them right to him. He was interning at the vineyard where they'd taken a special tour of the wine caves and, of course, he was their guide. "I guess we were just destined to be together because we found out that we were both living in Wilmington. I mean, doesn't that just give you goose bumps? We haven't been apart since he came back here and opened Sandy Britches."

"It's a small world," I murmur, knowing that's what she wants me to say.

"Isn't it, though?" she exclaims as Brandon smiles lopsidedly at her.

"Were you planning to open the winery here?" I asked him.

"I was. It would have been nice to relocate after my divorce, but my son was still here in high school and I didn't want to leave him, so I came back and found my little spot in the strip mall. We import our grapes and pretend it's Napa."

Jewel giggles and I smile. They're really cute. He gives her hand a squeeze as the evening breeze picks up and blows my hair. He notices. Now is the time I expect a question about my love life, but that doesn't happen, as Jewel picks up the divorce topic and launches into her own story. *Stop!* I really don't want to hear this. It's too much information. She's focusing on how hard it was for the kids so maybe she'll leave out the gory details so I can digest my food. The salads arrive so Brandon and I munch away while she drones on and on. *How can he stand this?*

Now she's telling about all the guys she went through before she found Brandon. "You know, it seemed that I always had about a month with each guy and then, boom, it was over. There was my September guy and then there was my November guy. I thought I'd never find anybody, and then Mama and I just happened to pop into the winery that day, and there he was. It's been two years now."

"Wow!" After a month, most guys would be sick of hearing her talk. It doesn't take a genius to figure that one out. Either Brandon is deaf, or Jewel is one hell of a lay! I don't believe there's a match made in heaven for each of us. We're all screwed up in our own ways, and we all have our peculiar insecurities. So I think I've just figured out Brandon's.

The seafood lasagna is by far the best part of this evening so far, that and the view. The sky is fading to pale pink as the boats slowly cruise by in the harbor, leaving little V-shaped ripples you can almost hear. It's so lazy and peaceful. Voices float across the water with a clarity that would be lost on land. The wine is making me feel heady and drowsy after my long day, and Jewel's ongoing monologue is almost hypnotic. I'll bet I have not uttered fifteen words, other than "mm-hmms" and "ohhs" since I sat down. I threw in a couple of "wows" to be polite and she seemed to appreciate them. *Oh, Brandon, what is your deal with this chick? And not only do you live with her, but you work with her as well.*

Randy appears at our table, asking how our meal was, and delivering a plate of key lime pie with three forks, on the house. We all give our compliments to the chef, so he takes a minute to sit down. Apparently, they really are friends, like I previously thought. The ever-present perspiration on Randy's upper lip seems to have disappeared since the sun has dipped behind the clouds. He and Brandon discuss business. Just as it does in the mountains, it's picking up here, now that the college kids are here for the summer, to train and prepare for the tourist onslaught that will commence once public schools are out in June. I glance around for the hung-over would-be waitresses, but see none of them.

"How's your bakery coming along?" Randy asks, arms propped on the table, doing that little thumb-lift thing he does.

"Good. I hope to open by June first. Jimmy's been an enormous help already. I posted an ad today to hire some employees for the start-up. I've ordered my sign, and they came to put my logo on the glass door, so I'm coming along. I already have an order—actually two," I add, remembering about Mr. May's birthday cake I'll have to bake next week. My supplies should be in by then.

"Good deal. What's your specialty?"

"Wedding cakes, birthday cakes, cupcakes…. Whatever you want really. I'll have coffee and breakfast items, and I have other specialty cakes."

"I'll have to check it out."

"I'd love that. If you like something, maybe I can contribute to your menu here on a regular basis. I'll bring you some samples when I get set up if you'd like." It's bold, I know, but I'm going to market myself to everybody I think can help me, and so far, the Dockside seems like the place to be. Brandon gives me a shrewd nod of approval while Randy catches my train of thought.

"Good marketing ploy," Randy says, drumming the table and looking me over as if he's underestimated me. I look him over right back, letting him know I think he's a definite possibility. He is, in fact, rather sweet and attractive, although somewhat heavier than I prefer. As I take a bite of the key lime pie, which is delicious, I let the fork linger in my mouth for a suggestive moment. He gets the implication immediately and then excuses himself to get back to work. I will be as busy as he is, but surely there will be time to play, and I haven't had proper male attention in such a long time!

Jewel has not spoken in at least two minutes.

What a miracle!

Chapter 9

MR. MAY

Surprisingly, I slept quite soundly during the night, lost in my own midsummer night's dream, pleasantly dead-heading roses with Mr. May in the flower garden outside. What a change for me! Over the top of my coffee cup, I glance out the window, looking to see whether he has arrived. Wanting to thank him for my peonies, I wander outside after listening to the weather forecast and the morning news. Perky Amy has held my attention on the show this morning for all of two minutes, as she is teaming up for today's human interest story with a local gardening expert, who is teaching us morons how to plant tomatoes. Although Amy's infidelity with my neighbor fascinates me, I can stand her irritating voice for only so long. The chill morning air and sounds of the crickets and the birds' morning conversation compel me outdoors. Granny and I used to sit on the porch and have our breakfast, listening to the birds, before she got so sick and had to take her meals, what little she could eat by then, inside.

More agile than I'd previously given him credit for, Mr. May is strolling the perimeter of the rose garden, clipping the spent blossoms, and dropping them into a large white bucket. There's a lot of exercise involved in gardening, I think, looking around at the expanse of the front and back yards, and all the tools there are to go and get, debris to dump, and dirt to haul around. Then there's the bending and squatting, and the lifting, not to mention the sweating. He appears to be deeply absorbed in his task, and seems not to have heard me come out, despite the scrape of metal on concrete as I slide out my chair to sit down. I take a sip of coffee and pull my hair back into a ponytail, thinking that this is the second day in a row I have planned to go without makeup to a public place and haven't cared. Mr. May's broad-brimmed hat rises as he steps to the next rose bush in the circle, and it is then that he sees me, giving a little wave with his gloved hand. I wave back while he completes his dead-heading and then makes his way to my part of the driveway.

"Good morning, Miss McLarin," he says, giving me a nod. How can he remember my last name?

"Good morning, Mr. May. How are you?"

"Very well, thank you, and you?"

"I'm doing great, thanks."

"How is your bakery?"

"It's wonderful. I'm going in this morning to work on setting up my office since I have already taken an order. I need to organize my paperwork." I have almost mentioned that I have two cake orders, but for his sake, I will keep his birthday cake a surprise.

"Well, good for you. I see you've been taking care of your window box."

"Yes. I watered it yesterday. I was wondering…do you think AB would mind—and is there a place I could carve out a little cutting garden? I'd like to bring in fresh flowers every day for my tables in the bakery. I wouldn't need much space, and I would take care of it myself.…"

He watches me carefully as I talk, making me aware that he could be hard of hearing. "Oh, of course! I'm sure she'd be happy to let you do that. I can help you if you'd like. What did you have in mind?"

"Oh, just some daisies and cosmos, and maybe some zinnias."

"How about some dahlias? And mums for the fall, maybe. Sure. We can work that out. There's plenty here to cut in the meantime, before your garden can get established. I don't think AB would mind at all."

"Oh, wonderful, and thank you for the peonies. They're beautiful! What variety are they?"

"You're welcome. They're called 'Bowl of Beauty'."

"I haven't seen that one. We grew peonies at home. Granny loved the Sorbet peonies."

"Yes, they're quite lovely. Where is home for you?" asks Mr. May, setting his bucket on the pavement and cleaning the blades of his pruning shears on his shirttail.

"I'm from Valle Crucis. Have you ever heard of it?"

"I know it very well. It's one of my favorite places in the world." *Mine, too.* "There's an inn there—I can't remember the name of it—where they grow their own vegetables and herbs and flowers, too, in a spectacular kitchen garden right across the road."

"Yes! I know it. It's the Mast Farm Inn. Our house was very close by. It's pretty exclusive."

"Yes, it is. I took my wife there for our anniversary one year, before she passed away. It was marvelous. What brings you to the coast then?"

"My grandmother died, and my son joined the Army, so I thought it would be a good idea to live at the beach for a change, and just…start over in a new place. I don't have much family, and I've always wanted to live at the beach. It just kind of worked out."

Mr. May considers this. *You don't leave that kind of place*, he is probably thinking. "Well, I suppose it's quite different here for you then."

"Yes. It's much more humid and hot," I say, knowing the heat will start up in about an hour, creeping up the back of my neck, but I really don't mind. "It's flatter and I've noticed that some of the flowers are different," I say, taking another sip of my coffee.

"Some of them are."

"What do you call those bushes along the driveway, the ones with the reddish blossoms?"

"Those are oleander."

"Oh! Like the street."

"Yes. They like our warm climate here, but they wouldn't grow in your mountains. You've missed our azaleas. They were very showy this year."

"I'm sure." Mr. May seems comfortable standing there and talking to me, but I offer him a seat, so he sits opposite me.

"Would you care for a cup of coffee?"

"No, thank you. I've had my quota for the day."

"So how did you become AB's gardener?" I ask. Usually, I'm not so nosy, but Mr. May intrigues me. And somehow, I don't think I'll mind if he asks me similar questions.

"Oh, I knew her husband, Monty. He was my student. Not in the film industry, as you could be imagining. He had his own extraordinary talent there. I was the county horticultural extension agent here for many years. I taught the Master Gardener class and Monty was a student. He was an avid gardener himself, and of course, he started all of what you see here," he says, waving a hand at the expanse of garden before us. "When he got sick, he asked me to take care of it all when he was gone. He was afraid Anne Borden would let it run to ruin since she has no interest whatsoever in gardening or getting outside where she could get hot and sweaty. So she and I made a deal when Monty became too ill to tend the garden. I'd work here three mornings a week until she decides to sell the place, although I can't really see her doing that."

"And the other two days?"

"I tend my own garden. It's not as grand as this one, though well-loved. I grow mostly ve-ge-ta-bles." I smile at the way he pronounces the word distinctly, making it four syllables.

"Monty must have thought a lot of you."

"Oh, I can assure you, it went both ways. He was a fine man. I'm glad to tend his garden in his absence. Although, being in his garden, it hardly seems that he's gone. I tend to believe our departed loved ones are never very far away, especially in a garden."

I nod, thinking the same thing about Granny and Pa. They don't seem to be far away either. Of course, I was sad when they died, and I wondered how I'd manage without them, but I still feel them with me. I can't say the same about my mother, who left me at such a young age. She never seemed *here* at all, much less gone. And then we heard that she'd died in a car accident when I was nine. I hardly think of her anymore. Granny was my mother.

My coffee cup is empty and Mr. May seems ready to move on with his day.

"I'm keeping you from your work again. It was nice chatting with you, Miss McLarin."

"Please call me Elle."

"All right, Elle. I'm off to fill my sprayer. Our roses need a little dose of mineral oil to keep the aphids away. You have a nice day."

"You, too, Mr. May."

I arrive before Jimmy and settle myself to the task of printing out forms and devising a filing system for taking orders, receipts, vendors, and purchase orders. Smelling the fresh paint excites me since it is one more sign that my business is really going to happen. The corner office in the kitchen seems adequate for what I need, even though it is a small space. I try to imagine how it will feel, once things get going and I have employees milling about, baking, and working in the kitchen and behind the counter, serving our customers.

A loud knock on the door reminds me I have locked it behind me and that Jimmy obviously does not have a key. "Hold on. I'm coming!" I shout, rounding the corner of the kitchen into the shop, where I can see a young African-American woman peering in the window, shading her hand over her eyes to get a better view. She must be a customer, wondering whether we are open for business. She looks to be about twenty and is dressed like me, in shorts and a T-shirt, and the requisite pair of beach flip-flops for living in this area.

Her bushy, black hair is pulled severely back from her head in a ponytail that looks like it belongs on an actual pony. She wears large black-framed glasses that remind me of Buddy Holly, and as soon as she sees me, she breaks into a huge smile, revealing an impressive amount of orthodontic metal wiring. Before I can get the door open, she seems to be hopping up and down in excitement.

"Hi. We're not open yet." I break it to her before she gets any more wound up than she already is.

"Hi! Oh, I know you're not open yet. I was answering your online ad for the job you posted yesterday."

It takes a moment for this to register. Yes, I did post an ad, but I never expected to have such a rapid response!

"I sent in my application online, but I guess you haven't checked your email?"

"Oh! I guess not. Wow."

"Yeah. Hi. I'm Monai," she says, sticking out her hand and grinning at me with wide, blinking eyes the color of sourwood honey. The girl can hardly keep still! Maybe she needs to use my bathroom.

"Monet, like the artist?" I ask, shaking her hand.

"Well, you say it that way, but it's spelled M-O-N-A-I. My mom was—I don't know—rebellious and kinda quirky back in the day, but not ignorant, just so you know. I really like the artist, too—all those water lilies and green bridges...." Her head and hands move as she talks and her feet shuffle too, as if she's dancing to her words.

"Yeah, Giverny.... Oh, I'm Elle, by the way."

"Hi. Yeah, so here I am, answering your ad. Bake My Day! I *love* the name of your place, man! I mean, it's so cool! I just graduated from the community college with my pastry arts degree, and I'm so excited that I saw your ad yesterday. It's like meant to be, you know? Don't you think?"

"Maybe," I say to this whirling dervish of a girl who has the biggest grin I have ever seen and more energy than five kindergarteners put together. "Do you have references?"

"Yes, ma'am, I do. I brought them with me," she says, handing me an envelope. Upon opening it, I find at least five letters of reference that I'd like to read.

"Come on in and have a seat," I say, gesturing to my newly painted black chairs. I need to slow the pace of this interview so I can keep up with her.

"This is so pretty in here!"

Opening the envelopes and glancing over the letters, I see they are written by her teachers, former employers, which include a bakery and an ice creamery that I've seen in town, all glowing reports of Monai's work ethic and her enthusiasm for her jobs and excellent customer relations. "I'm going to go and print your application. Can you wait just a moment?"

"Sure!"

"Do you need anything? Water?" *A bathroom maybe?* All that squirming around—I haven't seen anyone this hyperactive in a long time.

"No, thanks; I'm good!" I fully expect her to pull out her smartphone to occupy herself while I'm gone around the corner, but her eyes are glued to me as if I'm the most fascinating creature on the planet. In a moment, I'm back and I join her at the table, proudly admiring the honey-colored finish, thinking how Monai seems to belong here already, almost matching the décor. Her personality would definitely be lemon meringue! And those honey-colored eyes are just like the tabletops Jimmy has stained. Her dark skin is flawless, setting off the braces on her white teeth in a dramatic way.

Looking over her application, I begin our interview. "So. You live in Wilmington, not Wrightsville Beach, right?"

"Yeah. I live with my dad," she grins, clasping her hands on the table, taking a whiff of the stain. "Did you just do these tables? They look great!"

"Yeah. What do you like to bake?"

"Anything! But I love wedding cakes. Everybody's into cupcakes now, and they're really fun, don't get me wrong, but I love weddings. I want to be a wedding coordinator one day. I'm really good with ganache! Do you wanna see some pictures of some cakes I've done?"

"Sure."

Monai pulls out her phone then, and with a touch of her finger, she opens up her photos and slides her finger across the screen, showing me one impressive creation after another.

"Where did you work last?"

"I had a job at a bakery down in the historic district, which was great, but she could only give me part-time hours and I wanted to work full-time, plus your shop is much closer to my house. I can ride my bike over here from my dad's place."

"You ride a bike?" I wonder if she's a DWI casualty. Her background check will show it and anything else I need to be concerned about. But then, I can be forgiving, unlike some people.

"Oh, I have a driver's license," she says, pulling it out for me to see. "I can save all kinds of money on rent and gas, so I can start putting it away for a place of my own someday. My dad is all about me saving some money, and to tell you the truth, since I bake all the time and he has an enormous sweet tooth, I think he really likes having me around!" she grins again. Who wouldn't like having her around?

"I pay ten dollars an hour to start with."

"That's cool."

"I can start you at twenty hours a week and work up to full-time after we open."

"When's that?"

"June first."

"That's fine. Do you want me to help you do your marketing? I mean, I can run flyers all over town for you and stuff like that, you know, like, talk it up to all the right people?"

"Hmm. Yeah. You probably know all the right places. How about my competition?"

"Oh, yeah! I've got your back on all of that. And I know all the wedding venues and bridal shops. I know a lot of the other vendors too, 'cause when I was workin' at the other place, we were always running into the other vendors at the events we catered."

"Fantastic! Can you start tomorrow?"

"Sure! I can start today if you want."

"Well, I haven't got anything for you to do today. You'll have to give me a day or so to get myself together."

"Okay. I'll go to the printer for you too, whenever you get your flyers ready. There's a place right down the street that gives out coupons every time you go in there."

"Oh, good."

"Do you have a uniform?"

"Not yet. I have a logo I thought about having printed on some aprons."

"And you could do T-shirts too."

I nod. I could ask Randy where he gets his T-shirts done. The door chimes as it swings open and Jimmy Burns walks in, wearing his same ancient jeans and another paint-spattered T-shirt with yet another rock show advertisement underneath.

"Hey, Jimmy. This is Monai, my new employee."

Monai stands up to shake Jimmy's hand. After they greet each other, he sets his lunchbox down on the display case.

"Jimmy is helping me put the place together."

"It looks great!" she says, giving him her incredible metallic grin.

"Thanks. I'm going to bring in my power saw in a minute. Will the noise bother you?"

"Nope. I think Monai and I are about done," I say, turning to her. "Why don't you come in on Friday about ten and I'll have a plan for you. Maybe wear some business-to-business calling clothes, or whatever you can manage on your bike, and we'll take it from there, okay?"

"Okay, great! Thank you so much for hiring me. I'm so excited to be working with you, Elle!"

"Yeah, me too, Monai. Thanks for stopping in."

As soon as Monai is out the door, Jimmy is sawing away, cutting boards for my cabinet, so I tear off pieces of facial tissue to stuff in my ears while I work on grand opening flyers. By lunchtime, the deliveries have begun—boxes of paper towels and toilet paper. My purveyor arrives next, delivering flats of eggs, milk, oil, lemons, and butter. Salt, baking soda, baking powder, vanilla, food coloring, and lots of cocoa are stacked in boxes to be put away. There are fifty-pound bags of sugar and flour to go into my bins. My arms are well-sculpted from this kind of labor over the years. And I have a strong back to say the least from lifting all this stuff!

I can stand the saw's noise no longer, so I drive over to the Dockside for lunch and some advice. Randy is again at the host station when I arrive, and he seats me at a table where I order another bowl of blue crab and corn chowder, and request his company. He seems to sit down gladly, despite the many customers.

"Hey! What's up?"

"I wanted to see where you get your T-shirts. I want to order some for my staff and I think yours look good. They're good quality."

"I'll get you the information."

"Thanks. I just hired a girl this morning. Everything is starting to arrive so I can start baking and getting things ready for a soft opening. All I need is my cash register and a department of agriculture inspection and I'll be ready. Jimmy's working on my consultation cabinet and counter-top today."

"Man! You are rolling right along."

"Stop by sometime and see me."

"I'll need to return the favor. You've been here three times."

"You're counting?"

"Yep."

"I'm a good customer."

"I'd like to be a good bakery customer, but I'd hate to ruin my girlish figure," he laughs, giving me a wink that makes me giggle.

"Well, come in for coffee if nothing else. I know you need coffee. I've worked in plenty of restaurants to know how that all goes."

"I'll be sure to do it. Let me go get you that T-shirt contact," he says, patting both hands on the table, and then he is off and running again, picking up dirty dishes as he goes. His butt isn't that big, I think to myself, sucking my iced tea through a straw and watching him walk away. If nothing else, I need friends.

Before returning to the bakery, I decide to swing by and check the mailbox for my business cards. Maybe there will be a letter from my soldier. I park at the end of our driveway, noticing that Mr. May is gone for the day. Reaching inside the mailbox for 312-B, I am delighted to find the long rectangular box filled with my cards. There is an assortment of junk mail as well, and as I flip through it, I discover an envelope addressed to the house next door. It looks like a utility bill, so I'd better take it over there and place it in their mailbox. I feel so happy, I sing a song I've been hearing on the radio that has stuck in my head. Opening the next-door neighbor's mailbox, I see there is nothing inside. If they have gotten their mail already, they won't see this until tomorrow, so I walk up the sidewalk to knock on their door. Having a grandmother who worked for the post office, I have always been respectful of the mail system.

The appearance of the house makes me stop singing. It seems quiet and sad-looking, with its odd, painted, smoky blue brick. A fraction of the size of AB's house, it barely looks lived in. Overgrown shrubbery makes the place stand out on our street like an orphaned child, devoid of any kind of adornment. Weeds grow between the cracks in the sidewalk, untouched by the caring hands of the likes of Mr. May. An older person must live here, I think, maybe a sickly one with few friends or family. *Like me.* I'll be living in a place like this when I'm old, sick, and alone. It's inevitable.

I knock on the door, waiting and listening for some sign of life. I can hear no footsteps, just the monotonous chatter coming from a TV program in a back room as the door suddenly jerks opens and a man's dingy and dark face appears, making me gasp with surprise. He wears a blue work shirt with *Hector* embroidered in red on the pocket, the same blue as the house. His face is odd and suspicious at first, but then it morphs into a bright smile that somehow gives me the creeps. I can smell a reprobate from a mile away, and this guy is definitely one!

"Hello," he says, almost questioning, stepping forward and placing his hand on the screen door handle.

"Hi. I live next door and your mail was in my mailbox today," I say, holding up the envelope. He opens the door and smiles again, but it doesn't reach his eyes.

"Oh, thanks very much," he says and takes the envelope with a little nod and closes the screen.

"You're welcome."

"Have a good one. Bye."

"Bye...."

He closes the door and I strain to hear his footsteps walking back toward the TV. As I walk back down the sidewalk, I peer around the hedge to get a glimpse of the driveway, equally filled with cracks and weeds. Under an oak tree is parked a large work van with a carpet cleaning sign painted on the side. Hector whoever must clean carpets for a living, I think, with a little shiver.

I'm glad I won't need his services.

Chapter 10

OBERON

It is now twelve days to show time. In six days, I have hired three employees, set up a cash register system, gotten my inspection and licenses in place and all the supplies I need to run a bakery full tilt. I've even drawn out a plan for the flowers I will plant in the small garden plot Mr. May has tilled up for me. I could be missing something, but if I am, I don't know what it is. As I am putting the final touches on Mr. May's colorful birthday cake, Leon, the sign man, and his team are assembling the sign on my storefront—the icing on the cake.

"Oh. My. God! Elle! Come out and see the sign! It looks so awesome!" exclaims Monai, who has just returned from her latest grand opening flyer blitz. She has worked tirelessly, slapping the half-sheets of paper underneath every windshield wiper on every car in the parking lot in Lumina Station shopping center for the fourth day in a row, and this after baking pan after pan of pound cake, white cake, caramel cake, and devil's food cake. Tall, curly-haired Jordan looks up from the pans he's washing at the sink, and Anna, red hair pulled into a knot at the nape of her neck, glances up from packaging my cupcakes to see what I'll do.

"Hang on just a sec." One last stroke of the light yellow tip of my icing bag and I have finished the Bowl of Beauty peony that is the highlight of Mr. May's cake decoration. I must admit that in all its splendor, this cake is Shakespeare worthy, if ever there was one to depict *A Midsummer Night's Dream*. Wiping my hands on my apron, the others follow suit and we go together toward the front door, with Jimmy Burns bringing up the rear. (He stopped by to install a peephole in my back door—I kept forgetting to ask him to do it.)

"Okay, let's see this sign," I say, almost under my breath. This is the final piece of the puzzle, other than getting all the cakes baked that I'll need to represent my inventory, but we still have twelve days.

"Wait, wait, wait!" Monai squeals, seized with an idea and hopping from one foot to the other to emphasize how excited she is. "Don't look, Elle! You have to hide your eyes!"

"Oh, good idea," says blond-haired Jordan, who has clamped his hands over my eyes, while steering me through the front door to the laughter of the sign crew that is finishing up on the sidewalk. The sound of cars gliding through our parking lot, and the conversations of shoppers going into the Salt Marsh gift shop next door orient me as Jordan turns me around.

"Wait, no! Pull her out into the parking lot so she can get a better view!" says Anna.

"Okay. Oh, wow!" I hear Jordan murmur over my head.

"Okay, look!" shouts Monai, as Jordan's hands drop from my face, and I focus my eyes in the mid-afternoon sun, glancing up at the storefront. And there is my sign. My sign. *Bake My Day*, in large, stylized black letters, forms the pedestal for the three-tiered cake in mango, kiwi green, and yellow, outlined in black. It is exactly how I wanted it, but far better than I even imagined.

"Ohhh!" is all I can say. My trembling hands go to my cheeks, which instantly flame with a burst of pride. *My prize and joy*, I think to myself, echoing what Vada said to me the day I was released from prison. She'd called me that and I'd laughed. *"You're my prize and joy. It's what my mother used to call me when I'd done something that made her proud. And Elle, you've made me real proud. You're going to do just fine."* And I feel like I'm doing just fine. I have made this happen.

All of us stare at the storefront sign, awestruck, as if we are viewing Mount Rushmore for the first time. It is miraculous for me, and I think my companions feel it too, even though they have no idea the depth of what this means for me. Jimmy is the first to break the silence, although I can hear Monai fluttering and cooing beside me.

"Well. Ain't that somethin'?"

"Oh, Elle, it's beautiful!" says Anna. Our collective eyes travel from the bench and accompanying bright flowerpots to the plate-glass window above it that bears the name of my bakery with frosted letters, and then up to the door and over the eaves to the newly created sign that already seems to beckon, as passersby stop to admire it with us.

I shift my gaze to the sign crew and give them a thumbs-up.

"It's fabulous!" I say, grinning, knowing my face is telling them all they need to know. "Thank you so much!"

"Here! Let's take a picture and post it on Facebook!" says Monai, herding us together in our aprons, Jimmy in his tool belt, and the sign guys in their work clothes. Monai clicks away with her camera phone as we hug each other and grin happily.

"Post it on your page too," I tell them, and Leon, the project manager laughs in agreement.

"You can be sure this sign is going on our Facebook page. We brought you a free decal for your rear window if you'd like. It's like the frosted sign on your front window, only smaller and it covers the whole back window," he tells me and I cringe for a moment. He doesn't know about my bumper sticker aversion. A rear window sign would be a real stretch for me.

"Oh! You gotta do it, Elle! If you don't do it, I'll take it."

"Yeah, but you ride a bike."

"They can put it on the back of my Jeep," says Jordan, who is more than likely going to be doing my deliveries, but then a surge of pride floods in and overrides my current dislike for advertisement. This opportunity could be critical for my success. I'd be foolish to pass it up.

"Okay, I'll take it."

"All right! It'll take about ten minutes."

"Awesome. My car is the white CRV in the back of the building. I have to leave in just about ten minutes anyway." We shake hands and they go to their truck to take care of my car as Brandon emerges from Sandy Britches to take a look at my new sign. He sticks his head in at the bakery any time something new is going on over here—probably to get away from Jewel and all that talking. Shoot, I would, too.

"Wow! Nice! You're official!"

"Just about! I have Channel 3 News coming in on the thirty-first to do a story on the bakery, just in time for the grand opening."

"Super! That will get people coming in. I saw your website. You've been a busy girl!"

"And this is just the start. When the orders start coming in, we'll be completely submerged."

"That's great!"

We only need to establish our breakfast items and routine and we'll be ready for a soft opening in a few days. I'll do the staff's training tomorrow and we'll get to work on the pastries and muffins. I never thought this day would come. I'll have to call Judy and Marcus. I want to tell Joey, too, so when I have a moment, I'll write to him. I haven't heard from him since he thanked me for the camera last week.

"Okay! I need to get rolling on my cupcake tour. Thanks for the support, Brandon. Tell Jewel I said, 'Hi'!"

"I'll do it! See you!" he says, and ducks back in his door.

Back in the kitchen, Jimmy packs up his tools and gets ready to leave. "That's a nice cake you have there."

"Oh, thanks. It's for a birthday party tomorrow night."

"Huh. I'm going to a birthday party tomorrow night, too," he says.

"Birthdays and weddings. That's all we hear about in a place like this. It's a happy business," I reply and he shakes his head, considering that it would certainly be true in a bakery.

"Well, I'll see ya. Call me if you need me."

"Okay. Thanks, Jimmy. You know I will. By the way, I love the counter!" I say to his retreating back as he heads out my back door and he waves.

"This place looks fantastic!" says Monai, looking around at the café, with little glass vases filled with yellow, orange, and red zinnias from AB's garden. The blackboard with its mango and kiwi painted border is propped against the wall, filled with colored chalk offerings of cake flavors and coffee. A large glass decanter that will be filled with cucumber water sits on an old chest I found at a thrift store that is covered with one of Granny's vintage tablecloths. (She had to be a part of this!) The focal point of the room is Jimmy's large consultation cabinet, topped with a smooth honey pine countertop, sanded and polished to a rich sheen, and holding my cake books where people can sit on barstools to view them.

"It does look good," I agree, hands on my hips while I take it all in. I have even more plans, but I push them aside for now, slipping my apron off over my head and going back in the kitchen to collect my cupcakes. "Anna, let's put these in the cooler and then we can put them in the back of my car. The last thing I need is to have them melt all over someone's bridal shop."

"Got it," says Anna, her freckled face pink with all the excitement, the few minutes of sunshine from the parking lot, and the heat of our current frenzy. She helps me place the cupcake boxes on top of ice packs Jordan has brought from the freezer. Already my crew is working like a team.

"Have you got your list?" asks Monai.

"Oh, yeah. I'm all set," I tell her, taking my notebook with all the bridal shops and wedding venues listed along with the owners and managers I'll be visiting over the next three hours. Monai holds the door for us as Jordan carries the large cooler to the back of my car. The car feels like an oven, but the ice packs inside the cooler should keep my delicate cargo intact. The new logo is in place on my back window and Leon and his crew are gone.

My staff will ice all the frozen cakes while I am gone. I take a moment after I start my car, thinking about what to write to Joey. I jot it down on an old receipt from the gas station. *"Twelve days to grand opening. Sign looks great. Wish to hear from you. I love you.... You know that, right?"*

I sigh and back out of my parking space, distracted slightly by the sign in my rearview mirror, and head over to a bridal shop, the first on my list, and the closest to my place. When I arrive at the shop—it is blessedly cool inside—two overly dressed young women are bidding goodbye to a girl with a pink garment bag slung over her shoulder. Perfect timing! Everybody looks happy, and it will only get better when they see what I have in my bag. I can see the grand opening flyers that Monai has left on their counter as one of the women greets me. Junior League. I dressed for such an audience, in my patterned crop pants, crisp, sleeveless white blouse, and wedge-heeled shoes. I even polished my fingernails last night.

"Hello! Can we help you?" asks the younger woman, smiling at me, wearing pearls and a lacey, blush colored dress, with nude heels.

"Hi, I'm Elle McLarin, the owner of Bake My Day bakery."

"Oh, yes! We have your flyers," says the other woman, more toned down in her dress and her personality.

"Yes! I saw them. Thank you for putting those out for us! I brought you each a cupcake to give you a little sample of what we do, in hopes that you'll refer your clients to us if the topic of wedding cakes should come up." I set my bag on their counter, pulling out a box for each of them, one with a lemon cupcake and one with a white one, and decorated with different kinds of flowers.

"Oh, yum!" says the younger girl. "I shouldn't, but I'm gonna!"

"I guess a little taste couldn't hurt. These look delicious!" says the older woman, looking around as if she is concerned about soiling something with the icing.

The younger woman has already bitten into hers and is crooning with delight.

"This is fabulous! I'll definitely refer our brides to you! And I'll come too when I have a cake to buy or something yummy."

"Oh, thank you so much!" I gush back at her. "And here are some of my business cards. The grand opening, as you know, is on June first, but we're already taking orders. We'll be doing a soft opening in two days, so stop in and see us. We're right between the Sandy Britches winery and the Salt Marsh gift shop."

They nod and chew, and the older woman recovers first, saying, "I go to Sandy Britches a lot. It's a great little winery!"

The rest of the outing goes just as well, and by the time I have returned to the bakery, my three staff members have iced the remaining cakes and cleaned up. Jordan is sweeping, while Anna wipes and replaces the clean bowls on the fifty-quart standing mixers.

"You guys are wonderful! Tomorrow, we'll train for the breakfast crowd and prepare the pastries, and we can open on Friday morning. What do you think?"

"Bring it!" says Jordan, raising his hand to bump my fist with his. Joey used to do that with me. I wish my son would communicate with me. Just a letter—a word or two would be all I need.

"All right, you guys! Go home and rest, go to the beach, whatever you do to relax, and I'll see you in the morning."

When they are gone, I box Mr. May's cake and return it to the refrigerator, and then I hurry home to check my mailbox one more time.

Nothing.

It is a balmy, pleasant evening in the Montgomery garden. Crickets must chirp from dawn till dusk here at the coast, unlike what I know of late spring mountain days. A soft breeze wafts the humid air tranquilly about, cooling me off from another hot day's work in the bakery. Setting my fabulous cake on the table AB has shown me, I glance at the other food—chicken satay, barbeque sliders, pasta salad, assorted fruit, cheese and crackers, hummus with pita points, and a vegetable tray she's had catered on the covered tables on her patio. AB lingers for a moment, looking at my cake, but she doesn't say a word to me about it, which is a bit unnerving, considering I think it's a masterpiece. Her indifference is worse than flat-out dislike of my fine creation. Could she not say *something*? Is she just that snooty, or is she preoccupied with her guests arriving? To her, I just might be the hired help, but still.... At any rate, Mr. May's party is going to be lovely, I think to myself as guests continue to arrive and AB greets them all as long lost friends, and maybe they are.

Some of them seem well-dressed and super-attractive, so I assume they must be movie people. At least twenty people are milling around, drinking whatever they have been served by the bartender, who has set up shop at a long table in front of the garage doors. Patsy, Harley's owner from down the street, is here. She has cleaned herself up and looks very presentable. She reintroduces herself to me and pumps my hand profusely. We chat briefly about Harley. Then she explains that she knows Mr. May from her daily walks in the neighborhood, when she'd stop to ask him about gardening, picking up whatever tips he had to offer.

I suddenly have a sickening feeling that my hot neighbor might show up at this soiree. Somehow, I don't think this would be his crowd, but you never know. Still, my eyes dart nervously around as if I might spy him at any minute. I want my face to be ready so I don't look cowed. That wouldn't do at all. Three other men about Mr. May's age whom I don't know have arrived together, looking like the outdoorsy type, probably fellow gardeners. AB introduces us all around, and then my mouth drops open, as Randy and Jimmy come walking down the driveway, carrying a twelve pack of beer. The cavalry has arrived!

"Well, hey! I didn't know you were coming!" Jimmy says to me, as Randy breaks into a grin. His casual short-sleeved shirt and jeans give him a whole new, relaxed dimension, and Jimmy has cleaned up nicely as well. "So this is the party you were talking about," says Jimmy.

"Hey! Yeah, I'm a two-fer. I live here, and AB recruited me to bake the cake."

"Well, this is a surprise! You *live here*?" Randy echoes, laughing, glancing at Jimmy. "Did you know this?"

"Nope. I'm as surprised as you are."

"I'm renting the guest house until I figure out my next move," I explain, sharing their surprise, and wondering how they know Mr. May, when he arrives himself, causing a stir in the ranks. AB makes a fuss over him, and he does indeed look handsome, in a checkered shirt and khaki pants, without his hat and gloves. I've never seen his hair, which is sparse on top and a faded tan color, as if he is resisting going gray. I watch as Jimmy and Randy greet Mr. May with hugging and back-slapping as men often do, making me realize they have a close connection, again making me wonder why. Then Mr. May sees me and grins, reaching for my hand. *He thinks I'm swell.*

"Hello, Elle! What a nice surprise! I'm so glad to see you!" he says, beaming at me.

"You too, Mr. May! Happy birthday!"

"Thank you!"

AB gathers the odd assortment of guests around Mr. May and produces a large gift bag. There are other gifts on the gift table, but she lifts her hand to command attention. It takes a minute for the revelers to settle down so she can talk.

"Before we get started on dinner, I'd like to welcome you all to Mr. May's eightieth birthday party!" There is applause and she continues. "I know, darn it! He hardly looks his age, or acts it either!" There is laughter and a smattering of applause. "As the generous master of the garden that he is, I thought it would be fitting for him to have a little costume to go with our *Midsummer Night's Dream* theme, and as you know, I have a thing about costumes, so without further ado, Mr. May, I'd like to crown you Oberon, King of the Fairies, at least for tonight!" With that, she pulls a long purple cape from the bag and drapes it around his shoulders. The crowd breaks out into laughter and so does the guest of honor. He is the ultimate good sport. From the bottom of the bag, she pulls out a crown and places it on his head, his silent laughter shaking his shoulders.

"Oh, I forgot, there is one more thing. Your scepter, Your Highness," she laughs, and produces a toilet plunger, painted gold, from under the table and places it in his hand. He raises it high in the air and the crowd bursts into raucous laughter and applause.

"Oh, dear…my wife is probably rolling over in her grave to know I've been crowned king of the *fairies.*"

"You shoulda told her!" quips one of the gardeners, making the rest of them laugh.

"Well...."

"It's okay. She knew you were a king, at any rate," says Patsy, standing beside AB, and the group raises their glasses. "Happy birthday, Mr. May!"

"Happy birthday," the other guests echo.

They drink to Mr. May, and Jimmy hands me a cold beer so I can participate in the toasting.

Mr. May begins to speak. "Thank you for this, AB. And thank you all for coming. Most of you have been around and have known me for a while, and I'm certainly honored to be the center of attention tonight—actually I'm amazed to be the center of attention—of anything—and we all have Monty to thank for getting us all together as friends. He was wonderful that way. But some of you may not know the new person who's joined us tonight. I'd like to introduce you to Elle McLarin, our newest friend!" He raises his glass to me as a look of total shock registers on my face.

"Elle is a baker and is getting ready to open her new bakery in a few days, so you should all go and buy your sweets and desserts from her! Plus, she's awfully nice to have around! She makes you feel good!"

I've never been told I made anybody feel good.

"She baked your cake, by the way, Bernie," says AB, with a sweep of her hand in the direction of the cake table. All the eyes follow and there is a collective, delighted gasp at my creation. Then the group looks back at me, curious about the new girl. Even the movie people are noticing me now. Any other time, I'd be all over this like white on rice, preening and trying my best to rub elbows with them, but it doesn't feel right. Tonight should be all about Mr. May. My face is burning, but I'm trying to look unabashed.

"Oh, look at that! Good heavens, that's absolutely spectacular!" says Mr. May, going closer to get a better look at the cake. "Thank you so much! Young lady, your talent is even more impressive than I had imagined!"

"Oh, thank you. I'm glad you like it!" I say, lifting my bottle to him.

The guests begin pulling Mr. May into this group and that, to wish him happy birthday, and I feel myself gravitate to Jimmy and Randy since they're the only ones I really know. AB looks away from Patsy momentarily and shoots me a wink from across the patio, sending me her approval.

"Very nice job," Randy says, giving me an appreciative glance.

"Thanks."

"Hope you brought your business cards."

"I did. AB reminded me to put some out on the table. So, how do you guys know Mr. May?"

They glance at each other and Randy grins at me. The look they share is like the one that crossed Randy's face when I'd asked for a handyman recommendation. "Well, it's kind of a club. We're all fairies!" he says, making Jimmy snort, but I'm not sure how to react. Randy scratches his beard. "Nah, seriously, Monty had a way of connecting people. He was a real networker, very social, but unlike many wealthy people, his reach seemed to cross social boundaries, you might say; for instance, these kinds of parties with people like us and the film people were common when he was alive," Randy explains. "AB still gets us together from time to time. I think it helps her feel like he's still with us somehow."

I suddenly think of Marcus, and I have some idea of the kind of man Monty must have been. A savior. And maybe AB isn't so bad. Still, I wait for more. They seem unwilling to go on, so I ask, "So Mr. May must be very special?"

"Oh, he is," says Jimmy in all earnestness. "His own garden is legendary." Randy chuckles and they share a look. "He takes care of Mrs. Montgomery's flowers, but he raises his own vegetables at home and gives most of his harvest to the food pantry in town. He was doing that before it was the popular thing to do."

"Well, I guess I'm not surprised. He seems like a very kind person," I say, feeling a little honored myself to know such a gentleman, so well-respected, and someone who has publicly acknowledged me.

"He's about the kindest man you'll ever meet," says Jimmy. "I've painted his house, and they don't get much nicer than Mr. May."

"And Monty? How did you meet him?"

"I painted for him, too, after Randy introduced us."

"Monty and AB used to come into the restaurant all the time, and they'd been looking for a handyman and a painter, so of course, I sent Jimmy over and that's how they met."

"I've painted most of the rooms in their house, and in the guest house as well."

"You painted my house?" I ask, marveling at the way this well-woven fabric has unfolded before me tonight. Jimmy nods while Randy grins at me, seemingly pleased to see my incredulous reaction. I can't believe I have had the good fortune to stumble on such a solid and wonderful group of people, and they seem to like me. They could be my friends. Maybe I'm doing things right for a change. I haven't had the chance to disappoint them yet, but there is *that*. The breeze blows tendrils of my hair that have escaped my chignon across my cheek so I brush them back, studying the bottle in Randy's hand while he tries to catch my eye. He's probably thinking about asking me out. I sip my beer and look away. *It's best not to get attached, Randy.*

They're all going to be so let down when they learn I'm a felon. This midsummer night's dream I'm in could be over if the truth ever comes out. And it always does.

Chapter 11

PERKY AMY

Hello, Ms. McLarin! I'd be delighted to interview you at your new bakery the day before your grand opening—June 1, right? I can be at your establishment, Bake My Day—love the name by the way, with my camera crew at 5:30 a.m. on May 31 if it suits you. I know it's early, but that's the nature of the morning show. Best regards, Amy Stainback

You have got to be kidding! 5:30 a.m. I will certainly be there, baking my little heart out and every day that week, but nobody else in their right mind will be up at that hour! What's the freaking point at 5:30? Screw this! I type back the following email:

Hi, Amy! Thanks for your prompt response to my request. I am so glad that you will be able to cover our opening! Are there other time spots available? I was hoping for a time when more people might be tuned in, such as 7:00 for instance. If it's at all possible, that would be my preference, although I will be there baking from about 4:30 a.m. every morning that week. Looking forward to working with you! Elle McLarin

Hitting "Send," I rear back in my seat, folding my arms across my chest. I will not be jerked around on this. I'm sure she has other times available. If she won't cooperate, I might have to contact her boss, whomever the station manager is. Maybe a little pre-TV cupcake will be in order if it's a problem. Then again, there are other TV stations. I wonder how long it will take me to hear back from her, or if she'll just show up at 5:30 on the 31st and expect me to be happy about it. The worst-case scenario will be that we get pre-empted altogether by another story. It's already taken her two days to respond the first time. I refuse to sit here and be her captive, so I glance around the kitchen to see what's happening.

The two fifty-quart standing mixers are whirring along, with Monai manning the buttercream frosting, and Anna taking care of the cream cheese icing. Jordan is cutting strawberries at the table, laughing at Monai's enthusiastic and energetic rendition of one of the songs from our favorite play list—the song I like, "Let it Go," from *Frozen*. I was lucky to hire people with good musical taste. And they are competent bakers, with Anna being on the weaker side, but she is a quick study.

It's nine o'clock and already we have nine layers of pound cake in the ovens. When they come out, white cake layers will go in, and we'll ice the frozen devil's food cakes from yesterday while the pound cakes cool. The door chimes so I go to the front to wait on customers. We've been doing breakfast items and coffee for two days now, in preparation for the big day. People are beginning to find us, now that my sign is up. A lady with her newspaper tucked under her arm orders a slice of spinach quiche and a cup of coffee. We chat about the opening and she is glad to have us nearby. After I take care of her, she settles at one of my tables to read her paper, so I return to the kitchen to check my email at the computer on my desk.

And lo! Amy has replied:

Actually, there is a 7:15 spot available. As you can imagine, we like to offer the earlier ones first because most people would rather go on later, but I'll be glad to be there for a 7:15 shoot. Look for us around 6:45. Does this work for you? Amy

It takes me no time to type in:

Perfect, Amy. Thanks so much for adjusting your schedule for us! See you at 6:45 on May 31! Elle

That's the way to work it! I give a victorious whoop and then inform the staff of what's going to happen, and they are ecstatic with the news. This is how it's done, I think to myself, making a note of the event on my calendar. One week from today, we will be on TV. In eight days, the bakery will be officially open for business. Our new T-shirts will arrive in a couple of days, so we will look official while we work. Everyone will be here, doing what we normally do. Usually the staff comes in at 7:30, but that day I will expect them here at 6:30. I'll be coming in at 4:30 to get breakfast pastries baked and to have everything done for the grand opening. Right now, business hours are 8:00 a.m. to 6:00 p.m., but that will change to 7:00 a.m. after the grand opening and the weddings begin. We already have seven scheduled in June, which is pretty good for a brand new bakery. Word has gotten out, thanks to our cupcake blitz. I plan to hire three more people within the next two weeks, with the hours the weddings will require. The busier we get, the more staff I'll need. It will take two shifts to operate the bakery by then, since I can't see myself pulling fifteen-hour shifts every day. Some people can do it, but that's not what I have in mind. I sigh with the weight of it all.

"What's wrong, Elle? You look stressed," says Monai.

"No, I'm okay. Things couldn't be better. It's just a lot to think about," I say, putting my hand to my head and brushing my hair back. Standing at my spot at the icing table, I begin the crumb icing on the devil's food layers in front of me. It's a mindless and therapeutic task at the same time for me; I could do it in my sleep. The stroking back and forth and then around the curves of the layers puts me in a rhythm much like the ritualistic brush strokes of Jimmy Burns, Randy's smooth, social roaming of the Dockside deck, keeping everybody happy, or Jewel's pouring of wine—just the right amount in each glass as the description rolls off her tongue like poetry: the daily work that we each hold sacred, sustaining us and giving us a reason to get up every morning.

But there has to be more to life than just this reverent routine. What's left for me at the end of the day? What's Joey going home to? Or Aiden— although I think I know, and he doesn't need to be in the forefront of my thoughts any longer. I think of AB in her costume department, dressing her actors to perfection for each role. I think of Mr. May in the garden, pulling weeds or expertly examining leaves for pests or diseases only he can diagnose. Even Jordan, Monai, and Anna intrigue me, making me wonder what it is they go home to every night that makes it all worth it at the end of the day. And then there's Amy; she's the most intriguing of all. What does she do after work each day?

Imagining her leaving the television studio around 2:00 and slipping by to steal a little afternoon delight with my hot neighbor for an hour or so before she has to pick up her kids from school has me pursing my lips in displeasure, or envy maybe. If I'm right about their affair, and I think I am, I wish it were me, truth be told. The thought makes me shake my head, knowing that man is the last person in the world I should be fantasizing about, but I can't shake the feeling those blue eyes of his left me with the day Harley arrived at my mailbox.

Maybe if I did something fun for a change, I could stop thinking about him, but it's the forbidden fruit that always calls our name. Good

Elle reminds me that I need to squash all thoughts of him immediately. Sighing again, I realize I haven't taken the time to enjoy myself, even if it's just a solo trip to the beach for a quick little dip or some sunbathing. It wouldn't kill me to have some fun. I've sat in movie theaters by myself before, I think, glancing up at the twenty-somethings who work here. I wouldn't go out with them anyway. They're too young. Brandon and Jewel are nice, but they're a couple, and she drives me freaking crazy with all that talking! Randy's busier than I am, and who knows? He probably has a girlfriend. He hasn't asked me out, so that has to be the reason.

I need to go on the prowl! There is Bad Elle again, trying to stir up trouble. I have eight days until this place opens, and then I'll be so slammed I won't be able to see straight. It would feel good to get dressed up and go out somewhere. I've been to bars by myself too, and I usually didn't leave alone, either. It could be so easy. The scintillating thought of a man's naked body pressed against mine, penetrating my numb hopelessness for just an hour or two, makes me shake with yearning, as though I am starved for sexual intimacy. It's been months since I've been touched or kissed, physically moved by another human being.

The guilt that goes along with my thoughts brings an image of my son to mind again. When Joey stayed with Aiden on the weekends, I had the opportunity to go out sometimes, so he wouldn't know I was dating. What is Joey doing? What does he really want? Does he yearn for the same things I do? Does he think he did the right thing, joining the Army? What gets him up in the morning besides a feisty drill sergeant?

I take a break and write a quick note to him again. *This is your mother. I'd like to hear from you. Hope you're okay.* Should I add, *Do you care?* But maybe I don't want to know. A knock on my back door signals Jimmy's arrival. He has come to install my incredible, vintage crystal chandelier in the café that will place the crowning touch on my place. Joey's letter will have to wait.

"Hey!" I greet him. Maybe Jimmy likes movies. I don't want to see his half-naked body on any beach, but I wouldn't mind munching popcorn with him at a movie.

"Hey, there. Y'all look mighty busy!" he says, hefting a large box through my back door.

"We are! Oh, no! I just realized you'll have to cut the power to install that light, right?"

"Well, yeah, but only to the café area, so your ovens and mixers shouldn't be affected. I tried to get in here earlier, but I had a job to finish up first thing this morning. Do you have any customers out there?"

"No. We'll do what we have to do. You can go ahead with whatever you need."

"All right. I'll pull around front and bring the ladder in the front door."

In thirty minutes, Jimmy is finished and the effect of the new lighting is breathtaking.

"Wow! This completes the whole package."

"I think you're right. What's left?"

"Nothing, really. Amy Stainback from Channel 3 News is coming in to film us the day before the opening. I guess I just need to canvass a few more areas to distribute flyers and cupcakes. It never hurts to get out there and meet the people."

"That's what the politicians do—press the flesh."

"I guess."

"Well, I'm outta here. I'm heading home for the weekend."

There goes my movie plan. "Oh. Got plans?"

"Yep. Me and a buddy are gonna do some fishin' up on the west fork of the Pigeon River."

"Oh, that sounds exciting." That's the last thing I'd want to do, but then, I remember those few times when Pa took me and I did have fun. "I caught a rainbow trout one time."

"How big?"

I held out my hands to the best I recall, about a foot long.

"You probably caught a native. They don't have to be real big to be fun to catch."

"I guess. Well, have fun!"

"You have a good weekend too! See you next week. Call me if there's anything you need."

"I'll do it. Bye!"

Returning to the kitchen, I can hear the kids talking about what they're doing tonight, so apparently I am all by myself. My restless self.

"So what are some good bars downtown where I could distribute some flyers?" I ask Jordan, the most likely barfly candidate, but include the girls with a collective gaze.

"The Reel Café, definitely. It's on Front Street—on the corner of Front and Dock. They have a courtyard oyster bar and a rooftop bar, too. They usually have live music," he says.

"I've seen it. And those people probably play weddings and other events," I muse out loud, remembering from driving by the downtown's historic district and wondering about what it would be like to live down there—in my dreams. I don't want them to think I'll be going down there alone tonight, but that's exactly what I'll do.

"Then there's the Front Street Brewery down the street."

"Here, let's write down a list of all the best restaurants too," says Monai, pushing up her glasses, her eyes and mouth working overtime as she talks. It must be hard to get her lips around all that wire in her mouth. Who wears braces at that age? Still, she's as cute as pie.

"Oh yeah, there's Indochine, and the Dock Street Oyster Bar," says Anna, going to our pad and pen that sits out on the counter for listing anything we need, or new brainstorms that come to mind.

"And the Pilot House and Bluewater," says Monai.

"Don't forget Tower 7 Baja Grille," says Jordan. "That's my absolute fave!"

"I've already been to some of these, guys, but keep it coming. Write down everything you think is worthwhile. I've hit all the wineries, just so you know."

The Reel sounds like just what I need.

Chapter 12

NATE

At 9:30 p.m., I am rested and relaxed after spending a peaceful hour on the beach. (I found a nice college boy to rub sunscreen on my back.) I brought home fish tacos from Tower 7 on the beach for dinner, and then I dressed in a teal blue sundress that sets off my loose blond hair and gives my tan a spectacular glow. In short, I look like a million bucks and can't wait to hit the town. It will be a piece of cake to waltz in and out of the places on Front St. and elsewhere, armed with a purse full of grand opening flyers and business cards.

It's a beautiful evening in historic downtown Wilmington as I'm gliding in my car down Front St. in search of a parking place. I turn left, up a side street where I'm rewarded by the flash of red taillights, indicating someone is starting up and getting ready to leave the spot I need. Once I've parked the car, I stroll casually down the street toward The Reel, noticing crowds of people doing the same thing, heading from dinner to the local nightlife spots or just coming out to celebrate the evening. It feels odd and freeing to know I won't run into anyone I know down here. Every once in awhile, I wonder whether I'll ever run into one of my fellow inmates, but here in downtown Wilmington, it seems unlikely. But you never know. There was a doctor's wife who might emerge into my reality someday. I push the thoughts of those women away whenever they resurface, as I have done with so much of my past. Don't talk about it. *Let it go.*

The crowd that's out tonight is generally attractive and intelligent-looking, giving me a little charge at the possibilities. I'm doing legitimate business tonight, so I'm not out to pick up anybody necessarily, but if the opportunity presents itself, I won't be against it. I'm not due at work until 7:30 in the morning. The breakfast pastries are made for tomorrow.

The Reel is hopping! There's a brick wall around the corner courtyard, lit with white lights, which lend a festive air. A singer playing a guitar is audible from his perch in the back as I walk in, and I can already tell he's good. Half of the crowd is singing along to his excellent rendition of Van Morrison's "Brown-Eyed Girl." I have hazel eyes, but mostly they're brown, and Aiden used to call me his brown-eyed girl in the old days, when we really liked each other.

The girls in this town really dress up for barhopping, I notice, feeling a twinge of panic that I could be underdressed, but then I raise my chin and flick my hair back, putting on my best smile. Men usually prefer the more toned down look, so if that's the case, I'm definitely the standout in this place tonight. Maybe it's because of my age that I dress this way, but I definitely missed the dress code memo. Whatever; I don't care. Heads are turning my way so I relax and look for an open spot at the bar. It's still early, enabling me to find a place between a group of sunburned guys who look like they're celebrating, and a group of double-daters who are ensconced among each other. Someone will buy me a drink in the next ten minutes. Just watch.

The young man beside me turns my way. He's the one. I know he can smell my perfume—not too strong and not too sweet. I've been told it's a real turn-on. He's in his mid-thirties too, with short dark hair and a sunburn—and a decided buzz from the look in his eyes. He's definitely the one I'll start with.

Sliding onto the barstool, I place my purse on the hook under the bar. (I didn't even have to look. I knew it would be that kind of a place, having all the amenities.) "So…what are we celebrating?" I ask.

My charm works on him instantly. He looks me over and grins, turning his full attention toward me, as I rest my hand under my chin and grin right back at him.

"A sixty-five-pound yellow fin tuna!" he says, and the man beside him catches onto our conversation and slaps him on the back.

"Oh, wow!" I say, showing him I'm duly impressed.

"Yeah, boy! And he reeled it in all by himself, yes he did!" he says, taking my friend's face in his hand and squeezing his cheeks, the way grandparents sometimes do with little children, and then guffaws at the look on the dark-haired guy's face. These boys have been here a while. There must be four or five of them, sharing stories of the day's fishing trip out to the blue water and slurping amber beers from heavy mugs, wet with condensation in the outdoor humidity. They are rowdy and happy, and the camaraderie makes me envious, but hopefully, I can jump in here somewhere.

"Well, congratulations!" I'm showing my dimple now and the brown-haired guy sees it.

"You need a beverage to toast with, don't cha now?" he says, now focusing on me while his companion has taken up the louder conversation on his other side. His eyes dart toward the bartender and he nods his head to me.

"What can I get cha?" asks the bartender.

"I'll have a Dos Equis amber," I reply and my new friend nods with approval.

"Thanks," I say to him. "What's your name? I'm Elle," I tell him, extending my hand, and he takes it like he's going to kiss it, but then shakes it. (Less than three minutes on that drink.)

"Hey, Elle. I'm Bill."

My beer is in front of me. "Thanks," I say with a wink for the bartender. "You didn't ask me what *I'm* celebrating," I scold Bill.

"Oh! My bad. What are you celebrating?"

"I'm getting ready to open my brand new bakery in eight more days. It's called Bake My Day."

"Wow! That's awesome! Congratulations!" We lift our glasses and clink them together, and then I take a large sip. The beer is cold and sweet, just the way I like it, and Bill is rather good-looking and clean. Scanning quickly around the bar, I see I've taken the last seat in the house and people are milling about, standing and talking with friends, drinking, and laughing. I need this. Just let me get lost in a crowd and the music and I will be rejuvenated. It feels happy and boisterous here, and the ambience is catching.

The singer is on to a Jimmy Buffet song, and everyone is singing along about wasting away in Margaritaville. Bill's friends have noticed me now, and he's introducing me and telling them about my bakery. There are toasts to Bake My Day and Bill's big fish. Joe, the bartender, has come back around to Bill's friends, and we strike up a conversation about the bakery. Joe agrees to take some flyers to put at the bar and suggests that I take some inside to leave at the hostess station. He tells me what the manager looks like so I can leave some of my cards.

I catch a glimpse of a white-haired, heavy-set man with wire-rimmed glasses, in his mid-fifties, across the bar, wearing a dark polo shirt and a beer-induced smile that he's been directing at me since I arrived. Great. He is by himself, and I know it will only be a matter of time before he staggers over here to tell me the story of his sad, lonely life. That's the down side of solo barhopping, so I snuggle closer to Bill and prop my head on my hand so it makes us look more intimate. Bill doesn't seem to mind. He tells me they've been up since 4:30 in order to make their fishing charter. I can imagine that a day out on the ocean, some rigorous fishing, and several beers will make Bill pass out in another hour, so he's not going anywhere with me. We make more shallow small talk as I finish my beer and cast about for other potential conversationalists.

The couples on the other side of me are self-involved, but still I turn to interrupt them briefly, offering them flyers and business cards in case they are ever in need of a wedding cake or birthday cake or cupcakes. Bingo! The couple on the far side of the foursome has just become engaged and they've been discussing having their wedding at the beach. They are so glad to have run into me!

I turn back to Bill, who has bought me another beer, so I rub his back in a friendly way to thank him with an "Oh, you didn't need to do that!" I go back and forth with Bill and his funny friends and their fishing stories, and the double-daters who are talking weddings now. I feel sorry for the guys in this group. They are just not into it.

Something inside me loosens up from the core of me outward, thanks to the effects of my two beers. It's a good feeling, not caring as much, for the moment. I feel free—freer than I've felt since I came down here. The singer announces that he's going to take a break, and I take the opportunity to excuse myself to go talk to him so I can inquire about wedding connections he might have. We chat a moment and swap cards, and I give him a flyer, promising to post his business card in my bakery. (I will have to get a bulletin board to put above my wedding consultation counter.) The older guy is stirring, getting ready to make his move, so I dart into the ladies' room and take care of business, reapply my lip gloss, and return to the café, in search of the manager. She and I talk, and she agrees to take some flyers and my cards, letting me know they do a lot of private parties, and that she will be glad to help me spread the word.

My business here is done, but I need to thank Bill for the beers before I leave, so I make my way carefully and undetected around the big guy, whose attention is currently focused on the baseball game playing without sound on the TV screen in the opposite corner. My seat at the bar is gone, and I realize I've been replaced with a new member of Bill's group, and one who is being covered up with raucous greetings and apparently had something to do with the day's successful fishing trip. Good; I can slip out without causing too much of a stir. The flash of the newcomer's light blue shirt catches my eye, as I weave through the crowd to get to Bill to say goodnight.

"Hey, thanks for the drinks, Bill," I say, tugging intimately at his shirt to get his attention. Already, I am edging backwards.

"Hey, are you leaving already? We're just getting started! Our guide just got here!"

I take one more step closer to Bill and the guide turns to face me from his (my) barstool and speaks to me. "I'm sorry! I took your seat. Here!" he says, slipping off and holding his hand out for me, but I can't speak. The deep-set hot tub eyes have me completely paralyzed. It takes me a moment to recover, especially when his hand is on my arm, cradling my elbow so he can guide me back to the barstool.

Holy shit! Shit, shit, shit, shit, shit! It is my hot neighbor and he is *touching* me! That sandy brown hair and his face, tanned almost to the point of looking grimy, sets off his flash of a smile, and it is *definitely* naughty.

"Oh, no, that's okay. I was just getting ready to leave."

"Wait—hold on. Don't leave. Don't I know you?" He's squinting at me with those sparkling eyes under the lights of the bar, and I am fighting inside myself, trying to come up with a decent plan. *Oh, hell yeah, girl, you go for it!* Bad Elle is the first to yell out, while Good Elle is cautioning me with, *Now remember, we said you could never become acquainted with this guy.* Shut the fuck up, I say inside my head, while fireworks are going off somewhere south of my midsection.

I blink twice and swallow hard, trying to regain my composure, commanding his complete attention, while Bill has already forgotten me, gesticulating about another hilarious incident with another guy in their group and shoving me closer to Hot Neighbor in the process.

"Uh, yeah. I think we've talked briefly once. I'm your neighbor."

"Oh, right, right, right!" he says in that crisp, clipped voice that I like. "You're the girl who found Harley that day," he says grinning now, mesmerizing me completely with that grin. He is not like Kyle at all, I realize, noticing the soft light hair covering his arm, which, by the way, is still attached to my arm by his hand. He is interested and edgy, and I like the whole package. But what is going on with him and Amy?

"Yeah, that was me. I've seen you in your driveway with your wife."

There is a nanosecond of hesitation and he smiles again. "That's not my wife."

"Oh, fiancée? I was hoping I could tell you about my new bakery and then maybe you'd order your wedding cake from me." It's worth a shot to see his reaction.

He chuckles, "Smooth! But I'm not engaged."

"Neither am I," I find myself saying, and it is then that his hand moves away from my arm, while he signals the bartender. "What are you drinking?"

"Dos Equis?" the bartender asks, and I just nod like an idiot. I do not need even to be talking to him, much less drinking a beer with him. Three beers going into this tired body after a general drinking hiatus are probably going to result in bad drama for me. I'll just take a few sips.

"So are you a Montgomery?" he asks me.

"No. I rent their guest house, temporarily until I figure out my next move."

"Got it. I'm Nate," he says, extending his hand. "Don't say it—I hear it all the time," he warns, giving me raised eyebrows. *Nate the Great.* I won't.

"Hi, I'm Elle," I say, shaking his hand, liking the feel of it and holding it a little too long, but he seems okay with it.

"Here, please sit down," he says, offering me the stool as the singer starts back up for his second set with "The Story of My Life," making me chuckle.

Nate smiles too, quick blue eyes scanning me, taking in everything about my appearance, and I think he even notices the dimple. I can't help but look him over too, wondering whether I'm as subtle about it as he is. I try to breathe while attempting to look cool and calm.

"So tell me about this bakery of yours."

"The grand opening is in eight days. It's called Bake My Day."

"Get out!"

"No, really."

"I'm a huge *Dirty Harry* fan. I have all of Clint's old movies. I'll quote a few lines for you, if I get a few beers in me."

I laugh. "My grandfather loved him too. That's why I named it that," I say, my voice drifting, just thinking of Pa and how he used to laugh and rewind every time Clint said the famous line.

"He's gone—your grandpa?"

"Yeah, and my grandmother too."

"Well, that's a good name for a bakery. I can't say I'm much of a bakery person. I haven't got a sweet tooth in my whole mouth." The way he says it is just the slightest bit suggestive, or maybe I'm imagining it. His mouth is not bad. "But I'm sure it takes a gift to be able to turn out some of the cakes I've seen. You must be good at it."

"I've been doing it since I was in high school. It's fun. It's an up early kind of job," I say, thinking I'll segue into my exit speech.

"My business is like that, too," Nate says, looking me over again as he talks, maybe gauging my interest level. "I've been up since 4:30 with these *knuckleheads* over here," he says loudly for Bill's benefit, and he laughs when Bill turns around in mock resentment.

"Right; you're the fishing guide." I think to slide off my barstool and go, but I can't make myself do it yet.

"Not exactly. The guide works a lot harder than I do. I work for Bo Hauser, who is the host of the show. I do the filming and the production."

He chuckles at my blank look.

"Have you ever heard of Bo Hauser?"

"No...should I have?"

"Only if you're addicted to fishing shows like these guys are." Nate grins, turning his head toward Bill's group. "They're basically just like Saturday morning cartoons for grown-up boys. We have a show on the Sportsman Channel called *Carolina's Catch with Bo Hauser*. I'm the field producer. That means Bo's the host—he's the professional—and I film the trips and then produce the shows that go on TV."

"That's cool," I say, truly impressed. "How did you get into that?"

"When I got out of the Navy, I went to school and got a journalism degree. I worked at the TV station here and was fooling around on one of the fishing trips I went on and sent my footage in to an agency. They liked what they saw and invited me out to do a couple of shows. I got to meet Bo at a fishing expo, and I told him about my films. He watched 'em and got me on board—literally! And the rest is history. I'm gone about half the time, all over the Carolinas, sometimes Mexico when it's cold around here, Canada, or Alaska other times. We've even been to Scotland to fish for salmon. Then I'm here, putting the shows together. I have the best job in the world, going fishing all the time and telling the stories with my camera. These guys are going to be on TV and they're pretty stoked about it."

"Wow." I'm looking at him with renewed interest after his comment about being in the Navy. "My son just joined the Army," I say, pushing my hair back, and he gives me a somber look, and suddenly things turn serious. I'm not going anywhere now.

"How old are you?" he asks, those blue eyes boring into mine.

"I'm thirty-seven."

"You don't look it. What's your son's name?"

"Joey. He left on Mother's Day. I left my home in the mountains right after that and drove down here to start my business."

"Mother's Day. Bummer. Where's he based?"

"Fort Hood."

"Big bummer." I nod. I've heard all the stories about the shootings that went on there, about the soldier who became a radicalized Islamic terrorist a few years ago, and then the more recent shooting that left several dead before the shooter turned the gun on himself.

"Actually," Nate continues, "Fort Hood might be one of the safest bases in the country right now, but it's a tough time to be in the service. There isn't much support from the current administration for our armed forces, but don't get me started..." he says, and then realizing that it's a tough topic for me right now, he adds, "But we should be talking about happier things. How's he doing? Have you heard from him much?"

"No. We haven't been keeping in touch. Well—I've written to him, but I haven't gotten a letter. It's not that surprising. We aren't close." I drink some of my beer and then set the mug on the bar.

"Well, crap, this isn't going as planned," Nate says, and peeks under my lowered face to catch my eye. I can tell he's relieved I'm not crying. "You know, my mother told me once that she raised me through my boyhood, but she couldn't make me into a man. That was my job."

I look up. He's hit the nail on the head. How could he know exactly what I'm going through with my son? I give him another more direct, appraising look.

"So there's hope for Joey?"

"I'd say so.... Hey, I have an idea," he says. "But I should ask, are you by yourself?"

"Tonight?"

"Well, no...I mean all the time?" He looks seriously at me, making me want to melt a little. Damn it. I'm not falling for his irritating charm. I should just fricking leave.

"Yeah. You could say that."

"Since we're neighbors, how'd you like to take a little moonlight boat ride with me down the Intracoastal Waterway? I figure you're heading my way and it's a nice night.... I can't think of a more relaxing way to end the evening."

"But aren't you here with your guys?"

"Pshh! I've been with them all day! They should all be going home to bed anyway. Let's go, okay?" With that, Nate takes my arm to help me off my barstool and drops cash on the bar. For some reason, I don't resist, even though I should. We say our goodbyes to Bill and his group, and I take another moment to say goodbye to the double-daters.

"Are you all right to drive?" Nate asks, as soon as we have cleared the bar's exit. His hand is protectively at the small of my back as we get to the corner.

Of course I'm all right. I don't need him taking care of me. "Yeah. I'm okay. I'm just parked up the street here," I say, gesturing to the left.

"So am I," he says, taking my hand as we cross the street and then holding it as we walk quietly along the sidewalk, as if we're a couple. I must be hallucinating. This isn't happening, I think, shaking my hair out to clear my head. Nate is shorter than Kyle but better built, and his features are rounder and gentler, but he's scruffier in a way, even though Nate combs his hair and Kyle doesn't. There is a blunt openness about Nate that I like—and he's nothing like Kyle ever was to me. I need to stop comparing them. Maybe if I do, I will feel better about disappearing down this rabbit hole with Nate.

My hands have stopped shaking as we pull into Nate's driveway. I was almost expecting to see the slate blue Mini Cooper—all my life I've seemed to court drama, so why should tonight be any different? But, thankfully, we are alone. Alone. I am *alone* with Nate Whoever-he-is, and I'm nervous as a whore in church. How uncharacteristic of me not to have the upper hand, although maybe I do. Still, he's throwing me for a loop. Looking on the bright side of my situation, I have to admit he makes me feel prettier than I've felt in forever, prettier than I deserve. But then again, he doesn't know me. It's all a fairy tale. I will turn into a pumpkin in just a few more hours.

He gets out and walks back to help me with my door, reminding me of Marcus. I'll bet Mr. May always opened doors for his wife, too. I smile in spite of myself, making Nate give me that cute, naughty grin again. *Oh, he is going to be so much fun to unwrap!* murmurs Bad Elle.

Run while you still can, stupid! scolds Good Elle, but I squash her immediately. Why shouldn't I have fun? But then he does look like he-who-shall-not-be-named. My grin does not go unnoticed, even in the dark.

"What's funny?"

"It's just...you look like someone else I know—it's a little disconcerting."

"They say everyone has a twin."

"Yeah," I laugh at the cliché that is not a cliché as we walk across the street to the private dock.

"Is that a good thing?" he asks, taking my arm to steer me around a hole in the shoulder. (I saw it. I can walk all by myself, thank you very much.) *The uncertainty in his voice is sweet,* says Good Elle or Bad Elle—I am so fucking confused right now! Who the hell is talking to me!

"In my case, it isn't."

"Ah, a good juicy story, huh?"

Not one I'm telling. "You could say that."

We look toward the dock where a figure in a white T-shirt is hunched over the railing.

"Oh boy, this isn't good," Nate mutters as the figure comes into better view as we approach. An adolescent boy, at my best guess, is fishing off the private dock, and I assume from Nate's reaction, he doesn't belong here.

"Aubrey! What are you doing here?" Nate shouts, his crisp voice commanding in the dark. He's scolding, but doing it in a good-natured way, making me think this is a kid he likes.

"Fishin'"

"Uh, yeah, I see that. It's eleven o'clock. D'you sneak out?"

"Yup!" says the boy, grinning, a mouth full of braces glinting in the lights at the end of Nate's dock. He appears to be of mixed race and his oversized T-shirt hangs over his stout body like a feed sack.

"Patsy's gonna skin you alive, boy! What are you thinkin'?" Again a good-natured line of attack. This is the way you handle boys. I wasn't quick enough with Joey.

Aubrey continues to fish while Nate pulls his cell phone out of his pocket.

"Aw! Don't call her!" Aubrey pleads, an embarrassed smile crossing his face.

"You're makin' me, man!" Nate laughs, looking over the screen for Patsy's number. "You shouldn't be out here alone this late at night. Weird people do bad things late at night. Oh, Elle, this is Aubrey, Patsy's grandson. Our resident juvenile delinquent," he says, giving Aubrey his devilish grin.

"What's that?" asks Aubrey indistinctly, but I understand him from the context.

"It means 'little shit,' you little shit. What are you catchin'?"

"I don't know. But I've caught four or five of 'em."

"What are you usin'?"

"This stuff," Aubrey says, pointing out a plastic package on the table that looks like it's used for scaling and cleaning fish.

I peer at the packet, which contains little strips of pink bait. "That looks like fried baloney!" I laugh, and Nate chuckles, holding the phone while it rings on Patsy's end.

"Ha! It does."

"What's fried baloney?" asks Aubrey.

"Haven't you ever eaten baloney?" I ask. He shakes his head. "It's this gross pink processed meat that's round and flat. My mother used to make me fried baloney sandwiches when I was little," I tell him.

"Ew."

"Yeah, it's nasty. There's absolutely no nutritional value in it at all. Your grandmother has done you a big favor by never feeding it to you."

"Patsy! Hey, it's Nate.... Sorry; did I wake you? Look, I found something of yours down at my dock.... Yup, a little escapee.... Will do. I'll watch him from my end. Hold on; he's got a fish! I'll send him directly! See ya."

Nate ends the call and pockets the phone while Aubrey's shoulders squeeze toward his ears and he begins to reel. The end of the fishing rod bends over like a banana as he continues to reel.

"Keep the tip up...that's right. Don't horse 'im," says Nate, watching the line over the railing and letting Aubrey land the fish. "Whoa! There you go. Look at you!" he shouts as the silver fish flies toward us out of the black night.

"What is it? That's what I've been catchin'. That makes six of 'em!"

Nate grabs the line and pulls it close to us. "Listen. Can you hear it? It's a croaker. They make that noise." He holds the fish protectively, the way he had his hand at my back.

"Cool!"

"All right. Good job. Now, throw him back and get your tail on home. Patsy's mad at you, boy!"

"A'ight! I'm goin'," Aubrey says, struggling to get the fish off the hook.

"Careful with him. He's just a baby," Nate says, carefully guiding Aubrey's hand to take the hook out of the fish's mouth and tossing it back in the water. Aubrey reels his line back in and anchors the hook.

"Next summer…I'm comin' back for you," Aubrey mumbles to the fish. At least I think that's what he said. Nate has no trouble understanding him.

"A'ight. Don't forget your baloney," Nate says, winking at him and grinning at me.

"It ain't baloney."

"The fish don't know that. See ya, man. Stay outta trouble."

"Okay."

"Bye," I say, waving, wondering how many times the two of them have done this same activity together from this dock.

Aubrey turns and smiles. "Bye. Bye, Nate."

"Bye, buddy," says Nate, watching him go.

We watch him walk down the dock and go through the gate. Then he turns and walks through the yard toward the end of the street, where Patsy is lumbering along to meet him. She waves when she catches sight of us.

Nate waves to her and turns to me. "Well, that kind of sucks. I was hoping to take you for a little moonlight cruise…."

I should go home. I really shouldn't let this encounter continue, like I'd promised myself the first time I saw Nate. And besides, I have to pee.

There's no way I'm going in his house. We're bound to have sex if I go inside. It's so hard being good!

"Yeah, it's getting late. You've been up since four-thirty."

I glance down at the end of the dock where a large boat hangs in dry dock and another smaller boat is docked in the water. "Those are your boats?"

"The skiff is mine, the one in the water. The Grady White belongs to my uncle. He owns this place, but he's never here. I rent it from him and he stays here when he's in town."

"That's a nice arrangement."

"It is. I use one of the rooms for an office when I'm working from home, like I will at the end of next week, putting the show together. I have to go off on another trip, but I'll be back," he says, steering me over to the benches under another light. We sit at an angle to each other so I can see him clearly in the dock light. The night breeze has picked up even more on the water, and his hair moves in response. I grasp my own hair to keep it out of my face while we talk.

"So where are you from, Elle?" he asks, leaning forward and propping his elbows on his knees.

"I'm from a small town in the mountains called Valle Crucis."

A bright smile flashes across his face. "That's awesome! We've fished the Watauga River up there many times. And the New River near Todd, and the South Toe in Banner Elk."

"You know Valle Crucis?"

"Absolutely!"

"You get to fish?"

"As much as I can. I always try to get to our sites early so I can wet a line before the guide groups come. Yeah, there are some primo spots up there on the private waters. Other than that, though, the Watauga is over-fished for the most part."

"I don't fish. My son loves to fish."

"Nothing's better than teaching kids to fish."

"I figured that about you. So you don't have kids?"

"Nope. Never been married. Too busy, I guess."

"But the woman...?"

He runs his eyes over me a moment and says, "Look...it's not serious. I'm what you call payback, I think. Her husband messed around on her so she used me for payback." He shrugs. *Used*. Past tense. He said, "used."

"And you don't care?"

He looks at me with the sparkling blue eyes and breaks into a grin.

"Hell, Elle..." he says, reaching up to stroke an errant strand of hair out of my eyes in the breeze. "It's all a crapshoot. But I'm a risk-taker; aren't you? Haven't you made mistakes you knew better than to make?"

"You have no idea."

He grins again. "I thought so. You're a girl like that."

"Yes. I am."

"Then...you just gotta...go for it."

He looks at me again with those eyes that almost make me sick. My insides have gone straight to quivering jelly and I know we are at a major crossroads. On the one hand, I could—and should—walk away and never meet up with him again. *That would be the decent and proper thing to do. He might even get turned on by the tease and continue to pursue you.* (Thank you for your input, Good Elle.) On the other hand, I know that if I go inside with this man, I will be totally sucked under and ruined— right back to where I started, obsessed and deluded, nineteen years ago when I slipped Kyle the roofie. *Hell, yeah, you will, but you'll love every minute of the torture, you addicted fool. And if you don't let him lay you down tonight, you'll be kicking yourself for the rest of your life, wondering what could have been,* Bad Elle tells me.

It is indeed a crapshoot. If I don't go to bed with Nate tonight, I may never have another chance, especially if he ever finds out what I'm really all about. I glance one more time at that grimy, lascivious smile of his, and wonder what in the world I'm doing. But is it really a lascivious smile or just a raw, probing look from someone I should spend more time exploring? Or is he inwardly and dangerously weird, and I just don't know it yet? I honestly don't know. How can you tell after just two hours? This is usually how all of the mistakes I have made start out—that visceral feeling that if I don't act now, I'll never know what I'm missing. But then I find out I was wrong in the long run anyway, in that secret, sketchy, loathsome way I go about looking for love. I'm not that girl who gets roses, after all. What to do? *Life is uncertain; eat dessert first*, comes to mind. Oh, hell! Stall. I have to stand up. After almost three beers, I really need to pee again. I have no choice but to do something about it.

"Okay, I have to use your bathroom."

"This way," he says, eyes examining me, and leads me through the gate. I wonder why he doesn't lock it, and then he answers my thought. "I used to lock it, but people can just jump over the fence, so why even bother?"

We walk under the shadow of the trees and across the street onto the crunchy gravel of his driveway. Suddenly, he takes my hand and pulls me in to his chest, his hand at the small of my back, pressing me close to him, and kisses me. Who needs words anymore? His hand is in my hair, pulling my head closer as he kisses me deeply, and I kiss him back with the same degree of heat. We both know exactly what could be said.

Drawing away, I catch my breath and say, "I wasn't kidding about your bathroom."

"Oh, sorry!" he laughs, and we make it to the porch where he unlocks the door, letting me inside. "Down the hall, turn right, and it's the first door on the left."

After I have relieved myself, I wash my hands in his unusually clean sink and dry my hands on a clean towel. Wondering, and being my usual snoopy self, I open the medicine cabinet and look around for any telltale signs of Amy Stainback. I see a prescription bottle of cough medicine with his name on it—*Nate Aldridge*. There are two toothbrushes at the sink, one of them pink, but I can find no other feminine items that might belong to her. Until I open the linen closet and find the pink satin robe hanging on the back of the door. I doubt it's something Nate Aldridge would buy for himself.

When I come out, he goes in, oddly; I know he has another bathroom. I take a moment to browse around his house. It's nice, furnished in that way a man would do it, with earthy tones, wrought iron lamps, and rich wooden tables. Even his kitchen is tidy and clean, with the exception of stacks of mail, hunting and fishing magazines, and sportsman catalogs piled here and there.

In the living room is a large fish mounted on the wall, some creature from the ocean I can't identify. I wander past the fireplace and into the next room, which I recognize immediately as Nate's office. I hear a duck quack when I cross the threshold, one of those comical doormats with a sensor, maybe. The room is more like a lair really, I think, when I flip on a light, which reveals a six-point-buck head staring at me from the opposite wall, making me gasp with surprise. There is stuff everywhere, memorabilia from everything Nate has ever done—more dead animals mounted on the walls and tabletops—trout, a turkey, some kind of duck with a reddish head. There are fishing rods and a hockey stick propped on one wall, with a Denver Broncos football jersey autographed by Peyton Manning hanging on another wall beside a bulletin board, lined all the way around with orange University of Tennessee ticket stubs, framing his certificate of discharge from the Navy, and a faded UT ball cap tossed on the desk beside a gun safe. I look around for the sophisticated technical equipment that I expected to see, but all I can find is a computer with two monitors and several cameras in cases piled on the floor. A calendar turned to this past February is nailed to the wall, the sure sign of a busy man.

I hear Nate answering his phone in the hallway near the bathroom, so I dawdle, looking at more pictures on his wall to see what else I can learn. There is so much orange in his life! I can't help my aversion to the color that dominates his culture, but he is apparently from Tennessee and those UT Volunteers must love to flaunt their orange. A framed photo on the wall of three people in orange T-shirts catches my eye next. It's a page from a magazine article. On one side, a lovely twenty-something girl with chin-length wavy brown hair and pretty eyes stands with her arm around another girl who also appears to be in her twenties, with slanted eyes and a big smile full of tiny teeth like Tic Tacs in her round pink face. The obvious facial differences remind me of Down Syndrome. A slender young man with longish hair and glasses flanks the other side of her, grinning back at the camera. The caption reads, *"Sarah Grace is the inspiration behind our business. We're all like a big family now. Besides being the best dancer in the building, she teaches us patience and determination, along with her awesome sense of humor and purity of heart. You don't find people like her just anywhere,"* says September Nolan, director of Good Girl Dog Treats. I peer at the people in the photo again, murmuring "September—what a cool name," under my breath.

"Ah, you found my cubicle!" Nate startles me, making me jump.

"Oh! Yeah. The rest of the house is immaculate, but this takes the cake!"

He proceeds to give me the tour, describing what is special about each relic, explaining how he can never throw anything away. I look at more pictures on the walls, pictures he's taken of sunsets and sunrises, woodland scenes with fawns and moose as the subjects, snowy river shots in winter, and fishing trips with men and their trophies, some with women and their catches. He's telling me about the turkey he shot when my eye lands on a picture of a man holding up a large saltwater fish, with a woman and two small boys grinning beside him. It's Amy and her family. I look away as soon as it registers, and I try to follow his story about the turkey hunt.

We move from the office back to the living room, and I feel the need to contribute to the conversation. "You must have a maid."

"I do, but she doesn't go in my office—for obvious reasons. You've met her. It's Patsy."

"Really? Patsy lives in this neighborhood and cleans houses?"

"She only does it for beer money—or so she says. I reciprocate by taking care of Harley and watching her house when she's out of town. I love dogs, but I don't have time to have one of my own. It's a sweet deal for both of us...."

Nate stops talking for a moment. Letting his eyes run all over me in the lamplight, I hear him murmur, "Mm-mmm!" I don't have the hard body I did when I was an eighteen-year-old cheerleader, nor do I have Chelsea Davenport Davis's lithe ballet dancer's body, but it doesn't seem to matter to Nate. He takes me in his arms again, kissing me and running his fingers through my hair, breathing in my scent as he does. I feel his mouth in my hair. "Oh, wow...do you always smell like birthday cake?" he whispers hoarsely. (It's the vanilla and buttery sugar that all bakers reek of.) He kisses me, making it hard to answer.

"I thought you didn't like sweets."

"Oh, I'm up for trying all kinds of new things," he says. Then he's flipping off lights and walking me backwards into his bedroom. I can feel his erection pressing into my crotch and his hands are all over my neck and shoulders as he works his way to the straps of my dress, pushing them over my shoulders and down around my elbows. I kiss him back passionately and he tastes delicious, making me glad he has good oral hygiene, since our mouths have become one in the heat of this moment.

Finding his zipper, I grab the tab and pull it down and he groans with relief at being freed. I lift his shirt up and over his head and he pulls it the rest of the way off, while I pull off my dress. Next, I try to help him struggle out of his jeans, which results in both of us losing our balance and falling onto the bed, laughing and surrendering to our needs. Nate reaches in a drawer of his bedside table, producing a square, foil packet. "Will we be needing this?" he asks. Since I didn't turn out to be the best mother, I've done all of humanity a favor by doing my part to prevent further procreation. If I am guessing correctly, he keeps his supply of prophylactics for Amy, which means he has enough sense to protect himself from diseases. Who knows where she and her husband have been? And if Nate were any other tourist in the mountains, I'd definitely do the honors, but I hesitate. I want him raw. I want all of him.

"We won't," I say, swatting it out of his hand, kissing him again. He reaches behind me to unhook my bra, pulling it away and devouring my breasts. His hands and his mouth are going everywhere, and even though he's shaved, with the intensity of his attentions, his face is scraping the hell out of my tender, sun-exposed skin, but I don't care. It's been so long since I was ravished like this! It's delightfully painful, and he's so good at it!

We take turns peeling off each other's underwear so that finally we are naked and hot, skin on skin, kissing and groaning and pressing against each other. With my mouth pressed against his neck, I can feel his pulse racing against my tongue, as my fingers run through his soft hair. He smells like the ocean and lingering sunscreen even after his shower. My hands explore his shoulders and up and down his back, his fine, tight buttocks, the exquisite hollow of his hip…and oh, my God! He holds my face and looks into my eyes, smiles, and then kisses me again, plunging his fingers through my hair to cradle my head as he prepares to do the rest. This could be so good. This could be what I've always wanted, a man like this, loving me. It can't be possible, but here we are.

He thrusts himself inside me before I even realize how wet I am. He is so big it hurts, and all I can do is gasp. My heart is pounding. This could go on all night, over and over again until I pass out from sheer exhaustion. It's as if we are horse and rider, moving against each other, racing faster and faster. I hear myself scream. His face is pressed against my cheek and he lifts my hips away from the mattress, positioning my pelvis in a way that makes my eyes cross, blowing breaths like a horse himself again and again, and then he explodes, gasping and groaning with an "*Oh, God!*" We cry out together and exhale at the same time, coming down slower and slower until both of us go limp, our breathing slowing as our hearts slow too. He is heavy on top of me, like a bear. A big, hot, hibernating bear. He is asleep. Asleep. A dead bear, on top of me.

Two freaking minutes and it's over! What the hell! And I can't move. This guy is heavy as lead. It's as if Michelangelo's *David* has just fallen over on top of me. I will be trapped here underneath him all night long. I try to move, and rub my hands down his hairy back to wake him, but he doesn't budge. I groan with the weight of him, but he doesn't move. I know he isn't dead; I can feel his heart pounding and his breath is coming in slow ragged heaves, like someone who has been asleep for hours. I'll bet he snores.

Shit. How am I going to extricate myself out from under him? I'd be happy to fall asleep myself, but he is suffocating me! Fuck! I have to get out from under him or I will die. It takes some doing, but momentarily, I manage to wriggle free somehow, and he settles on the bed with a soft thud and does not move. I wait for a moment, thinking he will come to and cuddle with me until I decide it's time to go, but he is still out cold. After a moment, I collect myself and slip off the bed, covering him as best I can with the sheet, gathering up my clothes and making my way to the bathroom. Yes, just two minutes, but it was worth every second, even if I never see him again. I'll make sure I don't.

I clean myself up and get dressed, looking in a drawer for a hairbrush, and brush my hair. Just for fun, I throw Amy's pink toothbrush on the floor, laughing, and then I pick it up and toss it in the toilet. Poor Nate will pee on it before he realizes it's in there. I could do worse things with it, but I'm done being Bad Elle for the night, I think. Then I slip quietly out of the bathroom. It takes a minute to accustom my eyes to the darkness, so I sit on the couch to orient myself. I pick up Nate's phone from the coffee table and chuckle to myself, thinking I'll leave him a message. I give it a try, surprised to find that he doesn't have a security code to access his phone. Maybe it takes too much time to enter a code when you're trying to snap a photo of a fish some guy caught.

I go to Nate's photos and start to scroll through, finding just what I expected—Bill and his buddies crowding around a large fish hanging from a hook. More pictures of fish being held up by grinning men, the boat, the captain, a sunrise on the water, Harley, and then I stop scrolling. There's a selfie of him with Amy, shot in his very bed, taken by her, it appears from the angle of her arm. In the photo, she is grinning as he is sucking on her shoulder, but it's the two of them, barely covered by a sheet, nonetheless. I tap the screen for the menu and send it to myself. I don't know why, but something compels me to do it. The next shot is of Nate alone, wearing only boxer shorts in his kitchen, holding a frying pan at the stove, making breakfast for Amy. I send that one to my phone as well. Then, I enter his name and number in my contacts, reach for my phone, and send him a message:

I had fun. See you in the 'hood.

I listen a moment longer. I was right; he snores. Letting myself out the front door, I twist the lock to secure the property before I leave. Turning my key in the ignition of my car, I wait a moment, thinking Nate will hear my car and appear at the door, wondering what happened, but he doesn't, so I back carefully out of his driveway and pull into the Montgomery's drive. Parking under the crape myrtle, I yawn, but I'm restless and keyed up still. It's not fair for him to get to dump his hormones in one quick shot while I was just getting started on mine. It's the same old story that so many women can relate to. I thought Nate would be different. *That's not fair! The poor guy's been up since four-thirty!* says Good Elle, or is it Bad Elle? I'm so confused!

I walk to the mailbox, singing to myself John Legend's "All of Me," and flip down the mailbox door for 312-B. There is nothing inside, nothing from Joey, so I walk back, stretching my arms over my head, when I hear a *tap-tap-tap*, like a rock on glass. I stop, straining to hear in the cricket-filled night. *Tap-tap-tap* again. What is that? I don't think I'm imagining it. Maybe it's some strange, coastal night bird I don't know about, tapping a shell to open it like our cardinals did with sunflower seeds back at home.

Or then again, I could be hallucinating once more.

Chapter 13

A LETTER

Allyson, the woman I'm interviewing in front of me at the table, is wide-awake, and I'm struggling to feel the same way, but my wild night has caught up with me. I slept through my alarm, and bolted upright in bed with fifteen minutes to get to work. Needless to say, not having showered after my sex-filled night is making me feel gross and disgusting, not to mention the headache that's pounding inside my brain. Feeling this way only reminds me that I have committed a no-no with Nate, one that I'll probably regret, but I doubt I'll be hearing from him anyway. In my pocket, I can feel my phone vibrating, but I'll get to it after I've hired Allyson. She's a veteran baker about my age, mature, brilliant, and if her background check comes back clean, she'll be an asset once we get going—in a week. Just thinking of the opening makes my heart pound. Two more people and I'll have the staff I need to get through the summer. Anna, Jordan, Monai, and I are all practically dead!

Anna is working the counter where a line has already formed. Monai comes around to refresh my coffee cup. What did I do to deserve these people?

"Oh, thank God! And thank you so much!"

"Lookin' rough today, Elle! Did you have fun last night?" she grins widely at me, the metal in her mouth blindingly painful, as well as her usual bubbly personality in my current condition.

"Too much fun, but oh well, it'll never happen again," I say, my voice sounding uncharacteristically like Greta Garbo's.

"Jeez, you sound as bad as you look."

"Thank you so much!"

"Just kidding. We worry about you. You deserve to have fun."

"Maybe so, but fun's going to kill me. I'm not as young as I used to be."

She snickers and makes her way to the other tables, offering coffee warmers to our happy customers. I take the moment to check my phone while waiting for my job applicant to arrive. My heart drops to my stomach. There's a message from Nate.

I had fun too. Sorry I couldn't keep up. Would like a re-do. Nice touch w toothbrush btw.

There's a smiley face at the end of the text.

"Aw!" I cannot contain my reaction. Why does he have to be a decent guy? This makes it even harder to dis him like I know I should. There's got to be something wrong with him. There sure is something wrong with me, and he never needs to find that out, making me hesitate before responding. *Make him remember you with fondness*, says Good Elle. I'd like to remember him the same way. What should I say? I'll have to think about it. I can visualize him waiting on the other end, but maybe he's not. He's probably forgotten about me already. And he's probably leaving anyway to go off on some other fishing trip. It's for the best.

The phone is still in my hand when a young woman with bright pink hair and a pierced nose approaches—my second interview. I can see a tattooed flower peeking up out of her blouse. Don't be judgmental, I remind myself, looking away from her chest. I shake hands with Roxy, a classmate of Monai's, who comes highly recommended, and we begin the interview. Although I'm distracted by her black fingernail polish, my headache, and the previous text message that I'm trying to ignore, I am somehow able to focus on her qualifications. Roxy is a cupcake girl, which is good, because now each of my folks has a specialty—Jordan is the baker and delivery person, while Anna loves to bake breakfast pastries. Monai is the wedding specialist and Allyson is a former bakery manager like me, until she got fat and her husband dumped her because she was really too smart and practical for him, so she moved back home to be near her family who will help her raise her children. I totally get her. Life sucks, but I will help her make her lemonade. All I need is a birthday cake fanatic and I can sit back and watch the show. Not likely, but if I need to be gone for whatever reason, it will be much less stressful.

When Roxy leaves, I retreat to the kitchen and take my seat at my small desk to run the background checks. Our T-shirts have arrived in a large box, and everyone takes a moment to come by and check them out, each one finding his or her size and holding it up to check the fit. (At least Roxy's blossom will be covered up!) The T-shirts look great. Again, Randy has not steered me wrong. Randy...if Randy was ever going to make a move, I have ruined myself for him. But since he hasn't, I shouldn't flatter myself with expecting him to be interested in me. I am destined to be alone so I might as well get used to it.

I check the café again to see whether my third candidate—Scooter, a friend of Jordan's this time—has arrived, but no one new has come in. The door chimes and Brandon comes in, flashing that lovely smile at me and giving the almost wink. I wonder if it's a tic. I make a point to wait on him myself, and he orders a cheese Danish and a cup of coffee.

"Nothing for your sweet fiancée?" I ask, giving him a little half-wink of my own.

"Nope; she's swearing off sweets until the big day. Then she'll have a piece of that Italian cream wedding cake of yours, and no telling what will happen from there."

We giggle about it while I put his order together. I'm so happy they have chosen my bakery for their cake, taking a leap of faith in the new girl when there are so many established bakeries in town they could choose from.

"Got time to join me?"

"Sure. I'm waiting on a new applicant to arrive any minute now."

We sit at the available table by the window. Brandon looks around the room.

"This place looks incredible!"

"Thanks! Your business is booming too! You hardly ever come up for air!"

He nods, flashing those teeth, pulling an inaudible sigh out of me. His teeth are almost too large for my liking, and I have to admit, I've seen better recently. Then his smile disappears.

"What?"

He takes a sip of his coffee and thinks a minute. He looks as troubled as I've ever seen him.

"I don't know if I can do it." He looks at me with a directness that is brand new.

"What? Oh, God! You mean...."

"Yeah. I'm not sure if I can marry Jewel."

It takes a moment and several blinks of my eyes to process this news.

"You can't be serious."

"Oh, but I am."

"You have to. You're business partners."

"And therein lies the rub," he mumbles, rubbing the back of his neck.

Suddenly, I want to smack him.

"Well, that's pretty fucking unfair," I say, feeling a hot flush start at my chest, working its way up to my neck. Not the reaction he was looking for, judging by the look on his face. I'm not sure what has surprised him more, my vocabulary or my opinion, but the combined reaction has left him unprepared.

"What?"

"Well, what is she supposed to think? You're in this thing way too deep to back out now. What and when was your first clue?"

I sound so harsh that he can't fathom my reaction, making him flounder for a moment. I guess he thought all those little winky-winks back and forth made me sympathetic, or something. He wads his napkin in one hand with his fingers, thinking of how to respond to me.

"I, uh…I thought…it's just that she gets on my nerves so bad with…."

"All the talking?"

"Yeah. I can't stand it. There's never a silent moment. If there is, it usually means I'm in trouble." My opinion of Brandon has just fallen flat on its ass.

"Okay. Have you ever *told* her this?"

"I—I guess not. Not in so many words."

"Then just tell her, for God's sake! Tell her, 'Just shut the hell up.' She's so nice, that I'll bet no one in her whole life has ever told her she talks too much, in a very serious way, that is. I'd tell her in a heartbeat. Nobody likes to hear that kind of criticism, but my God, you're going to marry the woman!"

"I'm sure that's why her first husband divorced her."

"She never told you why?"

"She told me she didn't really know. She said they just weren't compatible."

"Who would be compatible with a motor-mouth like that? You have to tell her. Even if she chooses to end the relationship, you have to tell her how annoying her talking is. It's just a sign of her insecurity. The sweet, spoiled, pretty girls are like that sometimes." Ha! Some people would say that's the pot calling the kettle black, but it's the truth.

He doesn't respond and looks uncomfortable.

"Don't tell me you're afraid of hurting her feelings? It's okay to break off the engagement, and screw up your business, but you're worried about hurting her feelings? Come on, Brandon; I know you have bigger balls than that." Southern men can be so stupid!

He looks at me as though I *have* actually slapped him. "I wasn't expecting *this*."

"Well, sorry. I'm not sure what you were expecting, but it's what you need to hear. And it's what you need to do. I don't ever beat around the bush. My grandparents raised me this way and it's just the way I am. You can't hurt Jewel. I like her. God knows, I hate all that talking as much as you do, but I like her, and you need to man up and deal with it. You can work with her on her big mouth."

If he even thought...I can't even think it myself. As depraved as I am, I will not even consider having a roll in the hay with Brandon, and maybe I led him on in the beginning, but he sure knows it now. And I'm sure not going to talk to Jewel about all this on his behalf, if that's what he came in here for. He needs to grow a pair and do it himself. He is definitely not smiling.

"You're absolutely right," he says. Suddenly, I feel sorry for him. Why and how escapes me, but I do.

"Brandon...you're just having cold feet. Look; I heard about a study the other day on the morning news that said women talk three times as much as men do. They've measured the number of words and it's really true. You just need to keep that in mind. I know—Jewel talks six times as much as you do—hell, she talks six times as much as I do—so if she only reins it in a little bit, then just know that you can't expect miracles. It's just our nature. And she's…Jewel." I shrug and he laughs.

"Okay. Thanks for the counseling session. How much do I owe you?"

"Uh, you run a winery…."

"Yeah, but you don't seem to drink much wine."

"I'm not much on hangovers," I say, acutely aware of my throbbing head, especially after my diatribe. "And I'm usually too tired to drink, so that's why you haven't seen me in your place." And because I don't like your wine and I don't want in on your weird love affair.

He nods, as if seeing an illuminating truth.

"Still, if you need a time out or a little peace and quiet, you can always duck in here. I won't be too hard on you."

"Thanks. I'll keep that in mind."

The door chimes and I turn to see Scooter, a large African-American young man with close-cropped hair and enormous feet, coming through the door with his job application in one hand. He is as big as my grandfather, but I've never seen anyone with feet that size!

"Well, here's my next appointment. Tell Jewel I said, 'Hi.'"

"All right. Thanks, Elle. I'll see you."

I can almost see Brandon's tail tucked between his legs as he leaves. So he has his flaws. I certainly have mine, so now I guess that means we have bared our souls and we are truly friends on equal footing. It feels good. Who knew I could be the Joan of Arc for womankind? And me, the bitch of all time, standing up for another female. Vada, I *am* your prize and joy!

Finally, after I've returned home and had my long-awaited shower, the walk to the mailbox rewards me with a letter from Joey. I go weak at the knees upon pulling it from the mailbox. I hoped every day that I would find a letter from him, and now that it's finally here, I can't believe it. He's kept it short and sweet, but there is a sentiment there that I wasn't expecting, a mature sense of responsibility and fondness, but I wasn't expecting the reason for his letter.

Dear Mom,

Thanks for the letters. So far the Army is great and I'm trying to stay out of trouble. It's hell to pay if you mess up. I'll have to wait for after boot camp before I can have the camera, but I'm looking forward to using it. Hope you can come to my graduation. Eight more weeks. Will send you an invitation.

Did you know Dad has been sick? He wrote and told me he's had a fever and they don't know what's wrong with him. It's not flu season, so maybe he's just got a virus. Thought you should know. Do you talk to him?

Good luck with your bakery. When is the opening?

Love,

Joey

Love. I sit a moment, relieved and happy, enjoying the feel of the plain white stationery in my hand, this letter from my son complete with the endearment I have craved. He wrote to me once from soccer camp, but this is the only other letter I have ever seen from him. It is so good to hear from him. He sounds happy and well-adjusted; however, it concerns me that I haven't learned about Aiden being sick from himself. *Do you talk to him?* Joey is always wondering and hoping maybe we'll be connected. I place a call to Aiden's cell phone, and it rings several times, going to his voicemail prompt. I leave a message, wanting to tell him that I got a letter and ask about his health. Maybe he is better and back at work. Aiden never answers his cell phone when he's on the dump truck. And Aiden is never sick.

My luck with my stellar employees has finally run its course. By Wednesday, everyone on my six-person staff has started work. Scooter has turned out to be a disaster—not one that can't be fixed—but we have discovered that he is all thumbs. He was pouring sweet tea into the large metal dispenser while I was restocking the cabinet below him with paper cups, when half of the tea went down my back instead of in the dispenser, soaking me to the skin, flooding my hair, shirt, pants, and shoes. I am returning home at 11:30 to change clothes, waving to Mr. May who is departing for the day. Ten minutes later, after I have changed clothes, I decide to check the mailbox before getting back in my car. Walking down the driveway, thinking back on my letter from Joey, I start to sing— "Walking On Sunshine"—loudly—abandoning my irritation at the interruption in my work for a few more moments before I have to return to the fray. Joey and I used to sing it when he was little and liked me. Maybe he still likes me. More flowers are blooming, and the sight of them does me good. Hummingbirds, green as little leaves, flit about in a mass of coral honeysuckle growing over the hedge at the edge of the driveway.

Opening the mailbox, I'm not surprised to find the usual junk mail, but then I'm delighted to see a handwritten note from Judy. She's from the generation of people who still writes notes, the way I'm doing now. I remember her collection of notecards with all kinds of different artwork on them. Lots of our customers used to bring them to her as gifts. Maybe that's why she writes so many notes! As I'm opening the envelope, carefully, to avoid getting a paper cut, I hear that odd tapping again. It's louder this time, and definitely sounds like a rock on glass. Looking around and trying to orient to the sound, I realize it's coming from the second floor of the sad house next door, where the rainbow-painted windows are. As soon as I look up, one of the rainbow panes gives way with a crash, as glass hits the pavement below. Two large brown eyes in a face I recognize appear in its place and the accompanying voice cries out.

"Help me, lady!" The voice is frantic.

I try to fathom what is happening, but all I can seem to do is open my mouth, unable to form words at all.

"Help! Lady! Can you hear me? Help me!"

Chapter 14

RESCUE

Gasping, I look from the boy's face to the driveway, where the carpet cleaning van is parked under the old shade trees. My hand flies to my mouth, and all I can do is nod. Then I put my finger to my lips, a signal to him to keep quiet for his safety. His wide, dark eyes register complete understanding. I look around for any sign of the repulsive man I spoke with a week ago as I fumble in my pocket for my phone. Running back to the shelter of my house to escape detection, were the creep to show his face, I duck behind the house where I can call the police while keeping my eye on Jeremy. I can't see him from my vantage point now, but the side of the house is in clear view.

When the dispatcher answers my call, my entire body is shaking, including my voice. I don't dare tear my eyes away from the house while I talk to her.

"I think I just found that boy that's been missing—Jeremy something?"

There is a frisson of silence on the other end and then the woman's urgent voice.

"Jeremy Rayle? What's your location?"

I give my address and the address of the blue house. She asks my name and I tell her, and I explain what happened and that I have my eye on the house, and she takes it all down, telling me she is dispatching the police immediately.

"Did you see the boy? Did he appear to be harmed?"

"I just saw a part of his face. I don't know if he's hurt, but he could talk to me. There's a van—a carpet cleaning van that's parked in the driveway. I dropped off mail there last week and there was a guy there that answered the door. He was wearing one of those blue work suits with the name 'Hector' embroidered on the pocket. I don't know him. I only saw him that one time, but he's probably there."

"Can you get the license number of that van, miss?"

"I can try," I say, edging over to the back of our yard, looking through the unruly shrubbery at the van. I have to walk closer to the fence to peer through to see. "No. I can't see the license plate. It's backed in. I can't get over there because of the fence."

"That's okay, miss. Don't put yourself in danger. Do you see anyone on the property?"

"No. It's real quiet over there. There's another car there sometimes, too, an old, tan Buick, but the two cars are never there at the same time. I've never seen another person there. There never seems to be anyone home."

A dog begins to bark, and then I hear sirens from a distance getting closer.

"Tell them to turn off their sirens!" I say to the dispatcher. "What if the guy freaks out and hurts the boy?" As if on cue, the sirens stop, but I can hear car engines approaching at a good clip and a squeal of tires as the vehicle careens around the corner onto Waters Edge. Two cop cars are there in no time, pulling up to the curb. Four officers jump from the cars and split up in the yard, two taking the front entrance and the other two circling around to the back. Still on the phone with the dispatcher, I run up AB's back stairs where I can get a better view of what's going on. I can still hear the dog barking. *Harley.*

"Do you need me? They're here."

"Thank you, no. They'll take it from here. Spell your name, please."

"Elle McLarin," I say, spelling it for her since people usually ask.

"Thank you for calling this in."

The dispatcher is off the line, and in the next moment, I hear shouts and another vehicle coming down the street, this time an ambulance, followed by two more police cars, one unmarked, with blue lights flashing.

Holy cow! I murmur to myself, unable to take my eyes off the house next door. In the next few minutes, I can clearly see the police officers leading Hector out of the house, hands held behind him in handcuffs. He's wearing a pair of shorts and nothing else. His hair looks wet. Maybe Jeremy knew he was in the shower and took advantage of the opportunity to communicate with me. That brave little boy took a big chance knocking the glass out of the window. I guess he heard me singing and knew I'd be able to hear him, too.

Police officers go in and out. There must be eight of them, and a couple of paramedics that I saw go in have not come out yet. Hector has been placed inside the backseat of one of the patrol cars, where the two officers are standing over him at the car door. One is talking on the radio while the other one stands watch over Hector. Another officer comes out to tape off the area with yellow crime scene tape, and another plain-clothed one looks around toward my house. I swallow. They are looking for me.

I skitter down the stairs and walk over to meet the detective. He greets me with enthusiasm. "Hi. Are you Elle McLarin?" he asks, checking my name by looking down at his notebook through aviator sunglasses.

"Yes. I called in the 911...call...." I hope I can talk coherently. My mouth is completely dry. My eyes go back up to the broken window. "I was getting my mail when the little boy broke that window and called out to me."

The detective looks questioningly at me.

"I guess he heard me singing."

"Beautiful!" he says, breaking into a large grin. "We've been looking for Jeremy for four months. You just cracked the case."

I nod, unable to speak, and look around. Neighbors are starting to arrive, walking over from up and down both ends of the street. Patsy is the first to arrive with Harley on her leash. Cars drive slowly by with rubbernecking drivers that don't even live on our street. The officer introduces himself as Lieutenant Maxwell, and he takes down my statement, getting my phone number and my address, asking all kinds of questions about what I've seen, and letting me know I will probably be contacted on more than one occasion for follow-up in relation to the case.

"How about Jeremy? Is he okay?"

Lieutenant Maxwell gives me a grim look. "It looks like he's been through a really rough time; from outward appearances, he's thin, dehydrated, hungry, and overcome with shock, but overall, he's glad to be free. His parents are on the way. They'll likely want to meet you."

"Oh. Okay."

"And the news people will be squealing in on two wheels in the next few minutes, so be ready for some excitement in your life, Ms. McLarin. You're a real heroine now, and I wouldn't be surprised if this story makes the national news."

"What?"

Lieutenant Maxwell grins again and looks back at the house, saying, "Gotta go."

I pull my phone out again to call the bakery, letting them know I will be detained for a while. Patsy starts to make her way down the driveway when one of the cops stops her for a moment.

Monai answers the phone and I tell her what's going on.

"Wow! Only you, Elle! This is amazing! I can't believe you found him! Oh, my gosh! You're going to be famous. You know that, right? Everybody in the country is going to know about Bake My Day! Just imagine the number of people who are going to show up at the grand opening now! Holy *shit!*"

I giggle at her. It is unlike Monai to cuss.

"Look; it's starting to get crazy over here, so I'll call you in a little while. Are you all okay over there?"

"Yup! We good. You just take your time. If you need to walk me through the closing again, I think I can handle it."

"Thanks, girl." I press "End," just as Patsy and Harley have made their way to me in my driveway. Patsy is carrying my stack of mail. I must have dropped it when I saw Jeremy's face in the window.

"What in the world is going on?" asks Patsy, as Harley sidles up against my knee. I give her head a pat and she nuzzles my hand as if we are old friends.

"You won't believe it. Our neighbor here was the one who kidnapped Jeremy Rayle." I tell her how the windowpane fell and I discovered Jeremy.

It takes a moment to register, but then Patsy's face goes white. "Oh, my God! That little seven-year-old boy? We've had a predator in the neighborhood all this time and I didn't even know it! Oh, my gosh, and Aubrey has been sneaking around by himself out here at night! I can't even.... Oh, Lord!" she says, her hand covering her mouth as if she is going to be sick. When I see that she isn't, I reach out for her and we hug each other.

"I know! I just thought of Aubrey as soon as you walked down here. Is he still at school?"

"Yes, thank goodness! This will teach him a lesson, but oh, my! I just feel so blessed—and bad at the same time for that child! That poor little boy! Do you think he was abused?"

"Yes. Yes I do." Hector's sinister face at the door that day makes me imagine all the worst.

"Oh! It's just awful beyond words! The poor little thing. And his parents!"

I nod somberly. Thinking of Joey and how I felt after some of his exploits, I can only imagine how Jeremy's parents have suffered, and how finding him alive and well will be a long-awaited relief. But still, what he must have been through will be hard on his family for the rest of their lives.

"That was you—with Nate the other night, wuddn't it, when Aubrey was up at his dock?"

"Yes."

"I thought so…."

Our conversation is interrupted by the appearance of a news van that has just pulled up in AB's driveway. It's a good thing she is not here, but wait until she sees this on TV. If it were me, I'd be freaking out! Wondering how long this will go on, I see that it is a Channel 3 News van, and who should step out of the passenger seat but Amy Stainback!

"Oh no," I mutter to myself since Patsy has already gone back down the driveway to inform the other neighbors of what has happened. Amy stops at the foot of the driveway, where she and her cameraman look around to get the best shots, and she motions to the garden while the cameraman checks the lighting, moving her under the shade of one of Hector's trees. I wouldn't want to stand anywhere near that house. Just imagining the goings on inside makes me shudder.

Then Lieutenant Maxwell goes over and introduces himself to Amy. They chat a while, and I notice that he points to me. Amy writes down a few things and then she looks at me again, as if she recognizes my name.

Of course, you idiot, you're coming to Bake My Day in two more days to film the dress rehearsal of my grand opening! I can almost see the wheels turning in her head as she puts two and two together. Maxwell stands patiently while they do a test. Maybe it's a sound check or something, and then she starts talking to him, making me realize they are doing a live breaking news segment. Before I can react, another woman in jeans and a headset walks over to me and introduces herself as a news team production assistant.

"I'll get the preliminary information from you first, Ms. McLarin, and then Amy will be over to interview you for the next breaking news segment. Remember, this is live. Just stay calm and answer Amy's questions. She'll just be asking you to tell what happened."

My head is swimming. This is all happening so fast! We talk while I watch Detective Maxwell, who is talking to Amy, both of them standing at close proximity to the camera. She has to hold the microphone up to his mouth since she is so short. I watch as he gestures my way, while the producer guides me over to the tree in the shade beside Maxwell. I'll be next. She hands Amy the sheet with information I've given her.

"And next up we're going to talk to the person who found Jeremy and who is responsible for making the 911 call, Elle McLarin, who lives next door to the house in question. So tell us, Ms. McLarin, how did you discover that Jeremy was next door?"

It is so hard for me to focus on Amy. It's surreal with everything that's going on. I keep seeing visions of her pink toothbrush in the toilet, with Nate unknowingly urinating on it. And then there's the selfie of them in his bed, but I try to get it together.

"I—uh—I happened to be home early from my bakery business and I was getting my mail. I was singing while I was walking down the driveway and then I heard this tapping sound. It sounded like a rock on glass. Jeremy must have heard me out here singing…anyway, I looked up at the window, and suddenly, it just broke, and there he was, calling for me to help him…" I say, and my dry voice breaks unexpectedly.

"What did you do then?" Amy asks to fill the dead air while I compose myself. She glances at her producer with a glint in her eye. This is good drama. I don't mean for it to be. I just can't talk.

"I—I ran back over to my house and hid around the corner so I could see the house but not be seen, and I made the call. The police showed up in like two minutes. They went in and it was over—just like that." The camera is panning over to the Montgomery house, as if I live in the big house. I think to correct the cameraman, but this is happening live and it's too late. Everyone in Wilmington will think that beautiful house is mine. Anne Borden Montgomery is going to be so pissed off!

There is another wonderfully pregnant moment of dead air while Amy searches my face, pondering her next question. This should be good. Maybe she is better at this than I thought. "What were you singing?" she asks, making me gape at her in disbelief. *This is all she's got?*

"Walking on Sunshine," I murmur, and I see smiles go all around, from the cameraman to the producer to Lieutenant Maxwell. Hector Who-ever-the-fuck-he-is is sitting right over there in the back of a cop car in his underwear and she's asking me what song I was singing? What an idiot!

"So there you have it, live from Waters Edge, from the Sunshine Girl herself. Back to you, Jason."

The producer walks me away from the camera, and it looks like Amy wants to be done, but the anchorperson apparently has more questions, so she listens intently and turns her attention to the police car where the cameraman is shooting the first photo the world will see of the latest sexual predator caught in his sick world, and where thankfully, a little boy has gone free.

Amy is busy reporting, so I start to go back down the driveway, wondering if I can just go inside my little dollhouse and sit down and maybe faint or throw up, when from the corner of my eye, I see another figure striding toward me. Amy is watching him too. Turning slightly, I see that it's Nate walking briskly toward me, wearing an expression of shocked concern.

"Elle," he says, walking straight up to me and taking me in his arms. I feel myself collapsing into his chest, feeling his hot breath in my hair and his hand on the back of my head. "Good God! Patsy just told me what happened! Are you okay?"

"Yeah. I'm fine, I just.... This is all really overwhelming."

He glances over his shoulder at Amy, who is still reporting on the scene, but I know she saw Nate hug me. "Look; let's go sit down over there in those chairs," he says, gesturing to the little wrought iron bistro set in front of the guest house. We walk over and sit down in the welcome shade. I can hear the fountain bubbling behind me as we sit together. Oddly, I'm not shaking or trembling, but I'd kill for a glass of water.

I start to stand. "I'm going to get a glass of water. Do you want one?"

"No. Sit. I'll get it. You're *really* pale."

"Really?"

"It's called shock. Don't move."

He goes in my house, and in a minute, he is back with my water.

"Cute place, by the way," he says. He watches me drink and then gives me a minute. I can't help but stare at his well-developed, tan calves and thighs and the way they disappear up inside his khaki shorts. Maybe he'll think I'm just in a stupor. "Patsy filled me in...."

"Yeah, I was walking down the driveway with my mail, and all of a sudden, the window pane crashes to the ground, and there he is...those eyes. I've seen his eyes in those pictures all over town. Every bank you go in and every convenience store you stop in has his picture with those haunted, big brown eyes."

"Sad eyes."

"Yeah."

"I heard the cops talking with the EMTs. They said the little boy was naked when they found him," Nate says.

"Oh, God. I don't want to know."

"I know. It could get pretty gruesome, Elle, with all the details that are going to come out, but you saved him."

"I did what anyone would have done," I say.

"I know you did, but you were at the right place at the right time." Nate shudders. Being in the Navy, I assume he has seen grim and unimaginable things, but still he is moved by the gravity of this situation. "Can you believe, he lived right between our two houses, all this time, and all this has been going on right under our noses, and none of us knew? I mean, I'm never here, and when I am, I'm inside working or off fishing somewhere. I don't even cut my own grass. I drive right by and don't even look."

"AB and I are the same way. We're gone all the time, and Mr. May, the gardener, is so quiet…and I think he might be a little deaf. He never would have heard anything. And Jeremy would never have known he was out here. The way they had the windows painted, he couldn't see out."

"Patsy is freaking out over Aubrey, living two doors down from a sexual predator…."

"I know." My face clouds over.

"What?"

"There must be another person who lives there. There's always either that carpet cleaning van or an old, tan Buick in the driveway."

"Did you tell the cops?"

"Oh, yeah, and the description of the car. I've never seen anyone else, but I don't think Jeremy was ever left alone, if one of them was with him.

So now they've got to find the other person." We watch Amy, who is still on camera with the news crew. Apparently, this is being discussed on the breaking news segment. Maybe Amy will be up for an Emmy. The Sunshine Girl, my ass!

Nate is watching me. I've been up since 4:00 this morning, and I have on zero makeup, jean shorts, and a faded Appalachian State University T-shirt. My sticky, tea-soaked hair is pulled up into a makeshift bun that I didn't even check in the mirror. He must be thoroughly repulsed by my appearance, but if he is, he doesn't react negatively, and if he did, I wouldn't give a shit anyway.

"You never returned my text message," he says, chastising me.

"I know.... I wasn't sure you wanted me to."

"Really? Then I did a really bad job of making my feelings known the other night. I thought I'd made myself embarrassingly clear." He doesn't evade my incredulous stare.

My stomach flips over at my recollection of his epic, two-minute explosion. "Well, I didn't hear anymore from you either, so I didn't know what to think."

"I had to go out of town again on another trip. I thought I'd mentioned it."

"You might have."

"I've been with four men continuously for the past few days. I've been dying to talk to you."

"So it was a miscommunication."

"Absolutely. I'd like to see you again."

"Oh, I think you will. All over the news. And then I have my grand opening."

"Yeah. You're going to be really busy. I think you're about to get summoned again," Nate says. Another car has arrived, and an anxious-looking man and woman about my age get out and are directed over to the ambulance. Wrapped up in my conversation with Nate, I failed to notice that Jeremy must have been taken out of the house and settled into the back of the ambulance. Hopefully, Amy's producer has had the good sense not to air that on live television. We watch as the parents climb inside the ambulance and the doors close. The lights turn on, sending out flashes of red at intervals, and then the vehicle takes off slowly up the street. "Well, maybe not," says Nate. We look back at the house next door, wondering whether the cops will stay here all day and night, until the other suspect in the case is found.

It is my turn to shudder. "This whole thing really gives me the willies."

"It should. What are you going to do now?"

"I should get back to work. I only came home because one of my employees dumped a five-gallon bucket of iced tea down my back and I had to change clothes."

"Hoo-wee! Did you fire this person?"

"No, he was just nervous. His name is Scooter. He's as big as a moose, and I was probably in his way…. I should really give AB a call to let her know what's going on at her house. The way they filmed my part, it made it look like I live there," I say, waving my hand toward the big house. "Can you imagine? She's not going to like that."

We both laugh at the strangeness of the situation.

"Well, what I really meant was, what are you going to do tonight? You don't have to stay here," Nate says.

"I'll be fine."

"You might need protection."

I laugh, but then maybe he has a point. "I don't think the police are going anywhere just yet. At least not until pervert number two is caught. I think I'm living in the safest house on the street, don't you? Like Fort Hood….

Oh, and by the way, I got a letter from Joey," I tell him, feeling like sharing it with someone. It's important, and with my discovery of Jeremy, it feels like a connection in an odd way, like I've found two boys today.

"That sounds like progress."

"I hope it is."

He eyes me suspiciously, knowing I'm evading his offer of company throughout the night. I'd love nothing better than to experience his idea of a do-over, but it's probably not a good idea for him. Or me. What if his two-minute wonder is all he can ever do? Doubting that, still, it's not a good idea for either of us to get invested with each other. Especially since Amy is staring him down in my driveway. Like I said, I tend to court drama.

"I think you're the one being summoned. I'm going to call AB while you and your roving reporter have a chat," I say, taking the sunglasses off my head and putting them on, signaling an end to our conversation.

Up until now, Nate has been unaware that I know Amy is the one he's been seeing. I don't really know where they stand, and even though he's hinted that they're over, I have a feeling it might not be up to him.

Nate looks at me as if I've caught him with his pants down. It takes him a minute to process what I know, and then he exhales raggedly.

"A'ight. Be that way. I *will* check on you later," he says, pushing himself out of the chair to go and face the music.

"Thank you," I say, and he gives my hand a squeeze before walking down the driveway toward a grinning Amy, who is giving him her best cheerleading smile.

I watch them talk while I get hold of AB and go through my dramatic story one more time with the prelude that she'll be in for a shock. She has not heard the news and is appreciative that I was considerate enough to call her before seeing her house on the evening news. My call lasts all of ninety seconds; however, the conversation going on at the mid-point of the driveway, halfway between the shade tree and my range of hearing, where Amy has chosen to confront her lover about his apparent misbehavior, is still continuing. His arms are folded across his chest, head cocked to one side, and she has placed a hand on one of his arms. I can't hear what is being said, but she's asking questions and not liking the answers she's getting. He shakes his head. She drops her hand quickly, making me think he's just told her something she doesn't want to hear. I snort. We're in *big* trouble now! When she shoots a piercing look my way, I pretend to be texting on my phone so she won't see me watching under my dark glasses. They are apart now, and Nate glances back at me, but I ignore him too, so he walks back down the street toward his house and she goes back to the van to talk to her producer. She might be here for a while.

I open the forgotten letter from Judy.

Dear Elle,

I know you must be going crazy, getting ready for the opening of Bake My Day. I am so proud of you for going after your dream! Your grandparents would be, too. You did the right thing, leaving the mountains and starting over fresh. I hope you are learning that as well. You know I can't be there to celebrate with you, but I want you to know that I'll be there in spirit. We all will. Let me know how it goes. Best wishes!

Love you, Honey Bun!

Judy

I smile at the words from the only relative who still cares about me, placing her letter with Joey's in my purse. I will start my own box of letters to treasure. Getting in my car, I clean my sunglasses and back around in the drive, then make my way slowly and carefully out of my driveway, taking care not to run over any TV people or cops. I look to the left to make my turn onto the street and what I see makes goose bumps stand out on my arms.

Holding up her cell phone, Amy is glaring at me while she snaps a picture of my license plate.

Chapter 15

OH, NO YOU DIDN'T!

"Oh, hell, no, you didn't! You little fucking bitch," I mutter to myself and yank the gearshift into park, right in the middle of the road. I get out of my car and stalk back to see Amy, who is watching me with her mouth set for battle. Sometimes Bad Elle is needed in these kinds of situations, and I'm glad she hasn't gone far.

"What the *hell* are you doing, taking a picture of my license plate?" I shout at her, mostly for the benefit of her program producer, and hopefully, Lieutenant Maxwell. It was an effective move, since the producer, the girl in the jeans and headset, is turning our way.

"What?" Amy asks crisply, as if I have accused her of murder.

"Yeah, let's see your phone. Why were you taking pictures of my license plate? Let me look at that!" I am loud and accusatory and thankful that I had the sense to confront her now, before she got away with this shit and made me into a victim. Clearly, Amy's motivation for photographing my license plate must be fueled by my snaking her lover, but this is more than just a high school catfight. The last thing I need is some little bitch probing around into my shady past. Jeans Girl is all tuned in. She is walking over to see what's up, but the one I really want on my team is Lieutenant Maxwell. He is busy talking to the cops on the scene. Maybe I should ratchet it up a notch.

I have my hand out for Amy's phone, and the producer is there, looking back and forth at us, with questions all over her face. We need more commotion to make this thing a go.

Amy looks at me with the beady eyes I'd seen when she was trying to milk the emotion out of my shoot at the crime scene. A chill goes through me, but I'll be damned if I'll let her see it. Who *is* this chick?

I wait, hand held out, and so does the producer, validating my concerns. Amy holds out, creating a moment of tension. I have to do something.

"If you have a reason to photograph my license plate, tell me now, or erase that picture. I've done nothing wrong." *Lately.*

My voice was just loud enough and I've spoken long enough to create a bit more tension in the air, and Lieutenant Maxwell has finally picked up on it. Hell. I'm the heroine, as he said earlier, so Amy is up Shit Creek without a paddle right now, and we all know it. Maxwell is walking over, casting a shadow in his wake until its darkness has merged with the creepy tree shadow in Hector's yard. Even I am getting chills, and then, seeing the policeman coming over, Amy hands me her phone. I have to hand it back so she can enter her passcode to get in and access her photos. I watch as she taps her photos screen and locates the photo of my plate. I take the phone from her and hit "Delete" and then "Delete photo." It is gone. I slide my finger across the screen to check for more photos, but there are none, other than the pictures of Hector's sad blue house and AB's mansion to the left. I'm surprised she didn't photograph Nate and me, sitting at my bistro set, having our conversation about our tryst the other night. If she only knew!

Pulling my shoulders back and tossing my head in victory (there is no fabulous hair to toss, but I forgot), I hand red-faced Amy back her phone, shooting a glance at Maxwell, and then one at Jeans Girl. They all get the gist of what just went down, and I am satisfied that I am again in charge here.

The detective takes a moment to speak to me. "Don't worry about your safety here tonight, Ms. McLarin. There will be officers on the premises in case our second suspect happens to show up later. Until we've apprehended him, there will indeed be a presence in the area for your protection."

"Thank you, Lieutenant. That's reassuring." *Now how about protecting me from this irritating little bitch reporter?* Then I head back over to my car, which is blocking the street, and drive easily down Waters Edge as if I own it, on my way back to Bake My Day.

Trying to shake the feeling of dread I got from Amy, I pull into my parking spot at the back of Bake My Day and kill the ignition, set the parking brake, and get out of my car. A glance in the rearview mirror surprises me again, seeing the large decal that advertises my business. I'm not used to being so exposed. And now, everyone in Wilmington will know who I am, as soon as the evening news replays Amy's story. As Detective Maxwell has predicted, I'm sure the case will attract the attention of the national affiliate, and it's only a matter of time before I hit the big time. And I came to Wilmington to hide!

As Monai says, I should be glad we are going to get exposure for the bakery out of this awful situation. At any other time, I would be all over an opportunity for publicity like this, and it couldn't have come at a better time, with the bakery opening in three more days, but the reason for it is grotesque and horrible in reality. I sit in my car a moment, trembling, thinking about poor Jeremy Rayle, all alone with those two deranged men doing God knows what to him in that house for four months. Without clothes, he couldn't go running out into the street, and with one of them there at all times, he didn't have a chance to escape. If I hadn't been singing on my way to the mailbox, he wouldn't have heard me, and if Joey hadn't written, I wouldn't have felt happy enough to sing. I meant to call Aiden and check on him since I've had no word since Joey's letter. I check my phone to see whether Aiden has returned my second call, but there are no messages. I think about calling his mother, but I give up that idea as soon as it enters my mind. She would no sooner talk to me than she would treat herself to an enema!

I feel tired and rattled as I climb out of the car. It's already two o'clock in the afternoon, and I haven't eaten lunch. My mind is racing through all the day's events, and I wonder how the staff has performed in my absence. On top of all that, Amy's stare is burned into the back of my head, and even though I bested her at the scene, that odd, detached look in her eyes has me somewhat disturbed.

I unlock the back door and enter the building to find my staff humming along, doing the things I've trained them to do. Scooter is folding a cake box at the table and is the first to see me walk through the door.

"Oh! Gosh, Elle, I'm so sorry about dumping that tea on you!" he says, from a safe distance as if I am angry at him.

"Scooter, don't worry about it. I guess Monai told you the news about Jeremy? You were the one who saved that boy's life, you know? If I hadn't gone home to change, I wouldn't have seen him, so in a way, dumping that tea on me was the best thing that could have happened. But—please try not to do it again, okay?"

"You got it!" he says, grinning with relief that he's not getting fired.

Monai, Anna, and Jordan are finishing up the crumb icings on the wedding cakes we will showcase on Saturday, and Roxy and Allyson are tending to the customers in the café.

"We need to get a TV in here, Elle," says Jordan. "Do you know how hard it is to watch the news on our phones?"

"Yeah, we saw the feed of the breaking news on our phones. If you're going to be on TV all the time, we really should be allowed to watch you on a decent-sized screen!" Monai says, flashing me her metallic grin and pushing up her glasses. "You already have a cable hook-up and you'll be able to afford cable with all of the attention the bakery is going to get. Are you ready to be famous?" she asks me.

This is the kind of attention I used to want, like being on the stage and having applause and ovations for my acting and singing, but I realized long ago that it was the wrong kind of thing to desire. And today, it is absolutely the wrong thing to want.

"I just want people to like my bakery. That's all." My voice is raw—only because I'm tired and rattled, giving them all the impression that I'm something I might not be—someone decent and worthy of all the attention I'll be getting. This is wrong, isn't it? To want success is one thing, but if they really knew who I am and what I've done, then what would they think?

The phone is ringing and Allyson answers. She is going to be the mother here. I can just tell. She listens a moment and glances at me.

"It's Preston Frazier, from Channel 3 News."

Preston Frazier is a big deal. He's the evening news roving reporter, destined for stardom, in my opinion, and apparently, in all of my staff's from the looks on their faces.

I take the phone. "Hello?"

"Elle? Hi, it's Preston Frazier from Channel 3 News. How are you?"

I swallow. "Fine. And you?"

"Great! I wanted to let you know that we'd like to interview you, a little more in depth after the Sunshine Girl story that Amy Stainback just did." Duh. Even I know that was awful. "We have our ABC affiliate,

Phoenix Corbin, coming in tomorrow to meet with you and the Rayle family around 1:00 p.m. Can you meet with us?"

Phoenix Corbin? She's the shit on the national news. "Uh...sure. Where?" Amy is coming here on Friday morning, and they want me to appear on the national news with Phoenix Corbin tomorrow! Holy cow!

"We'll set it up...probably at the Rayles' home if Jeremy is there. The Rayles think he'll be released from the hospital in the morning. They want Jeremy to be a part of the interview, just a small part, you see, but if it's at their home, he won't feel too uncomfortable. Just be ready about noon and our staff will send a car for you. Where will you be?"

"At my bakery, Bake My Day, on College Road." They aren't taking any chances on me screwing up a national newsworthy appearance. By sending a car, they will ensure that I arrive without delay. It would be embarrassing for everyone involved if I didn't show up.

"Got it. I have the address. Wear something nice, if you like, a little makeup if it suits you. Stripes don't work well on the screen, but don't worry too much about it. Solids are best. See you at noon, okay?"

"Yeah. Sure." I'll be up at 3:30 a.m. getting ready for all of this. I hope I can last until the air turns black! And then there is the grand opening on Saturday.

I thank him and end the call, turning to my staff, all six of them waiting with bated breath.

"I'm going to be on TV again tomorrow."

"Yeah. Amy Stainback is coming, but that's Friday. You told us that," says Monai.

"But there's more, isn't there?" asks Allyson, taking a step toward me, as if predicting that I will fall over in just a moment.

"Phoenix Corbin is coming to interview me, as I meet with the Rayle family over at their house," I say, clearing my throat. "They're sending a car for me at noon."

The six of them begin to laugh and hoot and holler. I feel as though I am the quarterback who has just thrown a touchdown pass to come out on top in the last quarter.

"Okay. I have a TV I can bring," says Allyson. "It's smaller than you all want, but it's something, and since Elle is about to be on national TV, we need to see what's going on, right?"

"Absolutely!" says Jordan.

"We'll all see you, Elle. Look around at what you've made," Monai says, holding out her hands and gesturing about the room. "This place is really special. You should be so proud of what you've done. You found that little boy and you made this bakery happen. Look at this place. You *did it!* It's your prize and joy!"

Chilled to the bone at what she's just said, I blink at her as the others laugh.

"Don't you mean *pride* and joy?" Roxy chortles at Monai.

Monai laughs. "No, it's what my grandmother used to always say when she was proud of me. My mother said she'd tell her that too, when she'd done something good. You're my *prize and joy!*"

I feel myself going weak at the knees, but no one else seems to notice. "Didn't you say you live with your dad?"

"Yeah, but it was Mama's mother who used to say that. My mother lives in Raleigh. She and my dad are divorced—have been for about seven or eight years."

"Oh...what does your mom do?" I ask, a pounding in my ears beginning.

"She works for the state correctional system. She's a case worker at the women's prison in Raleigh."

"Whoa!" says Jordan, calling the attention away from my face, which I'm sure has drained of all color. "That's random." *Monai is Vada's daugh-*

ter? When my story hits the national news tomorrow night, it will only be a matter of time before Vada realizes who her daughter is working for and my cover will be completely blown. *What a small world!* I can hear Jewel saying it now. Panic rolls through me like the start of a large wave. The shit is about to hit the fan.

What in the small world should I do now?

Chapter 16

PHOENIX CORBIN

Sitting in the front seat with Jeans Girl in her car, I take deep breaths, trying to steady my nerves. My upcoming meeting with Jeremy's parents, and the thought of seeing him again after his unimaginable ordeal, are unsettling. Jeans Girl tells me that the police have followed up on one or two leads, thanks to my tip about the tan Buick, and it may only be a matter of hours before they are able to arrest the second perpetrator.

Cameron, Jeans Girl's real name, drives me to an area of Wilmington that I haven't seen. Turning onto a suburban street, she slows immediately, as both of us see the news van and a high-end rental car parked at the curb in front of a modest, but attractive white brick house with the obligatory palmetto trees and gardenia bushes blooming in the yard. In the driveway, I catch a glimpse of a tall woman with loose, dark hair, Phoenix Corbin, impeccably dressed, wearing designer clothes, standing beside the also impeccable Preston Frazier. Both appear to be waiting for me. Apparently, this story is bigger than Amy Stainback, who has definitely been upstaged by these two. I feel like Cinderella, having arrived at the ball in her pumpkin coach.

I reach up to smooth my hair, a nervous habit, before getting out of Cameron's car. This morning, to prepare myself for the most important day in my life, I've applied my best makeup flawlessly over hemorrhoid cream to camouflage the dark circles under my eyes, and styled my hair in a tasteful chignon, something nobody from home would expect me to do. Who will see me? Judy? Aiden? Kendra? Marcus? *Kyle?* It doesn't matter. None of them will see the information about my bakery opening on Saturday; if they see me at all, it will be today's story about finding Jeremy, and hopefully, they will all be able to see the transformation from my sloppy Sunshine Girl appearance yesterday, without makeup and sticky hair, to what I look like today. None of it matters anyway, except that a little boy is home safe with his parents again. I shiver with imaginings I'm trying to shake.

Cameron and I walk up to meet the others, and she introduces me all around to Phoenix and Preston, along with the camera crew and other staff. It's surreal, I think, walking up the sidewalk in my white blouse and trendy, patterned crop pants, the Junior League outfit I tried to emulate while blitzing the likely retailers in town on my marketing campaign. I even spent last night shopping for that pair of two-toned shoes that AB wore the night I moved into her guesthouse. Unable to bring myself to spend that kind of money, I found a comparable pair at a department store at the mall, and I don't think I look bad.

Phoenix shakes my hand, putting me at ease with her soothing network voice, "Hello, Elle. It's so nice meeting you!" Then Preston Frazier greets me next. I can hardly talk to them, I am so nervous. A lighting man hovers, holding a light bar at differing angles near our heads, while the cameraman warms us up as we exchange a few more pleasantries. Then an impromptu interview takes place in front of one of the Rayles' most impressive palmetto trees, where I'm asked to go through the events one more time that led up to discovering Jeremy's face in the window of the sad blue house. I tell her the story of having iced tea spilled down my back at the bakery, giving credit to Scooter for sending me home to change clothes so I could be in the right place at the right time to discover Jeremy. Phoenix asks me about the new bakery, and then about how I must have felt when the rescue all went down, and it's easy to answer her questions. I comment that I'd have recognized Jeremy's eyes anywhere, thanks to the posters all over town.

Breaking for a moment, the news team sends Cameron to the door, where she is admitted by Jeremy's family, and then signals for Phoenix and the film crew to continue. The cameraman pans over the lawn and the sidewalk, filming our feet as we begin walking toward the front door, making me glad I bought those shoes! Phoenix uses her carefully planned steps toward the front door as a segue into the thoughts and fears of the Rayles over the past four months, in constant touch with the police, waiting for news of Jeremy, worrying about the worst, yet hoping for the best. Her narrative voice is hypnotic, caring, and soothing, bringing the audience to a build up that won't disappoint.

We step through the front door where we are greeted by Jack and Andrea Rayle, who look equally as nervous and shy as I feel. Jeremy is standing between them, clinging to his mother's pant leg, and looking up at me with his amazingly large, brown eyes. I wave and he raises the side of his mouth in somewhat of a smile of recognition, and his big, brown eyes linger with me until the introductions are made. I'm then embraced by both of his parents and invited to sit on their couch across from Phoenix in her chair, as the cameraman, Preston, and Cameron take their places at a discreet distance from our intimate circle.

"What would you like to say to Elle for stumbling onto Jeremy in her driveway yesterday?" Phoenix asks in her mesmerizing voice, making my head swim as if we are all in some kind of love fest. I can almost smell the incense swirling around our heads.

Andrea is the first to answer. "I know that any mother in my position would want to express how eternally grateful I will always be to you, Elle, for finding our Jeremy, and bringing him back to us."

Jack nods, echoing her sentiment. "We'd almost given up hope of ever finding him, and then we got the call...." He stops talking and swallows, apparently unable to continue.

What do I say in response? "I'm a mother myself. I think I had some idea of the despair you would feel to have lost a child and then rejoice in having found him suddenly. My own son is in the Army now, so I have an inkling of how it must feel, maybe not knowing when and if you'll ever see him again." I feel the camera in my face but try to ignore it.

"You have a son in the *Army*?" Andrea asks, her own brown eyes growing wide. I nod. "You don't look old enough. But yes, I suppose in many situations when men go off to combat, it could be a much similar experience."

Phoenix lets the words sink in and then shifts the topic. "Elle, you've been called the Sunshine Girl because Jeremy heard you singing 'Walking On Sunshine' right before he had the courage to break that window. What made you sing that particular song?"

"I'd gotten the first letter from my son—Joey—just the day before, from boot camp, and going to the mailbox, I remembered how happy it made me, so I just started singing...."

"And it worked." Phoenix turns to Jeremy, who is sitting between his parents, looking shy and apprehensive. I wonder how she'll handle it. If it doesn't go well, they can always edit this part out. Jack and Andrea are smiling at him, encouraging him, so Phoenix continues.

"Jeremy, do you have anything you'd like to say to Elle?" Her voice is filled with compassion, but she does not make it sound sappy, or babyish, the way some people talk to children. Maybe she has children of her own.

Jeremy regards Phoenix with his large eyes and nods somberly. We wait a moment for him to speak, but instead, he stands and walks over to me, giving me a silent hug. I feel his bird-like arms go around my neck, wondering how much stronger he would be had he been at home for the last four months. My arm goes around his shoulders, and we hold each other for one wordless, powerful moment.

Chapter 17

SHOW TIME!

Alone at 4:30 a.m. in Bake My Day, I glance at my reflection in the bathroom mirror, swallowing down a nervous, nauseated feeling. So many things have got me on edge this morning, cops going in and out of the house next door, the meeting with Jeremy and his parents yesterday, my run-in with Amy Stainback on Wednesday. Putting the white apron over my head and tying it behind me, I wonder again who saw last night's national news and who will see the segment on this morning's local news program.

And again it doesn't matter, although I know if Vada saw it, she'd have contacted Monai by now. I dread seeing Monai this morning. Aside from talking to a newspaper reporter, Judy, and Marcus last night after the news, I've had no other personal telephone calls, so maybe that is a good sign. I start on the breakfast pastries, hoping the routine will slow my heart and prepare me for what's to come today. Along with the general unease resulting from the events of Jeremy's recovery, that unsettled feeling over Wednesday's confrontation with Amy has haunted me, even as I slept, tossing and turning every hour until I had to get up. I had to confront her the way I did, but I'm reasonably sure our encounter only further ignited any ill feelings she had toward me. She's the kind of woman who would dig around in my dirt, regardless of how I've handled myself. I have to be ready for whatever she plans to dish out. I have to be ready for anything.

At 6:30 on the dot, while I'm measuring out coffee in the baskets for the morning, my first shift arrives: Allyson, Anna, and Jordan, all wearing their new Bake My Day T-shirts. I dread Monai's entrance, wondering whether Vada has contacted her, after seeing the news last night. The day could get increasingly difficult. The other staff members have been invited as well for the TV appearance, and I expect Monai and Scooter to appear momentarily, but I'm sure Roxy will use the time to sleep since she'll be closing tonight. I'll be here for the long haul, and will continue the vigil until Saturday's grand opening is over. I plan to work on Sunday to catch the spillover, but on Monday, I will be taking a long, overdue day off. Nothing is on my Monday agenda but sleep.

Monai walks in with the camera crew, without giving me any other look than she usually gives me, thankfully. A moment later, Scooter comes through the door with Amy Stainback, chatting amiably, for which I am grateful, hoping for any reason to elevate her mood. Good Lord! She is flirting with him, and he is all of twenty-three years old! I try to arrange my face into its nicest expression while I go to meet her in the café.

"Hi, Amy," I say, my voice as smooth as sugared butter, trying to emulate what I remember from my encounter with Phoenix Corbin, extending my hand as if we are old friends.

She responds in kind, as polished an actress as I am, and even her dark eyes appear to have a warm glow about them. Maybe I was wrong. Or maybe she is cowed by me, after my smashing debut on the national news last evening. Preston Frazier, Phoenix Corbin, and I have all upstaged her and her pathetic attempt at a formidable breaking news story, which can't make her too happy.

"Elle! Good morning!" she says, scanning me quickly for telltale signs of animosity—and bags under my eyes. Of course, she wants me to look bad so Nate will see the error of his ways! I tilt my head up a bit and adjust my shoulders, standing squarely on both feet and suck in my stomach. With yet another expert makeup job, I look pretty damn good and she knows it!

"Welcome to Bake My Day!"

"Wow! It smells fantastic in here!" she says to the nods of the cameraman at her side, as he sets up more lights in the cafe.

While Amy instructs me on how to attach my microphone for the interview, Anna and Allyson bring in the breakfast pastries to add to the display counter, making Amy seem overcome with the aromas that fill the bakery.

"We can hook you up before you leave," I say casually. "And if you'd like to take anything back to the station with you, we can pack you a nice box of goodies—cake slices, cookies, whatever you want," I add, grinning at her, showing my dimple to the cameraman, who is already set up, and I see his lens trained on my face.

"We'll definitely take you up on that!" she says. "So, where would you like to start filming?" she asks, turning on her microphone and blowing in it to test it.

"Why don't we start in the kitchen where the staff is working on baking and icing some cakes? We have Monai, here, getting ready to ice a wedding cake that will be on display tomorrow..." I start, waving my hand toward Monai, who gives her broad smile, stretching her lips out of the way of her braces. The cameraman gets her in action, while I go on. "Jordan is working on mixing the pound cakes. We bake those first because they take the longest to cool, and then he'll start on the white cakes." The cameraman is rolling as I go, filming the whirring motion of Monai's mixer as she produces the frosting for the wedding cake that is sitting out on the table.

The smell of coffee from the café greets our noses, making the lovely ambience of Bake My Day complete, and I finally relax. Amy and I are back in the café, where it is quieter and the remainder of the interview takes place. She goes over my brief history, moving to the coast, starting a new place, getting everything set for the opening tomorrow. I have breakfast set out for her to sample on one of our tables, and we go over the ingredients in both the blueberry tart and the spinach quiche she's sampling, as she oohs and aahs about how good it all is. Then Anna appears with a slice of each kind of wedding cake we offer, arranged on a tray, and Amy samples the lemon cake, making a decadent moan, showing her approval. I intone that we are still taking summer wedding cake orders, and we can fit in any last minute brides still needing our services. We end the brief interview by reviewing our hours of operation, the grand opening event tomorrow, which will include a bridal raffle for a free wedding cake, as well as a free catered brunch for up to twenty people.

As we wind up the interview, Amy's demeanor starts to change noticeably, as the cameraman disappears and she switches off her microphone, and takes mine. Allyson has gone back into the kitchen, and for the moment, we are alone in the café. Amy congratulates me on my interview with Phoenix on TV last night, and then she fishes around with other questions about where I'm from.

"You know, I did a little extra research on you, Elle, and what I found out might not be so flattering," she says, her tone indicating that she hates to break it to me.

"Really? And what was it you discovered?"

"Well, did you know your mug shot is posted online as a matter of public record? Just like your criminal background? You were eighteen when you were arrested. It didn't take much digging to find out what you did to one of your classmates back in high school. Is that why you left those beautiful mountains, to come down here to the coast and start all over again?"

"As you say, it's public record. And it seems you've drawn your own conclusions."

"And I think it would be of great interest to all those people who are voting for you to be the hero of the week. Have you seen the interest your story has generated on Twitter and Facebook? Your interview with Phoenix Corbin is getting tons of hits on YouTube."

"I didn't know."

"People want to know all about the Sunshine Girl—thanks to me. So what would all those people think if they knew what you were really like, Elle? If they knew the things you've done? Never went to college? Served a year in prison? Had a baby out of wedlock? Your mother…well, and then, there's your father—"

"Stop!" *This is all about Nate.* She's lost him and she's blaming me. What better way to get revenge than to sink me on national news or in the newspaper? She obviously won't do it herself, but she'll leak it to the people who will make it count. "Don't even start with me, Amy. I know plenty about you that would destroy your sweet little family, and possibly your career," I throw back at her. I didn't want to have to expose her, but she's leaving me no choice. And this is a part I play very well.

"What do you think you know?" she shoots back at me. She studies me a moment and then tries to call my bluff. "You can't prove anything."

For a moment, I think she's right, but then I remember the picture I have on my phone. I'd never do that to Nate, but I might expose Amy if she pushes me.

"I know a lot, so don't be so sure I won't put it out there. All it would take is a little visit with your husband and a well-placed photo or two. Oh, I can prove it all right."

She looks at me with her beady little stare, unsure of what I've got. I stare back at her, giving her a knowing gleam in my eye that appears to unnerve her. I can be sure of one thing; she'll be contacting Nate Aldridge as soon as she leaves the premises. And if that's the case, I know it's over with us, if there was ever anything to begin with.

Why would Amy want to discredit me at this point anyway? My national TV interview is over, my bakery opening is hardly an earth-shattering event, and by this afternoon, my twenty-four hours worth of fame will have vanished into thin air. The Rayles are a middle class family with limited resources, so there was no reward money to track down to see what I'll be blowing it on. Jeremy is home. I'm moving on, and Amy will be back to reporting on recipes and what everyone's wearing to the beach this summer, so why the interest in ruining my reputation? Other than the threat of losing Nate to me, which is probably not my doing anyway—not that I'd consider us together by any stretch of the imagination. He hasn't called me after last night, so there is nothing even to think about. I knew it would turn out like this. What a mess I've gotten myself into! It's so typical of the way things go in my life. I scoff silently to myself and try to stop worrying about her. She's bluffing and I know it.

My bakery is moving on as if nothing has happened. It is 8:45. The white cakes are going in the oven and everyone is zipping around, doing what they are supposed to be doing, like the well-oiled machine I've wanted from the beginning. Glancing at my phone, I realize I have seven missed calls. People must be reacting to the story: one is from Marcus, two are from Judy, who has left me a voicemail message; there is one from Randy; one is from Jewel; another newspaper has contacted me, and the other is from AB. My landlady deserves the first call back.

"Elle, I just wanted to say that you did a lovely job on TV last night—and this morning! I was so proud of you! Oh, that poor family and what they've all gone through!"

"Thank you, AB. I hope the public understands that I don't actually live at your house…."

"Oh, don't worry about that! I've gotten a thousand phone calls about it, but it's okay. All that matters is that the little boy is home safely. Isn't it just horrible? There were three unmarked police cars parked on our street when I left for work. The police have been going in and out since

Wednesday. There's no telling what they've been finding in that house. Mr. May and I were just talking about you this morning—we watched you on TV again this morning—and he's so concerned about you. I hope you're all right."

"Yes, thank you. I'm fine. Tell him I'm flattered that he was thinking about me."

"Well, you're our heroine for sure! I thought the morning news spot was just fabulous! I hope you have a great opening day tomorrow! Take care, dear, and give a shout if you need anything!"

"Okay. Thanks, AB. Bye now."

"Bye-bye."

Putting my phone back in my pocket, I glance up at the small TV Allyson has brought in. The morning news team is back on after a commercial break, and I expect the next thing they'll discuss is the new movie out at the box office for the weekend. Instead of that, I notice the breaking news banner flashing across the screen along with the grim and attentive faces of the co-anchors as Preston Frazier's face appears. Monai looks up and Jordan and Anna follow suit. Allyson is the only one in the café tending to our customers, but I am unable to move to assist her, captivated by the picture and the caption on the screen: *Accomplice in the Jeremy Rayle case captured.*

I turn up the volume on the TV in time to hear the anchorwoman narrating the breaking news story, "And thanks to a tip provided by neighbor, Elle McLarin, the perpetrator's late '90s model tan Buick was traced to an apartment complex in Wilmington last night, where police held the armed suspect at gunpoint for a stand-off lasting over eight hours before he surrendered himself to police just moments ago." A picture of the tan Buick in front of a shabby-looking apartment complex flashes on the screen. She goes on to name the man, pictured on the screen, being led in handcuffs into the county jail in the live feed, and she reassures the public that he is going to be behind bars on a $250,000 bail. "SBI agents are on the scene now, combing the area for evidence that could possibly lead to other crimes involving young children in our viewing area who have previously gone missing...."

What a freak! I tune it out, unable to fathom that there could be more to this nightmare than I have previously imagined. And here I thought it was all over. I could be getting back into the fray again, however undesirable it seems at this moment. And Amy Stainback will be probably jumping right back in with me.

At lunchtime, Allyson sends me home to rest. "You're exhausted, Elle. Go home and at least take a break. We can handle it here."

Her kindness and competence are reassuring, so I take her advice and go home for a peanut butter sandwich and a nap. What I don't expect is my street to be crawling with cops and reporters. No sooner have I parked my car than newspaper reporters descend upon me, asking questions about the second suspect's arrest, and what I might have known. I have little to offer, but it seems that I'm a celebrity. Their questions are getting on my nerves, like, *Was there a reward? What are you going to do now?*

I catch a quick glimpse of Phoenix Corbin on camera in front of the house next door. I don't even want to talk to her. She is probably the only one who will handle the story with the dignity it deserves; still, I am really exhausted and just want to disappear. It seems to me that the whole world has gone on a feeding frenzy with the psycho men who happen to live next door to me. As revolting and disturbing as it all is, all I want to do is take a nosedive into my pillow and sleep for several days. It's then that I see Mr. May on AB's back porch, giving me a wave and motioning me upstairs.

Reluctantly, I climb the stairs to join him. It's nice to see him, but I don't have the energy or the inclination to tell my story again. Thankfully, he doesn't ask. He's heard it all anyway, and for him, the redundancy would be without purpose.

"Hello, Elle! You look like you could use a respite from the fray."

"Absolutely. Hi, Mr. May."

"I've found this spot to be an entertaining vantage point from which to observe all the frenetic goings on."

"I guess it is," I murmur, hoping I can hide for a few more minutes. "Wow. This is a great view of the garden, too."

"Yes, I agree. I believe a garden is a growing canvas—where a creative spirit can truly bloom as well."

"Mmm," I agree.

"I am the true vine, and my Father is the gardener," he says in a dramatic voice. I look questioningly at him, obviously confused. "John—15:2," he adds, clearing that up. I guess we could all use a little pruning here and there if Jesus thought He needed it himself.

"Ahh," I nod. Normally, people quoting the Bible would annoy me, but coming from Mr. May, it's so freaking cool. Granny would have loved him. I look away from the flowers, down at the driveway and the house next door, where there is indeed a clear view of police officers milling about, as reporters set up at different points around the house to broadcast the latest gory details about what was found inside the house as it relates to the second suspect. I guess I will hear all about it later, although I won't want to hear any of it. After meeting Jeremy, I can hardly bear to think of all the horror that was going on in there. And if he wasn't the only victim, it's truly unthinkable.

"Your friend, Amy, is having a busy morning, isn't she?" Mr. May comments, indicating with his hand the backyard of Hector's house where the carpet cleaning van that now may be impounded for investigation was once parked. I look over to see Amy, who is deep in conversation with someone, and I realize it's Nate. They are arguing, by the sound of it. I can't make out the words, but the uncomfortable tone of their discussion is clear. Her back is to me, and he stands facing her, hands on hips, listening to her, as she gestures animatedly near his face. I can see that his jaw is set and his eyes grow narrow as she talks. Then he looks up at me. His eyes are serious, discerning, and questioning. She turns suddenly and sees me, her face going slack with surprise. Then she turns back to him, telling him something else, reaching intimately for his arm. He doesn't shrug off her hand, but listens to her some more, the muscle in his jaw working; then he turns abruptly and walks away. I hear her call his name, but he doesn't go back. Before I can move to go down the steps to talk to him, he has walked out of the yard and back down the street toward his house. He had no intention of talking to me. He didn't even look back.

Chapter 18

GRAND OPENING DAY

It is 5:30 a.m. when I unlock the door of Bake My Day. I have over-slept—with "slept" being the operative word. It felt glorious to sleep for several hours without dreaming or worrying about anything at all for a change—until I woke up and realized I'd overslept on this important day. I'm here in my bakery T-shirt and my ponytail, with makeup on—one, because it's my grand opening, and two, in case someone from a news agency decides to show up and—make my day. The thought of Amy showing her face in here today makes me snarl with displeasure. I check my phone for my blackmail evidence, scrolling through the photos file, and sure enough, the picture of Amy and Nate is still there. I vow that I'll delete it if she leaves me alone. While I'm holding the phone, it rings. It's Judy, probably calling to wish me luck. And I need all the luck I can get today!

"Hey, Judy!"

"Good mornin', Honey Bun! How're you holdin' up?"

"Great!" I lie. "Did you call to wish me luck?"

"Yes, I did."

"I can use it. Thanks!"

"Listen; there's something else I heard yesterday that I wanted to tell you."

Oh, God, here we go! What has Amy done?

Judy continues, "One of Aiden's cousins was in here yesterday, and she told me he's in the hospital. Did you know that?"

"No. I haven't talked to him since Joey made it to base. Joey wrote and said Aiden was sick, and I'd tried to call him, but you know how he is. He never answers the phone when he's on that dump truck."

"Well, she thought it was kinda serious. She didn't know—maybe he's having some kind of surgery. Anyway, I thought you should know. You might wanna run him down later and see what's up."

"Yeah, I will. I meant to, I just—well, things have been so busy here and then you know...."

"Oh, I'm sure of that! Well, I didn't want to alarm you, but at least you can call and find out what's going on. Have you gotten any more letters from Joey?"

"No, but I'm sure he's busy, too."

"Well, you have a great day and call me and tell me how it was!"

"Thanks, Judy!"

"Bye, Honey Bun."

"Bye."

I won't be calling Aiden or anybody else at this hour. Before I start on the breakfast pastries, I fax in an order to my purveyor for more food supplies: flour, sugar, butter, eggs, milk, vanilla, and cream cheese. I open the safe to make sure I wrote the staff's paychecks. I think I did, but I might have dreamed it; things have been so crazy, I hardly know my own name this morning. The checks are there, so I get busy on the cheese Danishes, as Allyson surprises me by coming in early. I give her a relieved and grateful smile.

"Hey, Al! I'm so glad you came in early. I overslept."

"No problem with that, but have you seen this?" she asks, holding up a folded newspaper. I feel the color drain from my face. "Nobody I know even reads the paper anymore, but I thought you should see this," she says, unfolding it and turning to the local section. At the bottom of the page, the title reads: *Sunshine Girl Has Stormy Past.*

There is a picture of me, taken on Thursday during my visit with the Rayles. It could be worse; it could be my mug shot from my arrest, but apparently someone has shown me a slight bit of mercy. Amy will be disappointed. The accompanying article is only three short paragraphs: one, summarizing my finding Jeremy; two, the Rohypnol incident from high school, including my conviction and sentence; and three, the opportunity I took to move here and open my bakery, but there is enough damning information in the article to ruin whatever good reputation I might have earned in this town. Feeling my face flame with anger in front of Allyson, I scan the story quickly, realizing that there weren't any omissions, and whoever did the research was quite accurate in their fact-finding.

I thought I had this situation under control, but once again, some bitch has tried to sabotage not only me, but my business as well, all because I slept with her extra-marital boyfriend! And then I realize Amy is planning double destruction, taking revenge not only on me, but on Nate too. Her knowledge that I might retaliate and expose his involvement with her makes me realize how little she must care about him, were his name to be spilled in this whole mess. Feeling a mixture of overwhelming rage at Amy for leaking this story, and humiliation that one of my employees has found me out, I glance up at Allyson, trying to gauge what she thinks of me. Feeling like my life is about to implode, I start to give an explanation, but Allyson beats me to the punch.

"I'm sorry, Elle, but the past is the past. You paid your debt. Whoever did this should just be shot!"

Momentarily, I'm stunned. I blink and gape at her. Her reaction is not at all what I expected. Now that she knows all about my sordid past, I didn't expect support. But I'll take it. I roll with it without missing a beat.

"Oh, I know exactly who it was."

"What are you going to do about it?"

I fume for a moment, knowing precisely what I *can* do about it. In the old days, I would have hurled this flaming poison right back at Amy and made her pay, burning my own hand in the process. Whether I'll do it now is another matter. I ran to get away from all of this. If I drop the bomb on Amy, she'll get what she deserves, Nate will most likely be disgraced, and then I will be right back where I was, but this time, it will be without Granny's beautiful little house, and a new town full of people who will hate and scorn me and talk behind my back and pick on me at every turn. Still, she deserves to be put in her place. And who better to do it than me? It's what I do best. An eye for an eye.

It's not how we fall, Elle, but how we rise, I remember Vada saying to me.

I look up at Allyson, who seems determined to ride with me on this one, and it makes my heart swell to realize I have the beginnings of a posse. She's waiting for my answer. I take a deep breath, willing the courage to do something completely uncharacteristic.

"This is what I'm going to do about it," I say, tossing her newspaper in the garbage can next to the sink, not even believing it myself. She cocks her head and lifts her eyebrows, making me reach for the can. "I'm sorry! Did you need that paper?"

"Heck, yeah. There's a coupon for 50% off at Belk's today and tomorrow, and I've had my eye on this really hot new pair of shoes." We rifle through the paper in search of her coupon, tear it out, and then throw the rest of it in the trash, laughing. "You're going to be just fine, Elle. Nobody who knows you is going to give a shit. You're the Sunshine Girl, remember? Everybody has rainy days. Just keep reminding yourself of that."

I try to smile, but I'm not feeling her confidence. "I need to come clean to everybody. When the staff comes in, I'll tell them. I wish I'd done it before my story hit the press."

"It wasn't on TV," Allyson says.

"You've screened the TV news? How long have you been up?"

"I get up early every day. I always watch the news when I'm getting ready. When I saw this paper, I turned the TV on immediately."

I can't stand the thought of Amy Stainback's vindictive little rat's face on the TV, tattling on me. I sigh and shrug. "*Ugh!* I just want to get through this day on my own terms."

Allyson studies me for a moment. "Okay, suit yourself, but just so you know, I don't think I'm the only one on your side."

"I appreciate that, but you don't know my opponent."

"Your opponent's an *asshole*. I credit myself with being an excellent judge of character, so if you're not fighting, I'll take that as a sign that he or she isn't worth the satisfaction of a good smack-down."

Oh, I'd love to smack Amy down, but surprisingly Nate has turned out to be a pretty good guy, so I could really end up hurting someone who's worth a damn. I've made that mistake once and spent half my life paying for it. I might as well come clean to my employees and get it over with.

"I'd love to smack her down, actually, but there's more at stake than it appears."

"See, this is why I work for you," she says, grinning at me while she slips her apron over her head. "I like that you want to protect someone, but blackmailers are real stinkers in my opinion. If you decide to pick this battle, you just say the word and I'm in."

This is new. I grin at her, liking the way it feels to have a friend. Fifteen minutes ago, I was ready to run back to the hills!

"You must be one hell of a mother."

"Don't you know? Wait until one of my kids' teachers crosses me and there will be hell to pay; although, we've actually been lucky in that regard. My kids've had great teachers for the most part, and you couldn't pay me to do their jobs."

We get down to business immediately, fashioning the pastries, putting them in the ovens to bake, and setting out the wedding cakes that will be on display to promote the raffle. Thinking we'd have more business than we could handle today, I've frozen extra pastries over the last couple of weeks, so I take them out of the freezer to bake. If there are any left over, I'll donate them to the local food pantry, where they'll serve them to the homeless. Judy and I did that in her bakery in Boone, and it's a win-win for the community.

Anna, Jordan, and Scooter arrive at 7:30. Everyone is coming in at the same time today and working until closing, or until business tapers off and I can dismiss them one by one, as we need less help. I find that I'm holding my breath until Monai arrives so I can tell them what they need to know. So far, apparently no one has seen the paper, which doesn't surprise me, so everyone is going about business as usual. Finally, Monai comes through the back door, washes her hands, and puts on her apron as I'm taking the last of the pastries out of the oven. She gives me a wan little smile, so unlike her usual mega-watt grin, and I know. *She knows.*

"Good morning, Monai," I greet her, wondering how to proceed.

"Hey, Elle. Can I talk to you a minute?" she asks, pushing up her glasses.

"Sure," I say, giving Scooter a wide berth while he carries a five-gallon bucket of sweet tea into the café.

Monai motions me into the walk-in refrigerator so we can talk privately—the joys of working in an undersized space! There's no reason to beat around the bush, plus, it's cold in here.

"You're Vada's daughter, aren't you?"

"Yes. She called me last night and told me everything. I didn't want to rat you out in front of everybody right now, since I figured out you'd been in prison, but if my mother says you're her prize and joy, then you just are. Mama's always loved her job. She finds a lot of satisfaction in rehabilitating the women she counsels every day, and when she feels like she's been successful, she says there's no better feeling in the whole world. She knew from the day I took this job who I was working for, but she didn't say anything about it because she didn't want me to be prejudiced toward you in any way."

"Wow. That's ironic." In many ways, it's ironic, but knowing Vada, it seems perfectly typical of how she'd do things.

"I know. It's all ironic, isn't it? But yeah, that's my mom." I nod. "She knew we would get along great, and she was right. Knowing how happy I am here is just the icing on the cake to her about how you turned out—and I guess how I turned out, too."

I gaze at her a moment, thinking how proud Vada must be of Monai. I'm proud of her, and she's not even my daughter.

"Thanks, Monai. Thanks for not judging me. I know Vada is proud of you. I am too." I sigh. "The whole story is in the newspaper today."

Monai's eyes grow large beneath her dramatic black-framed glasses. "Why?"

"Somebody's trying to destroy me."

"Who? And why?"

"I don't know for sure, but I think I know who did it. If I'm right, it's an act of revenge for something I did. Or something somebody else did. Anyway, I have to tell the others. Sooner or later, they're all going to find out. I'd rather be the one to tell them."

"Okay. Wow. That's terrible. Well, I got your back."

"Thank you. Let's go then; it's freezing in here!"

When we emerge, the bakery is in full swing. Roxy and Anna are working the café counter while the rest of the staff is cranking out the cupcakes of the day—key lime with citrus buttercream frosting and little lime zest garnishes, the perfect prelude to summertime. The kitchen is loud with all the mixers going and the nervous chatter among the excited employees, not to mention the TV set in the corner, broadcasting the morning news that I refuse to watch.

Checking on the girls in the café, I realize we are already slammed, and there will be no time to have our little impromptu staff meeting. This could go down badly for me if the wrong person shows up and lets my secret out. After a dry swallow, I look around, watching a couple of young women filling out wedding cake raffle slips at the cucumber water table that's adorned with Granny's yellow-flowered tablecloth. "Help me, Granny," I murmur under my breath. There is a line at the counter as people wait for coffee to be poured and pastries to be presented on paper plates. Already, the seats are all taken, including the ones at the cake consultation counter. I start another pot of coffee, weaving in and out between Anna and Roxy, who are zipping around like automatons. Who would have imagined we'd be this busy before 8:30?

As I turn back around, I hear the door chime again, signaling more customers arriving. I'm shocked and delighted to see AB and Mr. May entering my place of business. Mr. May is holding a large silver pitcher filled with AB's flowers and greenery from her garden. Behind him, I see Randy and Jimmy, and through the plate-glass window, Brandon, Jewel, and her daughter (I can't remember her name), waiting to get in the door, give me a wave from the sidewalk. I'm so thrilled to see them all, out in support of our big day, but then I realize that maybe they have read the paper and have come with questions. My eye comes to rest on Mr. May and his flowers—peonies mixed with roses and lovely blue Baptisia, reaching its delicate fingers past the pink and coral blossoms. His kind, old eyes show nothing out of the ordinary, and I am deeply touched. AB looks around disdainfully at all the people. This kind of a hubbub is not typically her scene this early in the morning, but she is here, making me feel honored. Jimmy and Randy must have decided to stop by before they went to work at one of the houses Randy is flipping. I haven't talked to him in a few days, and I'm equally touched that he came by despite his busy schedule. There is room for Jewel, her daughter, and Brandon to get inside, and they slip in, grinning at me as if they are delighted with the crowd we have already. Brandon gives me a wink and a thumbs-up, as Jewel murmurs continually in his ear, which he doesn't seem to mind. I smile.

I begin to wait on customers as well, taking orders, retrieving breakfast items, and pouring coffee, counting change, and handing out napkins. It's going so well! I never thought our efforts would have produced such a turnout, and ironically, I feel a slight bit of gratitude to Amy Stainback for contributing; although, I remind myself, when she came here just yesterday, she had resolved to do me in. How life can turn on you in an instant.

"Hey! Thanks for coming!" Making my way around the counter, I greet Mr. May and AB with hugs for them both.

"Hello! This is so great!" says AB. "Congratulations!"

"Good morning, Elle! What a wonderful turnout! Congratulations!" Mr. May says, handing me the flowers. While I'm thanking him and deciding for the perfect spot on the display case for them, the door chimes again, and I gasp at who walks in.

Chapter 19

THE BAKER TELLS ALL

First, I see Cameron from Channel 3 News, holding the door open while Randy is talking to me. There are newspaper reporters in line behind the TV people.

"You need some tables and chairs out on the sidewalk to handle all this business!" Randy says, leaning over and giving me a hug. I manage to set the pitcher of flowers on the counter while I have the other new arrivals on the sidewalk in the corner of my eye.

"Yeah, I think you're right!" I say to him with a grin I'm not feeling. He senses it and looks back at the sidewalk.

Jimmy has seen the others and confirms what I see. "That's Phoenix Corbin, isn't it?"

"Yes," I say with a stiff smile, as Phoenix and her cameraman are positioning themselves on the sidewalk in wait for me, whenever Cameron can get to me to let me know they are there.

"Well, you certainly are popular with the press," says AB, and I can tell by her tone that she's read the newspaper, and after her shared look with Mr. May, he has too. I feel unsteady so I reach out to grab Randy's arm.

"Could you all step into the kitchen for a minute? There's a little something I need to clear up, and I might as well share it with everyone." The four of them look concerned and nod. "This is really bad timing, but I'll have to be quick about it."

I can feel them following me back into the kitchen, where the rest of my employees look up in surprise, as if I've just brought a field trip group back for a tour of the bakery. I make eye contact with Monai. "Would you mind switching places with Anna? Allyson, would you take Roxy's place?" They nod, understanding immediately what I'm doing, and make a smooth exit. The noise from the mixers is giving me a headache. "Jordan, would you turn off the mixers, please?" I ask, while I switch off the television.

Before I can even begin, Monai has stuck her head back inside the kitchen.

"Elle? The lady from the news is here. She wants to know if she can have a word with you?"

"Tell her not yet. Thanks, Monai."

She leaves, and Brandon, Jewel, and her daughter take their places in the already crowded kitchen, looking curious, and I know Allyson or Monai has sent them back to hear what I have to say. I take a deep breath and let it out. This is family. Just let it go.

"We don't have a lot of time. I wanted to let you know what's in the newspaper today—some of you may already have seen it," I start, as Mr. May and AB nod. "Back when I was a senior in high school, I made a very serious mistake. I committed a crime. I didn't know it at the time, but what I did was a felony. There was a boy in my high school that I was—let's say, obsessed with. I couldn't get him to like me, so one night at a party, I slipped a roofie in his drink, thinking I could be with him, but it knocked him completely out and somebody recorded the incriminating part of it—me talking about what I'd done. The evidence was presented, I got arrested and convicted, and then I served a year in the women's prison in Raleigh. I was pregnant and unmarried when I went in. I had a baby while I was there, and *Monai's mother*, of all people, was my rehabilitation counselor." Everyone looks around for Monai. "I served my sentence, and I am truly remorseful for what I did. So while I was in prison, I learned baking—I'd worked in my cousin Judy's bakery at home. I got my pastry arts degree at a community college and went back home to work for Judy. People always held it against me, what I'd done, and I got tired of always being judged for that and the way I grew up, so when my grandparents died and Joey went into the Army, I decided to sell my property and come here to start this bakery, and start over somewhere fresh. So…that's it."

There is dead silence. I'm aware that other people have filtered into the room, but there are so many of them, I can't see them all.

"I'm a felon. If any of you have a problem with that, I can't say that I blame you. If you want to resign, I wouldn't blame you for that either, but if you could be kind enough to stay and help the rest of us get through today intact, I'd really appreciate it."

There is more silence as all this sinks in. Monai has appeared again to listen. Apparently, most of the customers we had are now in the kitchen so Allyson must be handling the café counter by herself. It's then that I see him.

Nate has joined the group, standing on the side near my desk, listening with a grim expression, looking first at me, and then at the others. Mr. May glances at Jimmy and they seem to be deciding who should speak first.

"Well, ain't that somethin'?" says Jimmy. "I guess you think you're the only criminal in the room, Elle, but it's just not true. When you were at Mr. May's birthday party, we were afraid to tell you how we knew each other," he says, and Randy chuckles. So does AB, and then Mr. May laughs his silent laugh.

"Do you remember when you asked how we knew each other?" Mr. May begins.

I hardly see the humor in the situation, but I nod, relieved that at least no one has slammed down an apron and stormed out.

Jimmy picks up the narrative. "Remember? Randy told you there was a club. Monty had gathered us together—well, some of us and made us a club," continues Jimmy. I'm not following them. "See, I'm a felon, too," says Jimmy.

"As am I," Mr. May says in that professorial way of his. My eyes cast around to the others, who seem as surprised as I am, except for AB.

"What? Wh-what did you all do?"

You can hear a pin drop, and I am only slightly distracted by the fact that Allyson is manning the counter by herself, but I guess she's handling it. Mr. May begins.

"My wife was dying of cancer. As you know, I was the county horticultural agent at the time, so I knew a bit about plant propagation. Daphne had tried medicinal marijuana to help her through her chemotherapy sickness, and to help increase her appetite. She didn't like the side effects of the drug. It made her feel paranoid. Our son was what you might call...a *cannabis connoisseur*, and brought home some weed that she found much more palatable. I decided to grow some of it for her. Eventually, she told her other acquaintances at the cancer center about it and they started using it as well. I never sold it to them, but I grew a few plants—enough to share it with her friends. I thought I'd hidden it reasonably well on our property, but it was found and I was arrested, charged, and convicted. I served my sentence on probation under house arrest, considering Daphne needed me at home. The judge was lenient in light of our circumstances, but I was dismissed from my job, as you might imagine. Daphne passed away and Monty was kind enough to take me on as his gardener. I've continued in my community service by growing food and working with the food bank and serving meals to the homeless in our community. Fortunately for me, the people here have embraced me in a way I'm sure I do not deserve. So you see, you are not alone in your circumstances."

There is more silence as we all take in Mr. May's story. I look at Jimmy who clears his throat and begins.

"I'm also a felon. I was convicted of involuntary manslaughter and driving while intoxicated." He looks at me with the sad eyes I remember from when I asked him why he left the mountains. *The girl.* "I was engaged to be married. My fiancée, Leigh Anne, was riding in the car with me. We'd left a concert and we'd both been drinking. I'd had less to drink than she had and I thought I was okay to drive home. I took a curve in the road a little too fast and lost control of the car. It spun out and hit another car. She was killed and the other people were injured. I served my time too, and Randy and Monty helped me get back on my feet again, and now—thanks to Randy, who taught me how to buy a foreclosure—I own my own house. I saved my money from what he'd paid me on the work I'd done for him on his flips. You know, as a felon, I couldn't get a mortgage from a bank, but I was able to save enough to buy a small foreclosure. It's really small, but I can say it's mine. Like Mr. May, I've had good friends who took it upon themselves to forgive me for my mistakes and help me move on. You can do it, too. You have friends here. Monty set a wonderful example of forgiveness and compassion."

I nod, looking around at the compassionate faces in front of me, and realizing that I have many good friends who are forgiving me right now. My employees stir, realizing we need to get back to work. Out of the corner of my eye, I notice that Phoenix Corbin is standing in the crowded kitchen, but she is the last person I want to talk to right now. She has heard enough for a fantastic news story, but I have no desire to corroborate it for her.

I glance at Nate, wondering what his take on all this is, when my cell phone rings. It's sitting on my desk, where Nate is standing. He doesn't meet my eyes, but he picks up my phone and looks at the screen. Then he looks up, an odd look on his face. "It's Joey…."

Jordan, Anna, and Monai give me looks of solidarity, while Roxy nods and pats me on the shoulder on her way back to the café. My friends watch me with interest as I walk over and take the phone from Nate.

"Joey?" How can he call me when he's at boot camp under the most severe restrictions? His commanding officer took his phone and other personal effects as soon as he reached the base, or so I thought. Nate looks concerned which doesn't seem good.

"Mom? Hey. Are you having your big opening day?"

"Yes. How are you calling me? I didn't think you could make phone calls…."

"We can't at camp, but I'm on emergency leave. It's Dad. My CO said a representative from the Red Cross called him with a message about Dad. He's got a critical illness and he's in the hospital. They thought I should go. Didn't you know?"

"No. I haven't been able to get in touch with him. Wh-what kind of illness?"

"It's something to do with his heart—an infection; wait; I wrote it down. It's called *endocarditis*."

"Endocarditis?" I repeat and look at Nate. He raises his chin and looks even more seriously at me. AB and Mr. May are listening as well, and Mr. May shakes his head. What is this all about?

"They said he got an infection from something, probably the abscess they found in his tooth, and it went to his heart."

"What?" I can't take it in.

"Mom…they're saying he's going to die."

"No."

"There's nothing they can do. By the time they figured out what was wrong with him, it was too late. I'm at the airport now. I'm getting on a plane to come home. They gave me a week's leave. I'll be staying with Grandpa and Grandma. Grandpa's going to meet me at the airport. Are you going to come?"

"It's Aiden," I say to Nate, but then I realize he doesn't know who Aiden is. He is as confused as I am. "Aiden is Joey's father…" I murmur. Everyone nods gravely. This is my grand opening, but Aiden is in serious trouble and I have to leave. I feel myself sinking. Nate catches my arm and guides me into my chair. "Joey…what flight are you taking? When do you get in? Is he at Watauga Medical Center?"

Joey answers my questions and I write everything down. Monai is standing over me, rubbing my shoulder. Joey and I say goodbye and I end the call. I explain everything while my friends listen respectfully. Then I cover my face with my hands.

Aiden is dying.

Nate squats next to me and takes one of my hands, trying to look at me.

"You need to go, Elle. If the Army granted Joey a week's emergency leave, it's serious. It means Aiden is dying. You need to go."

"I know." I wipe the tears off my face and drop my other hand. He studies me and then glances at Monai.

"I'll go get Allyson," says Monai, taking Nate's cue that we need to talk privately. I'm aware that the others in the room are moving about; my friends are taking last looks at us before leaving the kitchen, while Anna and Jordan are getting back to work, looking at me to see whether the noise of the mixers will disturb my conversation with Nate.

"Listen," he says, stroking my hand. "I know this is a tough situation for you, especially today with your opening, and with everything that's been going on. You've got a long trip ahead of you…. Do you want me to drive you?"

"No. No! You don't have time for that. Besides, it's a six-hour drive and…I'm probably going to be up there for several days," I say, wondering where I'll stay. Judy would let me bunk with her.

"I insist. Look; I've got a show to produce, so I was hoping to stay holed up in my office for the next week working on it. I can do it up there as easily as I can do it here. We can get a…place to stay and you can take my truck to wherever you need to be."

I look at him uncertainly.

He shrugs. "Or we can take your car. All I need is my equipment, but I don't think you're in any shape to be driving six hours."

"No. Really, I'll be fine."

"Elle," he whispers firmly, in deference to my staff members who have yet to turn on the blessed mixers. "Let me do this for you. You're exhausted. And your ex is dying."

"We were never married."

"Okay, whatever—your *man* is dying. I know you need to go and you need to see your son and be with your family. We can go back to our houses now and get our things together. I'll do the driving, and you can sleep in the car."

For a moment, I regard his earnest look, a look that I never expected to see from him, and the sincerity in his face softens my resolve. He doesn't let go of my hand.

"Okay. You're right. I am too tired to make the drive by myself. But just so you know, aside from Aiden and Joey, I don't have a family—well, except for Judy…and one other friend," I add, thinking of Marcus.

"Families are whatever families are."

"Fine. I'll just warn you. You don't really know me. You could be walking into a real big mess."

Then he gives me that dangerous grin, shrugs, and squeezes my hand. "*Bring it.*"

Chapter 20

....

SIX HOURS

....

It took a firm hand and a few well-chosen words from Allyson to get the press out of my face when I left the bakery earlier in the day. The local and national TV news, along with the newspapers from Wilmington to Raleigh, had picked up on all the threads of my story, and everyone, it seems, is curious about the Sunshine Girl and her stormy past. Thank God for Allyson, and thank God I had the sense to hire her. I'm her bitch now, as we say in the clink. I've just ended a call with Allyson, one in which she's told me to stop calling and I have nothing to worry about and that they are rolling along nicely on opening day. *My opening day*. I trust her; I trust them all, even Scooter. I just wish I were there to enjoy the fruits of my labors.

I find it impossible to sleep, with Nate sitting beside me in the driver's seat of my car. Glancing at his extraordinary presence out of the corner of my eye, I still can't believe he's with me. Circumstances that are not of my doing have led him to want to help me, which I find unsettling, especially when he will soon see what's really going on in my life, but at least for now, I have a ride. I'm sure when Nate sees how Aiden's family and I get on like fire and gasoline, he will fling himself on the first bus back to the coast. I wanted him with me, and now that he's here, I don't really know how to handle it. In light of the situation, there's zero sexual chemistry right now. If there were, I would be as depraved as everyone thinks I am, so I guess it's a good thing I'm not feeling it. Anyway, however my circumstances and Aiden's have evolved, I hate not being the one in charge. Maybe that's why I love my business so much; I like being the boss.

Nate drives a lot faster than I do, and the worries I have about Aiden and Joey, and the complications I'm sure to encounter with Aiden's family and Kendra seem compounded by the distance between here and home, even though that distance is thankfully diminishing with each mile he eats up on this road. I have no idea what town we're near; for me, it's like being in a foreign country. All I know is the road is still flat and boring and unattractive, making my heart ache for my mountains even more. I'm going out of my skin; I want to be there right now. I want to see Aiden. I want to see Joey.

I make phone calls to Marcus and Judy, letting them know what's happening with Aiden and that I'm coming home. Judy tells me that she's seen me on the news and read about me in the papers. She's angry that someone ratted me out, and more than curious about my traveling companion, but I can't get into it with Nate sitting right beside me in the car. Marcus shares her sentiment about the media but glosses over it, offering to let us stay at Granny's house. It's in the final stages of renovation, so he will go over today to tidy things up for us. The Snow Drop Inn, one of his bed and breakfast properties, has an available room as well, but I figure with the work Nate has to do, Granny's house would be better suited for us, and I want to go home.

"You should try to sleep," Nate tells me when I'm finished making arrangements. I'm not used to this serious side of him yet; what do I really know about him? Less than he really knows about me. This whole situation is surreal, like being in a Fellini film—two biblically intimate strangers on a curious adventure involving imminent death, family estrangement, and probable calamity as soon as we reach our destination. If that's not a farcical movie trailer, I don't know what is.

"I can't sleep…. I can't stop thinking about Aiden." *I have so many regrets.* I can't even say it to someone I know so little.

He nods thoughtfully. He knows so little about our situation, even thinking we might have been married. Most people would think that. What has Nate gotten himself into?

"I can't imagine why you're helping me. The way you walked away in the driveway yesterday…I wasn't sure what you thought."

He looks over at me. "I had to walk away. I was angry—at both of you. Amy was trying to manipulate the situation and I couldn't let her see that you mattered. What did you tell her anyway?"

I matter? He is sadly misinformed from our brief rendezvous, but it sounds nice, just the same. I shake my head. "You don't know who I am…. I'm the last person on earth you need to be spending time with. I've just gotten you into a big mess with Amy."

He sighs. "Amy *is* a big mess. Like I mentioned before, things with her are over—and were over, for my own personal reasons," he says, glancing in the side view mirror in order to edge out into the left lane to pass the slow-moving car in front of us.

"So why were you with her in the first place?"

"I knew Amy from the TV station when I worked there in production. I knew she was married, but she made it clear she was available. Her husband was screwing around on her. She said she hated her life. For me, the turn-on was the forbidden sex and she wanted it bad." I feel him turn to me, but I can't look at him. "Haven't you ever had an affair with someone? When you both knew it was wrong, but that was exactly what made it so hot?"

A Girl Like That

I can feel his hot tub eyes on me, but all I can do is nod. I did allow myself that kind of indulgence a time or two before I knew the men were married and before Good Elle got the best of me.

He continues. "You know it won't last, and that's even more tantalizing, especially when you're the one in control."

Ah, he is like me after all. "Were you? In control?"

"I was until yesterday. It was my fault that Amy decided to ruin you."

"Your fault?"

"She's getting back at me through you. Amy was willing to discredit you, someone who saved a little boy from the clutches of a sexual predator. She said you had something on her—on us, but I figured whatever it was, you were calling her bluff. You had to. But you need to tell me if you do."

This is why he was mad at me. I sigh, resolving to make a habit of coming clean. In my experience, when you drag someone—like Amy—through the mud, you get twice as dirty and three times as tired, and I'm really tired. I might as well tell him everything. He asked for it. Still, Nate will hate me for sure when he hears this next bit. (It's over with us anyway, so it won't matter what he thinks.) "I went through the photos on your phone that night I was at your house. I sent the selfie she took—the one of you two in bed where you're sucking on her shoulder—to my phone—I don't know why...." After thinking about the picture again, I wonder whether I should get tested for any diseases. I may have made a big mistake not having Nate wear that condom the other night. I thought he was careful, but who knows? Who knows where Amy's been, where her husband's been, and where all Nate has been! Since I didn't turn out to be the best mother, I've had my tubes tied, so getting pregnant isn't on my list of worries with any man, but sexually transmitted diseases are another thing entirely.

258

Nate takes a minute to process what I've told him and clears his throat. "Huh. I don't know why you would do that, but I guess you had your reasons."

"Old habits…insurance, I don't know…and anyway, she sure had plenty on me," I scoff. "See? I used to be her. I was a girl like that. I would have used what I had."

"But you didn't."

"Well, I haven't had a lot of time to expose her since I just found out this morning that she leaked my story, but somebody should. She deserves it…but I know if I did it, it would just come back on you…and since you're giving me a ride home, that doesn't feel right." *And there are other reasons, but we shouldn't get too attached.*

He smiles. "So…you're not like her."

"I still don't understand why you're trusting me…why you're helping me."

"I told you already. You need help and *I'm an excellent driver,*" he says, grinning at his imitation of Dustin Hoffman in *Rain Man.* We do have something in common—we both like movies—and that makes me relax. Maybe I can trust Nate after all.

"Well, thanks. I mean it. I didn't expect you to be nice."

Nate looks at me, bewildered.

"I—I just thought you were a love 'em and leave 'em kind of guy is all…."

"And you're not that kind of girl—a love 'em and leave 'em kind of girl?" he asks, shooting an eyebrow up in reply.

"Well, yeah, I guess I am…obviously. But then we're not talking about *me* being nice."

"You're nice enough…for a guy like me, I guess," he chuckles. "Hell, you're the girl everybody wants to be. Everybody in America knows who the Sunshine Girl is by now. With the media attention you've garnered,

Amy can't touch you, regardless of what you did before. Your history makes you all the more intriguing to the public. You could be any one of them. They love you. Seriously, though? I need you to tell me everything. I mean, if you're not going to sleep, I need you to talk to me."

Nate has a point, and I might as well tell him everything. But before I can begin he continues.

"I can tell you what kind of guy I am. I go after what I want. I don't play games. And yeah, I love 'em and leave 'em if they're not worth my time. And when I'm done, I'm done. But when I'm in, I'm in." He turns to look at me again. It's a good thing we're on a straight, flat road. He couldn't look away from the road like this in Appalachia. "So tell me everything. What exactly did you do?" Oh, my God! Here it is: *What kind of crazy shit did you do back in high school?* And I was naive enough to think no one would ever ask me!

So I start from the beginning, telling him about my mother naming me after *Elle* magazine, how Mrs. MacLeod used to keep an eye on me and call my grandfather when she'd find me outside the trailer making mud pies in the rain because I couldn't get inside, and how my mother eventually ran off with Randy. I picked on the people who picked on me, the ones who needed putting in their places, but I never bullied the pitiful kids. I tell him about Granny and Pa taking me in, how Granny and I always watched movies, about how I loved to act and sing to escape, my sexual obsession with Kyle, how I'd drugged him at the party, and how I just wanted to create some control over my circumstances. I tell him about Aiden, and realizing I was pregnant with Joey when I was in prison, having him, and then giving him to Granny after Aiden had talked me out of giving Joey up for adoption. I explain how hard it's been for me to reach Joey lately. I tell him about Granny's ovarian cancer and taking care of her in our cabin until she died. Once I start talking, I can't seem to stop; it's like vomiting. Maybe I've needed a good, long cleansing talk to get it all out of my system. I've had no one to talk to really, in such a long time, and Nate is a good listener.

"When I was younger, I didn't even realize how my life was different than other people's, until I got to high school and saw how other kids lived." Nate is quiet so I look over at him. "I thought I could run things—and people—and change my circumstances. Still, it wasn't an excuse to have done what I did."

He nods, grimly taking in my story. We both watch the gray stripe of road as the car glides over it, and he is silent, so I continue.

"You and I weren't ever supposed to meet. I saw you that day with Amy in your driveway. You look a lot like Kyle. I've been running from him and what I did to him for half my life…and there you were."

"That's what you meant when you said I had a twin?"

"Yeah." I chuckle, thinking about Mrs. MacLeod's twin boys. "My neighbor, Mrs. MacLeod had twins, Eddie and Brian, but they were fraternal twins. I thought she was lying to me about it because they didn't look alike. God, I used to make her laugh! I didn't trust anybody when I was little." And it's hard now, but I'm getting there. Then I tell him about Aiden and how he took care of Joey while we both lived our separate lives. I tell him that Aiden was my best friend.

Nate nods, keeping his eyes on the road, evaluating my story, my life as I've explained it. He's quiet for a minute and I sit back, closing my eyes after my revelation.

"When are you going to forgive yourself, Elle?" he asks quietly.

"What do you mean?"

"It sounds to me as though you're still in that prison. You need to let go of your past and move on. Can't you give it up?"

I can't talk about this now. Staring out the windshield, I hope he doesn't notice the tears making their way to my eyes. I have to blink them back and pass it off, changing the focus of the conversation.

"Haven't you ever done something you can't let go of?"

"Yep."

"But you're not a criminal?"

"Nope."

"Not even a misdemeanor?"

"No. But I've done things that were difficult to live with."

I remember seeing his discharge papers from the Navy, and wonder whether that's what he's referring to. He doesn't elaborate so I move on.

"Huh. I have to say, I was shocked as hell to hear about Mr. May and Jimmy being ex-cons today. They're the last people I'd have ever thought would be on the wrong side of the law."

"Yeah, I can imagine. They seem like pretty decent guys."

"The best. I was thinking Jimmy might even be Jesus, the way he talks—it's like everything out of his mouth is gospel. And Mr. May is the prince of princes...."

"See? My point taken. You're not all that bad and neither are they. As for me, I wrecked a car or two, got in a few bar fights, slept with the wrong women—oh, but you already know about that. The worst thing I ever did that wasn't an act of war was to get thrown out of a campground because I didn't pay the fees at the office. It was raining and I didn't feel like getting wet...."

"Oh, you were so bad! What's your family like?"

"They're great. Sorry. I don't mean to rub it in, but we're very close."

"Do you come from a big family?"

"Four kids. My parents are still married. I have an older brother named Ronnie—he's married—and two sisters, Sarah Grace and Claire. Sarah Grace has Down Syndrome," he says, glancing at me.

"Wow."

"We treat Sarah Grace like she's anybody else, and she's living a happy and productive life. She still lives at home with my parents in Tennessee. She works and has friends. My parents were good advocates for her. She's awesome," he says and a wistful look crosses his face. "There's something so innocent about her even though she's an adult. We should all be more like that.... My first fight was over Sarah Grace when I was ten years old because another kid was making fun of her." He looks over at me and gives me a wicked grin.

"My first fight was about my mother. I was five. I hit a girl at Sunday school and made her nose bleed."

"Damn! Badass!" he says, offering me his fist to bump.

"My nickname in high school was Badass Barbie. I'm still trying to live that one down. Now you see why I had to move away."

He chortles. "Claire's my youngest sister. She's twenty-four—a special education teacher in Knoxville. She went to UT like I did."

"After you got out of the Navy?"

"Yup. I was unfocused in school. I liked to hunt and fish, shoot guns, and mess around; didn't take school real seriously. I didn't want to waste my parents' money farting around in college, so I joined up. I eventually spent my service in special ops in Afghanistan."

"Special ops?"

"I was a SEAL."

"Oh...." I'm awed, and this time, I don't mind showing it. I knew he was smart and well-built for a reason. And there's a lot more to be said for his character after this revelation. I wasn't as far off the mark as I thought. Maybe my judgment is improving. "I didn't realize…."

"I don't talk about it, probably for the same reasons you don't talk about your imprisonment."

"I seriously doubt that it's the same thing."

"Maybe…maybe not. I'm proud of it, don't get me wrong, but it isn't real pleasant conversation. Anyway, I wanted to do something completely different when I got out, you know—de-stress and try to live a normal life in a quiet place, so I went to school for journalism and you know the rest. I got lucky with my job, you know—doing what I love to do and making a living at it. I guess I was trying to regain some of the control in my life too, just like you are. And I needed to get out of the dark places."

"I can understand that. Sometimes I think it's the very things that shape our lives that we try so desperately to forget," I say, aware that he's nodding thoughtfully beside me. We ride in silence for a moment. My Fellini movie is over and I feel closer to Nate. Glancing over at him, I speak softly, "I'd really be honored for Joey to meet you." Sincerity doesn't come naturally to me and maybe Nate senses it.

"I'd be honored to meet him, too."

The winding road wakes me, my head snapping upright, as I realize with relief that I've slept for hours and finally we are on the approach to home. After taking a moment to orient myself, I check the clock on the dashboard. It's four o'clock and we are climbing the Blue Ridge escarpment, just thirty minutes from the hospital. The ugly reality of Aiden's illness comes springing back to my mind like a slap in the face.

I sigh, trying to focus on what's going to happen in just a few minutes. "Can we stop for flowers? There's a decent grocery store where I can get what I want quickly."

"Yeah, after we stop for food. I'm starving. I bet you are, too."

Nate's right. I realize that he drove on while I slept, not stopping for food even though he was hungry from fear of waking me. As soon as we arrive in the town of Boone, my heart begins to pound as my past life comes flooding in again. At the large intersection, we come to the famous double-decker Wendy's, where Nate pulls in so we can use the restrooms, and then he orders a cheeseburger and fries. I haven't eaten since five o'clock this morning, and the smell of burgers cooking makes my mouth water, so I get one, too. We have been in the car for six hours and both of us are stiff and ready to move. The familiar mountain air is fresh and clear, making me take a deep, cleansing breath. It's almost cool compared to the muggy, salty heat of the coast we left just hours ago.

"I love it here," I murmur, putting on my gray hoodie as we get back into the car and head to the store for flowers.

"I do, too," he says, barely audibly. I can't tell whether he is detached or keenly attuned to me; whatever the case, he is on a mission.

What was I thinking, leaving this place? Were there really so many obstacles I couldn't face? Nobody cares about a clichéd blonde cheerleader with a chip on her shoulder anymore, like an outdated movie character. Was that all there was to my life? I was blending into the woodwork here and I didn't even know it. Maybe that was my problem. Surely, I could've gotten by with Judy and Marcus to keep me company…and Aiden. But Aiden is not long for this world. I can't believe it. I can't deal with it. My fingers smell like onions as I wipe tears discreetly away. I direct Nate to pull over to the left and climb the hill into the parking lot at the Harris Teeter, where I know I'll find a fresh bouquet of seasonal flowers.

In just a few more minutes, we are at the reception desk at the hospital, asking for Aiden's room. We're directed to the correct floor, and at the nurse's desk, where several nurses are darting efficiently around, I ask again for his name. One of the African-American nurses who glances up at me looks familiar; it's Tia something-or-other from high school. She was the bitchy cheer captain on the squad, always sucking up to our teachers and making straight A's. She pretends not to notice me and buries her face in the newspaper, while an older nurse, a man in light blue scrubs, directs us to the proper room.

As soon as I go around the corner, I see a doctor talking to a soldier, making me catch my breath. *Joey.* He looks bigger than I remember. He never used to stand up that straight. His crisp white uniform shirt and black slacks fit him perfectly, showing the result of all his physical training, the black beret covering his neatly buzzed dark hair, which would ordinarily be wavy and messy, like Aiden's. He looks up and I dread his reaction, but it's not at all what I expect.

"Mom. Hey," he says, with a slight acknowledging look to Nate, and reaching out to give me a warm and welcoming hug.

"Hey, Boo," I whisper, unable to prevent myself from using his nickname, which sounds too childish and ridiculous. I feel as if I should salute him, but it would be so inappropriate. "Oh, look at you!"

Joey looks again at Nate. "Joey, this is my friend, Nate Aldridge," I say, knowing he's heard me refer to many men that way—my *friends*, but it's true today. It all feels different. "Nate served as a Navy SEAL in Afghanistan."

"Hey," says Joey, shaking Nate's hand, respect registering instantly on his face. "Nice meeting you."

"Joey," Nate says. "I'm pleased to meet you."

Joey looks back at the doctor, an older man with glasses, whose ethnicity I think must be Indian. "Mom, this is Dr. Chopra, Dad's doctor."

"Hello, I'm Elle McLarin," I say, shaking his hand. I watch his infinitesimal reaction to my name. *The natives have been gossiping.*

266

"We're limiting Mr. Caffey's visitors to just a few family members at a time. He tires easily. You can see him momentarily, but I would urge you to keep your visit short and try not to upset him. His heart is working very hard, and we're afraid he doesn't have much time left. The infection has worn away one of his valves, so it's difficult for him to manage much conversation," Dr. Chopra says firmly but with kindness. Still, I am not prepared for this.

"What?"

"I know," Joey says, understanding my disbelief. "I've only been here a few minutes myself, and I had to leave the room. I just…can't wrap my head around it." His eyes are filled with tears that haven't yet brimmed over, but he lets me hug him again, as much to steady myself as to comfort him. "You should go in," Joey says, and it's then that I'm aware that three people are looking at me from inside the room—Aiden's parents and Kendra. They are glaring actually, and it's not lost on Nate.

"I'll just be out here," he says, pointing with his thumb toward a small sitting room across from the nurse's station.

"Okay, thank you, Nate," I say, hesitating just a moment before heading into the room, where Kendra stands, holding Aiden's hand on one side of his bed, and his mother does the same thing on the other. I haven't seen Kendra this up close in eighteen years. They stare at me as if I am a skunk that has just waddled in to nose around.

"Oh, Lord have mercy, look what the cat done dragged in! It's the Sunshine Girl, comin' in to flaunt herself 'round for all of us to see and admire!" says Martha Caffey, her voice laced with bitterness and hatred. Ordinarily, I would be returning her best go-to-hell look with one of my own, but I try to refrain for Aiden's sake. His mother's mouth is wrinkled and drawn up like a sow's purse from years of sourness. "I knew it was only a matter of time…." She sneers at me. "Did you think anything was comin' to you? 'Cause there ain't nothin' for you, girl. Not from this family. Not now and not ever."

"Martha," Aiden's father warns her in a low but firm voice. He glances at me, not thrilled to see me either, but at least willing to heed the doctor's advice about not upsetting Aiden. Thank God he is a reasonable man. I set the bouquet of mixed flowers on a table by the bathroom door. They regard my gift as though it's just something I have brought to call attention to myself. Kendra's eyes fall for a moment on the Shasta daisies, and then she narrows her eyes with resentment. A high school memory flashes through my mind of when I'd asked Aiden to pick a daisy for me from one of the school's flowerbeds on the way to class. He made a funny show of bowing at the waist when presenting it to me, and I told Kendra he gave it to me, just to make her feel bad. She always liked him. It shouldn't have been a big deal, but it was. It still is.

Aiden is pale and clammy looking, his breathing clearly labored. "You came," he says, a slight smile turning up one side of his mouth. His pale blue hospital gown is soaked with sweat.

"Well, I had to. You didn't answer my calls." I can't think of anything else to say, and he looks confused. *They haven't told him I've called.* I want to rush forward and hold his hand, but Kendra glares at me as if I'm bringing the Ebola virus into the room. She's aged some and grown heavier, but she's still attractive, in her teacher kind of way, wearing the typical printed cardigan and cropped white pants. Her hair is still the same, straight as a stick, medium brown, medium length, and she has the same narrow brown eyes I remember. But there is no bright smile, her best feature, for me. She used to be my friend.

I reach forward and touch the end of Aiden's bed, letting my hand rest on his foot.

"I'll leave," offers Kendra, unable to stomach being in the same room with me, but Aiden's mother doesn't budge, hunkering down on her side of the bed, her doughy arms folded beside his.

"No, Kendra. I want you to stay," Aiden says. "Come here, Elle. I need to tell you something…and I want everybody to hear it." His mother glares at me. He seems so weak. I can't believe he's deteriorated this much since I saw him just weeks ago.

"Aiden…this isn't happening to you!" I blurt out.

"I know…. I should have gone to see about my teeth, like you said."

"It's okay." I try to reassure him.

"No." He looks up at me and speaks urgently. "You were a good wife," he says, measuring each word as if it hurts to talk. He must be delusional. I can't believe what I'm hearing. We weren't married; we never even lived together.

"No," I shake my head, wondering whether his illness has left him confused, glancing a little at his mother, who looks horrified.

"Yes, you were. I reckon we got along as good as most married people." He rests a minute before continuing. "And you've been a good mother. Look at Joey! I'm so proud of him," he says, gasping with the effort and the emotion.

"So am I."

"We've been a family…even though it wasn't the way Joey wanted it. Or me either, really."

"Aiden…" Kendra starts to protest, but he looks at her.

"No. It's true. I love you, Kendra…but I've always loved Elle, too, in my own way…. Elle's Joey's mother, and we are a family…. So when you have my funeral, I want Elle to sit with my family…. She'll sit by Joey and you'll sit by her."

There is a collective gasp, even from me, but it makes my heart swell the way he's taking charge, as sick as he is.

"It's what I want. You heard me say it. You'll both do it. And Mama, don't you go makin' a scene about it."

We nod and Kendra sobs, biting the back of her hand to try and stifle it. Martha is going to have a stroke any minute. Mr. Caffey stands stoically with his large, sun-worn arms crossed over his broad midsection, as though he were the presiding bailiff over this odd proceeding.

"Elle, I want that prayer…the one that we used at Granny's funeral."

"Okay." I nod.

"The Irish blessing. And all the same songs."

"Yeah, okay." I remember Granny's service like it was yesterday, and all the plans Aiden and I made.

"You can plan the whole thing…."

"Okay."

"Joey's good, isn't he?"

"Yeah, he seems to be."

"Hold my hand, Elle," he says. Kendra lets me over to her side of the bed so I can take his hand. "Get Joey," he tells her. His hand feels cold, but the same familiar calluses are there. Though I can't remember the last time I held his hand.

In a moment, I feel Joey move through the room and stand at my elbow.

"Joey, my house will be yours for when you come home from the Army. You remember what I told you, okay? You stay in touch with your mama, you hear? I'm proud of you, son, but you be good to her, and take care of her…like she took care of me and you, all right?"

"Yes, sir. I will. I love you, Daddy." Joey reaches for Aiden's shoulder.

There are too many memories of Aiden flooding into my heart right now—that goofy, shy boy who gave me the daisy, the brave young man who took me up on the mountain to help me save face the day I was turned in, the devoted young father, building block towers with Joey only to have them repeatedly knocked over, sending them both into laughter. He was the man who grew to resent me, but who always dropped whatever he was doing to traipse through the mountains in search of our lost son, the man who patiently answered all my questions about electronics, settling Granny's estate, and what to do when my car broke down…. I should have been nicer to him.

"Oh, Aiden…I love you too. You've been my best friend," I whisper to him, stroking his hair, while Martha averts her eyes. "I'm sorry…for so many things."

"I know…. You were my best friend, too." He closes his eyes. The male nurse is back in the room, moving about unobtrusively, checking the intravenous drip and the machines that beep periodically, telling him what he needs to know. He gives Martha room to swab Aiden's forehead with a washcloth.

"Let's give him a break now, okay, folks?" he says, softly, checking the bag of urine that hangs off the side of the bed and making notes in Aiden's chart. His nametag identifies him as *Jim*. Martha sobs into her hands and mops her face, as Ward Caffey takes her shoulders and guides her out of the room. It takes me a minute to get my feet working.

Aiden's eyes are closed. The nurse glances up at me, hearing me sniff.

"I wouldn't go far," he says to me kindly.

Chapter 21

THE WAY WE WERE

There is nothing more awful than hearing grown men cry. I understand it, and I expected it when Aiden passed, but watching his father cry out and crumble to his knees and seeing my son, the soldier, sobbing with racking shoulders is more than I can take. I should be used to losing people by now. Maybe I am. I'm not crying. Besides, someone has to take care of them all.

Nate stands in the small waiting room with us while I hold my son's shaking shoulders. Nate watches me for signs of similar collapse, but he seems relieved that I'm holding it together. I have never cried when people pass. I figure it's all out of my control, and it's not for me to understand why, so I just accept it. Even though I feel sorry for myself, knowing I'll miss them, it seems useless to shed tears. Crying never brought anybody back as I can recall. Granny told me I'd see her in heaven, and I hope she's right, though I kind of doubt I'll be invited if I understand what heaven is about. The Caffeys and Kendra have chosen to have their own bereavement gathering in Aiden's room, but I can't be in there anymore. I can't look at what's left of him, and they don't want me.

"You can come and stay with us tonight," I tell Joey. "Nate and I are staying at Granny's house. Marcus got it ready to rent and it was still available, so…."

Joey draws away and wipes his eyes with the palms of his hands. He takes the tissues Nate offers and sighs deeply.

"I told Grandpa I'd stay with them when he picked me up at the airport. Chip and Speck are there, so…."

"Okay. Whatever you want to do…. Chip and Speck are Joey's bird dogs," I explain to Nate, who doesn't need an explanation, but I feel the need to prattle on, to fill the awful silences. He nods. Poor Nate. What a disaster for him. What a disaster for *us*. I can't believe any of this.

Glancing outside the door, I'm aware that the nurses at the desk are talking about us. Of course they are; Aiden has just died, and they are discussing our situation. Tia has her eyes on me, which makes me uncomfortable, as if I shouldn't be here. But like Aiden said, I'm part of this family too. Jim has collected Aiden's personal belongings and has come into the room.

"I have Mr. Caffey's things. Would you like to take them?"

"I think his mother would prefer to be the one to take them."

"She said to give them to you." Something in his face tells me she's not dealing with this well.

"Oh, okay." I reach for the bag. For such a big man, it's such a small bag of clothes—a pair of jeans, a shirt, underwear, shoes and socks, a wallet and a watch. "Thanks, Jim. And thank you for everything you did."

"I'm so sorry for your loss, ma'am," he says, laying a hand on my shoulder. "You too, sir," he says to Joey and shakes his hand.

"Thank you," says Joey, pulling himself together, the way the Caffey men do—the way soldiers do. This is the third person in Joey's life to depart this world, and he is so young. I suppose being in the Army, he will get used to losing those he cares about.

Nate senses this too, so he puts an arm around Joey's shoulder. "I'm sorry, man."

Joey nods. "Well, I guess I'll go on with Grandma and Grandpa."

"Okay, honey. We'll talk in the morning, all right?"

"Yes, ma'am," he says and hugs me one more time before he leaves the room.

Nate packs his computer back into his backpack, slinging it over one shoulder.

"Are you all set?" he asks gently.

"I think so…" I say, as we head out the door of the family room. Joey has never called me *ma'am*. I hesitate and peer back into Aiden's room, where his parents and Kendra are watching him, as if by some great miracle he will wake up and it will all have been a bad dream. "We're leaving," I announce to no one in particular, but Ward looks up and gives me a silent nod. "I'll call you tomorrow." Another nod. The women do not look at me. I feel numb. Joey gives me a press of his lips. I wave.

Nate's hand goes around the back of my neck in a supportive gesture as we walk out of the nurses' station, where I feel Tia's eyes unmistakably glued to my back, or maybe they are on Nate. I've noticed that women look at him when he enters a room. I certainly did. Then it dawns on me that she might notice his resemblance to Kyle. It is rather obvious, and here I am, back in Boone with someone who looks like the boy I drugged in high school. Maybe that's what she was reading about in that newspaper. I will never get away from that. And now my best friend is gone. Joey's father is gone. There will be no more ties to this group of people for me. It was for the best that I left this town.

In the elevator, Nate takes me in his arms and wraps me in the most comforting hug I have ever felt. I feel his hand stroke the top of my head and the brush of his lips. For a moment, I let myself drift in the solace of his embrace, letting my tears flow. It's awful that I'm crying for myself and not for Aiden. Or maybe I am. I don't even know. "I'm so sorry," he whispers.

"Thank you," I say, hugging him back.

As the doors open and we walk into the hall leading to the lobby, there seems to be somewhat of a commotion. In a nonchalant gesture, Nate pulls my hoodie up over my head and tells me to look at my phone and pretend like I'm texting. I dig it out of my purse and do as I'm told. In the next moment, he steers me over near the door of the gift shop and pulls me into one more of those hugs, murmuring into my ear, "I think you were set up for a media ambush." I can't see, but I can sense that several men and women move as a pack past us toward the elevator, where they are apparently waiting for me. *Thank you, Tia.*

"Come on," he whispers again, his arm draped casually around my neck, holding me close and slowing our pace to a saunter out the front door, past several parked media vans in the drop off area under the portico and to my car in the parking deck. It's dark now, so it's unlikely that anyone can make out who I am in this hood, and they are probably expecting me to be alone, or with Aiden's family.

Nate starts the car. "Keep your head down—go through your purse or something, like you don't care about their vans," he says, driving right by the vehicles where a news team is getting its equipment together, maybe taking a different tack by staking out the parking lot. I think for an instant about the decal in my window, but no one has noticed it.

"So long, dudes!" Nate grins as soon as we've cleared the vans.

"Very smooth." I want to smile, but it evades me. He sighs and takes my hand.

"Food?"

"Eh, I guess we should eat."

"Absolutely. Our safest bet is drive-thru."

"Okay, but not another burger."

"A'ight, tacos it is," he says, and in a few minutes, we are exiting the local Taco Bell parking lot with our late night snack. It's the only thing open at this hour. Quietly, I direct Nate to my grandparents' house, where several minutes later, we pull up into the driveway of their enchanting cabin nestled into the dark hillside. Marcus has been gracious enough to leave the porch light on for us.

"Wow!" Nate says, that bright grin of his spreading across his face in the moonlight. "What a great place!" He's impressed by the stone foundation and bent twig front porch with rocking chairs where we all used to sit and talk on long, cricket-filled summer evenings, including Aiden. The sloping roof with three matching dormers at the top gives the cabin a cozy, welcoming look, as if lots of love waits inside. I'm aware of a widening of Nate's pupils when he looks at me again, as if he's catching a glimpse of the kind of woman I am, the kind who would give all of this up, and wondering why.

"I know; it's pretty great, isn't it?" I am smiling now, remembering, yet seeing it from a new perspective, until my eyes come to rest on the dumpster at the top of the driveway. "Except for that monstrosity. Marcus wasn't kidding when he said they'd just finished."

"Well, at least the inside should look good."

"Let's go see," I say, removing the hood from my head and getting out of the car. Nate manages our bags while I carry the bag of food, Aiden's belongings, and my hang-up bag with a couple of dresses. My body feels like lead. I climb the stairs like an old woman and sort through the keys on my ring. "I still have my key."

"Of course you do," Nate grins, his eyes glinting at me in the light of the half moon. I open the door and switch on the light, surprised by what I see. The original wall has been knocked out, opening up the main living area into the kitchen. The furniture is rustic and new, complementing the warm pine walls. In the kitchen, I run my hand down cool, smooth granite countertops. They are dark brown with lighter, warm designs in the stone, like unexpected, underwater blossoms peering up at us. Cabinets have been updated with windowed doors, displaying pretty dishes, and fashionable new drawer pulls replace the others. Stainless steel appliances stand efficiently in place of Granny's old ones, tying the room together.

My mouth is hanging open and I laugh at Nate's assessment of my reaction.

"I can't believe this! Their place never looked so good. It's really different," I say, noticing the hand-built farm table with a green glass bowl of my favorite bronze-colored pears waiting in the center. I remember Granny's old table that's in storage, waiting for me to use for myself—the one where Aiden and Joey and I used to sit when he'd come over for dinner on Sundays. I set down the bag of dinner and go into the bedroom to see what changes await there. I notice a new mattress on the queen-sized bed and new bedside tables and lamps. Granny's homemade curtains are still at the windows. In the adjoining bathroom, Marcus had the good sense to leave the 1950s ceramic tile in place, while updating the vanity sink and replacing fixtures and mirrors.

"I love it," I murmur, hanging my bag of dresses in the bedroom closet and dropping the bag of Aiden's clothing. A quick tour of the upstairs reveals nothing much new other than updated bathroom fixtures and new mattresses on the beds with the same handmade quilts I grew up with, along with Granny's cutwork curtains at the windows. Most of our personal pictures, the ones I have in storage, are gone. Instead, there are fresh, pleasing paintings of the mountains on the walls and mirrors and lamps in just the right places. One picture, a familiar framed magazine cover in my bedroom catches my eye, making me laugh. I should have kept that one, too. The whole thing is simple and not overdone, and I like the changes.

"This was my room, and Joey's was across the hall."

"Where would he stay now…now that you've moved?" He must think I'm awful for giving up this place, leaving Joey stranded.

"Aiden's. Joey stayed there more than he stayed here—when he got to be a teenager. He had his own room there, and they kept his dogs over there in Aiden's fenced in yard." I chuckle. "I think they slept in the bed with him, actually."

"Does it still feel like home?" Nate asks, running a hand behind his neck. He must be exhausted. I know I am. My body aches all over. I almost feel sick.

"Yes, in a way…only better. Granny and Pa would have loved all this." I hug my arms, thinking Marcus was sweet to leave Granny's quilts and curtains like he did. It's still her place after all, and people will like her charming touches. I lead the way back downstairs and we settle at the new counter on barstools, where I force down a taco and watch as Nate makes quick work of his two burritos. A bottle of wine and two glasses sit out on the counter with a note from Marcus.

Food in fridge for breakfast. Cold cuts for sandwiches. Dinner coming tomorrow from your cousin Judy. Welcome home! M

"How nice!" I say, fingering one of the pears in the glass bowl. I am too tired to eat it.

"That is nice. But that wine is going to wait until tomorrow," Nate tells me.

"Yes, it is. I'm so tired now, I can hardly hold my eyes open." My face falls into my hands as I prop my elbows on the counter.

I watch Nate take our trash to the sink and explore the cabinets, finding the trashcan, the way Pa used to clean up for Granny after a meal. Suddenly, I want Aiden to see all these changes. My heart sinks again, for the hundredth time today, knowing he's gone now, and he won't ever see it. They are all gone, and none of them will ever see it. A sob comes from some unexpected place and I cover my face, letting myself cry for a minute. *How could I have left this place?*

Silently, Nate flips off lights and takes my hand. In the bedroom, I slip off my sandals and wipe my eyes and nose with tissues from a box on the bedside table. He moves our bags to the floor with Aiden's clothes as I collapse onto the bed, fully clothed and without brushing my teeth. This is Granny's bed, the same one in which my mother was conceived, from where she gave me her best advice, and where I'd held her hand until she'd gone across.... Remembering all that is oddly comforting, making my eyes fill with tears again, but I am too tired to cry anymore. Then the lamp goes off and I feel Nate's comforting arm come around me from behind as he draws me close to him. I sniff, feeling a kiss on my head and a blanket settle softly over me, then hearing words whispered tenderly into my ear.

"Goodnight, sweetheart."

There is light coming through the crack between the curtains when I open my eyes. I have not moved all night. It's hard to open my eyes; they feel glued shut. Wearing waterproof mascara for over twenty-four hours will do that to you. Then it hits me that Aiden has died. I want to squeeze my eyes shut and go back to sleep, but I know there is no escaping what waits for me today. Realizing I am alone, I sit up, wondering what happened to Nate. Maybe he ran for it while he had the chance. I would have.

My feet land on the soft shag rug beside the bed, and then I walk stiffly across the familiar, worn wooden floors into the kitchen where he apparently fixed coffee before he fled. A pottery mug sits on the counter, so I pour myself a cup before wandering around looking for Nate. The front door is open, through which I see him standing out on the porch, wearing the same jeans and his pullover from last night, gazing out across the valley where sheep are grazing in the lush green pasture across the road: summertime in my mountains. The smell of fresh mountain air is like no other.

Hearing me come out the door, he turns, a hand in his pocket, his own pottery mug halfway to his mouth. "Oh, good morning. I didn't hear you get up. I was checking for paparazzi. I believe the coast is clear."

"I thought you left."

"I tried. Couldn't get a cab all the way out here," he says without missing a beat.

I chuckle and make my way to my favorite rocking chair. Nate joins me and takes the one beside me, Granny's chair. We creak back and forth companionably for a minute, taking in Granny's summer flowers in the front yard, where Nate silently points out a hummingbird darting in and out of black and blue salvia. In the sun, three yellow swallowtails pick their way over the crowns of echinacea and asclepias—purple coneflower and butterfly weed—helping themselves to nectar, while pollinating the flowers in front of the showy, green Christmas ferns that edge the woods. I look for the May apple and wild trillium that hide in the shade beneath the trees, making a forest for fairies, like Granny used to tell me when I was little. The familiar rhododendrons pay homage around the yard and bloom at the base of the porch, their full saucer-like pink blossoms fashioning corsages for the wildwood princesses they are, lending a lush coolness at our feet. Seeing it all comforts me, making me breathe more deeply here. The sweet, musky scent of dew-kissed earth and decomposed flora is my reward.

"How are you?" he asks tentatively.

Resting my head against the back of my chair, I close my eyes and feel the warmth of the coffee mug in my hands. Strangely, I feel comfortable around Nate, as if I could tell him things and he would understand. "Oh, I don't know. Awful."

"I can imagine. Your man died."

"I can't believe Aiden's gone. But somehow I slept like a baby."

"I don't think you moved. When I checked on you this morning, you were right where I left you."

"Where did you sleep?"

"In your room…. I wasn't sure that Joey might not show up and want his room, so…."

I think about his previous offer of a do-over, which makes me smile. That is definitely not happening now. I know that sex and love are entirely two different things. I've had enough sex in my life and not enough love, so I do realize the lack of love in my life, and so should Nate. So why is he still here? I glance at him.

"You didn't know what you were getting yourself into, did you?"

"What? With Aiden's family or with you?"

"Well, both."

"Yeah, I figured it would be like this." He glances at me and then returns his eyes to the pastoral scene. "I read that article in the newspaper. You told me everything. And if you don't like Aiden's family and they don't like you, then you only have to deal with them for a few more days."

I nod. "Yep."

He takes a sip of his coffee. "And like I told you, I need some time to get some work done, and you needed a ride, so I figured I'd kill two birds. Plus, the scenery here is off the chain!"

"Well, I'm real new to this hero stuff, but you seem to have it down real well."

He laughs.

"Is this like a mission for you, or something?"

"Are you trying to give me a big head?"

"No, it's just…in my experience, people aren't usually this helpful."

"I wouldn't say that. Seems to me, from what I saw in your bakery yesterday morning, you have a ton of fans in Wilmington. And Marcus let you stay here. Judy's bringing dinner." He shrugs as if his point has been made. He is still wondering why I left.

"Huh. Yeah. I've always been able to count on those two. They're the best…. Maybe things are changing for me."

He turns and gives me his molten, blue-eyed gaze. "Yeah, maybe they are."

While I gulp quietly, his cell phone rings in his pocket and he takes it out, checking the screen.

"Sarah Grace," he says to me and answers with a cheery, "Hey, girl! What's up?"

It makes me smile to imagine his sister on the other end of the call. Watching his eyes dance at the sound of her voice, I can hear her talking to him when a large, brown SUV pulls into my driveway. I sip my coffee and watch, thinking the driver will back out and turn around the way people sometimes do. Or not. Crap! Surely it's not another reporter!

"I'm in the mountains with one of my friends…. Yes, it's a girl. A very nice girl. You'd like her," Nate goes on, grinning at me, as I watch the vehicle come to a stop, and the driver's door opens. I stand to walk down the steps to greet the driver, whose eyes are on the monster dumpster in the yard. Hopefully, whoever it is will do something about getting it removed.

Halfway down the steps I freeze, half-listening to Nate's conversation with Sarah Grace, asking her what she's got planned for the day. The man standing beside the SUV, wearing jeans and a short-sleeved shirt, runs fingers through his unruly hair and closes his car door. When he removes his sunglasses, I realize that it's Kyle Davis. Numbly, I walk toward him, for lack of a better alternative. Normally, I would turn and run, but he's seen me already and I'm halfway there. I can feel the caked on makeup from yesterday screaming out to be noticed—and my hair—oh, what the hell!

"Hi. *Elle?*" He looks as shocked and confused as I feel.

"Kyle…. Hi."

"Hey. Uh—Marcus told me the guys had left the dumpster here. We'd specifically told them to remove everything before the guests arrived last night. I'm sorry about the mess. I've got a call in to the company to come and get it right now."

"You're working on this project?"

"Yeah. Marcus hired my firm to do the renovations. We, uh, work together a lot. I didn't expect you to be here, though…." He looks at me with such bewilderment. I must look awful since I've slept in the same clothes I've had on for almost an entire day. I don't even know what time it is. I try to hoist my shoulders back and look decent. *Play the part.*

"Oh! This is my grandparents' house—well, my house, or it was. I sold it to Marcus and moved to the beach to open a new bakery and…."

"Really? I think I heard something about that. Where?"

"Wilmington."

"Right…Chelsea's sister lives there. I didn't know this was your house. I've driven past it and admired it for years, but I never knew that you lived here."

I'm sure you were expecting a trailer. Well, there was that, too. "Yeah, I've lived here since I was five years old…." Kyle glances at the porch, making me follow his gaze. Nate is still on the phone with his sister, but standing now, leaning casually over the rail, as if he belongs here. Good lord, he might as well lift his leg and pee on the porch post to mark his territory! I can't determine whether they notice their resemblance, but I'm starting to feel as if I'm back in that Fellini movie again.

"Well, the house looks great! Did that girl, Elise, design the renovation?" Now it's all coming back to me. Elise worked with Kyle. She was also Michael's baby mama, and they were dating while Michael and I were dating. I guess she didn't know he wasn't exclusively dating her because one night she came over to see why he didn't show up for the opening of Marcus's Snow Drop Inn, and when she saw me there in my tank top and yoga pants, the shit hit the fan. When I heard that Elise and Kyle worked together, I thought it was just par for the course, given the drama I tended to attract. Marcus never made the connection between Kyle and me, and I sure wasn't going to tell him! So here we are again in another awkward, small town moment.

"Oh, no, Elise doesn't work with us anymore. Faith Maynard designed it. I'm glad you like it."

"Well, Marcus was really nice to let me stay here," I say while Kyle's eyes drift back up to Nate. Nate, who is still listening to his sister on the phone, gives me a little pump of his eyebrows and a special kind of smile. I feel myself straighten up just a little. Suddenly, I feel prettier. I'm rather sure I have the better of the two of them on my porch.

"Yeah, Marcus told me a family member was in the hospital."

"It was Aiden."

"Right, Aiden. You and Aiden...."

"We have a son together. Joey."

"Is Aiden okay?"

"Um, no—he isn't...." *How do you tell people something like this?* "Aiden passed away late last night."

"What? No!"

"I'm sorry to be the one to tell you, Kyle. He had endocarditis. He was sick for a while, but they didn't know what it was. When the doctors figured it out, it was too late."

Kyle looks dumbfounded; I could easily have slapped him in the face.

"Oh, no! I'm so sorry, Elle," he says. He doesn't hug me, but he looks like he wants to. It's what nice people do, and he's always been a nice guy. But then we haven't been on the best of terms for obvious reasons. The two of us flounder for words, and I can hear Nate going discreetly inside the cabin. Kyle gestures to the dumpster. "You don't need to be dealing with this mess while you're going through something like this. Again…I apologize. My guys are on their way and they'll clear it out in no time, and you can get on with your business. I'm sorry I disturbed you."

"No, it's—it's fine. It's nice to see you again."

"Yeah, you too. I wish it were under better circumstances."

We've never had this civil a conversation before and it feels good.

"I know…. I guess you need to tell Glen, huh?"

"Yeah, absolutely. Glen'll be crushed. They were good friends. We were friends in high school, too, but I hadn't seen Aiden in years. So how are you doing?"

I shove my hands in the back pockets of my jeans. "I guess I'm on auto-pilot. Gotta plan the service and all…with his parents. We don't exactly get along…and Kendra's back in the picture."

He nods. "Yeah, I heard that too—from Glen."

"It's still a small town."

"Yeah, it is."

"Listen…Kyle; I've wanted to talk to you for a long time…about what happened. I was so awful to you and to Chelsea back then. I know what I did to you was horrible. You could have died. I knew it back then and…."

"You apologized to me already…that night at the prom—yeah, it was you and Aiden."

"Right, but after I went to prison…." He winces slightly at the mention of prison. I doubt anyone he knows has ever been on the wrong side of the law. He's lived a charmed life since high school, even marrying the princess of charmed lives, and their lives have been perfect ever since. They probably live in a perfect house on their perfect mountain land that none of them will ever be forced to leave. I can't think about it while I try to make amends. "I really did learn a lot about myself and a lot about what I'd done. I just wanted you to know that whatever good I can do can't make up for what I did."

Kyle gives me that stoic look that I'm used to seeing from him. You can never tell what he's thinking. "Yeah, well, you served your time, Elle. Maybe it's time to just turn it loose, you know?"

"I've heard that one before, believe me. It's harder than it seems."

"Well, from what I hear, you're doing some pretty good things. I saw you on the news about saving that little boy. I've been following the story in the newspaper too."

"And I guess you saw in the paper what they wrote about me and what I'd done to you."

He looks away. His name wasn't mentioned, but it must have been a shock to read the article, all the same, just when we were all trying to forget. "Yeah. I saw it. I guess you feel as though you'll never get out from under it."

"Sometimes I do." *And actually, I feel as though I'm wearing a scarlet letter, but in my case, it's a blaze-orange "P"—for prison.*

"Well, even when I read it, I felt bad for you. Nobody needs to dredge all that up again. Maybe you just need to know that I forgive you. But you also need to forgive yourself."

I have heard this as well. Maybe it's true. Coming from Kyle, it should mean more, but it's Nate's voice that resonates in my head.

"That's really sweet, Kyle. Thanks for saying that."

Another car approaches and slows, making a crunchy turn into my driveway and pulling up beside Kyle's vehicle. This may be Aiden's father's car. I spot Joey's black beret, realizing that wherever he goes on leave, he has to wear his uniform.

"Oh, this is Joey now."

"He's in the Army?"

"Yes. Boot camp. He's on emergency family leave from basic training at Fort Hood."

"Wow! I can't believe he's that old."

"Your kids are how old now?"

"The twins are nine—and we have a baby girl."

The emotion in his voice when he mentions the baby girl makes me feel a little stab of envy. Could his life not be more perfect? I play it off as most women in my position would. "Aw! I always wanted a girl." *What would it be like to be you?*

"Well, I can vouch that it's not too late!"

"Nah, I think all that's over for me." *Now that my tubes are tied, I'm pretty sure of it.* "But that's real nice for you."

Joey has walked up to join us.

"Joey, this is Kyle Davis. Kyle and his company have done the renovations on the cabin. You'll love it," I say, giving him a hug before he shakes Kyle's hand.

"Hi, Joey. It's nice meeting you. I'm sorry to hear about your dad. We knew each other from high school, where I also knew your mom." Oh, boy.

"Hey," says Joey. If Joey recognizes Kyle's name from what he knows about my young adult criminal behavior, it doesn't register on his face, nor does the fact that Kyle looks like Nate. Maybe it's just me. Joey looks tired and pitiful, even for a soldier, and I hug him again. He needs to get inside.

"Thanks, Kyle, for everything. It was great to see you again. Tell Chelsea I said hello."

"Sure. You take care, Elle. I'll be seeing you in the next few days, I'm sure. Let me know if you need anything," he says, taking a card from his wallet and handing it to me.

"Thanks," I say, giving him a relieved smile. We could be friends one day.

Maybe.

When pigs fly.

Chapter 22

HOLD ON LOOSELY

When Joey and I enter the front door, we are greeted by the smell of bacon and eggs cooking. The corners of my mouth turn up at the memory of the photo I stole of Nate in his boxer shorts, cooking Amy's breakfast, and here he is in Granny's newly renovated kitchen—that Kyle did—wielding a spatula for my son and me. So weird.

"I was getting hungry. Hope you don't mind," Nate says as toast pops up from the toaster. I always made toast in the oven using the broiler, but we have modern conveniences now, it appears.

"Thank you! I'll pour the coffee. Need a warmer?" I ask, feeling an intimacy with Nate that only bacon and eggs can create. He seems comfortable, commandeering breakfast in the newly remodeled kitchen. Marcus has left Granny's seasoned cast iron skillet, which Nate lifts effortlessly. I forget that bachelors have to cook for themselves.

"Sure. Joey, how do you like your eggs?"

"Over easy," shrugs Joey. I wish he could get out of that uniform.

"Me too. Over easy," the way Nate says it makes it sound like more than the way he likes his eggs, but maybe I'm imagining it. "Elle?"

"Over easy, please," I say, preferring mine scrambled, but why be difficult?

"Over easy it is…. My twin?" Nate murmurs as I set his coffee beside the stove within easy reach. I noticed that he drank it black from before, like I do.

"Yeah…. That was Kyle. We had a nice talk. He and Aiden were friends so he'll probably be at the funeral."

"And you're okay?" Nate asks discreetly in my ear.

"Yeah," I murmur back, enjoying the closeness.

"He's why you left, isn't he?" Nailed. Before I can draw breath to answer, I realize that Joey appears to be listening.

"What's all this?" asks Joey, referring to the laptop computer and the arrangement of hardware on the kitchen table. There is music playing from the computer. It sounds classical, but like nothing I recognize.

"Oh, that's my work. I'm putting together a show."

"Huh. What kind of show?" asks Joey.

"*Carolinas' Catch…with Bo Hauser.*"

"Whoa! Really? I watch—well I used to watch that every Saturday morning. Daddy and I did," says Joey, his voice dying out.

"I'm the field producer for the show."

"No kidding?" My shy son perks up as Nate slides our eggs out of the pan and onto three plates while I place forks and napkins on the table.

"Yep. I get to fish all over the world, and then film the shows and put them together, so you have something to watch on the weekends." Nate sets Joey's plate on the table and my son sits down, totally enraptured by my friend.

"Cool. How'd you get a job like that? What does this do?" asks Joey, pointing to a contraption on the table.

"That's one of my external drives. I have five of them. Each one has a different thing, like music, or a particular film sequence. There is so much material I have to name the drives to keep them straight."

Joey looks at the different devices, reading the titles. "Woolly Bugger, Ugly Mother, Fat Albert?"

Nate picks up one of the drives, which is about the size of a deck of cards. "Yeah, I named them after my favorite fly-fishing lures. It's easier to keep up with the drives if I name them—outwardly and internally. That way, when I'm integrating all the parts as I'm building a show, I can find what I'm looking for. I have so much music and video to keep up with. See, I write the show as a story, like you would if you were writing an article, and then I can find the pieces of video and music I want, and insert them where I need them. This is a special, built-up computer that uses terabytes, since I use so much memory. It costs about four grand. You and most people use gigabytes, but I use terabytes, which is a lot more space than you'd ever use—in your whole life, probably."

"Wow. Cool," says Joey, taking a bite of his bacon, while Nate slides the various apparatuses out of the way so we can all sit at the table.

"So, what's going on at Ward and Martha's house this morning?" I ask Joey.

He looks uneasy. "They want us to meet them at the church around one-thirty to plan the funeral...after church is over. The funeral's probably going to be on Tuesday."

"Okay." My heart races when I think about being gone from the bakery for that long.

"I had to leave. I didn't like the conversation. Grandma's taking Valium so it's better than it was last night."

Nate and I share a knowing look. The talk must have been about me.

"You can stay here, you know," I tell Joey.

"Yeah. I brought my bag," he says, looking down at his eggs. He looks at me, confirming my impression that I've been the topic of conversation.

Joey shifts his eyes. "I can't go back over there. Is it all right with you if I bring the dogs over here?"

Hell, I'm not doing the cleaning. "Of course." I feel my face grow warm with embarrassment in front of Nate. I'd rather not discuss this anymore.

"Can we drop Grandpa's car off on the way? I told him we would."

"Sure."

Suddenly, I've lost my appetite, but I try to finish my breakfast since Nate was nice enough to cook it for us. When we've finished, Joey and I thank Nate, remove the dishes, and start washing up at the sink. Nate begs off to take a shower and heads upstairs, giving us some privacy.

Joey surprises me by starting the conversation. "Mama, I know Daddy was right, telling them that you're part of the family. Just...don't get your feelings hurt if Grandpa and Grandma don't see it that way."

"Look; I stopped letting them get to me a long time ago, Boo," I tell him, as he hands me the frying pan from the stove. Running the warm sudsy water in the sink, I'm reminded of how mundane chores often lend themselves to intimate conversations, as if a holiness exists within the ritualized motions of the washing, rinsing, and drying of dishes, the same way it is when Jimmy Burns paints a wall. Despite the fact that Joey and I have done this task countless times before with limited conversation, I feel a budding, new connection with him at this particular moment.

"What did your daddy mean in the hospital when he said, 'remember what I told you'?"

Joey is quiet for a moment, making me think he won't answer, the way he does sometimes. I know he hears me, but he has this irritating habit of not responding, like Pa used to do. Maybe Joey is the apple off Pa's tree. I never thought of it that way before. Finally, he speaks slowly. "Daddy talked to me before I left for boot camp...about you. He said if I ever fall in love with a girl like you, I should try and let go if I could. But if I couldn't, then don't plan on holding on too tight. I think that's what he was trying to do."

It all makes sense now, like in Aiden's favorite song—38 Special— "Hold on Loosely." He liked that old song and used to sing along when it came on the radio. I didn't think it had to do with me. I guess I was wrong. I was wrong about a lot of things.

I begin tentatively. Joey and I haven't talked this much—ever. It must be the soap suds. "I'm sorry our lives didn't turn out the way you wanted, Joey," I sigh, rubbing the sudsy sponge over the pan, rinsing it, and handing it to him to dry.

Joey nods. Again, I don't think he's going to respond, but then he says softly, "You know, when I used to go off into the mountains by myself, I'd have this fantasy that you and Daddy'd get back together. I thought if I stayed away long enough, you'd have to get together and come a-huntin' for me. I guess I never really thought it would happen, but then you left." He turns narrowed eyes toward me. "I was mad at you."

"Yeah, I know you were. I was mad at me too. I guess all of us were wanting to live out our what-ifs and continually being disappointed. You know I had to leave, honey. Nobody was ever going to let me live down my past up here."

He nods. "I know." Then he says, "I saw Aunt Sally. She told me about you, and how you found that little boy. I don't get to watch TV, but she told me. She saw you on the TV. They're calling you the Sunshine Girl. She said you saved him. They're saying those men did awful things to that little boy, and that there were other kids, too. She showed me the newspaper articles—and the one about you, too."

"Did you know all the details—about why I was in prison?"

"Yeah. Grandma told me." *Of course she did.* "She told me a long time ago. She told me about your mother too, and how she ran off and left you with Granny and Pa…and…."

"I guess she told you I never knew my father."

"Yeah. She said he blew himself up in a meth lab…. Is that true?"

"I guess it is. That's what I heard, too. It doesn't matter, Joey. None of it matters, except for what we do from now on, okay? Even though you and I are in different places, I'm not going to *leave* you like my mother left me."

Joey studies me, maybe trying to believe what I've said. Then he speaks. "When I was a kid, hearing stuff about you from the kids at school really pissed me off, and I was mad at you too—for a long time. I didn't like it either that you dated other guys and not Daddy. My buddies at boot camp tell their stories too…stories that make ours sound like a fairy tale compared to some of the crazy stuff I've heard lately. Right now, it makes me angry that Grandma and Grandpa are still mad at you, when Daddy forgave you for all of that stuff."

I have a rare opportunity to make my relationship right with my son. "I'm sorry I was such a disappointment. People say you can't choose your family, but you can choose how you want to relate to the people in it." I watch him wiping the counter with the sponge, with slow, deliberate motions. "You've changed, Joey. I'm so glad you finally wrote to me. It made me feel so good to hear from you. I was singing that day that the little boy heard me and broke out the window, yelling to me for help. I wouldn't have been singing if it hadn't been for you and your letter. You can take part of the credit for me discovering him."

Joey looks at me while he dries the coffeepot with the dishtowel. "I'm glad it was you, Mama. I'm glad you were the one who found him."

"Me too, baby." I smile and then shake my head. "Gosh, I can't call you that anymore. You're a man, a soldier. I'm so proud of you, and so was your daddy."

Joey gives me a wan smile, and for the moment, he's not a soldier, but just my boy. He is eighteen years old, but he is my child. He has just lost his father and he doesn't know what to do. I need to call in at the bakery, but even more than that, I need to take care of my son. He hangs the dishtowel on the hook at the sink, and I rest my hand on his shoulder.

"I don't want you to feel alone, Joey. I promise you, you'll always have me. I'm not really going anywhere." It must be little comfort for him, thinking that was what he expected of Aiden as well. "I guess it's hard to make plans now, isn't it?" I ask gently.

He shrugs. "I don't know. Grandpa said that I'll have to wait until they settle Daddy's estate. He's the executor of the will, and then whenever things are all settled, I'll have the house to myself. I'll have to make the house payments, but maybe by then I'll have a job in the service. Grandpa will help me manage it, and he'll take care of Speck and Chip until I can get back here to do it. Or…maybe I'll just sell the house, like you did."

I study him for a moment. "You weren't really planning to come back here—ever, were you?"

Joey's eyes meet mine. "No. I wasn't going to come home—well, to live anyway. I figured everything'd be right where I left it 'til I was ready to visit. I never figured on Daddy dyin'…" His voice breaks off.

"No. I guess not. No one did."

"You just never know, do you?"

"No. You have to make the best of everything you do. I can't say I did. I'm trying to start over and make things right. I hope you can see that, you know?"

"Yeah, Mama. I can. I mean, you have your life to live," he says, shrugging his shoulder and his eyes cutting to the upstairs of the cabin.

"Oh—no, Nate isn't a part of my life. He's just—a neighbor, and he was kind enough to drive me up here because I was so tired, you know, with the bakery and all...."

"Oh. I thought he was that guy's brother—you know the one in the driveway who did the work on the house. Well, whoever he is, I like him." It's somewhat flattering that my son thinks Nate and I are together.

"You can come and visit. Come to the beach. It's so beautiful and different there. I have a small place...just a guesthouse really, for now, but I have a comfy sofa you can sleep on. I hope you'll come."

"I'd like that," he says.

"Sometime, I'll have a better place, but for right now, I'm never home, so it works for me."

"Yeah, I guess. It put you at the scene of the crime."

"Yes, it did. It's all so—weird, you know?"

"So the bakery is open now?"

"We just opened yesterday, but it was going great when I left."

"When are you going back?"

His question leaves me wondering. I know there are weddings next weekend, so I should get back to Wilmington as soon as possible. I need to call in and see what's going on. "As soon as I can...I guess when the funeral is over. Whenever you think you're ready for me to leave."

"I don't want to stay here if you're not going to be here."

"Same here. We'll see about it today, I guess."

"Okay. I'll need to book my flight."

Joey leans in to hug me, making a new warmth spread over me. We haven't been this close since he was a little boy. I feel Nate's presence as my son and I separate. Nate re-enters the kitchen, fresh from his shower with a clean-shaven face, wet hair combed into place, and clean clothes I haven't ever seen. I know so little about him. For a moment, I try to pretend we are together, the way Joey thought, but it doesn't come to me. I can't even fake it. It's all too real. I'm almost embarrassed to be standing here in my slept-in clothes and makeup from yesterday, my forever ponytail seemingly cast in stone. Joey is used to the way I look, but Nate must be thoroughly disgusted.

"I guess I'll…get my shower now," I say nervously, while Nate goes to the table, setting his computer back up and checking the connections to his external drives.

I close the bedroom door, but as I bustle about, readying my toiletries for my bath, I can hear their deep, manly conversation through the door.

"What do you miss most?" asks Nate.

"Woodlands Barbeque," I hear Joey chuckle. Thank God for another man to rescue my son, and a man who knows the score about a lot of things.

"I know what you mean. It's always the food.…"

They are still talking when I emerge with clean hair falling around my shoulders, wearing a gray printed dress that seems appropriate for the occasion. Both men's faces brighten with my new, clean appearance.

"Nice!" grins Nate, while Joey notices his reaction.

"Thanks," I reply, and then I notice they are not alone. Judy has taken a place at the table, where several foil-covered pans are stacked. Dinner.

"Oh, *Judy*! God, it's good to see you!" I exclaim, truly delighted to see her, letting her wrap me in her mother's hug. "How *are* you?"

"Oh, I'm so sorry about Aiden, Honey Bun! I hope the food will work its magic and cheer you up, or at least fill your belly so you can get through the day."

My eyes well up with tears at the sight of her, and the thought of her being so nice to us. Just her solid and loving presence makes me want to cry.

"I guess you've met Nate."

Judy makes no overt facial expression, but I can tell she approves. "Yes, I have, and I've enjoyed seeing this young-un of yours, so grown up and a soldier—right here!" Judy rubs her hand across Joey's big shoulders, and all of us look proudly at him, even Nate. "How long are you going to stay?"

"We're not sure. The funeral is on Tuesday, and I need to get back to the bakery as soon as I can—we've got weddings next weekend—and I'm sure Nate needs to get home and see to his own life. Joey and I have decided we don't want to hang around any longer than we have to, but for now, it sure feels good being together."

"Of course it does." She nods, understanding my need to return as soon as possible.

I really need to call and check in with Bake My Day. They don't even know that Aiden has died. I feel so anxious, worrying about Joey, the bakery, and the upcoming meeting with the Caffeys at the church today, the people we will have to see, and what we have to do, while the weight of Aiden's absence sits grimly in the room. I feel myself trembling slightly and try to take hold of my emotions for Joey's sake.

Judy continues. "I just can't believe it...." It's a statement we'll hear over and over during the next couple of days. "Anyway, there's plenty of food here—it's a pot roast with mashed potatoes and green beans and some rolls. I brought your favorite chocolate cake, the one with the buttercream frosting."

"Mmm!" Suddenly, I'm hungry again.

"And bless her heart, she brought us a case of beer, too," says Nate with a glint in his eye, making Judy chuckle. As usual, Judy has thought of everything.

"Oh! Thank you, Judy!" If I eat my share of what she's brought, I'll look like a bowling ball when I return to the coast, but there are men here, who need this kind of sustenance, and Judy knows it. And I am truly grateful. These men need taking care of too. I am truly grateful for her generosity.

Before she leaves, we chat briefly about the bakery and my discovery of Jeremy. She tells me that everybody's been following the story, that she thought I looked great on TV, and that she doesn't think anybody here thinks badly of me anymore, so I shouldn't worry about it. Nobody except the Caffeys. And Kendra. And Tia, the nurse.... I need to get out of this town as soon as I can.

I retreat to the bedroom to call in at Bake My Day. Monai answers, and after I explain the situation, she instantly goes into mother mode, asking me how I'm doing, and reassures me that everything is fine there. "That nice Randy stayed yesterday and helped out in the café with the morning rush, taking orders and ringing people up until he had to go to work. Oh, and Mr. May was here this morning asking about you. God, he's just so cute! He said for you to keep the silver pitcher with the flowers. It was his wife's and he's got tons of that stuff and no use for any of it."

"That's nice of them. Well...the funeral will be on Tuesday. I guess I'll be back Wednesday. We've got to get Joey—that's my son—on a flight back to Texas, and then Nate and I will drive back."

"Okay. Don't rush on our account."

"Yeah, but we have the weddings coming up on the weekend, so I want to be back in time to decorate the cakes."

"It'll all be fine. Do you want to speak to Allyson? She's right here, dying to talk to you."

"Sure."

Ten minutes later, my mind has been put at ease, knowing that Allyson and Monai have taken care of everything, including telling the press to take a hike. Maybe by the time I get back, the news reporters will all have forgotten about me and I can get on with my private life. If this is what it's like being a celebrity, I don't think I'd really want it. Whatever the case, my brief moment of fame has had the desired effect on my business, and Allyson has had the good sense to come up with lemon cupcakes today, calling them Drops of Sunshine. Jeez! So far it's a hit.

"It's nice to see you smiling," says Nate, looking up from his computer screen as I walk out of the bedroom.

"I don't know how you're going to get any work done with all the coming and going around here."

"It's okay. When you guys leave this afternoon, I'll get crankin'." He threads his fingers together and pushes them away from his chest, making them crack. Then he gives me that smile that I'm starting to get used to. Still, it makes my stomach do a little sick flip every time I see it. He's so edgy and sexy and invasive that it hurts to look at him. He's exactly the kind of guy I could get addicted to, but I'll never let him see it. *Cut it out! You know better. You know way better,* says Good Elle in my head. I try to raise my eyebrows just faintly, as if I'm being aloof, as if he doesn't matter.

Then I think of Aiden again, and my fantasies involving Nate go right down the tubes. I sigh, wondering what it would have been like if I'd been nicer. What would it have been like if I'd let Aiden love me? What if we'd gotten married? A whole life of *what-ifs* I'll never know about. I'd have been married to a guy who drove a dump truck for a living, resenting him every day, with a witch for a mother-in-law who'd constantly meddle in our lives, and I'd be even more miserable than I am now. I'd have wanted so much more, like I still do. We'd both be having affairs, and Joey would be as messed up as ever. That's what it would be like. There's no sense in romanticizing it.

It is what it is, like Marcus says about things.

And I am who I am.

Chapter 23

WHAT'S LOVE GOT TO DO WITH IT?

It's six o'clock when Joey and I drag ourselves up the front porch steps, weary from an emotionally charged afternoon. The tan and white English setters follow close on Joey's heels, delighted to be included in our soiree. It's warmer than I'd thought it would be today, and I'm tired from the oppressive heat as well as the effort of trying to rein in my feelings. During the course of the day, I'll bet Joey and I have hardly exchanged twenty-five words, yet we have shared a tremendous amount of angst. I couldn't have made it through this day without him; I hope he feels the same way about me. The cabin feels welcoming and safe in its simple beauty, and I imagine smelling Granny's pot roast as I walk in the front door. Then I realize that the smell is real. Nate has Judy's dinner for us warming in the oven.

Glancing to the left, I see that he has made himself at home at the small desk in the corner of the living room. There is no view, but he doesn't seem to need one, absorbed as he is on his computer with earphones covering his ears, tapping rhythmically on the keyboard. He is in his lair.

Sensing we are here, he takes off the earphones and pushes his chair back, standing and stretching, as if he's been in that position for hours, which I don't doubt.

"Hey," he says.

"Hey." His eyes are still that maddening blue that makes me want him. "How's it going?"

"Good. Where's Joey?"

"On the porch, feeding the dogs."

Nate looks interested, standing to look out the window to see, like a kid about to meet a new puppy. Then he runs a hand across his jaw and gazes at me, focusing on me. I must look like day-old shit, but he regards me kindly.

"How was it?"

"Oh, weird as hell, but par for the course, I guess. Martha was heavily drugged so she didn't say much, but she was able to shoot me about a million condescending daggers while we were meeting with the minister. Oh, and by the way, *his daughter* is the girl I told you about—the one whose nose I busted at Sunday school when I was five. Awkward."

"Ha!" he laughs at the irony that is my life on this mountain. "Did you get everything planned?"

"Yes. They let me do it all…. It was almost like they were trying to see if I could do it, like I'd sink myself or something, but I had it all together, the music, all the prayers and the scriptures that we used at Granny's funeral. I even ordered the flowers—certain ones that Aiden would've liked. Red roses for deep love, Bells of Ireland for Aiden's heritage, white sweet peas for shyness, daisies for his funny sense of chivalry, green hydrangea for perseverance—all the attributes that made him the man he is—was—Martha wouldn't have known the meanings of these flowers. Granny taught me all of that. And Ward wouldn't have had a clue." At least Kendra wasn't there. It could have been worse.

Nate searches me again for signs of collapse, but again, there is none.

I toss my hair. "Then, after we were done there, I took Joey by Aiden's house to get some of his clothes from his room and we picked up Chip and Speck. That was hard on him, being there and all, but he held it together," I say, figuring Nate's heard about enough. "Dinner smells good. Thanks for heating it up. You're always cooking...."

"I'm a good wife," he quips good-naturedly, grinning and making me chuckle. "I figured you guys would be hungry," he says, looking at me as if he's going to hug me, and frankly, I could use it, but it doesn't happen when Joey comes in with a gym bag full of clothes, and they greet each other, shaking hands casually. Even Joey is connecting with Nate, which is a relief. We don't need any more awkwardness.

I look at him in his uniform. He looks so brave but so uncomfortable. "Why don't you change out of that uniform, honey?"

"Really. Nobody's gonna see you and we won't tell your CO," Nate adds.

"Yeah, I might do that," Joey says with a little smile, the first I've seen on him today. He's been so tense around everyone. So have I.

"Want a beer, Joey?" Nate asks after his retreating form.

"Yeah! Thanks." I hesitate, remembering that Joey isn't old enough to drink, but considering he's about to put his life on the line for our country, I let it go.

"And you, milady?" Nate asks. No one has ever called me that, making me smile in spite of myself. Here at home, everyone presumes I'm a heartless bitch, but my coastal friend has assumed I'm worthy of chivalry. The change of venue has indeed done me good.

"Sure!" I think to go change my clothes too, but I linger a moment, hoping for that hug, and Nate does not disappoint me. I feel the charge of electricity between us before I let him take me in his arms. His hands go up and down my back, massaging the tension magically out of my body. I feel his fingers working up my neck and through my hair as I drape my arms around his waist. A sensual memory of Robert Redford washing Meryl Streep's hair in *Out of Africa* flashes through my mind as he strokes his fingers through mine. And then he kisses me, surprising me with his passion, turning me to mush in seconds. I can't let myself dissolve the way I want to with him now, not with Joey coming back in a minute for that beer, so I pull myself away, trying to compose my face and seeing that Nate is struggling to do the same.

I clear my throat. "I—uh…I think I'll go change, too. Before dinner."

Nate nods and goes to the kitchen for the beers. He and Joey are petting the dogs on the porch when I join them. I get the feeling that Nate is a man's man. He must be, being the former Navy SEAL that he is, and given the profession he's chosen, immersing himself in fishing trips and spending days on end with groups of men, listening to their stories and capturing their escapades on film. Right now, he's telling Joey about some kind of time-lapse photography he's done of a night sky, filled with stars.

"There was a shooting star at one point, so I took that and used it as a transition piece to the next day's sequence," he says, absently stroking Speck's head, as if he has spent his whole life with Joey's dog, who at the moment is glued to his leg. Nate must have so many stories. I have so many questions.

"Cool," Joey nods as they turn to acknowledge me.

Nate hands me a bottle of something cold and amber. It tastes like heaven.

"Feel better?" he asks, eyes flicking up and down my dress, a comfortable short T-shirt thing that feels better than anything I own. My hair is brushed and I've freshened my face with a warm washcloth. He's smiling at me and Joey notices again.

"Yes, thanks."

We chat for a moment about photography. Joey tells him that he's looking forward to using the camera I gave him for his birthday.

I walk back inside the house to set the table and pull the food out of the oven to serve. Sitting around the table, Nate keeps the conversation going.

"So where is all your grandmother's stuff?"

"Most of the furniture here is hers—with the exception of this new table and the new mattresses. I kept some of the special pieces for us—in storage," I say, nodding to Joey, who looks surprised. "I have her Christmas ornaments and some of the old pictures and all of Granny's movies. She and I had quite a collection of movies and magazines."

"I saw the one in a frame in your room," Nate says.

"Yeah—the *Elle* cover from back in 1978—that's the year I was born. Granny had it framed after my mother named me that."

Joey is quiet. We've never talked much about my mother. Nate senses this and nods.

Joey surprises me by asking, "Mom, do you think that cover's a collector's item?"

"Farrah Fawcett—yeah, probably."

"You kinda look like her," Nate says, eyes sparkling at me again.

"No, I don't. It's just—the blond hair," I say, taking a bite of Judy's excellent pot roast.

"I always heard it was Barbie," says Joey.

Nate laughs and points his fork at me. "I knew you reminded me of her—especially when you wear your hair up in that ponytail!"

They both chuckle as I roll my eyes, passing Joey the butter when he picks up his roll. I sure don't have Barbie's figure, but then, who does? I try to dispel the image of my mother's boyfriend Randy with my Barbie doll and change the subject.

"I have Granny and Pa's love letters. Did you know they wrote to each other?" I ask Joey. "It was when Pa was in the Army," I continue when he shakes his head. "Nothing much was really going on then. We weren't at war at the time, but he was stationed in Germany, and Granny was here, working for the post office as a mail carrier. They both complained about how much snow there was, trying to outdo each other—here and over there, but they wrote really sweet letters to each other."

Joey scoffs, chewing on his roll, trying to imagine Pa's letters being sweet. Pa was a tough but quiet man who could be belligerent at times. He worked hard, chewed tobacco, and drank moonshine (what the local bars and restaurants market these days as *white whiskey*, as if it is a unique specialty drink suddenly worthy of tourist exploration). Pa loved his Clint Eastwood movies. And he loved Granny.

"Pa was sweet, in his own way. You would know that better than anybody. And I think it's special that Granny saved their letters. I'll save your letters, too," I tell Joey.

"I'm glad *somebody* will," mumbles Joey, chewing his roll.

"It's good to write letters—and to get letters," says Nate seriously, making me thank him inwardly for reinforcing the importance of letter writing with Joey. "Who else are you writing to?" he asks with a grin that says he knows he's opening a can of worms.

"Nobody," says Joey with a sad smile that tells the story of his zero love life.

"It's just as well. Save yourself for later." Nate winks at him. *I'd love to know what that's all about.*

"Yeah."

The three of us do the dishes together and then search on Nate's laptop for flights leaving the airport on Wednesday, booking one that doesn't leave too early. The air has cooled pleasantly, so we sit on the porch with the dogs beside our rocking chairs for company. When the guys start telling fishing stories, I step back inside, deciding to check in with Allyson to see how things are going at the bakery without me. It's late, but I still place the call, and she assures me everything is fine. They miss me. They've done a ton of business, and everybody is asking about the Sunshine Girl. She hates that I'm missing the grand opening weekend, and she asks how I'm doing, as if Aiden and I were married. It's hard for me in some ways, dealing with the shock of his death, and knowing how hard it is for Joey to have lost his father, but Aiden was not my husband. I don't want to appear cold about it, so I play along and speak about him with the respect I felt for him that people possibly misinterpret as matrimonial love. Nate certainly thinks there was more to our relationship than there was. So does Allyson. They don't understand how it was. No one did. Only Aiden and I knew what we were to each other.

I'm disturbed by what I feel, or the lack of what I feel, as always, but now that Aiden's gone, it's worse somehow. We weren't in love, although we loved each other. I've always coveted that deep love that people like Kyle and Chelsea have. The way Kyle talked about his family this morning catapulted me back to high school again, wanting what I've never had, and what people like them have so readily—a solid, multigenerational family that crowds around a large table with mismatched chairs every holiday, talking, laughing, praying, eating their special, traditional food together. I'm sure they have their share of family drama, but at least they are a family. *Who will I spend my Thanksgiving with this year? Or Christmas?*

I know I won't sleep a wink tonight. Surely, I will toss and turn and let my poor choices and their spoils torture me as they usually do. For now, miraculously, Joey and I seem to be on good terms, but after tomorrow, he will fly off to finish his basic training and then go on to deployment somewhere in the Middle East. Listening to the news these days, I get a bad feeling that our country is about to become embroiled in one conflict or another that we've ignored, and my son will be a forgotten pawn in someone else's great game. Hopefully, whatever sacrifices he has to make will be worth it. None of us has the power to control any of it, and

I hope these next couple of days together will not be our last. Uncertainty is our only certainty, but I am thankful for what I have with Joey today.

My bare feet make no sound as I slip out of the bedroom and make my way to the front door, where I can hear Joey and Nate talking. I stop for a moment to listen, but they don't know I'm here. Their conversation has taken a serious turn, I think, from the sound of their voices. Nate is talking.

"You never know what you're going to be asked to do on a mission, or when you're going to have to go, but you just do it. And you *can* do it. I had to do some hard things—things I wasn't sure I'd walk away from—but I never felt like I compromised my integrity. You'll be ready to put your life on the line, but it'll be okay. You'll be ready."

My heart leaps into my throat at the sound of Nate's words, but I quell my gasp before I give myself away. As much as I'd like to spend this time with Joey, I know that the two of them need to have this conversation together. And as much as I really need to be in Nate's arms, I know it won't happen tonight. This is a discussion they need to have. Joey needs to hear this kind of manly counsel from Nate, a fellow soldier. Before I turn away, I hear Joey ask a question that surprises me.

"You said you'd wait for…you know, finding a girl? I mean, not that there is one for me—but…."

Nate chuckles briefly. "Yeah, well, for me that was just the way it worked out. I had a girl, or so I thought. I thought she'd wait, but she didn't."

"But you loved her."

"Well, sometimes love isn't enough. Then I turned into one of those guys who thinks he'll never live to be an old man. I went into every mission figuring I might not ever come out, and it was okay with me if I didn't. I'd made my peace with it. If I had to put my family through something like that, it would be bad enough, but why drag a woman through it too, you know?"

I turn quietly and walk back into the bedroom, sinking down on the bed. *Thinks.* He said "thinks," not "thought." Maybe Nate still feels that way—that he'll never live to be an old man. That's why he pursues girls like Amy. And me. Even now, after he's left the service, he continues to settle for unavailable or undesirable women to avoid commitment. However classic or cliché, I'm used to being on the other end of that, but the bigger elephant in the room is the discernment Joey is going through right now. They're talking about killing and being killed, fear, courage—important things Joey needs to discuss. He needs Nate more than I do.

My head reels from the possibilities my son is facing, but I am thankful that Nate is here and can fill in as Joey's mentor since Aiden no longer can. Tears roll down my face as I wonder what will happen to my son. I cry for Joey and the loss of Aiden, for myself, and for Nate. Nothing is certain. This is why Nate came. When he took the call for me in the bakery kitchen, he knew he'd be needed, and not just by me. I was right; coming here was a mission for him. Here I was yearning for him sexually and emotionally, when he came here to help me help my son. Still, I don't want Joey to expect—like Nate—or even to accept—that his life will be short. He has made choices based on whatever limits he has placed on himself. I want him to know how much I love him. He will come home, and he will have an abundant life. If he survives, I will make sure of it. Whatever happens to all of us, we will move on with our lives.

Nothing has changed for me, really. I'm still working in a bakery, slogging away every day in my mundane middle class existence, but I'm satisfied with my new choices. I just need to sleep tonight. I need to get through Aiden's funeral tomorrow, and hit the road on Wednesday after taking Joey to the airport. Looking for a sleeping pill, I go into the bathroom and rummage through my toiletry bag. I need to knock myself out tonight, and when the funeral is over tomorrow, I'll go back to Wilmington, forget these mountains, and get back to work.

I have friends now whom I can see every day, nonjudgmental friends who support me and don't hate me for what I did. I'm not that bad, but I'm not that good either. Even finding Jeremy was a no-brainer. I was just there. *Just there.* Anybody else would have called the police just like I did. It certainly doesn't make me special. All that Sunshine Girl nonsense will be over and I can get back to normal. Amy Stainback has played her hand, but I didn't play mine, so she will disappear as well. She is the last person worth worrying about. Nate will do whatever Nate will do. I have no expectations from him. Looking down at my phone in my hand, I scroll through the pictures, finding the picture of him with Amy. I press the trashcan icon, then *delete photo*, and the image disappears.

I sniff and wipe my tears with the back of my hand. Readying myself for the funeral tomorrow, I hang my black dress over the closet door and smooth out the wrinkles with my hand, listening again to the men on the porch, catching only the low buzz of their voices through the open door. Setting my taupe pumps on the floor, I listen again. Then I search through my bag, finding the long silver chain I'll wear with the single teardrop pearl, Granny's Christmas gift from years ago, and lay it out carefully on the dresser. I should say goodnight before I go to bed, so I swallow my sleeping pill with a sip of water and walk back out onto the porch. They are still deep in conversation, leaning forward on their rocking chairs with their elbows propped on their knees, empty beer bottles and dogs curled at their feet. *Men's men.*

"Hey, I'm going to turn in. It's been a long day," I say when they turn to look up at me.

Nate's lips part as if he'd like to say something to me, but I can tell the two of them are in the middle of another important topic.

"Goodnight, Mom," Joey says.

"Goodnight, Elle," Nate says, eyeing me and giving me a smile. "Sleep well."

"Night," I say, giving my arms a rub and turning away from them.

Chapter 24

TIME TO SAY GOODBYE

I steer my car skillfully out of the church parking lot, attempting not to run over Aiden's departing relatives. They peer at me as if I'm some kind of blasphemer, having the nerve to appear in church after all I've done. Isn't this where girls like me are supposed to be? Repenting? What the hell is church for anyway? Look at them. Being the Sunshine Girl up here apparently doesn't count. I'm alone since Joey is going to Martha and Ward's for a wake after the burial. I wasn't invited.

"How's the hostage?" I ask Nate on the phone as I hit the road.

"*Hostage*—ooh, I like the sound of that!" Nate laughs in his usual clipped voice, the upbeat crispness of it a welcome sound.

"I'm on my way home and I was thinking about picking up something for dinner for us at the grocery store."

"Your friend Marcus beat you to it. He came by here a little bit ago with some filet mignon and more red wine—dinner for two."

"Oh. Wow. Marcus is so cool."

"Yeah, I thought so. Or maybe he was checking me out to see if I'd pass muster."

"Ah, yes, you could be right. He's very protective—and just the slightest bit nosy." *And kind.* Which may explain why he came to the funeral in the first place. He didn't really know Aiden, but he said he'd come to check on me. "I told him at the funeral that Joey was going over to Aiden's parents' place for dinner with the family—all forty-five thousand of them, crammed in their little house. Thank God it's summer and they can all spill out into the yard."

"Hmm, big family."

"Yeah, you wouldn't believe the size of their clan—and some of them even have most of their teeth!" I chuckle. "I'm sorry; that wasn't nice, was it?"

"Okay…maybe I'll let that one slide. You might be due one unseemly remark."

"Oh…it's just been a really long day, and you know, I'm the uppity and infamous outcast. I promise to behave for you."

"Don't do that. Remember? I like girls who misbehave. Just come on home and tell me all about it."

My insides flutter at the image he implies. *Come on home.* I could get used to hearing that. Misbehave with me.

In less than fifteen minutes, I am home. I find Nate on his cell phone, walking the flowerbeds barefooted, inspecting the fruits of Granny's labors—and mine, in shorts and a light green shirt with Chip and Speck sniffing around at his heels. Walking over to join him, I step out of my uppity pumps to avoid aerating the yard, letting my toes spread gratefully over the cool green grass under my feet. Nate grins at me and ends his call, promising whomever is on the other end that he'll talk to him or her on Thursday.

"Work," he explains. "I'll be heading out of town again on Thursday—as usual. You look great," he says, reaching up to my loosely styled chignon and cupping it in his hand, biting his lip and giving the bun a little squeeze, like he could yank it right out. I hope I'm reading him right—it's also like he wants to throw me right down in this luscious green grass, which I'd be more than okay with on any other day, but it seems inappropriate, given the circumstances, and he senses that as well.

He gives me a friendly sideways hug instead, asking, "How'd it go?"

"It was so…lovely, really. The music was so pretty." Strains of *Amazing Grace* on the bagpipes played by Pa's cousin in our family's church were so moving. "It was everything Aiden would have wanted. The minister knew Aiden well, and spoke of him eloquently. And then several of his family and friends got up and said nice things about him. Martha was still medicated, I guess. I had to keep finding her a place to sit so she wouldn't fall over. And Kendra was so upset. The whole time we sat together throughout the service, I had to hold her shoulders, she cried so much. She was so upset she didn't even care that it was me who was doing the comforting. And then there was the endless hugging and pressing of the flesh in the receiving line. Kyle and Chelsea and Aiden's friends, Glen and Abby from high school, were there."

They hugged me too and were surprisingly civil. Getting a hug from Kyle was nothing to write home about. And all this time I wanted it so bad. They even made pleasant comments on my discovery of Jeremy. It was so odd, being embraced by people who'd scorned and talked about me behind my back, who'd declined from making social overtures toward me in school, but I guess I brought all of that on myself. It was slightly hurtful, but I'm trying to disregard my own feelings, which aren't the focus of today anyway. Their sympathy was for Aiden today, not me. I know I'm appearing to be lost in my thoughts, but I guess that's what's expected at a time like this. Still, Nate presses me for more information.

"How'd Joey handle it?"

"He was good, I think." I have so much admiration for my son, but he's still my son. "He's so brave. And he looked so handsome in his dress uniform. All the people there were rather amazed by him. He really is a soldier now. I'm seeing that clearly…. Do you think he'll be ready for what he's getting himself into?"

Nate studies me for a moment and nods solemnly. "He'll be ready."

I finger the solitary pearl on the silver necklace that hangs below my chest. Tears are forming in my eyes, but I blink them back. "I don't think he was really looking forward to being over at Ward and Martha's, but there will be plenty of his cousins around for him to talk to. Who knows when he'll see any of them again…."

Nate folds me into his arms, resting his chin on top of my head. I can feel Chip pressing against my leg, as if he senses he should comfort me as well.

"It's been a tough day for you. Why don't we go in and I'll start the grill. Are you hungry?"

"Maybe. It's hard to tell."

Nate smiles and steers me toward the porch. In the kitchen, the steaks are resting in a glass dish and a plastic bag of green beans and a smaller one of almonds sit beside the dish.

"Marcus said you'd know what to do with all this," he says, gesturing to the food.

"More green beans. You'll be sick of them after tonight. I make green beans with almonds—one of his favorite dishes. I see he brought potatoes, too."

"So, you cooked for him?" *Do I detect a hint of jealousy?* "Were you and Marcus like a *thing*?" Nate is so direct, and I like it. I like looking at his mouth when he talks, trying to remember what it felt like exploring my body.

"No, we were not. He was more like a father figure to me—sort of. Marcus helped set me up in my business in Wilmington. I dated his son Michael, before he got run out of town for trying to scare off the mother of his child." Nate scoffs. "And you thought *you* could pick 'em!"

I'd hate for Nate to know about all of my past transgressions involving undesirable men, so that's the last I'm saying. Let him imagine what he will. It can't possibly be as bad as my reality.

"Okay...'nough said."

I snicker, going to the sink with the green beans to rinse and snap them, putting them in a baking dish with a little sea salt and water. Nate brushes the steaks with olive oil he's found in a cabinet while I microwave the beans. Standing close enough to him to feel his heat, I arrange the almonds in butter to go in next, feeling his eyes on me for a moment. I always find this kind of kitchen chemistry so seductive, me in my little black dress and both of us with no shoes on our feet.

"Shall I open this wine? We have two bottles...."

"Sure," I reply, watching his strong, hairy arms and suntanned hands go to work on the bottle. I tear my eyes away long enough to find two goblets from another cabinet, and he skillfully pours us each a glass. I look at the label—a Spanish Tempranillo thankfully, and not the local winery product I was expecting from Marcus's association with Kyle's brother-in-law's winery. I've had enough small town moments for the time being, thank you!

We toast, clinking our glasses lightly together, and Nate further endears himself to me by saying, "To Aiden."

"To Aiden." We sip and approve Marcus's choice. Nate goes out the back door to start the new gas grill while I check the refrigerator for Judy's leftover mashed potatoes, finding enough for our dinner, to my delight. As usual, she's cooked for an army.

During dinner, I'm relieved to shift the topic from the funeral, asking Nate about his day and gladly hearing about his work. He's a good storyteller and relates the show in progress to me, explaining the location of the shoot, the relationship of the participants, highlighting Bo Hauser's expertise, and the challenge of the drum fishing expedition that took place in the Chesapeake Bay. As usual, he explains, there is always an antic or two that makes for a good story, and the personalities of the people involved tend to emerge in an entertaining way. He adds just the right music to enhance the situations and voila, a television show is produced. There must be quite an art to what he does, being able to capture the story, in addition to appreciating nature, knowing fishing, and the skill involved in filming all those sequences on a rocking boat without falling into the water. Once again, Nate leaves me remembering to close my mouth.

After placing our dishes in the dishwasher and wiping off countertops, we take our wine and wander out onto the front porch to watch the last of the sunset. Birds flutter toward dark trees, settling in to roost for the night as cicadas and crickets begin their evening serenade. My mountains are beginning to take their deep exhale. Pulling the pins from my hair, I let it tumble from its confinement and run my fingers through it. Chip takes the opportunity to lick my bare toes while Nate and I rock and drink our wine. I reach down to stroke the dog's tan and white spotted head.

"So tell me everything."

"You ask me that a lot."

"I told you. I want it all."

The words—along with his stare—sear into my psyche in a way I wasn't expecting, making me catch my breath and sense that there is more to Nate's motive for being here than I'd previously deduced. Normally in these kinds of situations, I'd make some provocative comeback like, *Oh, do you, now?* Which would lead quickly to clothes being strewn like Hansel and Gretel's breadcrumbs on the bedroom floor. But I can hardly speak for the pounding pulse in my throat and the aching sensation awakening between my legs. I seem to have a novel and astonishing lack of self-confidence around him. I stroke Chip's ear to stall for composure. *Who is this man?* The emotion Nate has brought to the surface seems to push my limits with the remains of the day, and I catch a sob before it takes hold in my throat.

"It's just that…. First of all, it was hard enough to be saying goodbye to Aiden, but I kept imagining that I was sitting at Joey's funeral." I cast my eyes over the pasture and above the treetops at the deep watercolor sky, as more dark birds flutter across to their trees. Unwanted tears flood over my eyelids and spill down my cheeks. I sweep them away with my fingertips and try to heave my feelings back inside unsuccessfully.

"Mmm," Nate says, nodding gravely, then sighing. He leans forward in the rocker, resting his elbows on his knees and placing his hands together. "I always knew my mother would think about that when I was deployed…and my dad and my siblings. You can't help but imagine the worst. It's the way we prepare ourselves for the worst. I always felt badly for them whenever I'd call them before I'd leave for a mission. You never knew whether it might be your last conversation…."

"I have a bad feeling about things that are to come. I just hope he survives."

"I know. You have to be as brave as Joey is going to be throughout this whole ordeal. Believe me, I understand what you're going through. My family was so thankful when I was done. They prayed every day for my safe return."

We sit quietly for a moment, the rockers still, while I try to regain control of my emotions. My crying simmers until I can get it under control. Nate doesn't tell me not to worry. He doesn't tell me it will be okay. He watches me carefully. My face contorting into tears has never been a good look on me so I struggle to compose myself.

He reaches over and takes my hand. "What else?"

"Well, then when I tried to focus on Aiden, I guess I started having so many regrets. I wish I'd been better to him."

"Grief is our last act of love. The more you love, the more you grieve. It's okay. You loved him, Elle. You should let yourself cry for him."

Nate's words are comforting, but I want to tell him everything.

"Aiden was such a good guy, but an unsung hero in so many ways. I had more stories about him than anyone, but I never thought about telling them. They were too personal, but the things he did for Joey and for me spoke volumes about who he was as a man. I could never have married him, and he certainly did the right thing for himself by not marrying me—we would have killed each other—but maybe because of that and the devotion he still showed us, Aiden had a grace about him that…I'll never have…" I say, my voice breaking at the end.

"Ohhh…" Nate whispers, setting his glass on the table between us and rising to his feet. He takes my glass and pulls me up beside him, holding my hand. "I wouldn't say that at all, Elle. I've seen nothing but grace from you from the moment I saw you break the news to your staff at the bakery—even before that, with Amy, of all people. You've shown plenty of grace to Aiden's family and especially to Joey. However distant you were from him, you certainly aren't anymore. You can't give away what you don't have, and I'd say you have plenty of your own grace."

I sigh, a small laugh escaping with it at the idea. "Oh…well, that's something I never considered. Thank you for that. But his *family* still loathes me…."

"Ah, what do they know? So you've been cast out into the outer darkness, where there will be *wailing and gnashing of teeth*!" he says, laughing softly, entwining his fingers in mine, providing a needed bit of comic relief. Thank God! I can't take much more of anyone's sincerity. I toss my hair.

"Oh, please don't tell me you're a church-goer too."

"Yep. Spent every Sunday of my childhood in the Presbyterian Church until I became a SEAL. And then, boy, did I do a nosedive from there."

"How did you live with—whatever you had to do?"

"There's this thing in church—I'm sure you've heard of it—it's called *forgiveness*."

"Oh, right. I *have* heard about it. They have that in Wilmington, just not here."

Nate chuckles and hugs me again. "Elle, I wish you could see yourself through my eyes. I mean, okay, you've made your share of mistakes, but here you came out of prison, an unwed mother, who never went to college, and you raised a great kid who's turned out to be a brave man...you took care of your grandmother when she needed you, and you've started your own business. You're a self-made entrepreneur, for God's sake. You've turned yourself completely around...yet you don't even see it. I've only known you for a week, but you've absolutely blown me away."

I'm touched, but I shouldn't be. I know how to fish for compliments, but I wasn't trying to this time. I'm just trying to explain myself. Nate shouldn't invest himself in me.

"That's just it; you don't know me." I look at him in the twilight, the bright blue of his eyes sparking further at my challenge.

"I know a little. And the best part will be peeling back all those layers to see who you really are. It could take me a long time."

Nate lifts his hand, touching his thumb to my lips, tracing their shape. He smiles and cups my face in his hand like a flower. My heart races and I hope he can't hear it, or sense the sudden flood of my insides at his touch.

"I guess the really dangerous part is, you don't know me either," he says with a little chuckle. I swallow, trying to look unfazed but failing miserably, the way his thumb feels stroking back and forth over my lips and my cheek. I close my eyes to avoid giving myself away. "Elle...I've been trying really hard to be a good guest. I know you're grieving and I've been trying to be considerate of your feelings, but I don't think I can hold all of this in any longer."

"Please don't," I hear myself say. It sounds ridiculously desperate, but I don't care.

"Are you sure? I need to know if you're ready. Do you want this?" he asks.

Yes, I want this. I want you. My emotions have certainly gotten the best of me, but I do want him, and all I can seem to do is wipe my tears away and nod, hoping he can see how much I need him. I raise my face to give him the sign he needs, and then slowly, he leans in to kiss me. His open mouth is sweet and tender, with roughness around his lips where he hasn't shaved, and I kiss him back with complete abandon. *What could possibly be wrong with this man?* Other than his brevity in the bedroom, which I think I'm about to find out may have been just an unfortunate and unexpected fluke!

Shuddering and kissing him in the almost darkness, I feel myself letting go and falling naturally into Nate's embrace, letting him know my response is completely mutual. I stroke my fingers into his hair as he lifts me toward him, pressing the small of my back into his hips. His kiss is delicious. I can't stop kissing him. I've never been kissed like this before. My eyes are closed, but I hear a vehicle slow and tires crunch at the road, making us both pull reluctantly apart to look.

It's a car turning into the driveway. Joey is home. I hear him open the door and emerge from the car, thanking whoever has brought him home. He straightens and walks up the drive to the cabin, his form sharp and tall in his dress uniform. When he reaches the porch, I can tell that he reeks of cigar smoke. I can't abide a stinking, smoking man, and I never thought Joey would succumb to the likes of those who choose a slow and deliberate suicide with cigarettes, but at Aiden's wake, farewell cigars must have been the order of the evening.

"Hey," he greets us at the top of the stairs.

"Hey. How was your evening?" I ask.

"Okay. Aunt Sally drove me home. She was the only sober one there. They got to passing the jar around...."

"Oh, I'm sure." Cigars and *hooch*, even more charming, but men handle grief in their own way. "Did you get enough supper to eat? There's more green beans, and some of Judy's chocolate cake left over." Without food, the night could go south for him quickly.

"Yeah, I had aplenty."

"We were just having some wine. I don't suppose that'd be a good idea for you. Coffee, maybe?" asks Nate.

"Nah, I'm good," says Joey, seemingly aware that he's interrupting. "Actually, I'm pretty beat," he says, and I can tell he's had his share of sips from the Mason jar as well, the way he's slurring his speech, and tipping slightly back and forth. "I haven't slept real well the last few nights, and I'm gonna go pack and hit the sack so I'll be ready to go in the morning."

"Okay," I say, relieved that he's amenable to going to bed. I was fully prepared to offer him one of my sleeping pills, but it won't be necessary now. "We need to be out of here by eight to get you checked in at the Greensboro airport by ten."

"Right. Okay. Will you wake me up?"

"Sure will." *Good idea.* Nate shakes Joey's hand and waits politely while we say our goodnights and I make sure Joey has everything he needs to head off to bed for the last time in Granny's place. Then I lift up my chin and think to myself, *It won't be the last time.*

Chapter 25

LOVE ME TENDER

I try to gain my bearings before I can bring myself to open my eyes, trying to hold on to sleep, willing myself to dream about Nate. My alarm hasn't yet gone off. I must have been dreaming, which means I must have been sleeping. Granny appeared to me in my dream, imparting pearls of her wisdom, the way she did at the end of her life, when her medication let her relax and say the things she'd held inside most of my life. *"You are worthy of so much more love than you can even imagine you deserve."*

I feel warm in so many ways. Again, awakening and lying in Granny's bed must lend itself to communing with her from the other side, which feels completely natural and comforting, although with Nate's soft snoring in my ear, and his face nuzzled into the back of my neck, it's an odd little ménage a trois we have going on in this bedchamber! My eyes spring open. It's amazing what a steak dinner, a little rest, and some delayed and torrid foreplay can do for a man's stamina. We have hardly slept, and when we did, I was jolted awake by Nate's crying out, paired with a jarring lurch during his own sleep. Maybe that is the dangerous side of him that he mentioned. Who knows what he dreams about in the depths of sleep that he tries to shun during the daylight?

"Never believe what a man says; believe only what he does." Granny's second pearl. If that is true, then Nate is doing everything right. Surely his deeds over the past several days and throughout the night have shown me everything I need to know about him. He has given me all the tenderness, passion, and attention I want, everything I could possibly need, and yet, lying in the darkness, I look around, wondering whether this turn of fate is really happening to me. This man, who should be with someone else worthier of him than me, with little children to raise up into adults like him, has chosen to spend his last few days providing both compassion and counsel to me and my evolving son on my humble hillside, and he has taken me to bed in the most satisfying of ways. I am the personification of peace at this moment, a feeling that leads me to wait momentarily for a lusty retort from the cynical sister inside me, but there is nothing; it appears that she has left the building. Perhaps the scene is too maudlin for her to digest and she has gone on her way, overpowered by Nate's charms and our consensual lovemaking, to be displaced by someone warmer, more tender and hopeful—me, perhaps?

Lovemaking. I've never actually made love until last night. No one has ever made love *to me*, but I am sure this happened over the course of the night, making me shudder now with the memories of the vulgar version of what it was I used to do with men. Everything feels new this morning. Even the birds. A wood thrush is singing its sweet, fluted song outside the open window, a magical, soothing sound I haven't heard in weeks. A tear meanders down the side of my nose from the corner of my eye. As if on cue, Nate's arm, warm from its sequester under our covers, encircles me from behind, and he settles himself around me as if we are two spoons in a cozy drawer, making me relish our nakedness and the intimacy we've earned over the night's repeated coupling in this perfect place. I want the world to stop for just a moment. There can be no turning back now, and I know this is indeed real. It occurs to me also that I haven't had a malicious thought or said a profane word about anyone in almost two days. *What is happening to me?*

I am living in the moment, something I've only read about but never had the chance actually to do. Nate does this, giving me his full and undivided attention in whatever we're discussing or doing. He showed me in the way he loved me last night, demonstrating the art of tasting and caressing every inch of my body in his own good time, watching my reactions, not rushing the way he did on our first meeting; the way he looked deep into my eyes, seeing right through to my soul, as though someone even I am not fully acquainted with was there. It is as though the morning of Joey's call led him to be devoted totally to me—every part of me, as though I need him and he knows it. We have fallen together—into what, I'm not sure, but if this is love, then I want it all. As surely as Edna Pontellier was awakened, I believe I have been awakened as well. Would I walk into the ocean if Nate were to leave me now? I honestly don't know, but if this feeling were to be yanked away from me, I can't say how I would conduct myself, being cut away from the very being who makes me feel alive and worth loving—and quite possibly worth living. Maybe it wasn't a stupid book after all. But then, I have not known love like this from any man—ever. Maybe it is just as well, given my circumstances up until now. I realize now that over the past week, Nate, and possibly many other choices I've made leading up to him, have changed my life.

I swallow a lump in my throat and ease out of his slumbering embrace, feeling a brush of his sandpapery chin on my shoulder. Looking back in the first of morning's light, I can see his skin, dark and masculine against the white coverlet. I watch him for a moment, so peaceful in his well-deserved sleep. I'll let him rest while I rouse Joey and fix us all breakfast. *French toast.* It's sensual—as sexy as eggs over easy, but sweet and sticky like me. I hope there is syrup in the cupboard. Slipping carefully out of bed to keep from waking Nate, I search the floor in the half-darkness for something to wear. The morning chill turns my skin to gooseflesh. In my haste to leave on Saturday, I didn't think to pack a robe. Thinking absently about Amy's pink silk robe, I find Nate's shirt on the floor and slide my arms through the sleeves. Buttoning it, I hesitate, wondering how Joey will react to seeing me in it. I'll wake him up and come back to change, once I've surveyed the kitchen for breakfast ingredients.

"Joey?" I whisper, shaking his shoulder, acutely aware of the smell of alcohol and dogs filling the room. Chip and Speck stir first, stretching and thumping their tails, yawning as they wake. Joey opens his eyes, regarding me and taking a moment to orient himself. "Hey, honey. Time to get up and in the shower, okay?"

His military training kicks in as he rolls onto his back, stretching and wiping his fingers across his eyes.

"Okay. I'm up."

"I'll let the dogs out."

"Okay."

"Breakfast in ten minutes."

Padding barefoot down the cool wooden hallway with Joey's setters at my heels, I open the door to let them greet the misty morning. The air is cool and moist, making me shiver slightly. I wash my hands and begin the coffee, searching through the cabinets, finding a jar of local sourwood honey that will do instead of syrup. Putting slices of bacon in the new microwave, I set to work on the egg and sugar wash, wishing I had nutmeg, heating a pan on the stove for the French toast, while two showers start in both directions of the cabin. My hair is a tousled mess—I can tell from my reflection in the microwave's glass door—but my appearance will have to do if we are to make it to the Greensboro airport on time with full stomachs. It will take an hour and a half if there is no traffic, which should be the norm for this time of year and this time in the morning.

I find myself humming my favorite John Legend song, "All of Me," as I flip the French toast in the pan. It is a soulful melody, filled with emotion that spills out of me. I am a contented woman, my body feeling completely sated and more than just a little raw in the tender place between my legs, but it is a pleasant kind of soreness. I hope my counterpart feels the same way, and I suppose I will know when he emerges from his shower in just a few moments. A shadow of doubt crosses before me in an ugly cloud, making my song go silent for a second before I continue. I decide not to let myself think that way.

The dogs are back, so I pour food in their bowls and refresh their water. I can hear Joey bumping around in his room, and a cloud of soapy-smelling mist merges with the morning smells coming from my kitchen. The ritual of fixing breakfast is like no other cooking, the aromas of coffee and bacon and sweet breads frying in a pan giving wakefulness and hope to the start of a new day. How Granny would have loved this new renovation—after she'd gotten over the shock of all the expense that was shelled out for the tourist invasion that will surely follow! I am glad we are the first to enjoy the fruits of Marcus and Kyle's creation here. How odd, though—Kyle was in this very home, transforming it into something I love. I wonder how he would have done it if he'd known it was our place. It was best that he didn't know. It's a happy place.

My lover is suddenly at my side, giving me an exhilarating nuzzle with a minty "Good morning" that lets me know we are on the same page. His damp hair is combed, and I can feel that he has shaved. "How can I help?"

"Pour us some coffee? I think it's just about ready."

"Sure. Is Joey up?" His voice is rough and raspy from the sleepless night we've shared, and it makes me smile, knowing I was the cause.

"Yeah. He's out of the shower and packing from the sound of all the bumping around in there," I reply, taking three napkins from a stack on the counter and placing three forks beside them.

A cup of coffee settles on the granite countertop by the stove, and a large, competent hand encircles my waist, migrating to just under my breast.

"Thank you," I say softly.

I'm aware of him sniffing my hair for the scent of birthday cake possibly. I would think that by now, my sugar and vanilla fragrance is long gone. This morning we smell like each other. Just the thought of that sends a ripple through my midsection.

"How are you this morning?" he asks.

"Excellent. And you?"

"The same…. The same," he murmurs in my ear, rocking me gently back and forth, giving my neck a kiss. So I wasn't imagining it.

The French toast in the pan is almost finished. I find a large bowl to cover the rest that sits on the plate to keep warm.

"Do you mind keeping an eye on this while I change? I don't want Joey seeing me in…just your shirt."

His smile sends me again. I am hopeless. His eyes rove over the spectacle of me in his shirt, with just enough legs and chest visible to start a slow smile across his face.

"Absolutely. I like it that you're modest around him. You're a good mother, Elle," he says, gathering me in a suggestive embrace that could start things all over. His compliments aren't of the usual sort, making me appreciate that he digs deeper inside me, letting me know he sees what is important to me.

When I return, Joey is there, dressed in his white uniform shirt and black slacks, shoes shined after last night's outdoor gathering.

"Mornin' Mom."

"Hey, Boo. Did you sleep?"

"Like a rock. You?"

I can't help the blush that instantly colors my face, and I watch Nate turn away to keep from making it worse. "Yes. I got a goodnight's sleep." *For a few minutes, at least.* I can't help but smile, making Joey wrinkle his forehead.

After breakfast, the men clean up the kitchen while I shower. Nate and Joey have packed the car in the time it takes me to apply my minimal makeup and do my hair. We leave right on time, with me tucked into the backseat with a magazine and a book that I'll attempt to read once we're down the mountain. After dropping off the dogs at Ward and Martha's, Joey and Nate talk casually while Nate drives and we all look out the windows, each of us taking in the summer majesty of these hills. I feel myself drifting into a peaceful sleep, once the road straightens enough for me to doze, while their conversation rises and falls like breathing.

I feel the car slowing and going off the interstate, which brings me out of my slumber. I have slept the entire trip to Greensboro, and I open my eyes, stretching as Nate pulls the car to a stop at the intersection of the highway leading to the airport. I feel irritated with myself for sleeping; I wish I'd stayed awake to talk to Joey, or at least I could have listened to his words with Nate. In minutes, we are pulling in front of the airport where a sign indicates the Delta Airlines drop off.

Stiffly, I get out of the car as Nate and Joey retrieve his Army duffel and hang-up bag with his uniform jacket. Joey's black beret sits jauntily on the side of his head, making him look seasoned and manly, the way others most likely see him. Tears well up in my eyes as I put my arms around him. *When did he become a man?* He holds me gently, patting me on the back.

"You'll come to my graduation, right?" he asks. "Third week of August? I'll send you an invitation."

"Of course," I say, wiping my eyes, wishing I had a tissue. I wasn't prepared to fall apart again.

Joey laughs softly. "That means you're gonna have to fly, you know?"

I catch my breath while Nate watches. It dawns on him now that I've never flown and that this is a big deal for me. Obviously, I've never been to Texas.

"I know. I'll be a big girl and do it. You just let me know when."

"Okay," Joey grins, now the expert with one, almost two flights up on me. He glances at Nate and hesitates, as if wondering whether to invite him, too. Nate saves him from the awkward moment.

"Best of luck, man!" he says, shaking Joey's hand. "I'll be thinking about you. Take care of yourself."

"You too, and thanks! Take care..." *of my mother*, he wants to say, but no one is sure how this is all going to go. Still, Nate winks at him and gives his back a slap the way men do.

"Got it," he says to Joey, making me think maybe I have a chance of a lingering relationship with Nate.

"Bye, honey. Text me when you land, okay? And don't forget to write."

"I won't. You too, okay?"

"Okay. You know I will. Bye," I say, reaching up to hug him tightly again. "I love you."

"I love you too, Mama," Joey says in my ear.

Nate puts a hand on the back of my neck and gives it a squeeze, the way he did in the hospital, while we watch Joey walk through the automatic doors into the terminal. He turns once and gives a wave and his new grin to both of us. When he is out of sight, Nate hugs me again and chuckles, his lips brushing my forehead.

"It's just basic training," he says in response to my tears.

"I know...I just...we had a new little moment there, that's all."

"I'd say that was a big moment." We get back in the car, this time with me riding shotgun. Nate must be tired but he doesn't show it.

"You know, Elle, we've never even had a *date*, have we? I want to take you to a proper lunch at one of my favorite places in Raleigh. We should get there right about noon."

Chapter 26

ALL OF ME

In the car by ourselves now, Nate and I talk nonstop, trying to catch up on the last thirty-something years. We take turns peppering each other with questions. Some are on the lighter side, like "What's your favorite movie, book, football team? What's your favorite food? Things like that. Nate likes all kinds of music and literature. We've read some of the same books: *To Kill a Mockingbird*, *The Perfect Storm*, *The Prince of Tides*, and the whole *Harry Potter* series, although we mostly like realistic novels. *Cold Mountain* is his favorite—a little too dark and hopeless for me, but I liked it. *Atonement* is my favorite. Now there's a great read—so utterly passionate and tragic and believable, and he's read that, too. I didn't even know how old Nate was until now. Thirty-three. I knew he was younger than me.

Some of his questions have been bold and probing, like last night when he'd asked what kind of birth control I was using. He'd looked briefly floored—a mixture of disbelief and dismay on his face, when I'd told him I'd had my tubes tied. Images of him with little children keep flashing in front of me. Little children I can't have. It hurts to think about him not having children. He would be such a good father. In the car, I ask him whether he wants kids, and he takes a moment to think about it. "Having kids would be great if it's in the plan, but if it's not, it's not. I don't do what-ifs. You've made a great kid, by the way."

I stick to the less invasive questions, afraid I might be scaring him off. "What's your favorite color?" I ask. "Whatever color the water is at any given time," he answers. "But most of the time, it's green. What's yours?" he asks, and when I look into those heart-stopping eyes of his, I don't hesitate. "Blue."

Nate is surprised that I've never heard of Cameron Village. He's surprised that I haven't traveled outside of Valle Crucis with the exception of Wilmington and Myrtle Beach, and if you count Mountain City as traveling. It's not that I don't want to travel; I've just never had the opportunity. I think he understands how mountain people are. He doesn't make me feel bad about my missed opportunities. "Well, if you're going to be marooned somewhere," he says, "I think Valle Crucis would be about the perfect place—about as close to heaven as you can get." I have to agree.

Cameron Village is a quaint little shopping center in an older section of Raleigh, our state's capital. I haven't seen Raleigh the way most people do, considering my view was from inside the state women's prison, along with closely chaperoned visits to the community college to learn the baking trade. Most schools take a field trip to the state capital at least once in a student's course of study, but I'd been suspended from school that week for making out with an older boy behind the gym and wasn't allowed to go. Go figure. Nate explains that the shopping area was even cooler "back in the day" when his father used to take the family there on weekend trips that centered around NC State University football games and visits to his grandparents' home near Cary. I don't know about Cary either, other than it's outside Raleigh and it's grown fast over the years, according to Nate.

"Dad's a veterinarian," Nate tells me, escorting me down the sidewalk, his arm around my shoulders. We are turning heads. An older woman smiles at us. "He went to State where he met my mother. They're both from North Carolina, but they ended up in Chattanooga, Tennessee, where he got his first job after he finished vet school. He and Mom have been there ever since. But you should see the village at Christmas. It's really special at night with all the lights and decorations. This place I'm taking you is one of my favorite places in the world to eat pizza."

We walk through the door at Piccola Italia, where the mingled aromas of garlic, sauce, bread, and meat baking fill our noses, making me realize that I'm starving. He greets the dark-haired Italian man at the door as if they are old friends, which I guess they are. I'm introduced to Frank, who grabs two menus and leads us to the only booth left at this busy time of day.

"You caught me out of the kitchen. I'm going right back to make the pizzas."

"Fabulous! That's what we're getting."

"I'll send someone right over. Enjoy!"

"Thanks, Frank!" Nate says, settling down in his seat and giving me a wink.

"Won't your grandparents be upset that you're here and didn't stop in to see them?"

"Well, I'd love for you to meet them, but I figured we both need to get home. Maybe next time."

He looks at me and grins at my incredulous expression. "There will be a next time, won't there?"

I laugh. "That's totally up to you."

"Not totally. But I want next times; don't you?"

I nod. His words, or maybe the way he's taking my hand, are making my head swim. He might as well have nailed me into my seat. I swallow as the waiter descends, asking what we'd like to drink.

"Red wine?" Nate asks me and hesitates since we're driving. I nod. He orders us water and one glass of pinot noir to split—after all, it *is* our first date. He orders a pizza as well, asking me what I'd like on it. He goes along with my plan for a veggie pizza and then adds Italian sausage to half of it. "And make it a large," he adds to the waiter. Then to my raised eyebrows, he says, "You better believe we're taking the leftovers home with us. I can promise you this will be the best pizza you've ever had." *Home.*

He watches me, the way I'm trying to get used to his attentions. His eyes go soft.

"I'm glad you got to go home again. It seems like it was a good thing, wasn't it? Even with the circumstances being what they were."

"Yeah. I guess it was really good. You must wonder why in the world I would leave a place like that."

"I think I have an inkling. At least you can go back whenever you want. Marcus made that clear. Judy would obviously let you stay with her. And you'll have Joey's place eventually...."

"Yeah." I let him take both of my hands in his, even when the waiter returns with our wine. I love having wine with pizza, but I hope he'll be able to drive after the effects. Maybe I'll take over the driving since he needs to sleep.

I can imagine him at home around that Christmas dinner table with his family, all of them grinning and messing with each other as his dad carves the turkey, the way the movie families do it. *Could I be a part of that?*

"I'll bet you go home a lot."

Nate's eyes drop and he studies our hands. "Not really. I try to go home for celebrations like birthdays whenever I can and the usual holidays. But I stay gone a lot."

"Going home for you is easy, isn't it?"

"Not always, it wasn't." He doesn't look at me, making me wonder why.

"Was there someone special for you at home?" I pry boldly, needing to hear from his vulnerable side. This could be my only chance and I want to know. Other than Amy, I know nothing about Nate's former women, and his comment to Joey the other night has aroused my curiosity. Apparently, I've hit a nerve because he looks at me suddenly, with that move of the mouth that people make when they don't want to talk about something, and that slight narrowing of the eyes that means the same thing, as if I've poked at an old sore.

"The girl you were telling Joey about?" I ask, raising the glass to sip our wine, realizing he's staring at it, as if the color of it is a total surprise.

"You heard that?" I nod. He clears his throat and begins. "There was a girl. From high school. She was way out of my league. She went to college and I didn't. I went into the Navy and she started dating this really dweeby little guy with glasses, and she picked him over me. Turns out he wasn't such a dweeb after all, and he's a really awesome little guy with glasses. But I was too stupid and insecure to see it then. Too selfish to try to understand," he says, taking a sip of wine. *He was like me, so sure of himself and thinking he'd always get the girl.*

"Is she still there?"

"Yep. She married him in college. Among other things, they run the bakery where my sister—Sarah Grace works. I didn't tell you that Sarah Grace is a baker, too, did I?" The magazine picture in his office of the couple flanking Sarah Grace pops into my mind and it starts to make sense. *The lovely girl named September.* "Actually…my mother started the business—as part of her being such a fierce advocate for Sarah Grace. It's a dog biscuit bakery where young adults with special needs can work under the direction of September and Justin. They both had business degrees and good jobs, but September wanted to do something more meaningful. Mom always liked her and they had kept in touch, so… several years later, Mom contacted her, and there you go." He shrugs.

"That's the picture I saw in your office?"

"Yeah. Good Girl Dog Treats is the name of the company. One of our rescue dogs was named Good Girl. Sarah Grace named her," he says, grinning, signaling an end to our discussion about September. "It's a good fit for Sarah Grace and her friends. They're actually starting to get their product into lots of grocery stores and specialty stores in Chattanooga and some other places."

"So you have your own ghosts at home, too?"

"Nah, I'm over it. That's the price I paid for being a late bloomer." Still confident, still hurt.

My heart goes out to Nate, and I reach over for his hand again, just when the pizza arrives. September was important. Important enough to make it painful for him to go home.

I drive the rest of the way home, hoping Nate will nap in the car, but he uses the hour and a half to make phone calls and check emails, preparing for his upcoming trip, which from what I can glean is an offshore excursion with pro football players, departing from Charleston, South Carolina. He is as direct and humorous with his colleagues as he is with me, and I can tell he is well-liked, especially by the legendary Bo Hauser, whom he is presently cutting up with on the phone. There are so many text messages coming in that Nate ignores some of them while getting on with making plans for his trip. He ends the call with Bo and sits back, relaxing at last, or so it seems. He closes his eyes and I hope he will sleep for a while.

I use the quiet time to reflect on what is happening between us. When I used the restroom at the restaurant, I saw a new woman in the mirror. She was actually beautiful, prettier than usual, peaceful and happy. I haven't looked happy in a long time. Happiness for me—I thought—was getting to drive some drunk guy's expensive sports car home from a dinner date that got out of hand, or spending a weekend in a fancy mountain cabin with another summer tourist looking for a sexual adventure.

But I think happiness was really those days tending Granny's flowers in the garden, or all those evenings we spent rocking on the porch and talking, helping Joey catch his first lightning bugs in a jar, or going into the wintry woods with Pa to cut down a Christmas tree.

With Nate, there could be a whole new world of possibilities opening up for me, for us. *I want next times; don't you?* Some people I know would begrudge me this kind of happiness—a girl like me with a guy like him. How did this turn out for me? I don't deserve him and I know it, but what if I love him? I'm pretty sure I do. But what do I know of love? I don't have experience with love that way. I'm a virgin when it comes to really loving someone and having love in return. I think I have been starved for the kind of attention he has given me for…all of my life possibly. I'd like to tell Nate how I feel, but I find myself holding back. After last night, I think he feels the same way. He has to. I saw it in his face. I felt it in his touch. But I don't want to push my luck. So as usual, I'll just wait it out and see what happens. If I don't put myself out there, I won't be too disappointed when nothing happens. All this intimacy and emotion could just be my imagination anyway, and maybe Nate treated me so well because he felt sorry for me, losing Aiden the way Joey and I did. Or maybe he just needed to experience a little ecstasy with someone who was willing. Still, I can't imagine that he'll be two doors down and just ignore me for the remainder of the time I live there. Or could he?

I look over at him. Another text message has come across the screen, and this time he responds. Maybe a change in plans has arisen, judging by the look of displeasure on his face. We are coming into Wilmington, and I feel the same surge of excitement that only the ocean can elicit in me. Nate looks at me and smiles, catching my vibe. It's nice to be with someone who seems to understand what I'm thinking. He reaches over to take my hand and gives it a squeeze. Suddenly, he turns to me and speaks.

"Thanks for letting me be with you. I enjoyed sharing your little piece of heaven. I mean, I know it was hard for you, with Aiden's passing and all…."

"I know. Thank you for being there. I couldn't have gotten through this without you. It means a lot to me—how good you were with Joey."

"He's a great guy, Elle. You should go to his graduation."

"I will." I think to ask him to come along, but maybe I'll wait and see where we are in a few more weeks. Still, he'll need some notice to get free from his work commitments. I have to bite my tongue to keep from asking. There's more I want to say. I want to tell him I love him. Do I love Nate? I think I do. I'm happy for the first time in my life, not just because of him, but he's a large part of the reason.

We turn down Waters Edge and I creep along, hoping to prolong my time with him. We both have laundry to do, and I should get over to the bakery and check on things. I haven't called in today, but I will as soon as I drop Nate off. A familiar lady in a pink tank top runs by with her dog on a leash. We look toward the water, glistening in the afternoon sun like hammered silver, making me realize that Nate is drawn to water the way a moth is to the light. Water is in his blood like the hills are in mine.

"I need to take you fishing." It's a pronouncement. Nate will baptize me with all he thinks is good if I will just pick up a fly rod and go with him. And I am not against it.

"Okay."

"Tide's coming in," he observes absently, watching a boat gliding slowly up to its dock just before we reach the Montgomery house. I check to see whether Mr. May is still there, but not surprisingly at this hour, his car is gone.

Next door, the yellow crime scene tape is still in place, making both of us groan. It will be a good day when the reminders of what happened in the house between us are removed. And then I start to pull into Nate's driveway and catch my breath.

"Oh, God!" he whispers to himself.

The slate blue Mini Cooper is parked under the mimosa tree.

Chapter 27

THE BITCH IS BACK

I look questioningly at Nate, who seems almost as surprised as I am. *Almost.* What is he not telling me? I look at the car again and then swing my eyes over to his and the guilt I see there catches me completely off guard.

"What?" I can hardly say the word.

The all-knowing seriousness on his face makes my heart plunge to my stomach, making me instantly sick. "Elle, I'm sorry.... This isn't—it's not what you think." His hand goes up in defense.

I feel the breath drag through my lungs as I prepare to fall yet again into the deep sinkhole that is my life. I fall headfirst into a downward spiral as Nate watches me, with half a glance to the car and then to his front porch. He can hardly wait to get out of the car.

"Did you know she was going to be here?" I hear myself ask, the dryness in my voice making it sound like someone else talking.

"I—no, I—told her not to show up."

"Oh." I freeze, my hands glued to the steering wheel, my body seeming to float in the air as if it too belongs to someone else. They've talked. This is news to me.

Nate moves quickly, getting his gear together and opening the car door. I could help, but I can't move. This isn't happening. He doesn't talk, but I can feel the anxiety coming off of him in waves. He goes to the rear of my CRV and opens the tailgate, removing his bag and camera equipment. Stopping at my window, he bends to speak to me.

"Look; I'm so sorry. I'll call you later," he says, laying a hand briefly on the door.

Words I wanted to say are stuck in my throat. All I can manage is, "Okay."

I watch Nate walk quickly up the driveway, glancing in her car and then up the steps of his house. Dropping one of his bags on the porch, he opens the door and disappears inside as the door closes behind him.

She had a key. And he knew it. He didn't even fish around in his pockets to pull his keys out. Amy Stainback is in his house waiting for him in her pink silk robe. I wait for a moment, half-expecting him to come back and wave to me at the door, or at least to pick up his bag off the porch, but he does not appear.

After a few moments of sitting in limbo in his driveway, I try to move. I shift my car into reverse and turn methodically to back out into the street. My insides are swimming in a sea of confusion and hurt. I manage to drive the short distance to AB's house and down the driveway. I should check the mail, I think vacantly, but I drive past the mailbox. My foot is shaking on the gas pedal. I feel myself emerge from the car and collect my bag and hang-up clothes from the back of the car. Shutting the tailgate, I drift like vapor to the door of my guesthouse and work the key around in my hand to unlock my door.

Glancing to the left, I notice a new, dark patch of mulch with a small wooden sign marking the front. *Elle's Garden*, it reads, and amid the fresh sweet-smelling mulch are flowers planted in neat rows up and down. Daisies, zinnias, marigolds, chrysanthemums, and cosmos are present to greet me. Mr. May has been here, paying a tender tribute to me in my absence. I gaze for a moment at the results of his kind labor, knowing how much thought he put into each shovelful of earth, each plant he seated with his trowel, each handful of mulch he spread around the new flowers, tucking them in, all gifts to surprise and delight me upon my return. My heart aches with the kindness of his gesture. My heart aches. Period.

Once inside my house, I take my bag and the plastic bag with Aiden's clothes to the bedroom and hang up my dresses. I can't let this setback interfere with what I need to do. I need desperately to get to the bakery to see what is going on with my business. I need routine and constancy. I need people I know and trust. I need my sanctuary. I need to be distracted. It's stuffy and warm inside the house, and that musty smell has returned. Trying to move my mind past images of Amy and Nate together in his house, I go to the thermostat and turn up the air conditioning. I glance at the telephone at the end of my kitchen counter and the phone book catches my eye.

I have not played my hand with Amy, but an idea leaps to mind. Flipping rapidly through the large telephone book, I find myself looking through the S listings, my index finger scrolling down the page until I find the name Stainback in the left column. Edgar Stainback, not likely. Herbert Stainback, not it either. Jim Stainback. *Jim and Amy Stainback.* Setting the open book down on the counter, I realize I am trembling. All I have to do is press in seven digits on my screen and I can make all of this go away. My breathing is coming in deep calming waves now. This is what I would have done just a few short months ago, and I wouldn't have thought twice about it. I would have called Amy's husband and ratted her out, poured myself a glass of cabernet, and laughed about it for days afterward.

What's stopping you? Bad Elle is back. Why not? Amy is back and playing with me, pulling my chain, and Nate's—or not. Maybe he is playing her game with her. No. It can't be that way. Slamming the phone book shut, I put it back in its place, grab my keys and my purse, and head out the door. I will go to the bakery and do my job. Fuck them.

At the end of my driveway, I look to the left, seeing what I expect; the blue Mini Cooper is still there. What was I thinking? *This is why you never let your guard down, fool.* Bad Elle is back, my cynical sister.

I drive dully through town and arrive at Bake My Day without really knowing how I got there. Parking in the back of the store, I notice Jewel, dressed in a matching turquoise top and shorts and perfectly accessorized down to her shoes, getting in her car. She waves and waits a minute for me to get out of mine. I'm not up for talking, but I can tell she wants to pay her condolences, so I suck it up and drag myself out.

"Hey, Jewel." My expression must be exactly what she's expecting for what I've been through, but it's odd that the cause is not at all what she thinks.

"Hey! Oh, Elle, I'm so sorry about your boyfriend!"

"Thanks," I say, not even dreaming about explaining it all to her. It doesn't matter. We hug, and her embrace is fierce and oddly protective in a way I don't deserve.

"Are you okay?"

"Yeah. I will be. Thanks. Are you leaving?" It seems odd for her to leave now with the busy time at the winery just approaching.

"Well, yeah. I'm on a new schedule. Brandon and I are kind of divvy-ing up our time here. We don't both need to be here all the time so I'm out and he's in."

"Oh. Are things slowing down?"

"Lord, no! We're busier than we've ever been. We're just doing things a little differently right now is all. Brandon and I are breaking up. It's a little difficult since we live and work together, but the big jerk had the nerve to tell me I talked too much, so we're working in shifts."

My mouth falls open. "Oh, my God!"

"I know! Can you believe that crap? All this time I've been smothering up under him—he's always in my business and watching every move I make. And then there's all the flirting he does. All that winking at the women who come in and out of here. And he thinks I don't see him looking at everybody's rear ends and their cleavage. I'll tell you what; I've had enough. And if you've started on our cake, just put it in the freezer for somebody else, 'cause there's probably not going to be a wedding. You can keep the deposit."

"What?"

"Yeah."

"Are you going to keep working with him?"

"Only until I can find another job, but I'm outta here as soon as I can."

"I'm so sorry."

"Don't be. It's okay. I have an appointment at a sweet little boutique over at Lumina Station in about twenty minutes. Do you know, he even tried to blame it on one of his friends? Yeah. Somebody told him he should just tell me to shut up. Like I don't know I'm a big talker, right? Well, whoever told him to talk to me did me a big favor. It's just not meant to be, and I'm okay with it. I'm talking to Randy about finding another place to live, too. Brandon can just cram it right up where the sun don't shine. Who needs a man anyway, right? They're a lot more trouble than they're worth. You just never know about men, do you?"

"No, I guess you don't. Look, Jewel...."

"Honey, I won't keep you. I know you want to get in there and hear all the good news about your place. You guys have had a steady line in there since Saturday morning. You're the Sunshine Girl and everybody in Wilmington wants a piece of you! Congratulations!"

"Thanks."

"Bye-bye!" she says and hugs my neck again, giving me a perfume-infused smooch on the cheek that I don't want, but I must suffer with it until I can get a shower. Jewel and I will have to talk later. I have more to come clean about, but now is not the time. I promise myself to set up a lunch date with her. Or not. Maybe it's best to let sleeping dogs lie.

As soon as I open the door to my place, I'm greeted with more condolences, smiles, and hugs—and the sweet smell of a bakery. Maybe I will start to smell like myself again. Allyson and Monai are there, as well as Jordan, and Scooter, who is on his way out for the day. Allyson takes a break from the cupcakes she's decorating for tomorrow and gives me a big hug.

"I've thought about you so much. And oh, my God, girl, you won't believe our numbers! I've got to show you our sales figures for the past few days. I can't get supplies in here fast enough to keep up with the demand. But first of all, how are ya?" she asks, looking concerned at my dazed expression. First the situation with Nate and then this bombshell that Jewel has dropped on me must have scrambled my face into quite a picture.

"Well, I think I'm okay. I just really need to be here, you know?"

"Yeah, getting back to the routine sometimes helps." We watch Monai flying around the kitchen, her ponytail billowing out behind her like black smoke—her own personal rocket booster—helping herself to several of the freshly decorated yellow cupcakes, settling four of them into a cardboard carryout box.

"Sorry! They're selling like crazy!" Monai says, her metallic grin taking over her face as usual. It's great to be back. I have to smile. "Drops of Sunshine!" she says before she buzzes out the door. Brilliant.

Jordan checks the walk-in refrigerator for a birthday cake and carries it past us, winking at me. "Hey, Elle. Great to have you back!"

Allyson grins, placing a hand on her hip, tossing her head toward the others. "They're so frickin' great, aren't they?"

"Yes, they are. So are you. Thanks for running the place while I was gone."

"Hey, it's a well-oiled machine you got here. All we have to do is show up. Everybody knows what to do. And all your friends have been in here. Randy comes in every morning and works the counter."

"No way."

"Oh, yeah. He loves it. He goes around pouring coffee refills and sweeping up, making sure everybody's happy. He's great. And his friend Jimmy comes in about every day, checking up on you. And that Mr. May. He's a real sweetie. I told them all you'd be back today. I guess they'll all be here in the morning to welcome you back."

"Wow."

Allyson turns away conspiratorially. "Yeah, wow. And speaking of wow, tell me about the guy who whisked you out of here on Saturday morning, the smoking hot one with the incredibly blue eyes and body to die for?"

"That's Nate, my neighbor."

"And...."

"He's just my neighbor. He gave me a ride home." Or, *he took me for a ride*, I should say.

"All the way to the *hills*? And then what?"

"Stop. Really. There's nothing to it. He was just being nice."

Allyson studies me, the way I tossed my hair and folded my arms just now.

"Okay. Well, nice neighbors must be good to have."

Her tone is unmistakably suggestive, making my stomach roll, but I let it go.

"Show me the sales figures."

Amy's Mini Cooper is still there when I get home. Why? What are they doing? *You know what they're doing.* I can't even park my car I am so agitated. There is no sign of AB, so I back around and drive over to the beach. *It's a beautiful day*, I think to myself, which is ironic. A day filled with all these strange and depressing events should be gray and foreboding, with a rainstorm ready to break forth at any moment. But for June, the sky is a brilliant blue—*cerulean*—my favorite color. Sighing for what feels like the fourteenth time today, I parallel park and deposit quarters in the meter from my change purse in the glove compartment. I leave my flip-flops and walk across the hot sand, past the last of the beach-goers, packing up for the day. There are others like me out for an evening stroll, but none has my same agenda. College boys toss a Frisbee in my wake, but they stop momentarily to let me pass. I walk straight out to the water, letting my feet sink in the pebbly sand as the tide sloshes around my ankles, waves splashing foam onto my shorts. My hair whips around my face in the wind, and I feel the sun baking my cheeks. I let it soothe me, and I sigh again, raking my hair away from my face.

I feel sick with an unfamiliar heaviness. My malaise is characteristic of the broken-hearted, as I have read about, but I have never felt this way in my life. Was I so wrong? I thought I had Nate all worked out. I know how he was with me, the way he looked at me, the way he touched me; I *felt* it. It was real. The questions he asked me made me think he cared what I was all about. I remember one of my favorite stories from middle school, Antoine de Saint-Exupery's *The Little Prince*. "It is only with one's heart that one can see clearly. What is essential is invisible to the eye." I wanted to understand it then, and I tried to understand it as an adult. Even when I was in prison, I wanted to know what this passage meant in my life. It wasn't until yesterday that I actually felt I knew. But I must have been wrong. I wanted next times. My heart actually does feel ripped apart. That I do understand. *This is what happens when you open your heart.* Waves of doubt and hurt crash through it, dragging the sediment of your self-confidence away with every surge of the tide. I will never be able to trust myself after this.

Tears begin to roll down my face, one after another, as if they will never stop. My body heaves with sobs. I have never cried like this. Is this why people walk into the ocean to drown themselves? Is this what Edna Pontellier was feeling? I sniff and wipe my face, only for more tears to fall in their places as the waves lap around my thighs. No. *Hell, no.* I will never let myself feel that way, that desperate. No man on this earth is worth anyone's life. I was in love, but I was wrong. Was I? I wanted so much more from Nate. Was I wrong to be so greedy? There are too many questions. I have no answers. And then it comes to me again in one simple precept, the way I've gleaned it over and over in my life, so I should have learned: *If something seems too good to be true, then it probably is.*

The ocean swirls in and out around my legs, soothing and beautiful, a place to begin, not a place to end things. I can begin again. It's what I do. I will let Nate go. I will suck it up and move on. I will forget him, the way I forgot my mother and my father, and all the others of little importance in my life who made me turn out to be who I am, who *I* have made myself to be. I am not alone. I think of Mr. May's flowers in my new garden, connecting me to the future. I am reminded of Randy and Jimmy coming by the bakery asking about me. I think of Jewel, bucking up and getting rid of sorry old Brandon. Who needs a man? A man can't make you happy. Only you can make yourself happy. Damn right. Good for her. Good for me.

The waves wash over my thighs, pushing me to and fro in the surf, making me struggle to keep myself upright. From somewhere, the bagpipes play "Amazing Grace" in my head as I stare out at the water. I have friends. I think of Judy and Marcus and even Glen and Abby, and Kyle and Chelsea, and even Kendra maybe. There is a possibility that we could all be friends, or not, but it could all be up to me. Maybe with my initiative, and the energy I have put into this business, and my relationship with my son, I could make friendship happen with all of them. I have Allyson, Monai, Jordan, and Anna…and even Scooter when he is not drowning me with sweet tea.

Maybe friends are like flowers that fade away in the winter only to reappear in fair weather. And then there are the Judy and Mr. May variety, hardy hellebores that you admire throughout the winter months for their courage and character, bravely bearing up under ice and snow, blooming first as Lenten roses to give us hope for spring. Randy and Jimmy are like early bulbs that pop through the snow—crocuses and snowdrops, surprising us in the spring when we forgot they were there. I have AB, the dramatic heirloom rose, her flamboyant blossoms requiring painstaking care, always noticed, and probably worth the work. Aiden…my tree, my evergreen, is always there, even now, loving Joey, loving me, even when I didn't know it. Granny lingers delicately in my memory like the bleeding heart pressed and preserved between the pages of old love letters. Best of all, now I know I have myself. And I'm not that bad. I am a good mother. My son loves me. I am worth loving. I am a vine that won't die. Honeysuckle—invasive but sweet, if you like that sort of thing. People are always trying to rip me out by the roots, but I always come back.

And then there is Nate. I don't know what Nate is—Venus flytrap maybe? An alluring, attractive carnivore at best? I laugh. A man can eat me up and spit me out, but I will not be squashed like a bug. I do feel eaten up and spit out, but I will never be squashed. A larger wave crashes over my legs, rocking me backward, forcing me to step back and steady myself. I haven't paid attention. My shorts are soaked. Enough of this self-pity and useless introspection. Trudging out of the tide takes some doing, and I walk back across the hot sand to my car and drive home. Glancing down the street to Nate's driveway, I see that the blue car is still there, making my spirits dive again as doubt floods over me once more. How did I not see this coming?

At home, there is not much to eat and I am not particularly hungry, but I should eat something, so I decide to scramble an egg. Interestingly, as I daydream, the egg turns out over easy in the pan, and I close my eyes as I eat it with salt and pepper, savoring each bite as though it is my last supper. Joey sends me a text, saying he's landed in Texas and that he loves me. At least there is one good thing about this day. I stare at his message and then text him back, telling him that I love him too, with two pink hearts at the end of it, happy that we are communicating after so many years of estrangement. It occurs to me that Nate has not called, and in vain, I check my phone to see whether I've missed it. After starting a load of laundry, I set the coffeepot for the morning, take a sleeping pill, wash my face, brush my teeth, and go to bed with a cold compress over my eyes so I will not look bad tomorrow.

Chapter 28

CLOSURE

So much for my cold compress. Looking in the bathroom mirror, I see one of those amusement park mirror faces, distorted and swollen from all my crying. I take a couple of Advil, use eye drops, nose spray, and lie down once more with a cold washcloth over my face to see whether I can restore my looks for the busy day ahead. I have decorating to do today— wedding cakes for the weddings that will take place this Saturday. I can hide in the back, lose myself in the icing, and watch my staff go about the business of baking someone's day.

It's a gray day, just what I ordered, making me laugh at the irony. Maybe it will rain later and my movie will be complete. A shower makes me feel better, and a cup of coffee gets me out the door. My Barbie pony-tail is all I care to manage, but I have tried to cover my train wreck of a face with makeup as best I can. Everyone will understand. I am grieving and they will expect me to look this way. Ashamed of why I do, I get in my car and make it to the end of the driveway, waving to Patsy who's out walking Harley. She hesitates, as if she'll stop to talk, but I look away and check my watch to let her know I'm on my way to work. She waves again and continues down the street. Thunder rumbles, so she needs to get home before it rains anyway. I can't look to the left. I don't want to see what's there, so I decide to check the mailbox instead. Getting back in my car, I thumb through the stack of mail, mostly cards—sympathy cards from everyone I know, it seems. There are cards from Judy, Monai, Mr. May, Marcus, AB, Roxy, Jimmy Burns, one with a return address from Raleigh that I don't recognize. Another card from Kyle and Chelsea Davis catches my eye, and I rip open the envelope. It's a lovely card with a beach scene and a nice message, signed with neat script written in blue ink—*Thinking of you and Joey, Chelsea and Kyle*. Wow.

There are cards from others—Randy, and Glen Dunham, Aiden's friend from home. I go back to the card from Raleigh and pry open the envelope. There's a beautiful mountain scene and a Bible verse, Psalm 121, the same one we used in Aiden's memorial service. *I will lift up mine eyes unto the hills from whence cometh my help. My help cometh from the LORD, which made heaven and earth.* Reading it actually makes me feel better. There is a note underneath in a messy hand that I have to struggle to read.

Dear Elle,

I am so sorry to hear of your loss of Aiden. You and Joey are in my thoughts and prayers as you endure this difficult time. Monai calls me at least once a week, telling me all about you. She has never been so happy. I am so pleased to hear about the success of your bakery and that the two of you have connected in such a serendipitous way. I knew you would be my prize and joy. Don't ever doubt it for a minute.

Love, Vada

Well. Wow. I don't know what to think. My life seems to have come around full circle. Vada is the Dahlia in my garden, bold and brilliant, blooming in late summer through autumn, a sturdy perennial. I consolidate the pile of mail and put my car in gear. Checking for traffic to the left, I have to look. I realize that as I'd feared, the Mini Cooper is still there in Nate's driveway, reviving the dull ache in my chest and sending a lump to my throat, but I am done crying.

Who in their right mind wants gaudy, orange ribbon on their wedding cake? Clemson graduates, apparently. Of all the colors to deal with today, it would have to be prison-jumpsuit-orange, but I'm somehow able to let it roll off my back. I guess the card from Vada made the difference today. Somehow the ritual of decorating a cake has calmed me down, that and the sweet smells of cakes baking. Scooter sings passionately along to Marvin Gaye's "Let's Get It On," as he washes mixing bowls and utensils in the sink next to me, making me chuckle. Life isn't so bad today. I just might live.

Roxy swings through the door from the café to address me, hands on hips, her pink hair styled more dramatically than usual.

"There's a hot guy out front asking for you."

I look up from my orange ribbon with questioning eyes and a sinking feeling. She shrugs.

"He's sniffing the cake."

"What?"

"I don't know…he ordered a cup of coffee and a piece of *birthday cake*," she says, making quotation marks in the air with her fingers, "but he's not eating it; he's just *smelling it*." She looks at me as if to ask, *What kind of friends do you have?*

My heart pounds as I wipe my hands and go out front. Spreading my hands across my apron and smoothing stray hairs back into my ponytail, I look through the large collection of customers in the café, spotting Nate at the other end of the counter, blowing on his coffee. Monai sends me an inquiring look as she's ringing up a purchase. I lift my eyebrows and shrug in response as she asks to help the next customer. There is quite a line.

It takes me a moment to make my way around the counter and approach Nate, who has by now found a table. Setting his cake slice on it, he senses I'm here. His grim and exhausted face tells me what I need to know. At least he has the decency to dump me face to face. The air leaves my lungs and I place my hand on the chair to steady myself. This must be what it feels like to have the ocean close over one's head after that final exhale.

"Hi," he says without a smile, but I detect a glint in those beguiling blue eyes—desire, guilt, regret, whatever it is—I try not to look at them. It hurts too much. I know what's coming. I find myself praying for discretion—from Nate as well as from myself. At that moment, there is another low rumble of thunder, and I almost laugh—it's the sound of God's jaw hitting the ground. My movie is rolling and Fellini has nothing on me.

"Hey."

"Do you have time to sit with me a minute? I know you're slammed."

"Yeah, sure." All I can manage is a whisper. *Let's get this over with.* Glancing around, I realize we are sitting in my place of business where I'm about to get the absolute worst news of my life. Silently, I make a plan to bolt out the back door and throw up or scream, or whatever it is I'll have to do when the time is right.

We sit across from each other, watching the steam drift upward from his coffee cup. I feel suspended in time, aware that we are both lost in the tendril of vapor. Finally, he speaks.

"I'm sorry I didn't call you last night. I—there was a lot going on."

I give my automatic response, the one that will get him off the hook, but then my real feelings spill out. "No, it's fine…. Her car is still there." I look at him and shrug.

He looks pained. "It's gone now. I came down last night but you weren't home."

"You did? What happened?" Do I really want to know? *He came by?*

"You asked me once what was the worst thing I'd done?" Nate whispers, looking out the window. He looks down for a moment, and then he covers his face with his hands. A glimmer of hope springs into my heart, paired with concern for him, the way he looks. He lowers his hands, letting out a ragged sigh.

"Amy cut herself."

It takes a moment for his words to sink in and the shock that follows. I was not expecting this. "What? You mean she tried to…."

"No, it wasn't a suicide attempt, but she injured herself pretty badly…. She's done it before," he says gravely, and I think I see apology in his eyes. Still, this isn't sounding good. From the look on his face, I try to imagine the scene, their interactions, what she was wearing, if anything. (There was a girl in prison with me who was a cutter—the doctor's wife. Her husband ignored her like Amy's husband did, but she finally got his attention by stealing his prescription pad and writing all her friends prescriptions for oxycodone. I knew I shouldn't have been, but I was proud of her, standing up for herself that way.)

"She'd figured out I was with you. I'd packed some of her things in a bag before we left on Saturday and she found them." *The pink robe, the missing toothbrush, important pieces of Amy's secret rebellion with Nate.* "It must have sent her over the edge and…." He gives a mild shrug.

"Oh, Nate…. What did you do?" I ask, feeling my hand go to cover his.

"I bandaged her up and called her husband. Jim came over and they had a long talk, after we beat the shit out of each other." It's then that I notice the side of his face is slightly red and swollen. Still, he can't look as bad as I do. We study each other's faces.

"He hit you first."

"Yeah. I can't blame him. This was on me, Elle. I did this. This is the worst thing I've ever done."

"But…it's not all on you."

"I shouldn't have gotten involved with her. I knew she had rejection issues, and I never should have played into her sickness. But I did. I knew better. I deserve whatever beating I got. Just not from *him*. But I can tell you, I gave as good as I got. He deserved it, too."

"You said he was cheating on her, too?"

"Correct."

I want to say, *Then they deserve each other*, but it wouldn't help matters. "They need counseling, then."

"Yes. They're going to give it a try. They have kids…."

I watch him compose himself. Nate could get sued for alienation of affection, but then, backing up a step, Amy could sue Jim's mistress for the same thing. It's complicated, but Nate has tried to be the peacemaker, and quite possibly it has worked.

"Then you did the right thing."

"I hope so," he says, doubt edging his voice as he takes a sip of his coffee. "Listen; I came here because I owe you a huge apology, Elle. I'm so sorry for leaving you hanging like that. I'm sorry for making you doubt me and wonder what was going on…. I can't imagine what you've been thinking. I didn't know where you'd gone. I wanted to call you, but by the time I finished cleaning up from all the blood and all the mess from me and Jim knocking stuff around—and drinking—I was too drunk to make any sense. I had a lot to work out with myself last night. You deserve so much better. I needed to tell you this in person."

My hand tightens over his. His free hand runs through his hair as he continues.

"I thought I was coming clean, you know? I'd finally met you—someone I could really relate to and trust, and then I go screw it all up again...." He looks up with his morose blue eyes, and I can't stand it anymore.

"No, Nate...let it go. It's okay. You did right by her. You did right by me, too. Forgiveness, remember?"

His hands go up again over his face, and he winces at the forgotten bruises. His hands go back to the table, steadying his also forgotten coffee cup. He looks up, unconvinced.

There is nothing else to do but tell him. "I love you, Nate."

He looks at me and blinks as though he didn't hear me right. Then he sighs with relief, taking my hands again. "Oh, thank God! I came here totally prepared to beg for your understanding. I didn't really expect forgiveness. Thank you. I thought you'd be kicking me to the curb by now.... I deserve that, after what I've put you through. But I love you, too, Elle. That night on the dock, after I sent Aubrey home...you were starting to pull me under. So I'm in." Finally, he smiles, laughing, refilling me with the joy I'd lost. I return the look and laugh with him. He goes on. "I've never felt this way—with anyone."

Not even September. For me, the hurt is gone, along with all the doubt and loneliness. I smile. "Me neither." I feel the sun on my face again, which seems peculiar because it's raining outside now, a light, misting rain that will probably last all day from the weather report this morning. Still, I can't hide the smile that's radiating off of me. I feel myself glowing. This is what happens when you open your heart. Warmth flows in and warmth flows out. I wasn't wrong. I knew deep in my heart that I wasn't wrong about him, about myself.

"Elle, I know trust is hard for you. I thought you were beginning to trust me, but after all this, *can* you...trust me?" he asks.

The question is: can I trust myself? Now I know the answer. The answer is yes. Can I trust Nate? Again, the answer is yes. I nod. "Yeah, I can do that."

"Good. I was hoping we were on the same page."

"I'd say we are."

He strokes my hand, making me notice the cake on the table.

"Birthday cake?"

"Well…I figured if you were going to boot me out, at least I could still take a piece of you with me."

"You're going to eat it, aren't you?"

"That wasn't the plan, but things are changing."

"Yes, they are."

He gives me that bright, randy smile of his, coloring it with a little gratitude, making me feel as though we have retraced our steps to who we were in the car just yesterday. He searches my eyes for a moment, looking deep.

"Have you heard from Joey?"

"Yes! Yes, he texted me when he landed last night." I smile, again feeling warmth in my face. *I have two men who love me.* Aren't I the lucky girl?

"Good…. Listen; I have to leave. I'm on my way to Charleston, but I had to stop and see you first. I'll call you when I start to head home on Sunday, okay?"

"Okay. I'd like that. I'll cook for you this time."

"Great…. I'll bring the fish." He grins, stopping my heart again.

"I'll have wine…." *And you can spend the night.* He is reading my mind, judging by his old familiar smile and the carnal flash of his eyes. *Joe-pye weed*—strong and wild and beautiful. That's what Nate is.

He stands to go, collecting his cake. I walk him out to his truck and he wraps me in one arm the best he can with his cake, kissing me in the rain with everything he's got, and I give it right back. When we come apart, I'm aware there's an ovation going on inside Bake My Day. Monai is grinning like a fool, and so is Allyson, and all the customers who seem to be cheering and raising their coffee cups our way. We laugh and Nate kisses me again.

"A'ight, Sunshine Girl, until next time." He winks and gives my hand a squeeze before he gets in his truck and cranks it up.

"*Next time*…. Be safe," I add, looking back and rubbing my wet arms, trying to keep the feel of his hug on my skin. I turn to walk back through the front door where all eyes are on me, but I don't care.

I'm walking on sunshine.

The End

Other Books by Mary Flinn...

THE ONE - BOOK ONE

"Is following your heart worth having it broken?"

"Powerful and timeless, *The One* is a heartwarming story illuminating a love that is, in this age, truly rare. Flinn's depiction of a young woman's ability to remain true to herself in the face of many trials is unrivaled as she powerfully proclaims the importance of faith, family, friendship, and above all, love."

**~Meredith Strandberg, Student,
North Carolina State University**

SECOND TIME'S A CHARM - BOOK TWO

"Forgiveness is easy. Trust is harder."

"Mary Flinn is the female equivalent of author Nicholas Sparks. Her characters are as real as sunburn after a long day at the beach. Hot days and hotter nights make *Second Time's a Charm* an excellent sultry romance that will stay with readers long after the sun goes down. The second book in a series, this story is a movie waiting to happen."

**~Laura Wharton, author of
The Pirate's Bastard and *Leaving Lukens***

Three Gifts - Book Three

"There is a Celtic saying that heaven and earth are only three feet apart, but in the thin places, the distance is even smaller."

"Throughout *Three Gifts*, you will be rooting for Chelsea and Kyle, young marrieds so appealing, yet real that you'll wish you could clone them. They settle in the mountains, near Boone, North Carolina, and when they are faced with tragedies, they handle them with courage and grace. Even those oh-so-human doubts and fears that threaten occasionally to swamp them are banished through humor and the abiding love that sustains them. This is a journey of hope, faith, and love that you'll want to share with them."

**~Nancy Gotter Gates, author of
the *Tommi Poag* and *Emma Daniel* mysteries,
and women's fiction *Sand Castles* and *Life Studies***

A Forever Man - Book Four

"There are friends and there are lovers; sometimes the line between is thinly drawn."

"Just when I thought I would never see Kyle and Chelsea Davis again, Mary Flinn brings them back in *A Forever Man*; they returned like old friends you feel comfortable with no matter how much time has passed, only this time with eight-year-old twin boys, and a new set of life-complications to work through. In this novel, Flinn provides a deft look at marriage when potential infidelity threatens it. *A Forever Man* is Flinn's masterpiece to date, and no reader will be disappointed."

**~Tyler R. Tichelaar, Ph.D., and author of
*Spirit of the North: a paranormal romance***

AND TWO STAND-ALONE NOVELS,
APART FROM THE KYLE AND CHELSEA SERIES,

THE NEST

"Mary Flinn realistically captures the ideals of an empty nest filled with rekindling passions of soon-to-retire Cherie and her rock-and-roll-loving husband Dave—then flips it all over when Hope, the jilted daughter, returns to the nest to heal her broken heart. Between her mother's comical hot flashes that only women of a certain age could appreciate, the loss of her laid-back father's sales job, and the good news-bad news of other family members' lives, can Hope find the courage to spread her wings and leave the nest again? Flinn's deft handling of story-telling through both Cherie and Hope's voices will send readers on a tremendously satisfying and wild flight back to *The Nest*."

~**Laura S. Wharton, author of the award-winning novels**
***Leaving Lukens, The Pirate's Bastard,* and others**

BREAKING OUT

"A harrowing incident involving her talented teenage son helps dermatologist Susannah realize she has kept herself from moving forward after the death of her beloved husband, Stan. At times humorous, at other times poignant, *Breaking Out* is an eloquent exploration of how difficult life can be following the unexpected death of a loved one. With a wealth of detail, including the complexities of family relationships, Mary Flinn creates a heartwarming story about the curious way two people can connect through grief and break out into a new life together."

~**Jane Tesh, author of the *Madeline Maclin Mysteries***
and *The Grace Street Series*

CPSIA information can be obtained at www.ICGtesting.com
Printed in the USA
LVOW10s0959040815

448543LV00003B/4/P